TIES THAT BIND

TIES THAT BIND

a novel

RACHEL ANN NUNES

Covenant Communications, Inc.

Cover photo by Maren Ogden

Cover design copyrighted 2002 by Covenant Communications, Inc.

Published by Covenant Communications, Inc.
American Fork, Utah

Printed in the United States of America
First Printing: February 2002

08 07 06 05 04 03 02 01   10 9 8 7 6 5 4 3 2 1

ISBN 1-57734-939-3

Library of Congress Cataloging-in-Publication Data

Nunes, Rachel Ann, 1966-
     Ties that bind/ Rachel Ann Nunes.
         p.   cm.
     ISBN 1-57734-939-3 (alk. paper)
       1. Mormon women--Fiction. I. Title
   PS3564.U468 T53 2002
                                    2001058449

For TJ, my husband and best friend.
I know it's not easy living with an eccentric author
who sometimes has rather crazy ideas, but you have been my
constant supporter from the very beginning.
I LOVE YOU!
And thanks!

CHAPTER 1

The tune wouldn't leave Rebekka Massoni's head. Even over the loud bustle at the airport in Paris, she heard it clearly—just as she had during Louis-Géralde Perrault's missionary farewell the day before. Over and over, the melody repeated itself in her mind.

She tightened her grasp on the worn set of scriptures in her hands, the ones with the pronounced teeth marks. The music in her head grew ever louder, as though she were playing it on the concert grand Steinway back in Utah where she had been working until the past week. But instead of bringing comfort, the as-yet-unnamed tune she had composed for her fiancé, Marc Perrault, chilled her.

Marc smiled at her encouragingly, his brown eyes glinting in the reflection of the overhead lights. He stood a few inches taller than Rebekka, with broad shoulders that tapered to a trim waist. He put his strong arm around her shoulders and she stepped toward him, revelling in his closeness.

She still couldn't believe he loved her, that he had followed her to Utah to beg her to marry him. Of course, she'd said yes. She had loved him for almost twenty years, since she was five and a half and he was fifteen. Finally, he had come to love her as well—as a woman, not only as a friend.

"He's about to leave," Marc said. As always, his dark eyes seemed to beckon her to lose herself in their depths. He smiled, so ruggedly handsome and dear that she longed to hold him. His fingers brushed the scriptures in her hands. "You don't have to give them up, you know."

Rebekka took a deep breath. "I want to." She had never expected to willingly give up the scriptures the Perraults had given her to take on her own mission years before, but this same set had accompanied all the Perrault siblings who had served missions. Even Josette, Marc's twin sister who had served in Portugal, had used them in her personal missionary studies. It was only right that the youngest Perrault brother took them to the Ukraine as well.

Rebekka wasn't exactly unhappy to relinquish the scriptures to Louis-Géralde. After all, she had only loved them because they had been Marc's and had saved him from a vicious dog attack on his mission. Now she had Marc himself, and didn't need them anymore. And the scriptures belonged in the mission field. Their well-loved pages fell open to the right scriptures at all the right times. They also warded off all danger, including Bible bashers and vagrant animals. Yes, with these infamous scriptures, Louis-Géralde would do great work for the Church in the Ukraine.

Of course, the fact that he had studied both Ukrainian and Russian for three years before his stint in the army would also go a long way toward making him a successful missionary in the Ukraine, where both languages were still used prevalently. Louis-Géralde had believed he would be sent to the Ukraine for as long as Rebekka could remember, and though she had doubted his inspiration at times, here he was on his way to the MTC in London. He would stay there for a very brief training session before flying on to the Ukraine Kiev Mission.

Marc's parents embraced their newest missionary with tears in their eyes. Other family members crowded around for support. Louis-Géralde had already been away from his family for a year as he served in the French army, and it was hard for them to let him go again. But the Perrault family would always make sacrifices for their faith—only one of many reasons Rebekka admired them. Could it really be true that she was marrying into such a wonderful family?

Rebekka stepped up to Louis-Géralde. "We want you to take these."

Louis-Géralde grinned, his green-brown eyes opening wide. "Wow! You still have those things? They must be ancient! Thank you so much! I promise I'll take good care of them." He fingered the bite marks reverently before tucking them into the new scripture case Rebekka had purchased before leaving Utah.

"Now we can sleep at night knowing you have those," quipped Marc.

Louis-Géralde hugged Rebekka. "I'm sorry I won't get to see you two hitched." He had wanted to, and both Rebekka and Marc would have loved to have driven immediately to a temple to make their commitment official, but Rebekka's parents were planning an elaborate celebration for their only daughter's wedding. Plans continued to escalate, especially since her brother—their only son—had eloped weeks before with a woman Rebekka's father detested. Not that he was too happy with Rebekka's choice either, since he couldn't enter a Mormon temple to see them wed, but at least he respected Marc as a person. By having a large dinner reception at one of the most prestigious restaurants in Paris, her father would get to show Rebekka off to all his important friends.

"Well, maybe you'll get back in time to see our first son blessed," Marc said as he took his turn embracing his brother. He glanced at Rebekka and winked. "Or maybe our second. You'll be gone two years, and we've got a lot of time to make up for."

Rebekka smiled, but felt embarrassed at the comment. True, she had been waiting a long time for Marc, but she had only recently turned twenty-five and he just ten years older—or almost ten years, since he didn't turn thirty-five until February. For the average French person, he was the perfect age to marry, and she was perhaps a little on the young side. They would have many years left together to raise a family. No need to rush.

Louis-Géralde gave another hug to his parents and headed for the international gate. The family watched him go—sadly, proudly, happily.

Marc turned to her. "I guess that's that." He stared into her eyes as if drinking in her presence. He did that a lot, and though it pleased her, she still had difficultly accepting that he really loved her. She returned his stare, loving him more than she could express. The sweetness of being with him was incredible.

The music in her head was softer now, but she still heard the notes. What did it mean? *It's probably because I've been practicing it so much,* she told herself. *It's nothing.* She had composed the tune for Marc before her mission, and had kept it a secret from him all these years, with the intent of playing it for him on their wedding day. Then, that day had been a far-away dream. Finally it would actually happen!

"Hello, Rebekka, Marc! Is anyone there?" asked Josette, Marc's twin sister.

Rebekka started, and dragged her eyes from Marc's.

"We gotta get these guys married fast," said Zack Fields, Josette's husband. In his arms he held the youngest of their four boys.

Josette, six months pregnant with another boy, threw back her long, dark hair and made a smacking noise with her lips. "That's right. They look like a couple of big-eyed cows mooning over each other, if you ask me."

"I didn't ask you," Marc answered good-naturedly. He took Rebekka's hand, caressing it. "Besides, I remember you and Zack doing an awful lot of mooning over each other a few years ago."

"A few?" Josette rolled her eyes. "Our oldest is almost eleven. That means we've been married for twelve years. And that means you're way behind at this family-raising business, dearest twin brother of mine."

"I wasn't ready to get married twelve years ago," Rebekka defended Marc. "I, for one, am certainly glad he waited." The others laughed.

"Well, you've been grown up for quite a while." This came from André, Marc's other younger brother who was married and had two daughters of his own. Like Marc, he had laughing brown eyes and dark hair. He was only a centimeter or two shorter than his brother, but he weighed a good ten kilos more. Strong, but definitely not silent, as Rebekka well knew. He opened his mouth to continue. "Marc was just too dense to see—"

"So are we going out for that brunch or not?" interrupted Marc's mother, Ariana, forever the peacemaker among her noisy brood.

Rebekka had grown accustomed to the teasing in the week since she and Marc had announced their engagement, and even enjoyed some of it, but she was relieved when Ariana spoke.

"Actually, we have to get back to Claire," André said, placing a hand on the shoulders of his young daughters. "She's not feeling well, and since I'm taking the day off, I kind of want to be with her."

His mother's brow drew in concern. "If there's anything I can do . . . Why don't you let us take the girls? We'll bring them back when we're done." The girls and their cousins cheered.

"Thanks, Mom." André gave his daughters a kiss and warned them to obey. Then he winked at Rebekka sympathetically. "Good luck with all those plans." He lowered his voice. "Better you than me. Personally, I think you should've eloped."

Rebekka grinned, sorry to see him go. André was her favorite of all the Perraults, except Marc, of course. Through the years, André had never treated her like a child, as the others had. They hadn't meant to be offensive when they talked down to her, but in her precociousness, Rebekka had been annoyed all the same. Even after earning two bachelor's degrees, one in English and the other in French, and having won many awards for her piano playing and compositions, she had still felt that her age separated her from most of the Perrault siblings.

"Then let's get going." Marc pulled Rebekka toward the exit.

The family met at a nearby restaurant, where all the children reminded Rebekka of Utah—there always seemed to be more children than adults in Utah. Marc's twin, Josette, had four sons, his brother André had two daughters, and Marie-Thérèse, their adopted sister, had one of each. *Eight children,* Rebekka mused. Of course in Utah all eight might have come from one family.

The talk didn't revolve for long around the new missionary, Louis-Géralde. *No one to tease anymore since he's gone,* Rebekka thought. The next topic at hand was, of course, The Wedding. Rebekka and Marc had set the date for the end of October—only one month away, much to her mother's dismay at the short planning period. To Rebekka, a month seemed more like an eternity.

"Imagine all those years of you two knowing each other and then suddenly falling in love in Utah," Josette said, taking a drink of her milk. She had her youngest son cradled somewhat awkwardly in her lap, making Rebekka wonder if being pregnant was as uncomfortable as it looked. "I mean," Josette continued, "I know you had a crush on him when you were little, but I thought you had grown out of that a long time ago." The statement was more of a question, which Rebekka wasn't going to answer.

"Well, a lot of people in this family fell in love in Utah," replied Zack, giving his wife a loving wink. His blonde hair and bright blue eyes contrasted with Josette's darker features. All of their four boys resembled Josette, though with slightly lighter hair. "We did. And so did Mathieu and Marie-Thérèse."

Marie-Thérèse's smile brought life to her narrow face, which was framed by light brown hair that she constantly tucked behind her ears. "Yes," she said dreamily, taking her husband's hand. "It seems like only yesterday Mathieu and I were there, falling in love." Her daughter Larissa giggled, echoed by the other children. As the oldest of the cousins at twelve and a half, Larissa was nearly worshiped by the others, but lately she had developed an attitude her parents—and all the other adults—found difficult to understand.

Rebekka and Marc shared a glance. They hadn't "fallen in love" so much as he had finally recognized his true feelings and come after her. In fact, their relationship had nothing to do with Utah, but she didn't like explaining it all, especially the part where she had given up on Marc and nearly married another man. Of all the Perrault clan, only Marc's parents and his brother André had any idea of the real situation between the couple.

At least it was finally happening! Rebekka had waited a very long time for Marc to come around, and she was so excited she found it difficult to focus on the conversation.

"The flowers are all set," Rebekka's mother, Danielle, was saying in response to a question. "They should cover the entire reception center. But I tell you, we had to practically pay double to get them to promise to have them done by then. Four weeks is not a lot of time." Her voice was velvet soft. She had gray eyes, high cheekbones and perfectly sculptured eyebrows. Her long, dark auburn hair showed only a few streaks of gray. People often said Rebekka resembled her mother except for the strong chin which so obviously came from her father, but Rebekka discredited their comments. Danielle was more than beautiful; she was stunning. *I could never look like that,* Rebekka mused.

As if sensing her thoughts, Marc reached out and tickled her arm lightly with his fingertips. His touch burned into her flesh, and she felt warm all over. Her depressing thoughts vanished immediately. Marc thought she was beautiful and that was enough.

"Don't you think next spring would be soon enough to get married, Rebekka?" her mother asked. "It's not too late to change the wedding date."

"Hey, I'm not getting any younger," Marc protested.

"Well, thirty-four is a good age for men to marry," Danielle replied. "Although, I admit it is rather late for Church members. But since you've already waited this long, what's a few more months?"

Marc's mother laughed aloud, obviously recalling private memories. "What is it, Ariana?" Danielle asked her.

Ariana's smile grew wider. "Even four weeks was a long time when I wanted to marry Jean-Marc." As she spoke, her husband cast her a gaze so full of love that it was almost tangible, and Rebekka felt goose bumps on her arms. Though he was shorter than Marc, Jean-Marc looked a lot like his son, and Rebekka could imagine what Marc would be like in twenty or thirty years. He would be as lean as Jean-Marc, with gray peppering the black hair and deep laugh lines on his face. And hopefully, Rebekka would have aged with at least some of her mother's gracefulness. The nearly ten years between them would be evident, of course, but there was nothing to be done about that. What would it matter if she spent a few years alone at the end of her life? They had eternity, didn't they?

Marc squeezed her hand and Rebekka smiled at him. He looked more tired than usual, and she wondered if he could still be suffering from jet lag. She, on the other hand, felt vitally alive, if a little preoccupied with the idea of marrying him.

"I love you," he mouthed, lifting his glass of water for a sip. Under cover of the glass, he added, "Let's get out of here."

She threw him a kiss with a teasing smile, causing him to nearly choke on his drink. In an elaborate gesture, he glanced at his watch. "Look at the time! I have to meet with some clients this afternoon."

"What?" Josette looked suspiciously at him. "I don't remember André saying anything about—"

"He's with Claire, remember?" said Marc. "And since our illustrious third partner, my soon-to-be brother-in-law, Raoul, is still out of town on his honeymoon, I'd better be there." He smiled at Rebekka. "And don't you need to check in at the American Embassy to talk to somebody about your old job? I can drop you off."

"That's right," Rebekka said, arising.

"But you haven't finished your food," her mother protested.

Marc's father gave them an indulgent smile. "I think I lost five kilos in the month before Ariana and I got married." Ariana gave a low chuckle and put her hand in his.

"Whatever you decide for the wedding is fine with us," Marc added. "Rebekka and I don't really care as long as we get married." He glanced at her to confirm, and she nodded quickly. How many times in the past week had she wished they had married in Utah before flying home?

"Well, the Swiss temple is the obvious choice," said Danielle. "It's close enough for many of the ward and stake members to attend, if they want. I thought we could hire a bus and . . ."

Rebekka stopped listening to her mother's voice. She'd heard it all before, and at the moment, she just wanted to be alone with Marc. Yes, for years she'd dreamed of the perfect wedding with him, but she had been waiting for so long that even one more minute was simply torture.

They kissed Marc's two grandmothers, one grandfather, Marc's parents, her mother, and then waved at Marc's siblings and the children before escaping outside to the cobblestone sidewalk. Even this late in the morning the streets were teeming with cars and people.

They walked hurriedly down the street together before Marc stopped. "Wait, not so fast. I'm already out of breath. And my heart's pounding." He took her in his arms. "Of course, that's probably because of you. Oh, it's been so long since I held you." He kissed her firmly, his lips warm against hers.

"We should have eloped," she murmured. "The temple was right there."

He groaned. "I know what you mean, but you were right making us wait. Your mother needs this wedding."

"But we could be married now," she said with a sigh. Instead, she was staying at her parents', trying to fill the gap left by her older brother, and wondering when her father would quit making not-so-subtle complaints about her upcoming marriage in a place he couldn't enter. Yes, she could get married civilly in front of all his friends and business associates, but she didn't want to. Being sealed to Marc in the temple of God meant everything to her, and it wasn't as if they lacked the means to travel to the temple, as had been the case with others in her ward. She was not going to let her father's desire to give her away ruin her eternal plans with Marc.

"Just tell me, and we'll get back on that plane," Marc said. His grin vanished and she knew he was serious. "We could be married in Utah tomorrow."

She smiled. "No, let's stay. I—I guess I just wanted to hear it from you." She lifted her lips for another kiss, uncaring of the spectacle they might be making. This was Paris, the city of love; the natives were accustomed to romance in the street.

"Rebekka, I would marry you at any time and place," he whispered huskily. A frown creased his face. "I've been such a fool for taking so long to recognize how good we are together."

"There's no looking back now." Rebekka took his hand and they began walking aimlessly.

"We may not have much time."

She stopped abruptly. "What do you mean?"

"Nothing. It's just . . . I'm so much older than you are and—"

"Only ten years. That's not much—"

"—men tend to die much earlier than wo—"

"—nowadays. We'll manage."

He pulled her close. "I love you so much, Rebekka." His breath was warm against her ear. "So much that it almost hurts."

He had voiced her thoughts exactly. "I love you too."

They strolled together toward the Seine River, a comfortable silence hanging between them. Rebekka realized that the last time they had come to this cobbled walkway, they had only been friends. Her heart had been full with his presence, but he hadn't taken her hand or declared his love as her thoughts had silently begged him to do. There had been couples lounging on stone benches or leaning against the wall, kissing or talking intimately, and Rebekka had envied them.

Marc released her hand and encircled her with his arms. "Want to stop a minute?" He motioned his chin toward a vacant bench.

They hadn't walked long and Rebekka was about to refuse, but noticed how haggard and pale his face looked. "Is something wrong?"

she asked, arching a brow. "I've noticed your eyes blinking sometimes, like you're about to go to sleep."

He rubbed a hand over his face and up through his hair. "Yes, I am tired—and that seems to be affecting my vision a little. Actually, I'm exhausted now that I think about it. I couldn't sleep well last night." He chuckled in self-deprecation, pulling her onto the bench next to him. "I can't seem to get enough sleep at all these days. I'm guess I'm too busy thinking about you."

She leaned her head on his shoulder. "It could be the time difference. You've had to change time zones twice in two weeks." He was rubbing her arms, sending tingles into her flesh.

"Maybe." His voice was noncommital.

That worried her. She remembered something he had written in an e-mail to her in Utah—something related to his transplanted kidney. His red blood cell count was lower than normal, but apparently the nephrologist hadn't been too concerned. Yet had Marc ever returned for the recommended checkup? She didn't know. Recently he had seemed so healthy—except perhaps for the unnatural tiredness he was experiencing—that she had forgotten the incident.

Before she could question him further he said, "I really don't have a meeting today. Must be the first time I ever lied about something like that."

"You weren't fooling anyone except my mother. Didn't you see that look your parents exchanged? They understood."

"I wonder how much I've missed seeing all these years." Marc's voice became suddenly forlorn.

Rebekka leaned closer to him, searching his eyes with her own. "We've been through this before. I thought we agreed not to look back. We've been friends all these years, that's important too. And now we're getting married."

He held her tightly, fiercely. "I'm going to make you the best husband, Rebekka. I promise."

They clung together silently, watching the water in the river, the occasional passing boat. A group of teens wandered by followed by an old lady in black, her large shoulder-bag filled with groceries.

"My mother used to bring us here a lot when we were children." Marc's voice had returned to normal.

"I remember your telling me that she used to come here with her brother all the time. And then with you and Josette and André when you were little. That's why you love it so much."

"Perhaps." He was quiet for a moment and then said, "But what I remember most of all was when you and I used to come here roller blading. Do you remember?"

"Oh yes." She felt his gaze on her face, but she kept her eyes on the water. "I do." So many memories—most of them wonderful.

Marc slid off the stone bench and knelt in front of her. "I know I asked you to marry me at the airport in Salt Lake, but I wanted to do it again here, where we have so many memories." His eyes locked onto hers and she said nothing, sensing his desire to continue without interruption.

"Will you marry me, Rebekka?" Out of his pocket he pulled a plush blue box that held a thick band with five large, channel-set diamonds.

Rebekka felt her eyes widen. "You bought it?" They had looked at rings the week before, and she had favored this one, but had been embarrassed at the cost.

"You liked it best. And we can afford it." He removed the ring from its cradle. "Well?"

Tears slipped from the corners of her eyes. "Of course I'll marry you, Marc. I love you. I've loved you since I was five."

Marc eased the ring onto her finger and then cupped her face with his hands, wiping away her tears with his thumbs. "I believe I'm the luckiest man in the world." He pulled his face to hers and kissed her tenderly and then with increasing emotion.

At last they separated reluctantly, staring deeply in each other's eyes as several heartbeats passed between them. Rebekka could still feel the imprint of his hands on her face, of his lips on her mouth. "This is going to be the longest month of my life," she murmured.

Marc grinned and moved as though he were trying to get to his feet. Abruptly he tensed, bringing his hands to his chest. His breathing came more rapidly. "Rebekka, . . . I'm feeling . . . odd. Like I'm going to throw up. My heart's . . . racing. And I'm having trouble seeing again."

A few seconds passed before she realized he wasn't joking. Cold fear swept through her heart. The song she had composed for him began again in her mind. With a strength she didn't know she possessed, she helped him onto the bench, pushing him flat. "Breathe slowly," she ordered, keeping her voice steady, though inside she was thoroughly panicked.

What was wrong? A heart attack? Maybe. More likely it was something else, something related to the kidney transplant he had received so many years ago. Every two years his transplanted kidney had been tested, and every test had shown that it had been working perfectly.

Except that something was not completely right the last time he went to the doctor, she remembered. The doctor's warning hadn't been severe, though; Marc would never have let it go if it had been. They both knew too well that the day would come when the donated kidney would stop cleaning adequate toxins from his blood.

She tried to remember the details she had read about kidney failure. Sometimes there was a slow decline, others were more rapid. The toxins in the blood would build up, causing tiredness. Blood pressure would rise, causing—what? Rapid pulse? A heart attack? Did it also do something to the vision? *Why don't I know these things?* her mind screamed. She loved Marc so much and yet she was ignorant to all but the basics of the care he needed—or even his daily medications. One thing she did know: many people died from the numerous complications that were possible with the loss of kidney function. And the failure didn't have to be complete to cause death.

"Marc," she asked. "Quickly, tell me. Could these signs be related to kidney failure—or some degree of it?"

"I—" He paused, and when he spoke again his voice was a moan. "Yes. I guess. I don't know. There's a huge list of what can go wrong. I've had some . . . symptoms, but I thought it was because of . . . us. I didn't stop to think it might be related to my kidney."

Of course not. They'd had other things on their minds. And obviously the discomfort hadn't been severe enough to cause him concern—until today.

His labored breathing was growing worse, as was his pallor. Realizing she had no time to spare, Rebekka reached for her purse, searching for her cell phone. Whom should she call? An ambulance. That's what she needed. Better to overreact than to lose him. She dialed the numbers and when her call was answered, she quickly explained her location and Marc's symptoms. "He's a kidney transplant recipient," she added. "It could be kidney failure."

"Our people are on their way," assured a calm voice that Rebekka couldn't identify as male or female.

"I thought it would be longer than this," Marc said in a rush. "In Utah I had the feeling our time together wouldn't be long, but I thought that was because—"

"You're going to be just fine. You aren't getting out of marrying me so easily. Now shut up and breathe."

A grin appeared on his pale face. "That's one of the things I love about you, Rebekka. You don't mince words."

Rebekka held his hand as they waited for the ambulance, keeping a close eye on his breathing and his pulse, which was far too rapid. For once she wished she had majored in nursing instead of languages.

"I'm feeling better," he said after a short time, lifting his head. "I think I just need to take a nap. Help me up."

"No." She put a hand on his chest and pushed him back to the bench. "You stay right there. And keep your eyes closed."

She could hear the ambulance now, and felt relief as men with a stretcher pushed through the growing group of onlookers and surrounded Marc. The relief didn't last long.

"Blood pressure 260 over 140," someone said.

"Is that bad?" Rebekka asked, already knowing from the grave looks around her that it must be.

No one answered her question.

"Well?" Marc demanded.

"A little high," a man told Marc as he inserted an IV. "Lie still and try not to worry. We'll take good care of you."

They whisked him through the crowd, and Rebekka followed. One of the ambulance personnel dropped back to walk with her.

"You should know that 260 over 140 is an extremely dangerous level," he said in a low voice. "But we don't want him to worry. That could make it worse. He could have a very serious stroke at any minute."

Rebekka stumbled and would have fallen but for the man's quick support on her elbow. Had she come this far just to lose Marc now?

She began to pray.

HAPTER 2

André Perrault was loath to leave the family gathering, but it was far more important to be with his wife, Claire, who had contracted the latest cold going around the neighborhood. In anyone else it wasn't something that would cause concern, but he was always careful when it came to her health. During the first five years of their marriage she had been sick to the point of genuine worry. The doctors had attributed her poor health to a lack of proper nutrition while growing up, and the quick births of their two daughters, Ana and Marée, now six and five respectively, had further weakened her.

Five different doctors had warned André not to allow her to have another child—ever. Though he would have preferred more children, he had vowed that he would not trade the chance of a son or another beautiful daughter for his wife's life. Claire was his world and he loved her deeply. Meanwhile, Claire had learned to choose her food and nutrients carefully, and for the past two years she had been well, if not completely strong. André believed her improvement was permanent, but he was careful nevertheless.

"I'm home," he called out as he entered their comfortable apartment. The quiet was almost tangible, and he began to worry. "Claire? Where are you?"

"In the living room." Sure enough, she was settled on their off-white leather sofa, reading the Relief Society lesson she would be teaching in two weeks.

He kissed her pale cheek as she swung her legs off the cushion to make room for him. Her white crocheted lap blanket fell to the teal-marbled carpet and he swept it up before sitting next to her. As a result of her lack of body fat she was often cold, so she had made this small blanket to pull around her when in the living room.

"How'd it go?" Claire's striking turquoise eyes met his. "Where are the girls?"

André put an arm around her and she snuggled close to him. "Louis-Géralde is off and the girls are having brunch with the family. My parents will drop them by when they're through."

"That's nice of them." She paused before adding, "You could have stayed. I know how you enjoy those things, and I've been just fine here."

He nuzzled her soft, fragrant cheek. "Given the choice, I'd rather be here," he said truthfully.

She gave a little sigh and laid the back of her head against his shoulder. Her lesson book shut of its own accord. Claire opened it again, rifling through the pages until she found the right one. Her movements were quick and graceful, reminding André of a small bird who, despite its nervous energy, was ultimately so delicate.

"How are you feeling?" he asked.

She glanced at him with a trace of guilt. "I took a painkiller. I couldn't bear the headache anymore." He knew Claire tried not to use over-the-counter medication because of her new healthy regime. She hated feeling ill and hated staying in bed even worse, but they had learned that taking medication was often a temporary fix which only masked the symptoms of illness.

"It must have been bad. I shouldn't have left you."

"I'm really fine. It's not like when I was sick before. Really."

André gathered her in his arms and arose, lifting her slight frame easily. "Well, I think it's time you got back in bed—just in case." Her fingers feathered over his arm, and without meaning to, he kissed the soft white throat and buried his face into her black hair. She gave a low chuckle, her arms going up around his neck.

He tucked her into their queen-size bed. "I'm going to get us something to eat."

She smiled at him, a ghost of her usual brilliance. "I'll be better soon." Her eyes appealed to him, begging forgiveness.

He lay on the bed with his arms around her, their bodies separated by the blankets. "I know, Claire. And don't worry about it. I love taking care of you." He kissed her cheek softly.

"What if I . . . go back to being sick? I just couldn't bear that—for me or for you. I want you to be happy."

He held her more tightly. "I *am* happy. Don't you know that? Being with you makes me happy."

He started to leave, but she grabbed his hand. "Stay with me. Please."

André held her silently for a long time until her eyelids drooped. Smoothing her hair, he realized that he had come home just in time to prevent her from working too long on her lesson. She was obviously exhausted, but hadn't returned to bed.

He felt her head, and it seemed hot to him despite the medication. When she awoke he would take her temperature and then decide whether to take her to the doctor. Of course she would protest, not wishing to give him trouble or add to their expenses. She never seemed to understand that as one of the three partners in Perrault and Massoni Engineering and Architecture, he made plenty of money. Her frugal upbringing was deeply ingrained.

Bestowing a final kiss on her head covered by the mass of black hair, he closed his own tired eyes and slept.

Only moments seemed to pass before an insistent buzzing filled his head. Claire moaned softly and murmured, "It's the door. Must be the girls."

André's hand went instinctively to her forehead.

"I'm fine," she insisted. "Really, I'm feeling better."

"Stay here. I'll get it." André pulled himself to his feet, rubbing the sleep from his eyes as he walked toward the door. He punched the white intercom button in the entryway. "Yes?"

His mother's voice came cheerfully. "It's us."

André pushed the buzzer that released the lock to the apartment building below. Then he opened the door and waited for his mother and the girls to mount the stairs to the first floor, knowing that for such a short distance they wouldn't use the elevator. He knelt and hugged the girls as they arrived, each a miniature version of her mother.

"We had so much fun," Ana told him. "But you know, Uncle Marc is acting weird."

"He keeps staring at Rebekka," Marée added with a giggle.

"Well, why not?" André stood, picking them both up in his arms. "Rebekka's pretty easy on the eyes, don't you think? Not as good as you guys, but close." The girls giggled and squirmed to get down.

Ana's large blue-green eyes stared up at him. "Is Mommy awake?"

"Yes, you can go see her, but don't be too loud."

"Can she read us a book?"

"Hmm." André pretended to think. "Mommy's kind of feeling achy and sick, so Ana, why don't you read to her? You know, one of those books your teacher gave you from school. That way, Mommy can close her eyes while you read."

"I want to read too," declared Marée.

"You don't know how as well as I do," Ana said. "I'm in the first grade."

"Take turns," André told them. Marée couldn't read well, but she was very good at describing pictures. Most of the time her make-believe stories were more inventive and interesting than the real ones.

The girls ran down the hall and André turned to Ariana, who had arrived more slowly behind the girls. "Thanks, Mom."

She smiled and inclined her head gracefully, causing her short dark locks to fall forward, softly framing her face. "We enjoyed having them. Are you sure you won't let them come home with me until Claire is feeling better?"

"No. She likes having them around—even when she's sick. She worries too much when she can't check on them. But once she's well I'm planning on taking her away for a weekend, just like we did in the summer. We'd be glad if you'd take the girls then."

"I'd love to." Ariana stooped to pick up a few bits of paper, her body limber and supple despite her advancing years. She straightened, and her brown eyes regarded him soberly. "Are you getting any sleep?"

He grimaced. "Not much. But Claire looks better today. I really think this is a passing cold bug—not like before."

"That's good." Ariana sighed before adding, "I know it was really diffi-cult those first years, but I was so proud of the way you took care of her."

He lifted a shoulder in a half-shrug. His mother had told him this before, and his answer was always the same. "I love her."

"I know. We all do. Claire's a wonderful woman. I couldn't have asked for a better daughter-in-law."

"Now you'll have two."

Ariana's dark eyes came alive with playfulness. "Finally! I thought I was going to have to hit Marc over the head. He's been so stubborn that he hasn't been able to see how much Rebekka loves him." She gave a low laugh. "Do you remember how he just about went crazy when she left for her mission?"

André grinned. "Wasn't that when he started dating that voodoo woman from Haiti? Thought he could convert her to Christianity or something."

"She did come to church for a while. Of course, it didn't take her long to realize that Marc was in love with someone else—even if he didn't realize it himself."

"I don't know why he didn't see how he felt about Rebekka sooner," André said. "Rebekka's a fine lady. I have to admit that after my mission, I had a pretty serious crush on her myself, but she never glanced my way. It was always Marc, Marc, Marc." André laughed, joined by Ariana.

She shook her head in reminiscence. "Marc was always stubborn and a bit oblivious to a lot of things. He was lucky to have Josette and you to steady him." A faint smile played on her lips, and her eyes were far away.

"And now he has Rebekka," André said.

Ariana's smile dimmed. "You know, I'm worried about those two. Philippe and Danielle are putting a lot of pressure on them to wait and plan an elaborate wedding and reception. They don't seem to remember the urgency of youth."

"Marc and Rebekka will be all right." He was so sure of this that even as he spoke, he was no longer thinking of his brother and Rebekka, but about Claire. She had been so healthy these past two years and life had been very good to them. But what if her health declined again? Those previous years of recurring illness had been so difficult for them both. No, it couldn't happen, not when they'd come so far.

"What's wrong, André?" His mother gazed anxiously at him.

"Nothing . . . I'd better check on Claire." He nearly ran into the bedroom, but stopped when he found her cuddled up with the girls, listening to their stories. Her smile was bright, but not unnaturally so.

"I'm fine," she said, reading the worry in his eyes. "My headache is gone."

André's knees felt weak with relief. Of course she was fine. Just because she had been ill for so many years at the beginning of their marriage didn't mean one minor sickness would cause her to regress to that point.

"I am a little hungry though," Claire added apologetically.

"I'll bring you something."

As André returned to the kitchen where Ariana waited, the cordless phone began ringing. He grabbed it on his way to the cupboard. "Hello?"

"André, thank heaven! It's me, Rebekka. Something terrible's happened. With Marc. I've tried to call your parents, but no one's home there or at Marie-Thérèse's, and Josette's line is busy."

André didn't have time to be offended that she had tried his number last. "My mom's here. I think my dad must have gone back to work. What happened?"

"I don't know. Marc sort of collapsed. We're going to the ambulance now. I'm calling from my cell." Her voice lowered. "His blood pressure's way too high. They're afraid he's going to have a stroke." Her voice was calm but held a thinly veiled undercurrent of terror. André could easily read the thoughts beneath the words: now that Marc had finally come around, Rebekka was afraid she would lose him after all.

"What hospital are you going to?"

There was a pause while Rebekka asked the ambulance workers. André took the opportunity to quickly explain the situation to his mother.

"We'll meet you there," André said when Rebekka returned with the information. "Don't worry about calling anyone else. We'll take care of it."

"Thank you." There were tears in Rebekka's voice. "I'm hanging up now. The ambulance is going to leave, and I need to go with them."

André pushed the off button and turned to his mother, who stared at him anxiously. "Better call Dad," he said. "We'll need to give Marc a blessing."

$\mathcal{C}$HAPTER 3

After leaving the family brunch Marie-Thérèse and her two children went to Josette's house. Since the cousins weren't attending school that day, they wanted to play, and Marie-Thérèse and Josette took the opportunity to get started on the invitations for Marc's wedding.

"Since I've been so miserable with this pregnancy," Josette said, "I wouldn't have volunteered to design them. But Danielle was looking very stressed."

"She's enjoying herself, though, I think." Marie-Thérèse sat on a padded wooden chair in Josette's kitchen. "After Raoul ran off like that, she's glad to have Rebekka doing it right."

"Too bad Philippe doesn't see it that way." Josette put a stack of papers and a phone book on the table. "Marc told me he's been pressuring them to have a huge, showy civil ceremony."

Marie-Thérèse nodded sympathetically. "That's tough. You know, that guy was always too persuasive." Marie-Thérèse had never liked Philippe, but out of respect for his family, had generally tried to keep her opinion of him to herself. Feeling guilty at her words, she added, "But he really seems to care for Danielle."

"Thank heavens for that."

There was a loud thump in the playroom where the faint voices of the children could be heard. Marie-Thérèse listened for a moment to see if there were any tears.

"Emery, Preston, Anton, Stephen—stop that right now!" Josette yelled. There was no answer. She shrugged and began sketching on a white sheet of paper. "Doesn't sound serious."

"Brandon would tell us if it were." As the oldest and the only girl, Larissa should have been the responsible one, but Marie-Thérèse had long ago perceived that her son, almost eleven years old, was a much better baby-sitter. In fact, the energetic Larissa was likely responsible for the disturbance. Fortunately, Josette and Zack had bought their apartment on the bottom floor so they could have a little yard and garden space out the back, and that meant there were no neighbors underneath them to complain of the noise.

"There's nothing they can hurt in there, or that can hurt them." Josette started in on a new piece of paper. "And Emery knows how to keep the little boys in line." She paused a moment before adding, "Does Rebekka seem different to you?"

Marie-Thérèse shrugged. "She's in love, I can tell that. But you know, she's always been so collected, so together. Even as a child. Sometimes she intimidates me."

"I know what you mean." Josette stopped drawing. "Two degrees and being able to play the piano as well as she does. *And* always the top grade in her class. She must be some sort of genius."

Marie-Thérèse scratched the top of her slightly upturned nose. "And beautiful. Her skin is so perfect and the color of her hair—not really red but dark brown with just the exact amount of red highlights and—"

"And young." Josette interrupted with a giggle. "Gee, we sound downright jealous."

"Well, not really. I actually admire her. She hasn't let her looks go to her head."

"It's not easy to be good-looking. Either men only want you for your looks, or they're too scared to ask you out. And those are usually the ones that are worth dating, if you know what I mean."

Marie-Thérèse knew Josette spoke from firsthand experience. Her sister still garnered stares from complete strangers—even when pregnant.

"If you think about it," Josette went on, "for all her poise and looks, Rebekka hasn't gone out all that much. I think she stays away from men purposefully."

"Why's that, do you suppose?" Marie-Thérèse peered at Josette's drawings. "Here, let me write the words on another paper and then you can copy them onto your design." She had always been better at grammar than Josette.

"Maybe Rebekka didn't go out because she preferred to be with Marc," Josette said thoughtfully. "They were always doing something together."

The two women looked at each other in sudden understanding. "Do you think that all this time? . . ." Marie-Thérèse left the sentence hanging.

"I thought she was over him a long time ago." Josette bit one side of her bottom lip thoughtfully. "But maybe she wasn't after all."

"If that's the case, I wonder why she didn't confide in us? We could have helped."

Josette nodded and her straight, waist-length hair tumbled forward. "Yes, Marc always was a little dense at seeing what was right before his eyes. I never thought, though, that we were just as dense." She sighed and rubbed her swollen stomach. "But I guess we've been a bit preoccupied."

"Could that be why she went to Utah?"

"I'll bet it is."

Marie-Thérèse thought the idea of the cool Rebekka pining away for Marc more than a little incongruous—calm, poised Rebekka, who always seemed so sure of herself and had always pursued exactly what she wanted. "Well, let's not say anything, just in case. I wouldn't want to hurt her feelings."

Josette grinned. "I just can't believe Marc is finally getting married. And he looks so happy." She brushed a sudden tear under her eye. "Darn hormones. They always make me so emotional." With her knuckles she again gently kneaded her large stomach, and Marie-Thérèse wondered if the baby was kicking. She didn't ask.

"They're going to have beautiful children," she said instead, tucking a lock of dark blonde hair behind her ear. She normally kept it shoulder length, but her hairdresser had layered the sides more than normal, so it constantly felt disarrayed. Her husband loved the new look, but Marie-Thérèse wasn't sure if the softening effect it had on her narrow face was worth the annoyance.

Josette threw back her head and laughed. "Oh yeah, beautiful kids. Give her a few years and she'll be hauling a brood around like the rest of us. It's hard to look poised with a ton of kids hanging onto your leg."

Marie-Thérèse's breath caught in her throat. A ton of kids, her sister had said, but Marie-Thérèse didn't have a ton of kids. Just two, Larissa and Brandon. Both had come quickly enough, but she had been through ten years of reproductive therapy since with no further pregnancies.

Clenching her jaw, she tried to will the emotions away, but they rippled through her with a dogged thoroughness she couldn't deny. She had always wanted more children. Oh, not six or seven—she didn't fool herself that she, with her obsession for organization, could handle that many, but certainly three or four. She had discovered early that Mathieu was good with children, much more patient than she was, and he more than filled up any gaps she might leave in her mothering. She tended to be too rigid and organized, but under his tutelage she had learned to allow the occasional mess in the name of fun. Marie-Thérèse had given her best efforts and then some to raising her children, and Larissa and Brandon appeared to be emotionally healthy individuals, despite Larissa's rebellious attitude of late. Why hadn't she been allowed to conceive more?

"Oh, Marie-Thérèse, I'm sorry." Josette left her drawing and scooted her chair closer. "I spoke without thinking. I didn't mean to . . ."

Marie-Thérèse struggled not to cry. It was a hard thing not to be given a child when every day babies were abandoned or abused by those who should have been their protectors, when unwed mothers visited abortion clinics or dumped their unwanted offspring onto aging parents.

"It's okay," she said, knowing it soon would be. Her emotions ran high on the subject, but daily prayer prevented the bitterness from consuming her every moment. Prayer—and her plan for adoption.

She rose suddenly and seized her oversized purse, which she had laid near the telephone, taking out a thin manila folder. Silently she handed it to Josette.

Her sister studied the documents, eyebrows raising in surprise. "Is this what I think it is?"

Marie-Thérèse pushed her hair behind her ears. "I'm tired of waiting. I'm tired of all the needles, exams, and disappointments. So

Mathieu and I've decided to adopt. And not here since there's too long a wait for young children. Instead we're going to the Ukraine. It's going to cost a small fortune, but we're approved for two."

Josette leapt to her feet and hugged Marie-Thérèse. "Why didn't you tell us?"

"Well, at first I wanted to be sure, and then I just wanted it to be closer so I wouldn't go crazy with everybody asking me when it was going to happen. But we'll be going next month to choose children from one of several orphanages. The youngest babies they'll let go are six months old, the oldest three years, but that's fine with me. We might even adopt siblings—that's why we got approved for two. I didn't want to separate siblings if we found any that were supposed to belong to us."

Having been adopted along with her blood sister Pauline by her aunt and uncle, Ariana and Jean-Marc, Marie-Thérèse knew what it meant to a child to preserve a blood-sibling tie. Since Pauline had been born with HIV and later died from AIDS, Marie-Thérèse suspected the decision to take on the girls full-time hadn't been an easy one for the couple she now called Mom and Dad. But it had meant everything in the world to her to have both Pauline and her adopted family. She knew Pauline had shared the feeling.

Josette was dancing around the kitchen with excitement over the pending adoption, and Marie-Thérèse felt her own joy bubble up inside, replacing the previous hurt. Over the past months while making this decision, she had tried to maintain a calm reserve in the event of possible disappointment, but now it seemed as though nothing could prevent it from happening. She would have another child after all!

"So when are you going to tell the family?"

Marie-Thérèse suddenly felt self-conscious. "Well, I did talk to Mom and Dad a few weeks ago. They've been very supportive. And we told the children last night. That's why I'm telling you now. I'm sure Larissa will talk to your boys, and I wanted you to hear it from me. André and Claire also know because I've asked André if he'll consider going with me for part of the time in the Ukraine, in case it goes over the time Mathieu can take from work."

Josette hugged her again awkwardly, maneuvering the weight of the growing baby inside her. "I'm so glad that we'll be having babies together again." She grimaced. "Although you won't have to get rid of the fat afterwards. Of course you never did anyway, not really. You've always been so thin." She clapped her hands. "Hey, maybe one of the children will be Stephen's age! You know he goes crazy with no one his age to play with."

"I've thought of that," Marie-Thérèse admitted. "But we'll have to see what happens. I'd like them as young as possible, but if it's a sibling pair . . . we'll see."

"And the Ukraine—Louis-Géralde's mission. When he gets home he'll be able to talk to them in their native tongue!"

"Well, at least he can help them understand their culture. I don't know how much Ukrainian or Russian such a young child—or children—will speak, or remember after two years of being in France."

"That's right. I didn't think of that. But still, it's neat." Josette began to pace. "Oh, this is driving me crazy already! I don't know what clothes to buy for them or anything!"

Marie-Thérèse laughed. "It's driving you crazy? What about me? I'm the one who's going nuts."

"Oh yeah," Josette replied dramatically, winking a brown eye. "You're the one who plans a whole month of meals at a time, the one who organizes her cans alphabetically—"

"I can find them better that—"

"—the one who would rather have a clean refrigerator than a new outfit—"

"—way, and remember I don't have someone who comes in to clean like you."

Josette grinned. "You're going to need it."

"We might not be able to afford it after the adoption."

"There!" Josette returned to her a chair, grinning in triumph. "That's what I'll give you. Two months of weekly maid service while you become adjusted to your new baby or babies."

Marie-Thérèse laughed, admitting that Josette had hit on the perfect gift. She touched her sister's shoulder. "I accept. Thank you."

"And I'm sure I can get Marc and André to spring for some baby clothes, and Mom and Dad can fork it over for the car seat and a new stroller, and Grandma Louise can—"

"I get the idea," Marie-Thérèse said dryly. Secretly she felt happy knowing her family would be there every step of the way.

Then, wanting to change the subject because the realization of her dream was still a month away, Marie-Thérèse picked up one of the papers Josette had been drawing on. "Now let's see what you've done with these designs. Hey, I really like this triple folded one. Let's call a few printing shops for prices before we run it by Danielle."

After checking on the six children, who were busying playing a rousing game of Monopoly, they bent to their task. Almost two hours passed before André appeared at their door, his dark hair disheveled and his brown eyes worried.

"We've been trying to reach you for hours," he said, the words tumbling over themselves. "Marc's had a collapse and he's in the hospital. They think his kidney is failing."

CHAPTER 4

André explained the situation to his sisters on the way to the hospital. "Mom should already be there by now. I knew you would want to come, so we took separate cars. I've been calling you since Rebekka called us, but your phone was busy."

"We were talking to printing shops," Marie-Thérèse said.

"Hasn't there been any news since then?" In the back seat, Josette chewed her lip nervously, her face devoid of color. "Oh, I can't stand not knowing!"

André nodded sympathetically. Marc was his business partner and his best friend, excepting Claire, and he knew exactly how Josette felt. "Mom called me once, but she didn't have any news," he told her. "They're still doing tests. But don't worry, they'll get his blood pressure down. Marc's too stubborn to die."

"Yeah. Too stubborn." Josette looked happier. Marie-Thérèse said nothing, but her lips moved as though in silent prayer.

"Is your cell on?" Josette asked. "We left that number with the kids. Mine wasn't charged—I always forget."

"It's on." Normally André would have teased her about the ludicrous question—of course he would have his cell phone turned on during such a crisis—but this time he let it ride.

"I'm going to kill him," Josette muttered into the abrupt silence. There were two spots of bright red on her cheeks now, which André hoped was a good thing. But almost immediately, tears started down her face. "I bet he didn't go in for testing when he should have. It's all my fault! I've been so wrapped up in this terrible pregnancy that I didn't check up on him—not that I don't love you, Baby." She touched her stomach fleetingly.

"He's a grown man," Marie-Thérèse reminded her.

Josette nodded, chewing on her lip. "That's why he needs someone to care for him. It's the whole macho thing—refusing to get help because he's a man. But Rebekka wasn't around and I knew . . ." She looked at André, her thoughts changing in midsentence. "How long have you known that Rebekka's been in love with Marc for like a million years?"

He shrugged. "Rebekka's always been in love with him. That's nothing new."

"It was to me." Josette's bottom lip poked out in a pout that was oddly becoming. André couldn't help but smile. Despite the passing years and all her children, his big sister was just as passionate and expressive as ever.

"This is the same hospital we came to with Brandon last month," Marie-Thérèse murmured as they arrived at their destination.

André pulled into the nearest parking space. "Has he had any more reactions?" he asked. Brandon had been swimming with his cousins when his entire body had became splotchy red and swollen. He had begun coughing, and experienced such difficulty breathing that his parents had rushed him to the emergency room.

"It happened again when the neighbor children got together outside for a water fight," Marie-Thérèse answered, slipping from the front seat. "Though not as bad. That kind of rules out an allergy to the pool chlorine."

"What I don't get is why it happened when he was outside your apartment, but it doesn't happen in the bath," Josette said. "It's the same water."

Marie-Thérèse shrugged. "I know. It's confusing. Must be something in the air. But the allergy testing hasn't yet revealed anything other than the food allergies we already knew. At least he seems to be okay now."

"Maybe it's a passing thing." They were at the hospital doors now and André held them open for his sisters.

In the waiting room of the ICU, their parents sat on a brown couch, hands linked as they clung to each other for support. They arose as André and his sisters entered.

"Any news?" Josette asked quickly.

Ariana shook her head. "Soon. But they let me in to see him for a minute." She paused. "It's bad."

Josette was aghast. "Where is he? Is he alone?"

"No, Rebekka's with him. She'll let us know the minute she hears anything."

* * * * *

"It's my kidney, isn't it?" Marc asked the doctor, his grip on Rebekka's hand tightening. She sat on the edge of the bed, as close to him as the doctor allowed. How grateful he was to have her with him!

The doctor's ruddy face was grave. "Well, it looks that way. Your creatinine is high, and that's caused your blood pressure to rise. The high blood pressure is, in turn, causing the capillaries in your retina to bleed, thus explaining the blurry vision you're experiencing."

"Creatinine?" Rebekka's finely shaped eyebrows rose in puzzlement.

"A measure of kidney function. Normal levels are point eight to one point four, but Marc's is over six." He paused briefly before explaining to Rebekka what Marc already knew. "The loss of kidney function is not reversible; Marc will soon need dialysis or a transplant."

"When?" Marc felt a pit form in the bottom of his stomach. Nineteen years had passed since his first transplant, but he vividly remembered the pain and lack of energy he had experienced before and after the surgery. Strangely, the memories of dialysis were even worse. His hand went to his abdomen, where he carried the scars of both the surgery and dialysis to forever remind him of the night he had pulled Rebekka's mother out of an underground train station that had been bombed in a terrorist attack, nearly entombing himself in the process.

He looked at Rebekka. *I know everyone thought I was irresponsible that day, but I'd do it again. If not for Danielle, then for Rebekka. She was only five at the time; she needed her mother.*

"Well, normally blood pressure medicine might be able to control or even stall your decline, but your kidneys aren't producing enough erythropoietin." The doctor glanced at Rebekka and added for her benefit, "That's a hormone that aids in the production of red blood cells. When you don't have enough erythropoietin, your red blood cell count declines, and fatigue and anemia set in. That means you're constantly tired. And since the kidney is losing its ability to cleanse the blood, impurities and toxins are left, making you ill." His attention shifted back to Marc. "I bet you've been feeling nauseated."

"I thought it was because I'd gotten engaged recently." Marc gave Rebekka an apologetic smile. "You know, nervousness. And that the tiredness was jet lag."

The doctor eyed their linked hands without speaking. Marc wondered if he noticed the ten-year age difference between them. No, maybe not—everyone always said he appeared young for his age.

Rebekka moistened her lips with her tongue and said, "The last time Marc had dialysis they were worried about finding access—I'm not sure if that's the right term—and that they wouldn't be able to clean his blood anymore. And he wasn't doing well on dialysis anyway. He got really sick, had no energy . . ." Rebekka blinked furiously, and Marc knew she was holding back tears.

The doctor met Marc's gaze. "Then it's probably important that you begin transplanting procedures. You've been through this before and know the routine. Do you have anyone who would be willing to give you a kidney?"

Marc sighed. He certainly had been through this before, and the only members of his immediate family who had a compatible blood type and were therefore qualified to give him a kidney were his father and Louis-Géralde. But at the time of his first transplant his father had been ruled out because one of his own kidneys was not fully functional, and Louis-Géralde had not yet been born. Because Marc's blood was relatively rare and hard to match, and because the dialysis was not going well, the doctors and his family had feared for his life. Thankfully, they had found a match in time.

"I'll give him mine," Rebekka said, pulling Marc from his thoughts.

He looked toward her in surprise. "But your blood type probably isn't—"

Rebekka lifted her chin stubbornly. "When my mother almost died in that train bombing, there was talk of your getting her kidney—the one that still worked—if she died. She wanted you to have it, but then your father gave her that blessing and she lived—our first introduction to the Church. So I guess that if she could have given you a kidney, there's a chance I probably can, too."

Marc opened his mouth to protest, but realized she was right. He also realized that he didn't want her to endure such a thing for him. Though the chance of complications for the donor were very rare, it was not a risk he was willing to take with Rebekka's life. They had already lost so many years together because of his stupidity. "You might not have the right blood type," he stalled. "My sisters and André don't. You could take after your father."

"You don't have to have the same blood type," the doctor put in. "Your blood only has to be compatible. That makes it a lot easier. Of course related donors are likely to have more matching antigens, but even most unrelated people have one matching antigen. There have been quite a few successful nonrelated transplants."

Marc ignored him. "It can be dangerous, Rebekka."

"I don't care." Her normally velvet voice was firm and unyielding, and her beautiful gray eyes resembled pieces of hard granite. "It's a risk I'm willing to take."

Marc glanced at the doctor helplessly, hoping he would explain the dangers to her, but the doctor only smiled. "Good. Live donor transplants are so much more successful than cadaveric ones. I'll write down a recommendation for a transplant center—though you probably already have one in mind, having been through this before. I'm sure you know that the center you choose will most definitely affect the outcome of the surgery. The more kidney transplants a center does, the higher its percentage of success. Meaning, of course, that the doctors in the high-volume centers are more skilled and the staff more equipped to handle any emergencies that may arise."

Marc looked away from Rebekka's stoney gaze. "I remember reading that. Or maybe my mother told me."

The cuff that automatically checked Marc's blood pressure every twenty minutes tightened around his arm again. The doctor studied the numbers intently. "Your blood pressure seems to be coming back down, although very slowly. In another hour some of that growing crowd out there in the waiting room can come in, perhaps two at a time, and hopefully you will be able to go home tomorrow." With a final smile, he was gone.

Marc saw a single tear sliding down Rebekka's smooth cheek. He caught it with his finger, enjoying the soft feel of her flesh, but hating the pain in her eyes. "I don't know about this," he said softly.

"You promised you'd make me the best husband," she rejoined, adjusting her position on the edge of the bed. "You have to fight. I know you can make it." No more tears fell now.

He had been going to tell her more about the feelings he had experienced in America, when he had felt that their time together might be short. How in response to that feeling, he had promised the Lord to be happy with any time he would be allowed with her. But as she stared at him with those luminous gray eyes, he couldn't share the experience. He had to comfort her.

"It'll be okay," he murmured. "We'll get through this."

A faint smile flickered on her lips. "If we do the transplant quickly we might be able to still make our honeymoon."

He frowned. "I don't know if Louis-Géralde's going to be so excited about having his mission interrupted before it even begins."

"You're willing to let Louis-Géralde do it, but not me?" Rebekka's soft voice rose a pitch. "Marc, he's on his mission, for heaven's sake! I'm right here."

"Rebekka, it's not as easy as that! The better the match, the longer the kidney will last and the lower the dosages of medicines I'll have to take each day." His voice lowered. "Besides, this kidney lasted me nineteen years. Even in a best-case scenario, I'll need another transplant in twenty-five to thirty years. You could always donate then."

"Or one of our children could," she said tersely. "A lot can change in twenty years."

"I know." Marc stared down at the white sheet and worn, off-white blanket that covered his hospital gown. "Rebekka, I just can't bear to lose you."

"*I'm* the one who doesn't want to lose *you*." Her voice plainly exposed her fear.

He put his arms around her, awkwardly with the blood pressure cuff attached, and clung to her slender form. "You won't."

"At least let me try. I might be almost as good a match as Louis-Géralde."

"Okay," he conceded, willing to do almost anything to ease her agitation. "But Louis-Géralde has planned all his life to give me a kidney. He might be a little jealous."

She smiled blandly at his poor humor. "Well, in another twenty years he can have his chance." She bent down to kiss him with those soft, sweet lips. Their kiss was achingly tender and promising. Despite his exhaustion, Marc wanted nothing more than to melt into her, but to his disappointment she pulled away quickly.

"Can't do anything to affect your blood pressure," she said, eyeing the monitor. "You nearly died today." Then her body started shaking, as if she were only now realizing the gravity of the situation. He held her hand more tightly.

Thoughts began to haunt him. What if he did die and she had to suffer losing him all over again? Perhaps it would have been better to let her marry that man in Cincinnati. For the first time, Marc almost regretted going after her.

Almost.

But life without Rebekka was no life at all. He had learned that the hard way.

He wished he could promise her a long life together. But all he could give her was hope . . . and his love. "I love you, Rebekka," he whispered fiercely. "Whatever happens, I love you." As if that made it all right.

Gradually she stopped shaking. "I love you too. So much." She bent and kissed him again, this time on the forehead. "I'm going to talk to your mother and the doctor now, to see about getting tested. You rest. I'll be back later."

Before he could protest, she was gone, the lingering scent of her perfume the only sign she had been there at all. He wanted her back the moment she had gone. The memory of her lips on his was vivid and tempting. Why hadn't he married her in Utah when he'd had the chance? At least then they would have the promise of eternity.

Marc shut his eyes and tried to think of something else. Self-pity would get him nowhere.

* * * * *

Rebekka hadn't returned when the nurses finally let his family in to see him, two at a time as promised. Marc expected his parents first, but Josette and André came through the door.

"Look at you!" Josette rushed to the bed and bent over awkwardly to plant a kiss on his cheek.

"You know me—anything for attention." Marc tried to smile, hoping she didn't hear the fear beneath the words. How many times had he made her cry as child because of his repeated crazy stunts? He wished he could take it all back now.

"You were just trying to get me out of the house without the kids," Josette said to him, wiping the tears from her cheeks.

Marc gave her a weak grin. "Well, I seem to remember a phone call you made to Mom last week. Something about needing a baby-sitter or you were going to jump off the balcony."

"Well, yeah, I was having a rough day. Everybody has them." Josette's eyes suddenly gleamed. "But remember, I don't have a balcony anymore in our new apartment. It was an empty threat."

"There's always the neighbor's," André said. Josette punched him in the shoulder.

They all fell silent, as though wondering what to say next. Josette settled on the edge of the bed, bracing herself with an extended arm as she leaned back, her stomach jutting out more noticeably.

"So, we're back where we started, eh?" André didn't meet Marc's eyes, but studied the monitor next to the bed.

"Yeah, something like that."

André met his gaze. "Rebekka says you need a new kidney."

"Or dialysis." Marc couldn't help making a face. He had detested every minute of his time on dialysis—four hours, three times a week, watching his blood go through a machine. "I'm thinking about doing that until Louis-Géralde gets home."

Josette bit her lip. "Not that again. I hated seeing you that way!"

"It wasn't that bad," Marc felt compelled to say. "I met a lot of people who didn't have problems with it. Maybe it was my age. Hey, at least I learned how to play chess."

Josette said nothing, but her fingers stroked a long scar on his arm, a remnant of his days of dialysis. Marc stifled the urge to hide it from view. Even as an adult the scars bothered him, and he usually wore long-sleeved shirts to conceal them.

"I was afraid you would leave me," Josette said finally.

He almost had. Like today. Marc swallowed, suddenly wishing he could drink a huge glass of water. But of course, his liquid intake was now, like his diet, carefully monitored.

"Zack and Rebekka are going to be tested," André said. "Mother's talking on the phone to Dr. Juppe right now."

Marc nodded absently, remembering the doctor who had not only performed his first transplant, but who worked at the most prestigious transplant facility in Paris. He had a high level of confidence in the man.

"That explains why Mom didn't come in first," he mused aloud for something to say.

"Yeah." André stared again at the monitor as the blood pressure cuff tightened around Marc's arm. What he saw must have pleased him because he gave a curt nod. Marc refrained from looking at the monitor, knowing it couldn't be too much different from the past six times he had checked.

"There's no use in calling Louis-Géralde yet." Josette rubbed the heel of her hand across the upper portion of her belly. "Wow, this guy's a kicker. What was I saying? Oh yeah, no use in calling Louis-Géralde to come home when Rebekka and Zack might be good candidates."

"There is a risk," Marc reminded her. "Are you sure you'd be willing to let your husband go through with it? I mean, you've almost got five kids now. That's a lot of responsibility."

"Very *low* risk," Josette corrected him. "And without a transplant you could die. Of course we're willing."

That was what it all boiled down to—Marc's likelihood of dying. The dilemma was exactly the same as the last time he had faced kidney failure. While a kidney was one of the easiest organs to transplant, he knew that each year many people with difficult cases like his own died before they received one. Marc hated the helplessness of his situation, but what could he do?

"Is Rebekka all right?" Marc had to ask.

André took his eyes from the numbers on the monitor, his expression stoic. "She's worried, but she'll be fine. We'll all help her through this."

"She's part of the family now," Josette added, tracing an invisible pattern on Marc's blanket.

André frowned. "She always has been, hasn't she?"

Marc didn't know to whom the question was directed. "I've lost a lot of time with her," he said. "I have to make it up to her. It's just . . ." Should he tell them of his premonition? He looked closely at Josette with the tears shimmering behind her large brown eyes, and André's faux impassiveness. No, he couldn't tell them.

Besides, my view of a short time might not be the same as the Lord's, he thought. Hadn't he always been taught that earth life was but a blink in the eternity of time? Perhaps his family would once again be going through life's refining fires, but that wasn't necessarily a bad thing. Their faith in the Lord would carry them through and they would become stronger—whatever happened.

The next family members to visit Marc were his father and Marie-Thérèse. The love in their eyes made a lump come to Marc's throat, and their hope buoyed his own. He felt fortunate to have such a close-knit and loving family.

"Your mother will be back with Rebekka soon," Jean-Marc said. "They're arranging a few things. I have to hand it to you, son. You sure took a long time finding a girl, but you've got a great one."

"I know, Dad." Marc felt pleased at his father's comment.

"Mathieu's going to be tested, too," Marie-Thérèse said. "He's Danielle's cousin, after all. He could even be a better match than the others. His family's genetic lines should be similar to ours."

"Thank you. Tell him thank you." Marc was beginning to feel drowsy, though whether it was a result of the low light level in the room or something the nurse put in his IV, he didn't know.

"Dad, will you give me a blessing?" Marc remembered how often his father had done so during his first bout with kidney failure.

Jean-Marc clasped his shoulder. "Yes, we'd like that very much. As soon as your mother and Rebekka return from their appointment making, we'll do it. André is still outside waiting. And Zack has probably arrived by now. Maybe Mathieu as well."

Within an hour, Rebekka and Ariana returned and the entire family received permission to be present during the priesthood ordinance. Jean-Marc laid his hands on his son's head. The words he spoke seemed to confirm Marc's premonition. "The Lord will give this family the courage to endure the trials and losses that may come."

Not exactly the promise of recovery Marc had hoped for, but it did hold hope of a sort. For now, it was enough to caress Rebekka's hand and feel his family's love.

Ariana touched Rebekka's shoulder. "I can stay with him for a while."

She shook her head. "I have nothing to do. I can stay here all night, if they let me." By the determined tone of her voice, Marc knew the hospital workers would have no choice but to give in.

"I'll call later then." Ariana kissed Marc on the cheek and softly stroked his forehead.

Marc noticed the new lines of worry on her face. "It'll be okay." He purposely didn't say "I'll be okay." He hadn't been able to promise that, not even to Rebekka, though he would fight to achieve their dreams.

Ariana smiled a wide, happy smile. "I know that. I'm glad you do, too."

CHAPTER 5

Marie-Thérèse left the hospital more depressed than she had felt in a long time. She hadn't experienced such sadness since before she decided to pursue adoption in the Ukraine. Marc had appeared so horribly frail and human in the hospital and for a moment, she had seen her mother in the bed, then her father, and lastly Pauline, her dear little sixteen-year-old sister. All taken from her, one at a time.

While she didn't dwell on their loss, she admitted to herself a deep fear of losing more members of her family. Because of this fear, she knew she overreacted a lot. Both Larissa and Brandon had been to more doctor appointments individually than Josette's four children all together. But her peace of mind was worth the extra trips.

"Is your phone back on?" she asked André as they arrived at his car. The hospital personnel had requested that cell phones be turned off while visiting, and she wondered if her children had tried to call.

"I forgot." He reached into his pocket briefly before opening the car door for her and Josette.

"I can't bear to see him suffer," Josette said, entering the back seat. Her voice was unusually subdued.

"He'll be all right," André replied gruffly. "Rebekka and the others will be tested tomorrow, and then we'll know. Louis-Géralde only had three matching antigens out of six, I believe. Not the best."

"Well, six out of six would be like identical twins," Josette said. "I'm his twin—I should have at least been closer." She bit her bottom lip and stared at her fingers in her lap.

"But even if you were compatible, you've had so many children," said Marie-Thérèse. "That makes the chances of success go down, doesn't it?"

"Yeah." Josette sighed. "Maybe we should call Louis-Géralde's mission president today, just in case."

"Well, it's not like he's going anywhere," André said dryly. "He'll be there for the next two years."

Josette's laugh was nervous. "I know but . . ." She shivered, though the late September day wasn't cold. "Sometimes it pays to be safe."

When they arrived at Josette's, André bid a hasty good-bye in order to return to his wife. Inside Josette's large apartment the children were peacefully playing another board game, except for Stephen who was asleep on the carpet and Brandon who was watching TV from the couch. Marie-Thérèse breathed a silent sigh of relief that everyone had survived their absence.

Larissa popped up from the floor immediately. "Well? What happened?"

"Uncle Marc's kidney is failing, but he's stable now. They're doing testing to see who'll be able to give him a new kidney."

"I'd do it," said Brandon.

Larissa shook her head. "You can't. You're not old enough."

"Well, I wish I were."

Marie-Thérèse reached in her bag for her car keys. "Come on, kids. We should go now. Your dad had to go back to work from the hospital, but he'll be home for dinner."

Larissa started for the door, but from his position on the couch Brandon coughed and moaned.

"What's with you?" Marie-Thérèse asked.

"He's been coughing, and he's got an ugly rash on his leg," Larissa said. "It's gross."

Marie-Thérèse exchanged brief looks with Josette. "Let's see it," she told Brandon. He sighed, coughed again for a long minute, and then rolled up his pant leg. Marie-Thérèse was shocked to see a swollen, ugly red rash line with deep, painful-looking groves. "When did this happen?" she demanded.

Brandon shrugged, his light brown eyes innocent. "Yesterday, I think. It just came."

"Have you been scratching it? That's what it looks like."

"No, it hurts if I try."

"Why didn't you tell me about it?"

"It just got bad today. I only noticed when you were gone."

"Pull up your shirt."

He gave her a horrified glance. "Mom!"

"Everyone out!" Josette ordered.

The kids grumbled as they ambled from the room. "Don't know why he cares," Larissa muttered, wrinkling her nose. "He's a boy, isn't he?"

"He has a right to his privacy," Marie-Thérèse answered. Brandon had always been rather modest and rarely took his shirt off, even at the swimming pool.

Brandon didn't seem to mind showing his chest to Marie-Thérèse and his Aunt Josette, who was his second mother. To their dismay, his entire chest was also filled with the rash, though it looked less severe. Further investigation revealed that the red patches on his legs ran all the way up to his thighs, and that he was having trouble breathing as well.

"You'd better take him to the doctor," Josette said, giving her a sympathetic frown. "Larissa can stay here."

Over his protests, Marie-Thérèse drove Brandon to the doctor, trying not to fear the worst. Brandon was coughing badly by the time they arrived.

After a fifteen-minute wait, the doctor examined the rash on Brandon's leg. "I think this was caused by a bite."

"A bite?"

"Yes. Has he been in the woods lately?"

Marie-Thérèse thought for a moment. "Well, ten days or so ago we went to my parents' cabin in the mountains. But he's been fine since then."

"It's not uncommon to have a delayed reaction," the doctor said. "Possibly his body fought off whatever it was, but then something he picked up in the past few days caused the breakout. It's difficult to know." He picked up a pad and began writing. "I'm going to give him a cream for the rash and he's to apply it twice a day to affected areas. Since the cream is rather inexpensive, I'm prescribing a large jar so that you can use it if he has any recurrence. And because the rash is fairly severe, I'm giving you another medication to take by mouth. Take it until it's completely gone."

Marie-Thérèse nodded. "What about his breathing?"

The doctor's brow creased. "That's probably related to his allergic reaction to whatever caused the breakout. Given his history, I'd like to do more allergy testing once this has all cleared up. Why don't you bring him back next week? Of course, if it becomes more severe in the meantime, please come in sooner."

With an inner sigh, Marie-Thérèse agreed.

As they walked out to the car Brandon asked, "So, how long is Uncle Marc going to be in the hospital?"

"I'm not sure. I mean, they'll let him come home as soon as it's safe for him but he needs a kidney transplant. He'll have to go back in."

Brandon shook his head. "That's bad. I'd like to go see him. Maybe take him a new book or something. I got a new one he'd like. It's sci-fi."

"I'm sure he'd like that." Marie-Thérèse started the engine. "But that's only if you're feeling better."

He coughed for a minute. "I will as soon as we get that medication."

"We'll be at the pharmacy in a minute. Just lie back and rest."

Marie-Thérèse let a few moments of silence go by before saying, "Brandon, I think you should know that your dad's going in to be tested tomorrow, to see if he's a good enough match for Uncle Marc."

"I hope he is," Brandon said. "If I was older, I'd try to give him my kidney. Uncle Marc's cool."

"There's no reason for you to do that." Feeling a little guilty, Marie-Thérèse silently thanked heaven that he was too young. "There are others who can donate. Besides, we've got to work on getting you better."

"Yeah, I guess." Brandon stared out the window, but Marie-Thérèse had the feeling he wasn't seeing the passing buildings.

"I wonder what it would be like to be dead," he said after a long pause. "I would like to see it for myself."

Marie-Thérèse breathed in swiftly. Brandon glanced at her, and seeing her expression, he added, "Not to stay dead. I'm just curious. To see what's there for myself."

"Well, I think you'll see for yourself *after* a long life," Marie-Thérèse forced her voice to be light.

It doesn't mean anything, she told herself. *Just a child's curiosity.* At times in her life, she had been curious as well. After all, her family was waiting for her in the next world, and she had often wondered what it would be like when they were together again.

They stopped for the medicines at the pharmacy and then returned to Josette's to pick up Larissa. As soon as Larissa was in the back seat of the car, she started in on her usual request. "Mom, can I play with Jolie when we get home?"

Marie-Thérèse wasn't impressed with Larissa's choice of friends, but she tried not to make an issue of it. "Well, it'll be dinnertime soon, and we might need to go over to Grandma's tonight. We'd like to begin a family fast for Uncle Marc."

"You just don't like Jolie," Larissa said, slapping her hand in indignation on the back of the front seat.

That's accurate enough, Marie-Thérèse thought, but she wasn't going to admit it. "Besides, we need to discuss some changes that we'll be making once the new baby is with us. Or babies."

Larissa gave a disgusted sigh. "I don't know why we have to adopt a baby at all. It's just going to be a lot of work. Look at poor Preston. With all of Josette's kids, he's always baby-sitting."

"Josette doesn't go out all that much," Brandon put in. "And Preston likes to watch his brothers. *I* wouldn't mind a brother, even if I did have to watch him."

"Well, I don't want a brother *or* a sister. It's too much work. Jolie's an only child and she gets anything she wants."

Marie-Thérèse was shocked at her daughter's comments and was about to say so when she realized that eliciting such a reaction had been Larissa's intent. "I'm sorry you feel that way," she said calmly, "because your father and I feel very strongly that we are supposed to have another baby."

"Well, just so long as I don't have to take care of it!" Larissa folded her arms and sat back in her seat, lips clamped tightly together.

Marie-Thérèse didn't understand her daughter. She had thought Larissa would love the idea of a little sister or brother to mother. But since they had announced their decision to adopt last night, Larissa had made no secret of her ill feelings toward the idea. *Maybe we should have told her sooner, to let her become accustomed to the idea.*

Sitting in the front passenger seat, Brandon's hand stole over the space between them to gently pat Marie-Thérèse's shoulder. "I think it's a good idea," he said in a soft voice. "Larissa's just mad 'cause she wants to go on that ski trip with Jolie's parents." He made a disgusted noise in his throat.

Marie-Thérèse thought that for almost eleven he was pretty smart. She smiled at him, and he smiled back.

"And I won't share my room, either," Larissa added loudly. "So you might want to think about moving."

$\mathscr{C}$HAPTER 6

The next morning, at Marc's insistence, Rebekka left him in Ariana's care and went home for a shower and a change of clothes before her appointment at the transplant facility. Marc looked much better this morning, and both his blood pressure and his hormones had leveled off considerably. The doctors hoped that with the added medications he would remain stable until his transplant. Since his body had not reacted well to dialysis previously, everyone felt this was Marc's best chance.

The doctors had planned to release him that afternoon, and under duress, Marc had agreed to stay with his parents until his health was stable. Rebekka reminded herself to move some of her belongings to Marc's apartment so that she could go there when she needed time away from her own parents.

Rebekka's cherry-stained baby grand glistened in the morning light as she passed the music room on her way from the bathroom. With her wet hair up in a clip and wearing a white terry-cloth robe, she sat at the piano and played the song that had haunted her the day before. Not a single mistake marred the beauty of the melody that today sounded much more hopeful than foreboding. She *would* marry Marc, and she *would* play this song for him. She would also find the perfect title for the piece, one that epitomized their relationship.

She felt someone watching her and turned around to find her parents in the doorway. "That was beautiful," Danielle said.

Philippe nodded in agreement. "How's Marc?" he asked.

Rebekka arose from the bench. "Better. Or stable anyway. They'll be letting him go home today. They told him not to go to work or anything, but André says he can handle the slack until Raoul returns."

Her father's blue eyes narrowed slightly at the mention of Raoul, but to Rebekka's relief he didn't comment on her brother's new wife.

"Does this mean you're postponing the wedding?" Danielle questioned.

Rebekka shook her head. "Not yet. I want to see how much time it'll take to get the transplant set up when I go in for testing today. If we can get it scheduled soon we won't have to change our plans, even if we are still a bit sore." She paused, feeling awkward as she added, "The Perraults have made significant donations to the clinic over the past years, so I think they'll be willing to work us in more quickly than normal, provided Marc has a live donor."

"What do you mean 'get tested'?" Philippe's left eyebrow rose as if he wasn't sure he had heard correctly.

Rebekka swallowed hard and forced a nonchalance she didn't feel. Staying calm was always the best way to deal with her father. "I'm going to give him one of my kidneys."

Danielle paled and Philippe reddened. "You're going to *what*?" her father boomed.

"Give him one of my kidneys." She was beginning to feel hot under her bathrobe despite the wet tendrils of hair that had escaped her clip and were sending droplets of water onto her neck.

"That can be dangerous," Philippe said.

"I know, but Marc doesn't have much time to live without one. He needs a kidney *now*. And Louis-Géralde's on a mission."

Philippe's mouth twisted into a sneer. "Is his religion more important than his brother's life?"

Rebekka stifled an angry retort. One simply didn't address her father that way. She never had and never would; the result might be too dangerous. Her mother had told her how harsh his own father had been with him as a child, and while Philippe had never allowed his anger to manifest itself physically on his family, Rebekka had caught too many glimpses of his inner raging inferno. By unspoken agreement, the family was always careful about angering him.

"Why should he come back when I'm willing?" she said, keeping her voice level, reasonable. "And when his two brothers-in-law are willing as well? Besides, Marc will likely need another kidney in his lifetime, so whether I give it to him now or later makes no difference. What does matter is that he needs a transplant right now. His medical history has proven that dialysis isn't going to work for him. He will die if something isn't done."

"You could become ill yourself," Danielle said, her pale hands gripping together in front of her stomach. "You have your future children to think of."

"I love him," Rebekka stated simply. She wasn't really worried about her mother's fear—Danielle would come around—but her father could make her life miserable. She lifted her eyes to his, "Wouldn't you do it if it was Mother? Marc needs what he needs now because he risked his life to save Mother's. Isn't it fitting that our family should repay the debt?"

She waited for his anger, the barely hidden fury held in check only by iron bands of will, to finally burst forth. But the fury died as Philippe looked at Danielle. When he spoke his voice was soft and controlled. "You do what you must, Rebekka."

In that instant, he seemed a bitter, broken man, and Rebekka felt guilty. He had certainly experienced his share of setbacks recently: Raoul had eloped and would likely stay away until their father was calmer; Philippe would not be walking down the aisle to give Rebekka away, nor would he be attending her wedding at all; and now she was using his love for his wife to demand his support.

For a good cause. For Marc! She knew she was right, but felt a deep pity for her father. If only he had joined the Church. If only he could see beyond today. The Savior could have taken his fury and the helpless childhood pain he'd experienced and changed it into something worthy of a son of God.

It was the first time in her entire life that she had thought of her father as an offspring of Deity. But he was, just like every other person in the world. Maybe it wasn't too late for him. Was there something she could do to help him find the truth? She hadn't thought about doing that for a long time, but it was something she would have to think and pray about.

"Thank you for your support," she said graciously. Holding her head high, she slipped past them to the hall and down to her room.

* * * * *

Days passed as they waited for the results from the tests. Since Marc's release from the hospital Rebekka spent most of her time at the Perraults' fifth floor apartment in the outskirts of Paris, leaving only to sleep and to run a few errands. Despite the seriousness of the situation, both she and Marc were enjoying their time together.

Because of Marc's illness, Rebekka had decided against returning to her old job at the American Embassy in Paris. She wanted to spend every moment with Marc. Besides, Damon Wolfe and Jesse Hergarter, the owners of the software company she had worked for in Utah, were pursuing the idea of having her work for them from France. Her job as a translator would have entailed her returning to France period-ically anyway, so it was possible that she could work on this side of the Atlantic, perhaps even choose her own working hours. With her family's affluence, Marc's company, and her own savings, money wasn't a concern.

Of course, returning to work for Hospital's Choice Inc., would mean she would have to occasionally speak with Samuel Bjornenburg, CEO of Corban International. Damon and Jesse had contracted with the Cincinnati-based company to manage their overseas programs and sales, but she felt this aspect of the job wouldn't be a problem. Her former romantic involvement with Samuel was no longer an issue since Marc had asked her to marry him. She hoped Marc would see it that way as well.

Early Thursday morning Rebekka received her results, four days after Marc's collapse. Glowing with triumph, she raced to tell him the good news. "Where's Marc?" she asked when Ariana opened the door to the Perrault apartment, smiling when she saw her future daughter-in-law.

Ariana sighed and shook her head, but the smile didn't leave her face. "He went to work. I tried but I couldn't stop him."

"To work?" Rebekka was amazed. He had been so tired since leaving the hospital. "Well he must be feeling better. When I left last night, he could barely see me to the door."

"He slept well." Ariana frowned briefly. "But I'm sure he'll be back soon. So . . . did you hear from the clinic?"

"Yes." Rebekka felt tears well up in her eyes. "I'm a match! Not a perfect match, of course, not even as good as Louis-Géralde, but almost. Zack's not compatible at all, and Mathieu's blood's compatible but none of the antigens match. But none of that matters because I'm a match!"

Ariana hugged her. "That's wonderful!"

"I know." Rebekka wiped a tear from her eyes. "I have to go tell him."

"Of course."

Rebekka moved toward the door, but Ariana's voice stopped her.

"I'm glad you're back, Rebekka. And not just because of the kidney. Marc was so crazy when you left for Utah. I don't know what he would have done if you had been lost to him." Ariana gave a little laugh. "Of course, I know sometimes it takes awhile to get things right. But when you finally get married, it'll be worth the wait."

"Thank you," Rebekka said to Ariana. "I'm glad too."

After a rapid drive through the busy streets of Paris, Rebekka arrived at Perrault and Massoni's narrow, five-story apartment building. She found Marc in his office, poring over a set of blueprints and talking enthusiastically with André. "This is great! Wow. You say Herbert did these? We have to get that guy a raise. That's going to cut a huge chunk out of our bid while keeping our standards. We're sure to win the bid *and* revolutionize the industry."

"That good, huh?" she said with a straight face. She had tapped lightly at the partially open door, but neither man had heard her until she walked in.

Marc grinned as he caught sight of Rebekka. "Better than good." He sighed and rubbed a hand over his ruggedly handsome face. "Boy, I forgot how much fun it was to work here."

Rebekka walked across to the room to the teak desk where Marc sat. As she bent for a kiss, he met her face halfway. "Don't get up," she said dryly. "I don't want you to strain yourself or anything."

She'd meant it as a joke, but André nodded seriously, his hands spread on either end of the blueprints that threatened to roll shut. "I keep telling him to go home."

"But I feel fine!" Marc protested.

Rebekka smiled and drew out a compact blood pressure kit she had purchased the day before. "Let's see about that." Marc held out his arm, his eyes straying to the blueprints on the desk.

"Hmm, slightly elevated, but not too bad." Rebekka had learned a lot about blood pressure in the past few days, and she wasn't about to let the knowledge go to waste.

She returned the blood pressure kit to her large handbag. "Well, I'm thinking we'll finish all the preparation this week and get your transplant next week and then we'll get married."

Suddenly she had the attention of both men. Marc grabbed her hand. "You got the results."

"Yes, I'm a match. Almost as good as Louis-Géralde. The others aren't, but that hardly matters since you only need one kidney."

"Congratulations!" André let go of the blueprints, which promptly rolled together and slid from the desk to the floor. He pounded Marc's back. "This is great news! Isn't it, Marc?"

Marc's grin had faded, but returned with less force. "Yeah, it is." He stood and took Rebekka's elbow. "And I think I should take my lovely fiancée out for lunch to celebrate."

Rebekka gazed at him sharply. *More likely he's taking me to talk me out of giving him a kidney,* she thought. Why was he so opposed to letting her donate? She had researched the donor statistics, and the complication ratios were very small. His fears seemed irrational at best, and paranoid at worst. Somehow she would have to make him understand that she was going to do this whether he liked it or not.

"Take your time, would you?" André called after them. "I won't be here anyway. I'm taking a long lunch to be with Claire."

"How's she feeling?" Rebekka asked, pausing at the door.

"Completely better, thank heaven. It was just a passing thing."

The love in his voice was tangible, and Rebekka felt a rush of emotion as she recalled the years he had stood by Claire. She knew from her experience with Marc these past few days that watching a loved one suffer wasn't easy. That was why she wanted to at least give Marc her kidney; if she could change places with him she would.

"See you later," she said to André. "Please give Claire my best."

"Come and see her. She's been asking about you."

"I will." Rebekka glanced at Marc, who held her hand. "Just as soon as I get this rogue of mine settled."

Marc's eyebrow rose. "Rogue? I'll show you rogue." He took a menacing step toward her.

With another wave at André, Rebekka escaped Marc's grasp and sprinted from the room. He caught up to her and, seeing they were alone in the hall, kissed her soundly. This time, Rebekka didn't try to break free.

* * * * *

The lunch crowd hadn't yet begun, so Marc and Rebekka were almost immediately shown to an intimate table on a large shaded patio overlooking the Seine. They shared an appetizer of escargo scampi followed by a delicious meal of veal piccata, baked potatoes with cheese, steamed carrots, warm bread, and the house salad. Afterwards, they ordered two fruit-filled pastries with melted chocolate drizzled on top.

Marc thoroughly enjoyed Rebekka's presence, and knew he would be happy to sit and watch her for hours. With her auburn hair, high cheekbones, and unblemished skin, Rebekka was a beautiful woman who consistently turned heads. Her large grey eyes reminded him of dark clouds on a misty day, and her satin voice called up emotions in his heart that he had never felt before. Oh, once he had considered himself in love with her mother, but now he saw that his feelings had only been a childish crush, misdirected because of his belief that Rebekka was too young for him. Mother and daughter had always looked much alike, despite their age difference—and it seemed only logical that he would have rejected feeling so strongly about the girl he had viewed as a child and put her mother in her place, especially since he had saved Danielle's life in the train bombing and felt very protective of her. But in reality it had always been Rebekka in his heart. She was everything to him, and it was almost too much to believe that the extraordinary woman she had become loved him enough to marry him.

He grimaced mentally. Not only did she love him, but she was willing to risk her life for him. Her determination to do so was steadfast and uncompromising.

Marc had assumed that his premonition about their time being short meant that he would leave Rebekka, but in the days since she had decided to donate her kidney, the thought struck him that she might be leaving him instead. The idea was unfathomable.

With determination he set his fork next to his plate. "Rebekka, I can't let you do this."

"Let me eat this pastry?" She glanced down at her slender figure. "Are you trying to tell me something? If you are, forget it, because I know you'll love me even if I weighed two hundred kilos. Right?" Her voice was teasing.

"Like you'd ever let me get away with a statement like that even if you did have a problem. And of course my love for you has nothing to do with your weight."

She seemed to sense his seriousness. "Okay, out with it, Marc. Why don't you want me to give you my kidney?"

"It's too dangerous."

"No it's not." She took his hand and continued earnestly, "Oh, I know your first donor had some difficulties, but that was nineteen years ago. Methods have improved tremendously since then. In fact, both you and I will be up walking within a few hours of surgery. I'm not saying we won't be in a pain, but other than that we should be okay. Marc, I want to do this for you. I know it's the right thing. And I think you would too, if you'd just pray about it."

Prayer. He hadn't done that, hadn't wanted to because of the risk.

"Well?" she asked. Her voice became teasing once again. "You do believe in prayer, don't you?"

Yes, he believed. Without prayer, Rebekka would have likely been in Cincinnati married to another man.

And not facing risky surgery.

Her eyes were on him, waiting, her full lips slightly puckered. As though reading his thoughts she leaned sideways toward him, and he instinctively met her halfway, kissing those intriguing lips.

He caught the interested stare of the college-age kids at the next table and broke off the kiss, feeling a wave of heat sweeping up his face. Kissing in a such a public place—when had he lost all reserve? Love was a wonderful, crazy, and miraculous thing!

Rebekka laughed, low and sweet. She stuck her fork into her pastry. "If we get the surgery done next week, we can still have our wedding as planned."

"Okay," he said.

She smiled, licking a bit of red fruit from her bottom lip. "You'll let me?"

"I'll pray about it."

Her smile didn't fade. "Well, then I'm not worried. By the end of next week you'll be feeling better than you've felt in a long time."

She was wrong; no feeling could ever equal the euphoria he felt on the day she had promised to marry him.

As they left the restaurant he put his arm around her tightly, possessively. She leaned into him, breathing a sigh of contentment. For a moment, all was right with their world.

Fears still tumbled about in his mind, but Marc forced them to stay hidden. He had promised himself to enjoy every minute he and Rebekka had together. He planned to do just that.

CHAPTER 7

André left his office and walked to the exclusive restaurant where he planned to have lunch, arriving only a minute later than he intended. He was greeted by the maître d', a thin, distinguished-looking man in his early fifties. "Ah, Monsieur Perrault, it's good to see you again today. I take it you received word from our waiter that Madame Allure is awaiting you at a private table in the back room?"

"Yes, indeed," André said with a smile. "Thank you." He tried to slip the man a tip, but the maître d' shook his head.

"The Madame already took care of it." He raised his hand to signal a waiter. "Please show Monsieur Perrault to the table where his lady awaits. And see that they are afforded all the privacy and service they desire."

The young waiter grinned, almost stifling a laugh, then sobered under the disapproving eye of the maître d'. "Of course," the waiter said, inclining his head. "Please, follow me." The maître d' gave a curt bow to André, which he returned with a smile.

André followed the waiter farther into the crowded restaurant and through a set of wide French doors to a large back room where the tables were sectioned off by portable linen screens—not completely private, but giving the illusion of such. The lights were dimmer and there was less noise. André could hear a faint strain of classical music. He searched for his date, eagerly anticipating their time together.

He found her sitting at the most private table near the back, wearing a gold outfit trimmed with faux fur. Her raven hair was piled on her head, and a shimmering gold cloth partially covered the shiny mane. Ruby lips curved in a mysterious smile and her beautiful eyes were hidden behind cat-eye sunglasses.

"I will return shortly with the food Madame ordered." The waiter's face was expressionless and his voice courteous, but André couldn't miss the envious gleam in his eyes.

Madame Allure held out her hand as he approached, and he took it, bending over to kiss the soft skin.

"So glad you could make it," she said, her husky voice heavily accented.

"So glad you invited me. It's been a long time, uh . . . Madame Allure."

Her smile widened and she pulled down her glasses so that her turquoise eyes peered out at him—shining with pleasure. "Hey," she said, dropping the accent briefly, "it's the only name that came to me at the time. I mean, eets de only name dat come to me at de time."

André dropped to his chair, still holding his wife's hand. "Ah, Claire. I love you. Did I tell you that yet today?"

She pulled the cat-eye glasses off and set them near her plate. "Yes, this morning before you left for work."

"Don't you mean, 'before you leefed to work'?"

She laughed. "Something like that. How long do you have for lunch anyway?"

"As long as we need. Raoul's still gone and Rebekka came and dragged Marc away."

"Kicking and screaming?"

"Almost. But there is good news. She's a very good match for the transplant."

"Wonderful!"

"Yeah, only Marc isn't happy about it. He told me today that he wished Rebekka would drop the whole thing."

"He's worried about her." Claire always seemed to pinpoint the problem.

"Exactly." He caressed her hand. "But let's not talk about them."

"Well, I think we could help. Let's have dinner tomorrow night and invite them. Maybe you can talk some sense into him."

"Okay. Are you sure you're up to that?"

She leaned forward. "André, I'm fine. Now let's forget about Marc and Rebekka and enjoy ourselves. I hope you like curried chicken."

* * * * *

On Friday evening Claire checked the pot simmering on her gas stove. She enjoyed cooking for guests and knew she was good at it as well. She also knew that her creative talent with food developed during her growing up years. As a poor child living with her mother and younger sister, she had learned to make almost anything palatable to avoid the empty feeling in her stomach and the hungry look in her sister's eyes. There hadn't been much to work with back then. Not like now.

Involuntarily, Claire shivered. The memories of her sparse childhood were not the most pleasant. All her immediate family had long since died, with the exception of an older brother, Basil, who had left France when she was a toddler, and for all she knew he was dead as well.

The Perrault family was hers now, and she loved them fiercely—most especially André. She had been very blessed. First the gospel had come into her life and then André. He was every bit as courageous and good as the heroes she had dreamed of as a young girl.

She smiled at the memories of how they had met. André, two years back from his mission, had visited her ward in Strasbourg where she had been baptized six months earlier. He had walked into the building, strong and handsome, but looking a little lost.

"May I help you?" she had asked.

"I'm looking for . . ." He stopped and stared at her, as if seeing her for the first time.

"Are you visiting?" she prompted.

He continued to stare. "I'm here to make a bid on a project. But I think—" He broke off. "Are you married?"

The question took her by surprise. "No, I'm not."

"Good," he replied, "because I think you are the most beautiful woman I have ever met."

Claire had never considered herself beautiful, certainly not in the way that other women were beautiful, but in that moment, she knew André spoke the truth. Maybe it was her new testimony glowing in her heart, or maybe her thin, pinched features had filled out with the food the sisters in the ward had shared with her and her mother as they grieved the sudden death of her young sister. Whatever the cause, Claire knew André wasn't simply trying to impress her. In fact, he looked more than a little embarrassed by his own boldness, though he didn't take back the words.

They had stayed together at church the rest of the day, and when he left her that night on her mother's porch he said, "I've waited a long time to find you, Claire. I'll be back."

She hadn't believed him, but had held the promise in her heart. And André, always a man of his word, had returned. At first she told herself his visits to Strasbourg were because of his engineering firm, and that she was a merely a distraction—but she was already so much in love with him that it didn't matter. When her mother died and she faced her terrible, lonely grief, he had begged her to marry him and go with him to Paris. She accepted his offer, living with his parents until she had been a member of the Church for a year and could marry André in the temple. He had been twenty-four years old then, and she only eighteen. The day they were sealed for time and all eternity was the happiest of her life.

"Mom," said Ana, interrupting Claire's reverie. "Can I help you?"

"Sure, sweety."

"Me too!" said Marée.

Claire set the girls to washing lettuce in the sink. With her tender beef cooked to perfection on the stove she would also serve boiled potatoes and a fresh lettuce and tomato salad topped with purple onions, salt, and olive oil dressing. André loved purple onions. She hummed to herself, smiling as the girls ran the green lettuce leaves under the cold water, giggling in delight as the water splashed over their hands and occasionally onto their faces.

When André arrived home from work, Claire met him in the entryway, leaving the girls busy in the kitchen. She wiped her hands on her apron. "Good, you're home."

"Smells great," he said, sniffing in appreciation. Wrapping his arms around her, he kissed her mouth until she couldn't breathe, then made a trail of kisses down to her neck. She shivered, loving him so much her heart was full. What a wonderful thing it was to be married to such a good man.

He put an arm around her and they walked together into the kitchen. The girls turned from the sink shouting, "Daddy, Daddy, we're helping! Look!" Scrambling down from their chairs, they hurled themselves toward him.

André picked them both up, one under each arm, and sailed around the room. Ana and Marée flailed their arms and legs, pretending they had wings. Then André collapsed in a chair and brought the girls onto his lap, submitting to their eager, smothering kisses.

Claire laughed at their fun, happy with the knowledge that he was a devoted father, although at times she thought he was much too easy on them. By their age she had learned to make full meals and clean the house. Her smile faded. She had also learned to wait on her ill mother until she died.

But my daughters won't have to go through that . . . I'm well now. Death won't touch them—not yet. No, they wouldn't have to see their father smoke himself into a carcinogenic grave, or watch a little sister die from the flu. Claire prayed daily that they would never experience any of that kind of pain. She would do everything she could to make their childhood happy.

André tickled the girls into submission and came to her side. "Okay, what do I do next?" he asked, removing her apron.

She grabbed it from him. "Oh no you don't. This is my dinner and you're not going to mess it up."

"Well, I can at least set the table." He drew her to him in a quick embrace.

"All right," she conceded, "but in the dining room. Tonight is special. And I want four extra settings, not just two."

André studied her. "Who else is coming?"

"It's a surprise." She kissed him and pushed him gently toward the door. "Hurry up, now. They'll be here soon."

"Okay, but this is such a big job, I'm going to need some helpers." The girls jumped up and down with excitement. Once again, André tucked them under his arms and they "flew" out of the kitchen.

Claire turned back to her meat, its juices bubbling fragrantly on the stove. She tasted it. *Perfect.*

Just like André. Oh, he was stubborn, and sometimes he worked too hard, but he was special, and she was the most fortunate woman in the world.

* * * * *

Rebekka sat with Marc on the edge of his bed as he bent down to tie his shoes. At that moment she wondered if she should have agreed to go to Claire's at all. Marc had slept badly the night before, and although she and Ariana had made him stay in bed nearly the entire day, she still didn't think he appeared well enough to go out.

"I'm fine," he insisted, still bent over. "Besides, we have to eat, right? And André said Claire was really looking forward to having us over."

"Yes, but I know he's worried about her overexerting herself."

"You're worried about me, you mean." He looked at her with a grin, and his eyes seemed to sparkle with a little of their old life. "Claire has recovered perfectly."

"So what if I am?" Tears came to her eyes and she impatiently blinked them away.

Marc was suddenly contrite. He slid toward her, pulling her close. "Dear Rebekka, I'm so sorry. I wish you didn't have to go through this with me. I wish . . ." He leaned in for a gentle kiss. Although she typically would have mocked him for avoiding the subject, Rebekka found that today she was content to let the matter rest.

A gentle coughing brought them apart. From the open doorway Jean-Marc watched them with an indulgent smile. "You know, that rule we had about never having a friend of the opposite sex in your bedroom while you were growing up was there for a good reason."

"The door wasn't shut," Marc pointed out as he held Rebekka more firmly. "And you are welcome to stand there and watch us kiss anytime." To prove his point Marc kissed her again, but Rebekka turned her head so that his lips found her cheek.

She felt her face redden. "We were just leaving," she said quickly, easing out of Marc's grasp.

"I thought you were trying to talk me out of going," Marc teased.

Jean-Marc laughed. "Are you sure you want to marry him?"

"Daaaad," Marc complained good-naturedly. "It took me long enough to convince her as it was."

Right. All of two minutes, Rebekka thought.

Jean-Marc placed his hand on Rebekka's shoulder. "Rebekka, I don't know that I've had a chance to tell you how grateful I am for what you've agreed to do for Marc."

"Maybe," Marc put in.

Jean-Marc looked at him steadily. "Son, when I found out I couldn't be your first donor, it just about tore me apart. Don't let your own fears get in the way of Rebekka's opportunity to do this for you."

Marc frowned, as though he hadn't thought of her offer in that light before. She prayed silently that he would understand how much it meant to her . . . and agree to allow her to go through with it.

"We'd better get going," Marc said to Rebekka. "We'll be late."

Rebekka shared a sympathetic smile with his father before following her fiancé out the door.

In the car Marc was silent, and Rebekka was glad she had insisted on driving so that she could pretend to be occupied. If Marc had been feeling better they would have walked the short distance to avoid searching for a parking place. Though Andre's building had an underground garage for residents, many of the nearby edifices did not offer such a luxury and at night the streets were usually lined with parked cars.

Marc's hand stole to her knee, squeezing softly. She placed her hand over his, allowing the tension to trickle from her body.

When they arrived at André and Claire's, they were greeted first by Marc's enthusiastic nieces, and then more sedately by their parents, who were dressed up more than usual for a home-cooked meal. Claire looked especially radiant and healthy. Her unusual blue-green eyes were bright and her dark hair smoothly coifed. She wore a blue, floor-length column dress with a matching duster that fluttered about her like short wings.

The two women hugged. "I'm so happy for you, Rebekka," Claire murmured. "I can't believe you and Marc . . . it's so wonderful."

"Isn't it?" Rebekka grinned. "And you look great, Claire! Thank you for having us over." She glanced at Marc, who was tickling his nieces to a chorus of delighted screams. She lowered her voice. "Maybe you two can help me talk some sense into him."

André glanced at his wife with a knowing smile that said, "What did I tell you?"

"So I take it he's still balking about your donating the kidney," Claire said.

"Yes, and look at him. The doctor told him today they would have to either transplant or try dialysis again next week. If he doesn't agree to let me donate soon your mother will call Louis-Géralde. There simply isn't any more time." She tried to clear the catch in her voice. "I'm really afraid. He looks so terrible, and he's so weak."

"It'll be okay," André said. "I'll talk to him."

The buzzer rang again and Claire flitted to the door to let the new visitor into the apartment building. Rebekka thought her movements graceful and quick, like a small bird. André's eyes also followed his wife. "She has a surprise planned, you know."

"A surprise? For whom?"

"I don't know." He grinned at her, looking a lot like Marc in his healthier days. "Claire is always full of surprises. I guess we'll see."

Absently, Rebekka searched for Marc, who was now reading a book to the girls on the couch. She was glad to see he wasn't over-doing the uncle act. In the past he had played tiger with them, a game his father had begun when he was little. How long would it be before he would play that game with their own children?

Rebekka sighed with longing. The life she had dreamed of was within reach. If only Marc would listen to reason.

"Rebekka, look who's here," trilled Claire's high, clear voice from the hall.

She had forgotten Claire's surprise and belatedly wondered who had arrived. As she turned, someone hugged her. "Raoul!" she squealed. "Oh, Raoul!" She wrapped her arms around her brother. "I've missed you so much! It's wonderful to see you!" The last time she had seen her older brother was on the morning she had left for America five months earlier. Two weeks ago, the day before she had returned to Paris, he had e-mailed her to announce that he and his fiancée had eloped.

As she held her brother Rebekka searched out their hostess, who watched them contentedly. "Claire, this is the best surprise ever!" She hugged Raoul more tightly.

Over Raoul's shoulder Rebekka saw a ravishing young woman with long dark hair and heavily made-up brown eyes. She was short, only a few centimeters taller than Claire, but her tall heels brought her to Rebekka's height. She was dressed in a sleeveless black tunic with a tasteful stand-up collar and button-front closure. The princess cut was certainly stylish and showed her curvaceous figure to advantage, though the hemline was a little too revealing for Rebekka's tastes. Rebekka herself was wearing a fitted, short-sleeved blazer and matching pants because of the increasingly cold evenings, but her brother's new wife apparently didn't allow the weather to dictate her choice of clothes.

Raoul broke away from Rebekka and reached for the woman's hand. "This, of course, is my wife, Desirée."

"Hello," Rebekka said, smiling. "It's nice to see you . . . again. We did meet briefly once before, do you remember?" She embraced the other woman without waiting for a reply. "Welcome to the family."

Desirée smiled with pleasure. "Thank you."

"So . . ." Marc came from behind Rebekka. He slapped Raoul on the back. "Just got back from your honeymoon, did you?"

Raoul grinned and his gray eyes shone. "That's right." He put an arm around Desirée. "It's official now. She's stuck with me."

Everyone laughed.

"Well, have you heard about us?" Marc pulled Rebekka into his arms. "We're getting married, too."

Raoul's gaze flew to Rebekka's, asking for confirmation. She nodded. "You would have known if you were checking your e-mail. Marc followed me to America—but I'm sure you heard at least that much before you went off—and he asked me to marry him. I said yes."

Her brother hugged her. "I didn't think he had it in him." There were tears in Raoul's eyes, and Rebekka had moisture in her own. He knew how much she loved Marc and how she had despaired of ever having him.

"We went to the Riviera for our honeymoon," Desirée inserted into the lull that followed. "We would have stayed longer, but Raoul was anxious to get back to work."

Marc winked at Raoul. "He'd better be—we might fire him. Or find another partner."

"Don't worry, I'm back," Raoul said. "But I might be taking more time off than usual."

"We all might," André said, his expression becoming serious. "Did Claire tell you about Marc's kidney?"

Raoul's eyes widened as he shook his head, and his dark auburn hair, cut slightly long on top, waved with the movement. "No, what happened?"

André led them into the sitting room and began recounting the story quickly. Marc spoke little, but when he did Rebekka noticed that he underplayed the gravity of the situation.

"I'm going to give him one of my kidneys," Rebekka said. She glanced at Marc. "I mean, we're praying about it, aren't we, honey?"

He clutched her hand. "Yes," he said, his voice terse.

There was a short, uncomfortable silence, and then Desirée said, "You know, I believe it's a full ten degrees warmer down south than it is here."

"Are you cold, dear?" Raoul began to remove his off-white blazer. "Here, take my jacket."

His wife watched him for a second as she contemplated his offer. "No, I'm not cold. I'm just commenting." She smiled. "Besides, that color is all wrong for my outfit."

Raoul slipped his arm back inside the blazer. "If you're sure."

"I am. Thanks." She snuggled next to him on the couch.

"Well, dinner's ready," Claire announced. "If I can just get a few volunteers to carry things to the dining room."

Rebekka, Marc, and André followed Claire into the kitchen, and in a few minutes the feast was ready. André asked for a blessing on the food and they began to serve themselves.

"This is delicious," Rebekka said, tasting the meat. "I could never make something like this."

"Oh, it's easy." Claire shrugged, but her face was bright. "I'll give you the recipe."

"I'm not good in the kitchen either," said Desirée. "I tell Raoul that we're going to have to hire a cook or something." She laughed and the others laughed with her. Desirée batted her eyes, enjoying the attention.

"So now that you're back, will you be at church on Sunday?" Marc asked Raoul. "Isn't it your time to go up?" The three partners had a long-standing agreement to take turns bearing their testimonies on fast Sunday. What began as a challenge had remained as a testimony builder.

"Of course I'll be there," Raoul said. "I want to show off my new bride."

Desirée blanched. "But honey, you know I'm going apartment hunting with my parents on Sunday."

"You're moving?" Rebekka felt a keen disappointment. It wasn't easy to find apartments within the ward boundaries, and she didn't want to be separated from her brother so soon, especially since he had married a woman who wasn't a member of the Church.

"We're not moving," Raoul said. "Desirée's just helping her parents."

Desirée's expression revealed that was not really what she had in mind, but she didn't contradict Raoul openly.

"Don't worry, honey," Raoul said to her. "My father won't be at church, so there's no chance of a run-in with him." For an instant, there was a deep sadness in his eyes, and Rebekka keenly felt his regret at his estrangement from their father.

"We've talked about this." Desirée's voice was icy. "Let's not do it again here."

The muscles in Raoul's face worked, but he acquiesced with a nod, his respect obviously overruling his desire to be right. He squeezed his wife's shoulder and kissed her cheek. The love in his eyes was apparent, as was also the beginning of a lesion that would not soon heal. Desirée smiled at him and took his hand possessively in hers. Her lips puckered slightly, as though sending him a private kiss.

Rebekka felt transported back in time, and it was as though she were watching her parents trying to resolve their religious differences. Through the years they had managed to hold on to their marriage and to continue to love each other. But it hadn't been easy, and despite their deep love, she knew her mother still longed for her father to take her to the temple.

Suddenly Rebekka felt like crying. She held onto Marc's hand—her lifeline in the face of her brother's bleak future. She knew Raoul had understood when he made the decision to marry Desirée outside of the temple that it wouldn't be easy. And feeling as lonely as she had without Marc—almost lonely enough to fall into a nonmember's arms herself—Rebekka didn't blame him for his decision. Even so, she wished it could be otherwise, and that he could avoid the pain which was likely to follow. She planned to give him all the support he would need, and every night she prayed for him and Desirée. More than anything she wanted her brother to be happy.

"Well, I'm glad to hear you're not moving," André said lightly. "My sisters love the wards they've moved into, but there's nothing like your home ward. Still, if you have to move, you have to move. Sometimes there's no getting out of it."

The rest of the evening went smoothly, although Rebekka was irritated to soon find Desirée flirting openly with André and Marc—or trying to. They were polite to her, while at the same time refusing to be pulled into her games. Or maybe they simply didn't notice. Claire didn't seem to see anything amiss, and Rebekka wondered if it was all in her imagination.

Desirée also seemed preoccupied with the value of the furniture and other items in the house, asking questions about prices—something Rebekka would never have dreamed of doing with anyone but a close friend—if at all. Claire became noticeably uncomfortable when Desirée asked about the china.

"Ariana, my mother-in-law, bought these for us as a wedding gift." Claire touched the side of her plate with the tip of her finger. "I don't know how much they cost. I went with her to pick them out, but I . . ." She trailed off, looking at her husband for support.

But Desirée spoke quickly. "They are very costly. I know because I was looking at some just like them. Your mother-in-law must be rich to buy you these."

"My mother has always been quite generous," André said in an attempt to cover Desirée's apparent lack of social graces.

Claire's chin lifted. "Ariana has been a second mother to me. I couldn't ask for a better mother-in-law."

"I wonder what my mother-in-law will give us," Desirée mused.

Rebekka felt repulsed, but she forced herself to be kind. "I'm sure my mother will give you an appropriate gift—eventually. But I think it's only fair to tell you that she's feeling a little disappointed right now at not being able to attend your wedding. Perhaps it's best to let things follow their own course."

"Well, it doesn't matter, really. Raoul will buy me whatever I want," Desirée said, dismissing the conversation altogether. "But tell me, Claire, where did you find that lamp? It's simply gorgeous. It reminds me of the time I met this lady at a store and she . . ."

Deep in thought, Rebekka missed the humorous climax of Desirée's story, but she laughed with the others all the same. She had to hand it to the woman—she definitely had charm and knew how to use it when she wanted. But was the charming Desirée the real woman? Or was she the pushy, obsessed person they had glimpsed before? Or was the real woman someone else entirely? *No one is all bad or good,* Rebekka told herself. *And she is very young. There will be time to get to know her, to find her good qualities.*

Not until dinner was over and it was time to leave did Rebekka have a moment alone with her brother. "Are you happy?" she asked as she hugged him good-bye.

"Yes, very." His voice was low but vehement. "I know it's going to be hard, but I have faith she'll come around."

"I hope so."

"I love her so much."

"I can see that."

"There's so much people don't see in her," Raoul whispered. "I mean, I know she comes across as a little flighty and . . . well, selfish sometimes. That's because her parents didn't have any money when she was young. She's had to look out for herself. But Rebekka, she's great fun—keeps me laughing all the time. Just as she had us doing here tonight. And I could just look at her for hours. I've never felt this way about anyone. Ever. I want to give her the world. I want to make up for the life she didn't have as a child. I know it's not going to be easy, but I'm willing to make it work. She's worth it—I believe it with my whole heart."

"I'm glad, Raoul. I just want you to be happy."

"I am," he said with confidence. "And I'm glad for you, too. Marc's been a blind, stubborn fool, but I couldn't wish for a better man to marry my sister."

Rebekka wanted to say the same thing about Desirée but couldn't force the words. In fact, she felt an increasing dislike for her new sister-in-law. But for Raoul's sake, she would continue to try to get along with her.

On the way from the apartment Rebekka continued to ponder Raoul's relationship with Desirée.

"Why so quiet?" Marc asked, taking her into his arms as they reached the car.

"I don't know." She paused, debating whether she should share her reservations about Desirée. "No, that's not true. I'm worried about Raoul and Desirée. When I look at them, I see my parents all over again. Desirée obviously has no desire to join the Church."

"She may in the future," Marc said. "And at least she didn't lie to him. Raoul knew what he was getting into."

"It would be different if I felt she really loved him." Rebekka continued earnestly. "Like my dad loves my mom."

"You don't get that feeling?"

"I'm not sure. Sometimes I did but then . . . Didn't you see her flirting with you and André?"

He laughed and drew a dramatic hand across his brow. "Whew, I'm glad you noticed. I was wondering if I was imagining things."

"You weren't. Not that either of you encouraged her at all, thank heaven."

He grinned. "Of course we didn't encourage her. Why would we when we have you and Claire? Really though, I think it was rather harmless. I mean, we have to realize they're new to marriage and that they've been in flirting mode for a while. Maybe she needs some adjustment time."

Rebekka sighed. "Maybe you're right. And maybe I just don't want to share my brother."

"Or me?" he added teasingly. "Weren't you just a bit jealous?"

"Maybe," she conceded. "My new sister-in-law certainly is attractive. Raoul is completely smitten."

"So would you fight her for me?" He was still teasing, and his brown eyes gleamed in the lamplight.

"Heck no! She's got ten kilos on me, even if it is in all the right places." She punched him playfully on the chest. "Besides, she's not willing to give you *her* kidney."

The smile deserted Marc's face. "No one will let me forget that," he said softly.

She lifted her chin. "I won't apologize for it. I love you. We all love you."

"I know." He leaned down and nuzzled her face gently. "I just don't want to lose you."

"I'm not going anywhere." Even as she said it, Rebekka felt it was true. Couldn't he? The risk of her life wasn't really an issue here. His was.

"I've prayed about it," he said, "and I didn't get a bad feeling, like you shouldn't be the donor or anything. Maybe it's just been my reluctance holding me back all along."

Her hands gripped his arms. "So you'll let me?"

"Yes." He paused, searching her eyes deeply. "And thank you."

She kissed him lightly on the lips. "I was hoping you'd say that because our surgery is scheduled for next Friday."

CHAPTER 8

Early Saturday morning after breakfast, Claire went to the couch where André was reading the paper in his robe. She read with him, and they occasionally discussed an article. In front of them Ana and Marée were sprawled out on the floor coloring, their dark heads nearly touching as they bent to their important task.

Abruptly André shut the paper and set it to the side. "What is it, Claire?"

She didn't know what tipped him off. "Nothing . . . really." She suddenly felt unsure, and wished she had on one of her "Madame" disguises and that they were at their favorite restaurant.

He put his arms around her and she felt safe and protected. "Well?" he prompted. When she didn't reply, he nibbled her ear playfully.

"You're tickling me!"

"I know."

She turned slightly and hugged him. "You're the most wonderful husband in the world."

"You're going to bring up the baby again, aren't you?" His voice was calm, but she detected a note of underlying distress.

"I'm feeling better now. I am." She looked at the girls. "I know two children are considered more than plenty here in France, but I can't help but think you need a son to carry on your name."

"My name's not important," he said gently. "You are." He caressed her face with his fingertips. "Oh, Claire, just earlier this week you were so sick I was afraid to leave you to go to the airport to see my brother off. I know you're better now, but remember what the doctors have said about another pregnancy. Please don't ask me to risk your health. I don't know how I'd live without you!"

His brown eyes shimmered with the strength of his emotion, and Claire felt the tangibility of his love.

"I need you," he continued. He motioned to the girls. "They need you."

She knew he was right, but told herself she could go through another pregnancy because she knew how much he wanted a son. "I just thought . . . I mean, we're not getting any younger . . . Now might be the best time."

"Is this because of me? Or do you want to have a baby for you? Because those are two very different things." His gaze bore into her, seeming to penetrate her very soul.

She looked at the carpet, knowing she couldn't lie. For her, the girls were enough.

"That's what I thought." His voice wasn't harsh, but understanding. "And I know you think I want a son, but I don't feel that way, not enough to risk you. The girls and you are all I need."

Claire wanted to believe him, but she wondered if he only said what he did to protect her. All her life she had longed for a daughter and had been blessed with two. But what if she'd had two sons instead? Would she have simply given up the dream of a little girl? Was this the type of sacrifice André was making for her?

"What if I said I didn't feel our family was complete?" she asked, rubbing her hand along the satin length of her dressing gown.

They had been talking quietly, but now and then the girls glanced at them, apparently keeping track of their words. Claire wondered how much they understood.

André was silent for a long moment, not with an isolating quiet, but one of deep and careful thought. Finally, he spoke, "If you feel that way, I think we should pray about it very hard." He hesitated. "And if we come to the conclusion that we should have another child, maybe we should consider adoption like Marie-Thérèse and Mathieu. How do you feel about that?"

Claire blinked twice, amazed. Maybe what André was telling her was true, that he really didn't feel some eternal loss because she was unable to give him a blood-related son.

"Well?" He looked at her earnestly.

She smiled. "I guess I want to think about it. And pray." She snuggled closer to him. "I still mean what I said, you are the best husband." He sighed almost imperceptibly, and she knew he was relieved. His lips found hers, and she sighed happily.

"Daddy, can you help me color this boat?" Marée asked.

He drew away from Claire. "A boat?"

"Yeah. And the guy on it. And a lady with a long dress." She arose and walked over to his knee, holding out a jumble of broken crayons on her small, open hand.

André took two and handed one to Claire. "Sure, Mommy and I'll both help. But let's go color by Ana, okay?"

Claire lay on her stomach with the rest of her family, thinking that her life couldn't get any better.

* * * * *

Marie-Thérèse sat in her kitchen reading through her adoption paperwork for what seemed like the millionth time. A gentle breeze moved the thin curtains above her sink, and fingers of sunlight danced on the papers like a promise. The months and years of waiting were almost over! Soon the baby would be in her arms. She would touch the soft skin and smell the sweet baby smells. Should she choose a little boy or a little girl? Girls were so fun to dress up, but a boy might grow to be just as solid and agreeable as Brandon.

She gave a drawn-out sigh and sipped the hot chocolate she was having with her breakfast toast. Why was Larissa being so difficult? Josette's children always welcomed the idea of a new baby, but Larissa's opposition seemed to grow with each passing day.

As though in answer to her mother's silent thoughts, Larissa shuffled into the kitchen. Her short hair was so dark it was almost black like her father's, though the shape of her pale face resembled Marie-Thérèse's. She was also thin like her mother, but her temperament was volatile and often rebellious. Marie-Thérèse hoped her daughter wouldn't have to endure much pain and trial before she awakened to what was truly important in life. But there was only so much a mother could teach a daughter, only so much time in a day that she could pray for her to find her way.

Marie-Thérèse slipped the adoption papers into a drawer, but not soon enough. Larissa tossed her dark head and wrinkled her slightly upturned nose. "Are you sure you want to do this, Mom? I mean, you don't know what kind of a medical heritage this kid'll have. What if he has some kind of inherited disease that doesn't show up until later? Or what if his father is a murderer or something and he grows up with a mean streak? Can't you just wait until Brandon gets married and has kids?"

"It's hardly the same thing," Marie-Thérèse returned dryly. "A child is always a blessing, and I hope you'll give your attitude some more consideration. This is something your father and I have prayed about and we feel it's right."

Larissa grimaced and rolled her eyes. "Well, I can't say anything to that now, can I?"

"No, you can't, so don't even try."

Larissa sighed dramatically and stalked to the breadbox on the counter, where she began making herself some toast.

Brandon came into the kitchen, rubbing his eyes with his fingers. His brown hair was tousled as though he had gone to bed with it wet. He kissed Marie-Thérèse on each cheek. "Good morning, Mom."

She hugged him. "Good morning. How're you feeling?"

Larissa slammed a cupboard door shut. Marie-Thérèse stared at her hard, but didn't reprimand her aloud, figuring the child already had enough challenges to deal with.

"I'm fine." Brandon pulled up the leg of his pajama. "See? Rash is almost gone."

Marie-Thérèse examined the skin to be sure. "Well, so it has—mostly. Better keep using that cream until it's completely gone."

"I think the rash might leave a scar." Brandon's voice held a hint of pride.

Larissa coughed rudely. "I still say that even if it's a girl, she can't stay in my room. I think we need to move to a bigger house."

"What?" asked Brandon, momentarily confused. "Oh, the baby."

"We're not moving," Marie-Thérèse said. "And your room is plenty big for two. Maybe it'll be a good thing for you to learn to share. When I was a kid—"

"I know—you and Aunt Josette shared a room. You've told me all week."

"And we were close," Marie-Thérèse stressed. "You could really learn to love a little sister."

Larissa muttered something that vaguely resembled "pest," but Marie-Thérèse chose to ignore it. Larissa turned on her brother. "You don't want to share your room, do you?"

He shrugged and gave her an I-don't-care expression. "The baby can stay with me. There's room."

"That figures," sneered Larissa. "Perfect little momma's boy."

"Larissa!" Marie-Thérèse was shocked. "We don't speak to members of our family that way. You're inviting a bad spirit here and I won't have it."

"Fine!" Larissa threw the rest of her toast into the garbage. After glaring in her brother's direction, she stomped from the room.

Marie-Thérèse felt like crying. Where had she gone wrong? Wasn't it only yesterday she had cradled her tiny daughter in her arms and sung her a lullaby? How she longed to hold her now! But someone had taken away her sweet little girl and given her this emotional stranger instead.

Brandon calmly buttered Larissa's remaining toast and began to eat it. "Don't worry, she's just going through a phase."

Unbidden, a smile came to Marie-Thérèse's lips. "A phase?"

"Yeah." His face was serious. "Pretty soon she'll have pimples, start wearing high heels, and begin dying her hair." He paused and she could see a grin coming. "We'd best leave her here and move to America to stay with Uncle Zack's family until it's all over."

Marie-Thérèse laughed aloud, her heart lightening. "Yeah, right. We're not going anywhere." But his observations brought her a few ideas. Larissa *was* growing up, and doing so in an increasingly confusing world. *So how can I help her make sense of it all?* Marie-Thérèse put it at the top of her mental list of things to pray about, followed by Marc and the new baby. *Or babies*, she corrected herself.

Her husband, Mathieu, wandered into the kitchen. "What's up with Larissa?" He came to stand behind Marie-Thérèse's chair and began massaging her shoulders with his strong hands. She lifted her face for his morning kiss, feeling the stubble on his unshaven face. A wave of love surged through her. As he sat at the table she hummed to herself. Life wasn't perfect, not even near so, but it was good. Really good.

A loud crash came from the direction of Larissa's room. Mathieu sighed. "I hope it's not the window again. No, you stay here, hon. I'll go see what it is this time."

Marie-Thérèse grimaced. He was too easy on Larissa, but she didn't feel up to facing her daughter again. Tears came to her eyes and the good feelings she had felt vanished. For a moment, she really wanted to move to America, away from Larissa. What was she doing wrong?

* * * * *

Larissa threw herself on her bed. First her Mom and Dad wouldn't let her go on the ski trip to Switzerland with Jolie's family, and now this bit about a new baby.

It would have been so great—days on the slopes with no one to tell her what to do. Jolie's parents believed in letting their daughter make her own decisions. And why not? Twelve and a half for a girl was almost an adult, wasn't it? Larissa knew how to cook—well, at least a few dishes—how to wash clothes if she cared to, and how to use the metro and bus system. What else was there to know? And it wasn't as if Switzerland was *that* far away.

She had been there last year when her family had traveled with the ward on a temple trip. She had been baptized on behalf of deceased relatives whose genealogy her mom had researched. She sighed. She had a wonderful feeling when she had gone down into the water, but when she'd tried to explain it later to Jolie, her friend had made fun of the idea of baptizing dead people. "What do they care anyway?" she'd said. "They're dead!"

Larissa no longer talked to Jolie about that stuff. Jolie was cool and she didn't want to be an outcast. Right now she was one of the "in" group, and she wanted to stay that way.

She sat up and picked up a large, hollow glass apple from her nightstand. Slowly, her gaze traveled the room. *I won't share it,* she told herself. *I simply won't.* Having another person in here going through her things . . . no, she wouldn't allow it.

Brandon would. He didn't care who touched his things. He didn't care if his books were stacked on the nightstand, on the shelf, or on the floor, while she enjoyed having everything in its place.

Like Mom, came a thought.

No, I'm not like her at all. She wants to fill up this apartment with little Brandons who do exactly what she says.

And why did Brandon do everything Mom wanted? She smiled grimly. *I'll bet he wouldn't if he knew the secret—if he knew that when Mom first got pregnant with him, she didn't even want him.*

Over the years, Larissa had heard her mom and Aunt Josette talking about this "secret" when they thought she wasn't listening. Apparently there had been some trouble between her parents— Larissa wasn't sure just what, except that it was about money—and Mom hadn't wanted another baby.

How funny! Now Mom would give anything to have a baby!

She knew that this was why her mother favored Brandon. She was still trying to make up for those first few months of rejection. Ha! As if Brandon had ever known.

The result was the same. Her mother loved him more than she loved Larissa, and he went along with everything she said while Larissa had to question everything to know for herself.

And she doesn't want anyone to question her church, she thought.

Her church?

Larissa shivered. Didn't she believe the Church was true?

Maybe she didn't even care.

Larissa's grip on the glass apple tightened as she contemplated her rebellion. The glass apple fell apart in her hands, spilling the several silver necklaces she had stored inside onto the floor. It made her angry, and in a moment of rage she hurled the apple after them. It slammed into the wood floor with a loud crash, and the apple shattered.

Tears flooded Larissa's eyes, but she didn't cry. She sat staring unhappily at the jagged pieces.

A tap sounded at her door, and then her father walked in. "What happened?"

"I dropped my apple," she said, blinking furiously.

"Oh, that's okay. Look honey, I'll help you clean it up."

Larissa wished he wouldn't be so nice because then she could get angry.

He was back in a moment with a broom, a dustpan, and a small plastic trash bin they kept in the bathroom. She picked out the necklaces and watched as he swept the apple up and into the trash.

That's what happens to people who don't believe, she thought. *Parents sweep them away and replace them with perfect little Brandons.*

CHAPTER 9

Rebekka lay in bed at the transplant clinic, staring up at the ceiling. She was so nervous she couldn't think straight. It had all been so easy, the decision to give Marc her kidney, calling in favors owed to their families, making the appointments. But now that the moment of truth had come, she wanted to run from the hospital and hide where no one could ever find her.

Of course, she wouldn't do that. People were depending on her: Marc's parents, his siblings, his friends. Not to mention Marc himself. She would never desert him. The love she felt in her heart had grown these past weeks until it filled her entire being, except the small part that was paralyzed with this overwhelming fear.

She was relieved when her parents came into the room.

"How are you doing?" Danielle asked, rushing to her side.

"Fine," Rebekka managed to say. "They're just about ready to take me to surgery. Marc's coming to see me first."

Danielle shivered. "You're so brave, and I'm so proud of you."

Rebekka wanted to cry. She wasn't brave, she was scared witless. But she couldn't tell her mother that. Danielle had experienced enough trials in her life being married to Philippe, and Rebekka wasn't going to add to them. Besides, she couldn't admit to Danielle that she wanted to run away, that she wished desperately *not* to go through with the surgery.

They talked of inconsequential things while Rebekka agonized inside. When they ran out of conversation, Philippe turned to Danielle and spoke, "Why don't you see what's taking Marc? I'll stay and keep Rebekka company."

Danielle kissed Rebekka. "I'll be right back, dear."

"Thanks, Mother."

After Danielle left, Philippe watched Rebekka for a full minute without speaking. Then he said, "How are you really?"

His perceptiveness took her by surprise. Of course, as a successful banker he had learned to read people. Why shouldn't he use his talents with his offspring?

"I—I'm . . ." She had been going to say "fine," but the words wouldn't come. "Daddy, I'm scared."

He stiffened. She knew it was because she hadn't called him anything but *Father* since before her teenage years. She clearly remembered making that decision. He had mocked the teachings of the Church, and she, burning with the testimony of youth, had purposely become more formal with him. Why had she done it? At the time she thought she was punishing him, but now she realized she had done it to protect herself from his mockery. The change hadn't been completely her fault either. He had encouraged her fear of him with the barely controlled anger beneath his smooth, educated surface.

"Do you want me to stop this?" he asked, relaxing slightly. He cleared his throat. "If Marc really loves you, he'll understand."

"No," she said without hesitation. "I love him. I would die for him, and he for me. If he knew how I felt right now he'd never let me . . . You won't tell him!"

"Of course not." The skin on his brow furrowed, and then he said awkwardly, "You know that I love you, Rebekka, don't you?"

Rebekka couldn't be sure, but she thought he blinked away tears. "I know you love me. You've never left me in doubt about that. And you have always taken such good care of Mother." Yes, despite the anger she often saw burning just beneath the surface, Rebekka knew her father cared passionately for her mother and deeply for her and Raoul. It was never his heart she questioned, only his methods. "Daddy," she said. "I need you to pray for me."

He looked surprised, but the expression quickly turned into one of dismay. "I can't . . ." He didn't need to finish the sentence.

"I know you're not a member of my church," Rebekka said hurriedly, "and you don't have the priesthood. But you do believe in

Christ. I know you do. Ever since that day when I was five and Marc's dad gave Mom a blessing and she lived. You believe in Christ or God or something. Can't you pray to them to watch over me?" Her voice trembled. "Please, Daddy. I need you to pray for me."

She waited, not knowing what to expect. Refusal? Anger? Embarrassment? Escape? What would he do? She reached out a hand, praying that he wouldn't leave. Her feelings of vulnerability hadn't been this strong since she had faced Marc in Utah before he had proposed.

But to tell this secret to her father? What had possessed her to open up to him? Yet Rebekka knew the answer. It was because of the defeat she had seen in his eyes the day she had told him of her plans to give Marc the kidney, because of her sudden understanding that he, too, was a child of God. The realization had made him human, capable of giving her the reassurance she so urgently needed.

He took her hand, and in a minute she was in his arms. "Rebekka, I wish you wouldn't do this. There's still time . . ."

She didn't reply, but relished her father's embrace. "I love you, Daddy," she whispered.

"I love you too. I love you very much."

Rebekka's fear seemed to lessen. "Pray for me," she pleaded.

"I don't know how."

There was a knock on the door, and Philippe drew away slowly. "Come in."

Jean-Marc and André entered. "We've come to give you a priesthood blessing," André announced. "I know you thought we forgot you, but we didn't."

"I'm rather unforgettable," Rebekka said lightly, squelching her fear.

André grinned. "Hey, I should've been the one to say that. It's certainly true. Anyway, Marc and Raoul will be along in a minute to help us, but Dad thought you might want another blessing beforehand."

Jean-Marc glanced at Philippe in apology. "Sort of a future father-in-law's blessing, if you don't mind."

Philippe appeared relieved. "We were just talking about that. Why don't I go and see what's taking Marc while you talk to Rebekka? I sent Danielle, but she's not back yet."

"I'll go with you," André offered. "I'm not needed here yet."

Philippe gave a final kiss to Rebekka and the two men left.

"I hope I didn't offend your father," Jean-Marc said.

Rebekka stared briefly at the door before meeting his gaze. "I don't know if you did or not. I have the strangest feeling that I don't know my father very well at all. Perhaps all these years I've seen only what I expected to see." She took a deep breath and tried to smile. "But thank you for coming. I do need a blessing. I'm rather nervous."

"I'll bet." Jean-Marc moved closer to the bed. "Rebekka, I've known you since you were five, and I have to say that I'm very proud of the way you've grown up. I know it hasn't been easy not having the priesthood in your home, but you and Raoul both have been very strong. I'm proud of you."

"You were always there for us when we needed you," she answered. "You or one of your family. Thank you."

Jean-Marc chuckled. "Well, now that you're finally taking my son off my hands, I hope to be there even more. Not to put any pressure on you or anything, but I don't have any grandsons who carry my name yet."

"I see. I guess I'll have to do my best to remedy that." Rebekka laughed softly. As Jean-Marc raised his hands to her head, she caught his hand in hers. "Thank you for making me laugh. I feel a lot better already."

"I'm glad."

As though able to see her thoughts, Jean-Marc blessed her with peace and with strength. Despite Rebekka's wish that her own father could have been the one to bless her, she was very grateful to Jean-Marc. The overwhelming fear faded to a nervous feeling in her stomach, not gone completely, but manageable.

* * * * *

After the nurses stopped fussing over Marc, he was allowed to see Rebekka. They took him to her room in a wheelchair, which would have annoyed him further if he hadn't felt so weak.

The past few days had been long and trying. He had experienced another collapse earlier in the week and the doctors had almost decided to give him a permanent catheter in his neck to receive emergency dialysis, if necessary. But after a priesthood blessing and an adjustment in medication, he was again stable. The doctor warned that if he had another collapse, or if Rebekka's kidney was rejected, they would have to begin dialysis anyway. It would be a last resort, given Marc's poor reaction to it in his youth.

Ariana, André, Raoul, and Danielle accompanied Marc to see Rebekka. She looked beautiful as always, despite the green hospital garb. But her grey eyes looked larger than normal, and her face was pale. He wondered if she was afraid.

"Are you all right?" he whispered as he hugged her.

She smiled. "Just a little nervous. I'm fine. Really." He knew her well enough to know it was the truth. If she had been fearful he would have called the whole thing off, regardless of what anyone could say. He wouldn't exploit her love.

"Where's your father?" Danielle asked Rebekka.

"He left to find you." Rebekka frowned and tightened her hand on Marc's. "I guess he's not coming back. I think he's a little worried."

After giving Rebekka a priesthood blessing himself, Marc felt much better. "I'll see you soon," he said, when the nurse indicated that it was time to go. He kissed her slowly, wishing the surgery was already behind them.

"I'll be waiting for you," Rebekka whispered against his mouth. Since her surgery began first, she would be awake long before him. "Afterward, we'll have wheelchair races down the hall," she added.

He smiled weakly. "Wheelchairs? They told me they'd make us walk."

"It's time to go," said a nurse for what must have been the third time.

He hugged Rebekka again, knowing that after this day their relationship would never be the same. By her sacrifice, she would be giving him the gift of life all over again.

"I love you," he said fiercely.

"I love you, too."

They wheeled her from the room, and Marc returned to his bed, where his sisters were waiting to see him. But he was unable to relax. He alternately prayed and stared vacantly into space.

After a few hours, a nurse appeared. "Well, your fiancée's kidney is safely out. Right now Dr. Juppe is preparing the kidney's blood vessels for implantation and Dr. Blainville is closing her abdomen. Everything is going perfectly, and she will be taken to recovery very soon." She smiled. "That means it's your turn. Let's go."

But Marc insisted upon hearing that Rebekka was in recovery and doing well before submitting to his own surgery. It would be too much to take if he awoke and found that something had gone wrong.

* * * * *

Rebekka awoke, feeling disoriented. She felt someone grab her hand. "Marc," she murmured, forcing her eyes open to see her mother next to the bed.

"He's still in surgery," Danielle told her. "But they said it's going well."

Rebekka felt as though she had been trampled by a wild horse. She closed her eyes again, thanking the Lord that her half of the surgery had gone well and praying that Marc's would also go smoothly.

She dozed for the next few hours until her father appeared in the doorway. Rebekka vaguely wondered when he had returned, and where he had been. "Marc's out of surgery," he announced. "Your kidney started working right away. They say he should feel better soon."

Rebekka breathed a sigh of relief. Until that moment, she hadn't realized the weight of worry she had carried. "Thank you, Father," she whispered.

She had meant it as a prayer to her Heavenly Father, but Philippe answered. "You're welcome. I—I'm just glad it's over."

"Can I see him?" she asked.

Philippe shook his head. "They'll let us know when he's awake and able to have company."

Five hours after her surgery, Rebekka still had not been allowed to see Marc. Meanwhile, two nurses came into the room and urged her to sit up in bed, then move to a chair, and lastly to take a few steps. Rebekka thought it was much too soon, based on the awful pain and weakness she felt, but the nurses assured her the movement would aid her recovery.

"I guess I asked for it," she joked. The nurses laughed, but her parents only watched her efforts wordlessly, concern etched on their faces.

Rebekka finally saw Marc after dinner. The nurses had put him through the same torture they had inflicted upon her, but he was smiling when they wheeled her bed into his room. He reached out and gripped her hand. His touch was warm and firm, and already he looked much stronger than before the surgery. "We survived!" he said triumphantly.

"Of course we did." She grimaced. "Except I think I'm going to make a complaint about the horse they allowed to walk all over me while I was unconscious."

He started to chuckle, but it turned to a groan. "I know exactly what you mean."

Now the waiting began as they watched to see if Marc's body would accept Rebekka's precious gift.

CHAPTER 10

Philippe Massoni left the hospital at dinnertime, knowing that Rebekka was in good hands. She was much more composed and happy now that the surgery was behind her. Philippe knew he certainly was.

"Would you like to stop at a restaurant, or should we grab a bite at home?" asked Danielle. Her silky voice slid over him caressingly in the way that it always did, but instead of bringing comfort, Philippe was reminded of the other woman in his life who had a similar voice: Rebekka.

Please, Daddy. I need you to pray for me.

"Actually, I'd rather go home," he managed to say to his wife.

He hadn't been able to help Rebekka, not in the slightest. He had held her, kissed her, and smoothed her hair, but it wasn't the prayer she had begged for.

Philippe didn't believe in organized religion. For a long time he hadn't even believed in God at all. But through the years of association with members of the Church of Jesus Christ of Latter-day Saints, especially the Perrault family, he had come to admit that some sort of God-type being lived and that He did care about the people on earth. At least some of them. As much as he wanted to deny it, Philippe knew Danielle had been healed by a priesthood blessing after her severe accident in the train bombing. But he credited the miracle to the faith of those involved, not to their religion.

Rebekka and Raoul had been baptized into the Church, and though Philippe remained unbelieving, he had attended the baptismal ceremonies. It hadn't bothered him to see another man performing the religious duty for his children, one usually reserved for a father or close relative. He didn't accept the religious mumbo-jumbo as reality anyway, so it hadn't mattered. Nor had he cared when they had been confirmed, or when Raoul had advanced in the priesthood. Those were simply things Philippe did not believe in. He saw to it that his children had medical attention, a more than adequate education, and had even given Raoul money to enter a business partnership with the Perrault brothers. Those were things Philippe believed in. Solid things you could see and feel.

But a few simple words from his cherished daughter had destroyed all that.

Daddy, I need you to pray for me.

Yes, it bothered him that he would not be giving his only daughter away at a spectacular wedding, but he had known that was a strong likelihood for many years. Ever since she began to call him *Father*, instead of *Daddy*, he knew she had moved, if not beyond his reach, then at least beyond his total control. She had joined the Church with both heart and soul. He hadn't let himself feel her loss then, but the anger in him had burned more fiercely. Oh, he certainly wouldn't let it lash into his family as his father had permitted his anger to scar the young, helpless boy Philippe had once been, but the fury . . . and yes, the hurt, was there, eating steadily into his soul. One more thing to blame on Danielle's church. While it may have given life back to his wife, it had stolen his daughter and his son.

Please, Daddy . . .

But she had only wanted a prayer—why couldn't he give her that? *I don't know how.*

Philippe had never prayed, and he realized now that no one had ever taught him. His mother had died when he was young, and his father—may God curse his soul—had been too stern, angry, or busy to make the effort, if he had believed in prayer at all.

A light sweat broke over Philippe's body. He was barely conscious of riding the elevator up the eight floors to their apartment. At the door, Danielle entered, but Philippe lingered in the hall. "I think I'm going for a walk, dear," he said lightly, so as not to betray his inner turmoil.

Danielle watched him for a moment, puzzled. "Would you like me to go with you?"

"It's okay. I know you're tired. I won't be long. Don't worry." He kissed her soft porcelain cheek, briefly amazed at the intense love in his heart. What had she seen in him all these years? She was so beautiful, patient, and intelligent, if a bit innocent. Oh, how he blessed that innocence! It was probably the only thing that had kept her with him, and he tried to make it up to her every day.

"I love you," she said quietly, as if knowing exactly what he needed.

Why? he wanted to ask, but was suddenly afraid of the answer. Why *did* she love him? Why *did* she put up with his inner seething anger? Why, when she was so strong in her faith, did she endure his unbelief?

Philippe walked blindly down the street, tripping occasionally over a loose stone in the cobblestone sidewalk or the curb as he crossed the streets.

But you do know how to pray. The thoughts were his own, and they told the truth. He had heard his family pray many times. Had God been listening, or did He only exert His power when it was a matter of life or death?

Rebekka could have died today.

Why couldn't I pray for her?

Philippe found himself in a remote section of his neighborhood. Night was falling quickly, yet the street lights hadn't yet lit. He was completely alone, though he heard laughter coming through a nearby window.

Abruptly, he was angry, furious, more than he had ever been in his entire life. He shook his fist at the darkening sky. *Leave me alone!* he screamed silently. *I was happy before You came along.*

Had he been? No, before Danielle's accident he had been teetering on the edge of leaving Danielle for another woman, and his anger had all but consumed him. Then the miracle of Danielle's life had brought them back together, and their love had burned brightly ever since. He knew most of the credit went to his wife—and her church.

Philippe stumbled into an alleyway, too caught up in his emotions to do more than register that he had wandered a long distance from home into a neighborhood that wasn't nearly as safe.

He fell to his knees, caring little for his expensive suit, and dropped his head into his hands.

Daddy, please . . .

He tore at his hair. *Why couldn't I pray for her?* He had wanted to, more desperately than she could ever know. Yes, she received another man's blessing, but that other man was not her father. Philippe was, and he had failed her.

Again.

Tears fell from his eyes to the pavement.

How long he knelt there he didn't know, but eventually sounds called his attention. A cat mewing, a disembodied shout, faint voices from a television set, the scrape of something metal. Footsteps.

Philippe raked his hand through his hair, bent almost upon himself in silent torment.

Dear God, he began. *Please bless my little girl . . .*

There was a rustling behind him, and then something heavy hit the back of his head. Philippe's world went black.

* * * * *

Raoul had finally left his sister at the hospital and was driving home when his cell phone rang. "Hello?"

"I just got a call from the police," said his mother, her voice frantic. "They found your dad in an alley. Someone beat him up. I—" Her voice cracked. "I have to go get him."

"Stay right there; I'll come pick you up." Raoul knew how much his mother hated to drive, and going on the metro this late at night was out of the question. "I'm turning the car now. I'll be there in minutes."

"Hurry," she pleaded.

Raoul stepped on the gas. Was his father all right?

Cold fingers gripped his heart. What would his mother do without his father? She loved him completely. With the exception of her involvement in the Church, her whole life revolved around him— especially now that her children were grown.

He knew that if Desirée had been found dead in an alley, he wouldn't want to go on without her; she was everything to him.

Everything? a silent voice mocked.

Raoul grimaced. Desirée wasn't a member, that was true, and though every day he earnestly prayed for a change of heart, he still loved her. Just the mere thought of her beautiful face and her touch made him weak in the knees. When he was with her, he was happy. She kept him laughing and his heart racing. He suspected that she didn't love him as much as he loved her, but she was young—twenty-two to his twenty-seven. She would grow to love him more once she settled down a bit.

His grimace disappeared as he recalled the day they had met—at the grocery store of all places. She had been buying a basket of fruit and had looked so inviting in her summer dress that he had been caught staring. Before he knew what had happened, they were talking and she was giving him her number. He loved how easily she kept the conversation going. He felt he had known her forever.

He hadn't known then that she was as friendly with everyone she met, not just with him. And sometimes it bothered him the way she talked so familiarly with people—especially other men. When he mentioned it to her, she just laughed and told him that he was cute when he was jealous.

I'm not jealous, he told himself. *After all, she married me.*

Why? asked that nasty voice. *Was it for money?*

He pushed the disturbing thought aside. When he looked into her eyes, he knew she loved him, and that was enough. He was determined to make their relationship work—even if it required a lot of patience.

Drawing out his phone again, he dialed his home number. There was no answer. He wondered if Desirée was still visiting friends. She had declined to go with him to the hospital, claiming that Rebekka would already have too many visitors. Her statement turned out to be true, but Raoul had been a trifle annoyed all the same. *Family should be there for one another.*

He dialed the number again, but there was still no answer. *Where is she?* He scowled. The first thing he was going to do the next day was get her a cell phone.

When he arrived at his parents' apartment building, Danielle was out front waiting for him. She jumped into the car. Her eyes were red from crying and the tissue in her hand was wet. Raoul handed her another from the dash compartment.

"Which hospital?" he asked.

She stared at him blankly for a moment, as though trying to process the question. Her face was eerily illuminated by the street lamp outside. "He's not at the hospital," she said finally. "We have to go to the police station."

Raoul sagged with relief. "Then he can't be hurt badly, or they would have taken him to the hospital."

A light appeared in Danielle's gray eyes. "I just thought that maybe he was too bad to move . . . or something."

"It'll be all right." He patted his mother's leg, more confident now.

They reached the police station fifteen minutes later, and were ushered into a backroom where Philippe lay on a padded table, surrounded by a small group of uniformed officers.

"Are you sure you weren't drinking, Morrie?" a female officer was saying.

"I tell you, I saw what I saw," insisted a short, square-faced policeman. "There were two thugs, and one of 'em had a knife in his hand. I could see that he was going to stab this here fellow—uh, Monsieur Massoni, I mean—but then the other perp said something and he up and dropped his knife and ran."

"Not before he got my money," Philippe said dryly.

"He musta heard you coming," one of the other officers said to the one called Morrie.

"And you're sure he doesn't have a stab wound in his back?" asked the woman.

"I'm fine," Philippe insisted, his voice irritated. He struggled to a sitting position. "Except for this blasted headache."

"Whoever it was hit 'im pretty hard on the back of the head. Found a piece of wood nearby that they must have used. Had blood on it. I chased 'em but they were too fast."

Danielle didn't wait to hear more. "Philippe!" As she rushed to her husband's side the crowd of officers parted to allow them through.

Raoul hung back. He hadn't seen his father since his marriage to Desirée, and wasn't sure how he would be received.

"Thank the Lord you're all right!" Danielle rubbed her hand lightly over his back. "I've been so worried."

"I'm sorry, honey." Philippe buried his face in his wife's neck, but not before Raoul glimpsed an unmistakable vulnerability.

"I don't know what I'd do without you," Danielle murmured. "Are you all right? Shouldn't we go to the hospital?"

Philippe shook his head. "No, I'm fine. Just a little headache."

"A little?" mocked one of the officers. The others laughed.

Philippe withdrew from Danielle and began to rise slowly. His movements froze as his eyes fell on Raoul. An internal battle seemed to ensue, but Raoul couldn't read the emotions on his father's face. Anger, resentment, hatred? All three, or none? Raoul simple didn't know, and he felt a deep sadness. *A man should know his father,* he thought. What was left between them?

Finally, Philippe nodded in his direction. "Raoul," he said, as though Raoul hadn't eloped with a woman of whom he didn't approve. As though their religious beliefs hadn't created a barrier over the years that neither had been able to bridge.

"Is he free to go?" Raoul asked, looking away from his father.

"Yes, we already have his signed statement," said one of the officers.

Danielle possessively held onto her husband's arm as they made their way to Raoul's car. After a brief recap of the events, during which Raoul learned nothing more than what the officers had said, Philippe fell into silence. With his parents riding in the back seat together, Raoul felt more like a chauffeur than a son.

He pulled up to their apartment building after ten o'clock, and jumped out to help his father from the car. Shutting the door behind them, he watched his parents walk toward their building. Raoul didn't go with them. Desirée would be home now, and he should get back to her. Yet he knew the thought was only an excuse. In reality, he was uncomfortable with his father and dreaded a confrontation.

Philippe paused, then separated from Danielle, taking a few steps in Raoul's direction. "Thank you for coming, son," he said. "I'm glad you're back."

Raoul felt a rush of different emotions. He tried to speak, but couldn't with the sudden lump in his throat. Besides, what could he say? He nodded.

To his utter surprise Philippe hugged him, and Raoul was unable to stop the tears. "Father . . ." he began, but again couldn't speak. He still didn't know what to say. His father felt infinitely frailer in his arms than Raoul remembered as a young boy; he probably outweighed Philippe now by ten kilos.

"I love you, son. I always have. Whatever words we had are in the past. You and your wife are welcome in my home anytime."

Raoul searched his father's face. He saw no burning anger there, only regret. "I love you too, Dad."

He watched his parents enter their apartment building, marveling at his father and the scene that had taken place between them. What would Rebekka say if she knew? But that would have to wait until Rebekka was feeling better. Besides, Raoul was reluctant to explain the event to her when he didn't understand it himself. Something had happened to effect a change in his father's attitude, and he had no clue as to what. Surely a mugging couldn't bring such a shift, so what had? Certainly nothing spiritual; his father had always rejected such things.

Yet images of happier times flashed before his memory: of the two of them staying up late with a school math assignment; of Philippe sitting by his bed when he was ill; of the day Philippe had given him the money he needed to start the business with Marc and André. And towering over all was the continual care and respect Philippe offered to his wife. There was no mistaking the genuine love and deep attachment between them. *Maybe I've been wrong about him,* Raoul thought. *Maybe I've been so caught up in what was wrong with him that I never saw the good.*

When it came right down to it, his father had always been there for him when it mattered. Except at church. Did that one lack overshadow all the rest? Had Raoul's resentment over that one thing prevented him from having the relationship he desired with his father? He had always blamed Philippe, but now Raoul was not so sure the blame rested entirely on his father's shoulders.

At least Desirée would be happy to learn that his father had retracted his verbal opposition to their marriage. Feeling much lighter, Raoul hurried back to his car. Inside, he dialed his apartment number to tell Desirée he would be home soon.

No one answered.

By the time he arrived home, he was worried, but Desirée came in shortly after he did. He met her at the door. "Hi, sweetie," she said, coming to him and wrapping her arms around him. She smelled of smoke mixed with perfume.

"Where have you been?" he asked, kissing her lightly on the mouth. She tasted strongly of mint.

"With Leesa," she said. "And some others."

He wanted to ask her if the "others" were male or female, but he stopped himself. Just because Desirée was beautiful and friendly, didn't mean he had to be suspicious.

"My dad was hurt," he said. He led her to the sitting room as he briefly outlined the attack.

"I'm sorry, honey." Desirée knelt on the couch, turning his body so she could massage his shoulders.

He began to relax under her ministrations. "I don't know, it might be a good thing. He—" Raoul turned around so that he could face her "—he actually told me that he withdraws his objections to our marriage."

Desirée's dark eyes flashed. "That's wonderful! I know that means a lot to you."

"To both of us," he corrected. She laughed as he gathered her into his arms.

CHAPTER 11

By Monday night Rebekka was up walking the halls, on Wednesday she was walking around the hospital grounds, and on Thursday she was released. She didn't go home, however, unless it was to sleep. Instead, she spent every minute she could with Marc. As he was fighting boredom, he was very grateful for her company.

Unfortunately, his progress wasn't as rapid. His creatinine levels, though dropping from eight before the surgery to hover around two point five, still worried the doctor. "We'd hoped you'd be under two," explained Dr. Albert Juppe, the transplant specialist. The doctor was slightly shorter than Marc and stocky, with plump fingers and silver hair that had once been black. Marc felt a déjà vu every time he saw the man who had also performed his first transplant. "We have to be very careful that your body doesn't reject the kidney now."

Rejection? While he knew it was quite possible, Marc hadn't allowed himself to entertain the idea. How could he stand it if he rejected Rebekka's kidney after all the suffering she had endured?

Seeing his worry, Dr. Juppe added, "It might just be that the kidney was traumatized and needs a week or two to recover from the surgery." He smiled, his intense black eyes showing an apparent concern. "Don't worry . . . yet."

Marc was worried, but he grinned to cover the feeling. "You know that I'm getting married in about two and a half weeks—dead or alive."

The doctor snorted. "I heard you Mormons baptize for the dead, but I never believed you marry for the dead as well."

"That's not exactly what I meant." Marc launched into an explanation of his beliefs, and Dr. Juppe listened with a practiced patience.

When he excused himself twenty minutes later, smiling, Marc wondered if the doctor hadn't brought up religion just to keep his mind off the possible rejection.

Before he could dwell on the issue further, Rebekka glided into the room, looking healthy and so beautiful that Marc longed to take her into his arms.

"How are we today?" she asked, bending over gingerly to give him a quick kiss on the mouth. As she straightened, her hand went to her side and she grimaced. "Ouch."

Marc grinned sympathetically. He pointed to the sign above his bed that read *NO LAUGHING PLEASE.* "Brandon brought it today. He made it for me after he came to visit that first day and Josette made me laugh so much that I cried. I felt like she was digging sharp rocks into my stomach."

"Sneezing's worse," Rebekka said, sitting close to him on the bed. "After I left you last night I had a sneezing fit. I thought I was going to rip out the staples and start bleeding."

"Ouch."

She nodded. "Ouch."

They sat in silence for a minute and then she asked, "Any more news?"

"No. They'll take another test today. I may get to go home next week."

"You'd better hurry if you're going to make our wedding." Her voice was light, but he sensed an underlying worry.

"It'll be okay, Rebekka."

"I know." She didn't sound convinced. "It's just . . . well, we've been waiting a long time."

"Hey, I'll be at that wedding if I have to drive to the temple in a hired ambulance."

She chuckled, and then clutched her side and moaned, "Stop."

"I can see us now," Marc continued with a laugh, followed quickly by a loud groan. "There we are on our wedding night, lying in bed and moaning while we watch TV—something depressing so we won't laugh."

Rebekka smiled. "It'll be the best day of our lives."

Marc agreed with his whole heart. "I love you, Rebekka Massoni."

Her eyes misted. "I know."

Marc sighed. Despite the pain in his body, he was happy. And he would remain happy as long as she was by his side. Even so, his premonition of their separation hung over him, blurring the happiness.

With effort, he forced it from his mind.

CHAPTER 12

On Friday, one week after Marc's transplant, André had a particularly difficult day at work. Several crises had arisen and without Marc in the office, André and Raoul had their hands full. To make it worse, Raoul wasn't up to his normal standard, seemingly distracted with his new wife, who called at least four times during the morning alone. André ended up spending half the day on conference calls, and the other half running to two different building sites where he had heated discussions with two of the foremen about maintaining Perrault and Massoni standards. One of the men, a longtime employee, was chastened, and he immediately promised to right the wrongs in order to provide better service to the customer, but the other man was belligerent and André had fired him on the spot. This left him scrambling for a replacement. Fortunately, the assistant foreman, though young and relatively inexperienced, was knowledgeable enough to take over temporarily. André promised him the job permanently if he could deliver quality work within the budget and time frame stated in the contract.

When he arrived home, he was already irritated and very late. The girls met him at the door, and he was almost too tired to pick them up for their kisses. All he wanted to do was to fall into bed and sleep.

"Claire?" he called. There was something odd about the house, but he found it difficult to put a finger on.

"Where's your mother?" he asked the girls.

Ana shrugged her thin shoulders. "In bed."

Worry gave strength to André's weary body. He stumbled past the kitchen, noticing its utter silence. There was no pot boiling on the stove, no roast or cake in the oven, no beautiful Claire smiling at him.

The absence of cooking food made his stomach complain more furiously about the lunch it had missed.

"Claire?" he called again, his anxiety overwhelming him. His voice carried down the hall and into the bedroom, but there was no answer. The door was partially ajar and as André ran toward it, he felt as though it had never taken so long to bridge the gap.

Claire was lying in bed in the dark, facing away from him. Beneath the thin blanket, she looked like nothing more than a small lump with dark hair. The next thing he noticed was the terrible acid smell that assaulted his senses, making him gag. As he flipped on the light, she moaned and turned stiffly, squinting.

"The light, it hurts my eyes."

He turned it off quickly and came to her, a deep compassion and sorrow filling his heart. There was a white basin by the bed where she had been throwing up, but by the state of the blanket and the floor, she hadn't always made it. Her face glistened with fever and her forehead wrinkled with tension.

She began to vomit again, violently, and she lay with her head half off the bed as the spasms shook her frail body. Nothing came out into the basin except a thin squirt of yellow fluid. She shuddered and gasped in what he was sure was horrible pain.

André helped her turn onto her back, away from the smelly basin. "Do you want a drink?" She nodded and he sprinted to the kitchen and back again. With an arm around her, he eased her to a sitting position long enough to help her take a few sips of the water. "Why didn't you call me?"

"I did once, but your line was busy." Her voice was so soft he almost couldn't hear the words. "I didn't leave a message. I was going to call back, but then it got bad. I couldn't get out of bed."

"The girls could have called," he said, but without reproach.

She managed a thin smile. "I didn't want to worry them. They've been playing in their bedroom for hours." She gave a little sob. "They were hungry, so I let them eat all the cookies."

"It won't hurt them this once." André smoothed her hair and kissed her forehead.

Claire's body lurched, and she began to vomit again. He held her until the spasms passed. The fear that had been growing inside his chest since he entered the apartment consumed him. Years ago, she had been through terrible illnesses, several of which had prompted a quick trip to the emergency room, but none had ever made her appear this close to death. Or had he simply put those instances out of his mind?

"I'm so sorry, André. I don't want to be sick. I wish—I wish I could be strong for you."

"Nonsense. Don't say that. I love you just the way you are." It was true, though many times in the past he had longed for her good health, mostly for her; though if the complete truth were told, he had wished it at least once or twice out of pity for himself. "Besides, you haven't been sick for a long time, not really. That's in the past. This is just a little bug we have to work through. Come on, let's get you to a doctor." He picked her up, blanket and all. She felt as light as air in his arms.

"Girls!" André yelled, moving swiftly down the hall. "Get out to the car; we're taking Mommy to the doctor."

"I don't have my shoes," Marée said.

"Put them on—quickly!"

Claire's head lolled against his shoulder, though her eyes were open and glistening like blue-green jewels in a pond.

"I can't find them!" squealed Marée.

André opened the door to their apartment. "Get out to the car now!"

"But—"

"Go barefoot. Now!"

Marée looked at him reproachfully, but André didn't have time to soothe her wounded feelings. Ana, her eyes huge, pushed her stocking-footed sister into the hall and closed their apartment door.

Claire threw up repeatedly in the car. André hadn't remembered to bring anything for her to vomit in, but it didn't make a difference since she had nothing left inside her stomach except a small amount of digestive acids.

As he drove, he dialed his mother's number. *Please be home,* he prayed. She answered on the first ring. "Mom . . . ." He gulped. "It's Claire. I'm taking her to the hospital. She's really sick. She's throwing up, and I think she has a fever."

"When did it start?"

"I don't know. She seemed fine this morning except for a slight headache and a little stiffness in the neck. We thought she just slept wrong."

"Where are the girls?"

"With us. I didn't dare stop to leave them with the neighbors."

"Tell me where you're going and I'll meet you there."

Marc felt relief at his mother's words and silently thanked God that she was home when he needed her. Since she lived closer to the hospital, she might even get there before he did.

Claire was throwing up again where she lay in the back seat. Next to him in the front, Marée sobbed while Ana held her hand. André wished he could hold and comfort his youngest daughter, but there was no time. Instead, he squeezed her tiny knee. "Shush, baby, it'll be all right. Don't worry." Marée quieted some, but her sniffles still tugged at his heart.

When they at last drove up to the hospital, Ariana had arrived and was hurrying toward the doors. She stopped when she saw him park next to the emergency room. "I'll take care of your car," she said, waving him toward the hospital. "Go."

Leaving his keys and the girls with her, André hurried inside, carrying Claire. Her eyes were still open, but she didn't respond to him when he spoke to her.

"Help! Help me, please!" he called as he approached the desk. "I don't know what's wrong with her." Tears began coursing down his cheeks but he paid them no heed.

Two employees dressed in green rushed out with a gurney for Claire. They helped André settle her onto it, and then rushed her over the white tile into the back part of the emergency room. André followed them, not really noticing anything around him except the impression of cubicles sectioned off with green or white curtains, each filled with beds, machines, and medical supplies. As they arrived at the last of the curtain sections, two nurses began working on Claire, taking her vital signs and making her more comfortable. Claire opened her eyes and smiled at him weakly.

André's tremendous fear began to ease. *It'll be all right,* he told himself. She was in capable hands now and would be just fine.

But everything wasn't fine. After talking to André and Claire about her symptoms—fever, vomiting, severe headache, stiff neck, back and joint pains—the doctor-on-call ordered numerous tests, including a lumbar puncture, where a small amount of fluid was removed from around Claire's spine. Laboratory results were conclusive.

"She has meningococcal disease," the doctor told André. "It's a form of bacterial meningitis."

"It has a name—good, that means you can treat it."

The doctor inclined his head. "We can give her antibiotics intravenously, and we might even cure her, but the outcome is not always that positive."

"You mean she could die?" André could barely form the words.

"Well, now that she's receiving treatment, she has a ninety percent chance of pulling through, and that's fairly good. It would have been better if she had come in this morning or in the afternoon, but she has a better chance than if she'd waited until tomorrow." The doctor shook his head as his eyes shifted to his patient. "She's very sick. This is a rare enough disease, and I personally have never seen such a severe case."

An impossible lump formed in André's throat, and he struggled to speak past it. "What is it exactly—meningitis?"

"There are two types of meningitis, viral and bacterial. Viral is not usually life threatening. Bacterial meningitis, the kind your wife has, is much more serious. It attacks the brain and the spinal cord. About ten percent of cases are fatal and fourteen percent of the survivors are left with a significant handicap." The doctor hesitated before adding gently, "Last year there were only two recorded deaths in Paris from this disease."

André felt as though he were in a nightmare and couldn't awake. "But how could she have gotten it? She's been trying to eat right, she's been healthy."

The doctor shrugged, his face sympathetic and kind. "The bacteria customarily live in the nose and throat. Between ten and twenty percent of the population carry this bacteria at any given time, and many who do never develop the disease. We don't really know why one person gets it and another doesn't."

André thought of the past years when she had been sick. Could that be related? But she'd experienced nothing except a cold since

Louis-Géralde's farewell, and her immune system should be fine—or should it? How long did it take to rebuild an immune system?

"But she'll be okay, right?" André knew the doctor had already answered the question, but he desperately needed reassurance.

The doctor stared at him gravely. "I hope so, Mr. Perrault. We will do everything in our power. Meanwhile, we would like your immediate family to take antibiotics as well."

A sick feeling formed in André's stomach. "Are you saying my daughters and I could catch this?"

"The chance is less than one percent, but since her case is so severe and your daughters are so young . . . I'd feel better if they were protected. Of course, feel free to consult with your own doctor. Meanwhile, we'll get your wife admitted."

André was in a daze. He checked on Claire, who was sleeping, and then went to the lobby where his mother waited with the girls. Ana jumped up at the sight of him. "Is Mommy going to be okay?"

"Yes, honey. It's just going to take awhile."

Ariana stood with a sleepy Marée in her arms. "What is it? Do they know?"

"Ana, why don't you take Marée and go see the fish right over there in that tank? In a minute I'll come and we'll go buy something for you two to eat, all right?"

"A pastry?" Ana asked hopefully.

"Sure. Whatever you want."

André waited until the girls were out of hearing range. "According to the doctor, Claire has a type of meningitis. It's pretty bad, but—" His voice broke and he stopped to compose himself. "The doctor gives her a ninety percent chance of living." He felt numb as he spoke.

Ariana bit her lip, and her face creased with sorrow. "Then the odds are high that she'll be okay," she reminded him gently.

"He also said fourteen percent of the survivors have some sort of serious disability. That means she has about a seventy-six percent chance of recovering completely. Three out of four." He shook his head. "That's still too low."

Ariana hugged him, and André was amazed at the comfort he felt in his mother's arms. Her head went only to his chin, but he felt like a small child again. "Mom, I love her so much," he whispered.

"We'll get through this," Ariana answered, drawing away. "We will. Your father is on his way to help you give her a blessing. When he arrives, I'll take the girls home with me and put them in bed."

"The doctor wants to give them—us—an antibiotic just in case."

"I can get it at the pharmacy."

"Thank you so much, Mom."

She squeezed his hand and smiled.

They took the girls for a snack and then André returned to Claire's side. She was still sleeping, but restlessly. He bit back tears and fell into the chair by her side. *Please dear God,* he prayed. *Please help her.* Through his despair he felt his Heavenly Father's comfort pour through him and he knew that whatever the future held, his Father would make both him and Claire equal to the task.

CHAPTER 13

Before visiting Marc on Saturday morning, Rebekka stopped at the hospital to see André, who had spent the night there with Claire. He met her in the ICU waiting room after a nurse went to get him from Claire's room. There were deep circles under his eyes and his dark brown hair was mussed like a small boy's.

She hugged him, ignoring the pain it brought to her abdomen. "I'm so sorry, André." She felt guilty, too. Everything was finally going well for her and Marc. Poor André! And if there was any woman in the world who deserved an uncomplicated life, Claire did. She was a sweet, wonderful woman, whom Rebekka already considered a dear friend.

"Thank you for coming," André said.

"Can I see her?"

He shook his head. "No. Her condition is critical now. They're only letting in immediate family. I'm sorry."

"No, *I'm* sorry."

"She'll be okay," André said. "She has to be."

"Of course she will. We're all praying."

"How's Marc?"

"Good, so far." She forced a smile. "As long as you don't make him laugh."

André grinned, although the expression lacked his usual exuberance. "Well, you seem to be getting along all right for only being a week out of surgery."

"Nine days to be exact, counting the day of," she corrected. "And I feel fairly good."

"Good enough to get married?"

She uttered a short laugh, only to clutch her side. "Yeah. At least, I think."

André became serious. "For what it's worth, I want you to know how happy I am for you and Marc. I couldn't ask for a better sister-in-law."

Rebekka's eyes filled with tears. "Thanks. It hasn't been easy waiting all these years."

"I know," he said with a snort. "Marc was so blind. I used to get mad at him for not seeing what was right in front of him. The best thing you ever did was leave France. It certainly woke him up."

"Yes, but it might not have." She frowned. "When I left here, I thought I'd lost him for certain. It was the hardest thing I had to do."

"Well it worked out—for both of you."

She smiled and touched his arm briefly. "Speaking of Marc, I'd better get going. I promised I'd stay with him again today. He's going crazy in there."

"And I'd better get back to Claire."

She took a step away, and then paused. "André, let me know if there's anything I can do. Please."

"I will. But you have your hands pretty full with Marc."

"Marc's biggest problem is boredom. And he has a load of nurses to look after him when I'm not around. I'd like to help you if you need me. What about taking the girls?"

"They're with Mom."

"Well, let her know that I can watch them any time. I'm not even employed yet."

"Thanks. I will." He gave her a weak wave and turned back through the double doors into the ICU wing.

At the transplant hospital, Rebekka found Marc in high spirits. "How goes it?" She bent her head for a quick kiss. She began to rise, but Marc reached up and pulled her back for another long kiss. A delicious shiver ran up her spine

"Ahhhh, heaven," he murmured against her lips.

"Can you go home yet?" Rebekka asked, loving the way his eyes locked onto hers.

"They still won't let me go home, but they said I can take a walk around the grounds for as long as I can bear it, and then they'll let

you roll me around in a wheelchair—if you're feeling well enough."
His brow furrowed. "You are up to it, aren't you?"

She smiled, curbing the laughter that would shoot pain through
her abdomen if she let it loose. "Yes, for a while, anyway. And they
have some nice benches outside where we can rest."

"At least it's somewhere other than this room."

Within a few minutes they were outside in the small park that
was part of the transplant center. The early October day was warm
and beautiful, not too hot or cold. "This is wonderful," Marc said,
stretching gingerly as he stepped out of his wheelchair.

Rebekka's eyes tracked several other patients, walking or being
pushed by a family member or a nurse.

"It is nice," she agreed.

Marc took a few steps. "I can't wait to get back to work. André
mentioned yesterday morning that they have their hands full. I'm
thinking I might be able to do some work from here."

Rebekka realized that no one had told Marc about Claire. *Of
course they haven't,* she thought. Ariana had called and left a message
for Rebekka at her parents' late last night, and no one besides herself
had come to see Marc this morning. Rebekka had assumed that
Ariana had telephoned Marc as well, but apparently she had thought
it better to talk to him in person. Or perhaps she had hoped that the
morning would bring better news.

"Marc, there's something I have to tell you." Rebekka looked
down at the empty chair she was pushing—actually half-leaning on as
she already felt rather tired.

He immediately sensed the graveness of what she was about to tell
him and stopped in midstride. "What is it?"

She met his searching gaze. "It's Claire. She took ill last night and
André rushed her to the emergency room. She was diagnosed with
bacterial meningitis. I'm not sure what that is exactly, but according
to your mom, she was supposed to be significantly better today. Only
she's not. I stopped by there this morning on my way here and they
wouldn't let me see her. I did talk to André, though, and he said her
condition is very critical."

Marc's expression turned from disbelief to dismay. "Oh, no. Poor
Claire! And André! He doesn't deserve this—neither of them do." He

put his hand on hers where it lay on the handle of the wheelchair, and they walked slowly in thoughtful silence.

"Is this related to how sick she was before?" he finally asked. "You know, in the years after she had the girls."

"No. Your mom told mine that it's apparently not related except maybe because Claire has a weak immune system. But with how healthy she's been lately, the doctor doubts it's related." Rebekka heaved a great sigh. "Apparently anyone can get this disease. In fact, he said college students have a particular risk of complications related to the disease because no one's around to take them in to the doctor."

"I wish I could be there for him, as he's always been for me."

"Then get better," she said it half-jokingly, but there was fear in her voice too. The possibility of rejection grew more real to her each day.

"I'll do just that," he promised with a smile. "But meanwhile, will you keep checking on him for me?"

"Of course I will. Your whole family will."

Marc's gaze was luminous. "That's right. We Perraults are good at rallying around. I just hope . . . Let's get back to the room. With André out of commission, I'll bet your brother could use some help at the company. I can do some of that from my bed."

"You'd better not work too hard."

"Just a few phone calls," he assured her. "Believe me, I feel much better already. I think all this walking they force me to do is actually helping."

Rebekka left him before noon, happily talking to Raoul on the phone. To her surprise, she felt envious. Working had always been one of her greatest pleasures. Maybe she should call Damon and Jesse in America and see if she could do some work for them from home while she waited for Marc to recover.

* * * * *

Claire's eyelids flickered as though she were dreaming, but her face remained expressionless. André hoped she wasn't in any pain. At least while she slept, she didn't throw up or moan.

A succession of visitors had come and gone—his parents and his daughters, Josette and Zack, Marie-Thérèse and Mathieu. Even

André's grandparents had stopped by. No one had been let in to see Claire except for the little girls, and then only briefly. Claire hadn't been aware of their presence. The girls weren't overly concerned, as they were accustomed to Claire's illnesses, and André didn't have the heart to tell them of the seriousness. He sent his family home and prayed that her illness would pass.

His hopes continued despite the increasingly depressing prognosis. The optimism in doctors' and nurses' faces had been replaced by a subtle grimness that frightened André more than any of the monitors they had hooked to Claire's body. No one quite met his eyes either, but rather stared at the air a few centimeters from his face.

"André?"

His eyes rushed from the floor to the thin shell of his wife, lying so insubstantially on the hospital bed. "Claire? Are you awake?"

Her turquoise eyes rolled back in her head for a moment before returning to rest on his face. "Where am I?"

"At the hospital," he said, gently restraining her hand from pulling the oxygen tube from her nose.

"Why?"

"You're sick. But don't worry. You'll be okay."

"Where's Daddy?"

André was confused. "Do you mean your father?"

"Why won't you tell me?" A tear escaped one of her glazed eyes.

"He's dead, isn't he?" She began to sob softly. "I didn't get to say good-bye."

They had told him to expect odd behavior because the disease and the treatment might affect her conscious state, but he had figured that meant she would sleep until she was better. He hadn't expected this retreat into childhood.

He encircled her gently in his arms, careful of the IV. "Oh, Claire, your daddy's in heaven and he knows exactly how you feel. Don't worry, everything's going to be all right."

She clung to him as though her life depended on his touch. Gradually she relaxed, and he thought she had fallen to sleep again. But when he looked at her face her eyes were open, bright with unshed tears.

"Are you awake, Claire?" he asked.

She attempted to focus on him, but the medication they had given her for the pain and vomiting made it difficult.

"Will you find my brother?" she finally managed. "I always wondered what happened to Basil. I can't help but think he's out there needing me somehow."

"Sure. We'll do it together." They had discussed trying to find her older brother before, but over the years had been too occupied with their young family and his business to pursue the idea. Now he wished they had.

"I love you, André," Claire said faintly. "I love you so much."

"I love you, too."

He held her for a long time, positive that her return to reality was a good sign. "We'll beat this thing yet," he told her. She smiled at him and slept.

Some time after lunch he had nearly dozed off when a shrill alarm engulfed the room. André felt terror leap to the forefront of his emotions. In seconds, three nurses and a doctor rushed in, and he watched them with horrified detachment as they crowded around Claire's unmoving body. They gave her a shot. Nothing. They tried shocking her heart. Nothing. They tried everything again. Still no reaction. After a long time, they stopped their efforts and looked at him helplessly, almost guiltily. A steady scream still emitted from the EKG, and a flat line inched across the screen.

One of the nurses had tears running down her cheeks. She stared at André, begging him to understand.

"No," André said, suddenly realizing what it all meant.

"We're so sorry," another nurse said kindly. She turned off the monitor, while the others began to pack up the equipment. The nurse whose face was wet with tears turned off the IV.

"No! You can't leave!" André rushed to the bed, sure they were mistaken. Claire wasn't moving. He grabbed something—he wasn't sure what—from the small rolling cart they had brought in with them. He shoved it at the doctor. "Use this! Hurry!"

The man shook his head, sorrow etched on his face. "I'm sorry. But there's nothing more we can do. We tried everything—you saw that. I would do anything to bring her back, but sometimes it's not meant to be. I really am sorry." He put a light hand on André's back.

They left one by one, and André stared after them in a daze. When the door shut, he turned his attention to the bed. Claire looked as though she were sleeping. The only sound in the room was the oxygen hissing from the tube still attached to her nose.

"Ah, Claire," he whimpered like a small child. "Don't leave me. Please." He took her limp hand in his, willing it to move, to grip his own shaking hand. He touched her face. The skin was warm and pliable, soft. "Father, please!" he prayed aloud, his voice sounding empty in the small private room.

He clutched her to his chest, crying, pleading, aching. Though he had survived a loved one's death before, Claire was his beloved wife, his eternal partner, and he had never expected the complete emptiness that now assaulted him.

"It can't be," he moaned.

They hadn't shared a final scene together, other than the drug-induced murmurings earlier. There had been no opportunity to tell her what a difference she had made in his life and how grateful he had been for her love and companionship. Of how afraid he was of going on without her. She hadn't been able to promise to watch over him from above, or to remind him that their union was eternal. They hadn't discussed what he would do with the girls during his work hours, or brought them to say their final good-byes. There hadn't been time for any of it, especially because he hadn't believed for a minute that she would really die. Now he desperately mourned the loss of those unspoken words.

"Claire, Claire, I need you!" The plea went unheard.

The hissing air seemed to grow louder. André gently pulled it away from Claire's nose and threw it from her. With a slow deliberation, he lifted her eyelids to peek at the turquoise eyes that had fascinated him from the moment he had first met her, looking so young and frail and yet so beautiful in that ward house in Strasbourg. But they weren't the same. The life and love that had filled those incredible eyes had gone. Unspeakable agony pervaded his entire being.

Claire really was dead.

Better it was him.

He released her, slowly, as more tears wet his cheeks, and laid her gently on the white sheet. Her eyes were closed again, and for that he was thankful. Carefully, he arranged her hands over her breast. Time passed as he watched her, the incredible pain in his heart relentless. The tears dried on his cheeks, making his skin feel tight and dry.

At last he moved away from the bed and walked toward the door. Once there, he couldn't bear to leave her. A few steps brought him back to her side, where he let his rough hand trail the soft flesh of her cheek and down to her neck where she had so loved to be kissed. He lowered his face and kissed her once, softly. Then, resolutely, he left her and strode toward the door.

He hadn't planned on looking back, but he did, and the sight of her alone on the bed, chest unmoving, broke through his daze and once again released his formidable grief. He fled the room. Blindly and on shaky legs, he ran down the hall, stumbling slightly, and burst through the doors leading to the waiting room. No one tried to stop him.

I should call someone, he thought. But what could he say, "Hi Mom, Claire's dead. Will you tell the girls?" Or "Josette, it's over. Please tell me I'm having a nightmare." Or maybe, "Marie-Thérèse, I think you better help me before I walk off a bridge."

André felt the walls of the hospital pressing down upon him, squishing out his very life. While he would have liked nothing better than to join Claire in death, he couldn't tolerate the horrible pressure. Struggling to breathe normally, he headed for the elevator, plowing directly into someone. Unseeing, he tried to step out of the way.

"André!" the woman said.

He saw Rebekka through tearful eyes, but didn't know what to tell her.

"André, you're so pale. What's wrong? Is it? . . ." She glanced over his shoulder as two people emerged from behind her.

He didn't answer, but pushed past her into the elevator. "Gotta get out of here."

Dimly, he was aware of her following. "Oh, André!" There was a hurt in her voice that made him look at her. She launched herself into his arms. "I'm so sorry! I never thought—I can't believe . . . Oh, André!"

He began to cry with her, wrapping his arms around her as though she were a life jacket and he lost in the ocean. Rebekka smelled like fresh flowers, and she was vibrantly alive, unlike Claire's lifeless form lying so absolutely motionless in that tiny, silent room. He wanted to scream out his anguish, but he couldn't find words for his voice.

Rebekka held his trembling body for a long moment. When they arrived on the bottom floor, she quickly urged him into the lobby and from there to the street.

"I should go back," he said, though the pressure in his heart had lessened with the sight of the blue sky.

"Later." Her voice was firm. "Let's walk first."

He knew she was supposed to be taking it easy, not traipsing around the streets, but the endless torment in his mind wouldn't let him dwell on what was best for her; instead he greedily accepted any comfort she could give him.

She held his hand as they strolled, like brother and sister, into the Saturday afternoon. Without her support, André knew he would fall down and die right there in the middle of the sidewalk. They walked until they came to a more crowded area where the smell of fresh bread and coffee permeated the streets. André finally noticed Rebekka holding her side and breathing heavily, and he stopped near an outdoor table at a café.

She lowered herself gingerly into a chair, casting him a grateful glance. "I'm supposed to walk every day, but Marc and I did already . . ." Tears glittered in her gray eyes, like rain falling from dark clouds. "I'm so sorry, André."

He slumped beside her, a part of him thankful that the lunch rush was over and that no other customers were within hearing range of their table. The other part contended that it didn't matter how close people were because he was separated from them by an impassable gulf of grief. He was untouchable.

He stared at his hands folded together on the tablecloth, particularly at the thin band circling the fourth finger of his left hand. Though a welcome numbness was spreading to his heart, the grief was still overwhelming. *It's a part of me now,* he thought. *Never to leave. Nothing will ever be the same. Claire. Oh, Claire.*

He couldn't feel her at all now. Even when he was at work he had been able to feel their connection, intangible to his flesh, but real nonetheless. Now that connection was completely and utterly absent. "This is all a nightmare," he muttered. He looked up at Rebekka, eyes pleading. "Please, tell me to wake up."

"I wish I could." Rebekka's hand on his felt soft and cool to his touch.

"I didn't get to say good-bye." His voice broke and he struggled for control. He had cried for so long in the room with Claire—how could there be any tears left? "I didn't tell her how much I love her."

Rebekka rubbed his fingers. "She knows. Of course she knows. She's probably here right now."

He shook his head emphatically. "I would feel her."

"Feel her?"

"I've always been able to feel her. I can't now."

Rebekka seemed to understand. "She's on a different sphere now. It might take time to find her again."

"I would feel her," he repeated dully. But he didn't really believe it.

Rebekka's shoulders lifted in a delicate shrug. "Maybe she's a little busy with her parents and her sister. It's been a long while since she's seen them."

He hadn't thought of that, only of his own devastation and despair. For a brief, clear moment, he pictured Claire's happy face as she embraced those she had lost. Would she even think of him and the girls?

Of course . . . and yet he knew time was different in the afterlife, and that things mortals considered important might be low on a long list of priorities for those beyond the veil. Claire likely had duties to accomplish.

Duties he wanted to share with her.

In his peripheral vision, André saw a waiter approach. The absurdity of sitting at a café as though nothing in his life had changed drove him to his feet. "I have to get back to her." He sprinted a few steps away from the café.

Rebekka caught up to him, grimacing with the effort. André slowed to her pace and they walked in silence. "You were a wonderful husband to her," she said softly. "And Claire loved you so much." She paused, searching for words. "I can't pretend to know how you feel, but I know how I would feel about losing Marc. I'm so sorry, André. And I'm here for you, no matter what. Please let me help."

Strangely, Rebekka's words brought him comfort. André believed with all his heart that he and Claire would be together eternally, but the thought of living the rest of his earthly life without her was frightening. With the support of Rebekka and his family, it would likely be much easier.

"Thank you," he replied simply. How could he ever tell her how much it had meant to have her appear at the hospital precisely when he had been so alone? Perhaps someday he would be able to convey his gratitude.

Rebekka put an arm around him. "You're welcome."

André let her lead him back to the hospital. His father and sisters had arrived, notified by caring nurses. André fell into their arms and wept. Later he would talk to the girls. Later he would have to deal with everyday life. For now, he would grieve with those who loved Claire almost as much as he did.

CHAPTER 14

Two days after Claire's death Rebekka relaxed in a narrow recliner the nurses had set up for her next to Marc's hospital bed. Since she visited so long and often, they had worried about her obtaining enough rest to fully recover from her own surgery. Rebekka had to admit that the reclining position was somewhat easier on her abdomen than sitting. She was feeling better and stronger each day, but this morning felt tired and exhausted—the result of a lousy night's sleep. She had come into the hospital only because she had wanted to prevent Marc from spending all day on the phone working.

Dr. Juppe came in before nine. "Hello, pretty lady," he greeted Rebekka. He glanced at Marc. "This guy doesn't know how lucky he is to have such a faithful fiancée."

Marc grinned, but it was tinged by the sadness everyone felt from losing Claire. "Oh yes I do. I'm the luckiest man alive. So, have you come to break me out of here?"

Dr. Juppe's smile faded. "I'm sorry. Your creatinine levels are actually rising."

Rebekka's breath caught in her throat and her eyes flew to Marc's where she read the same dismay on his face. *Oh, Father, please,* she prayed.

"Are you saying . . ." Marc's voice trailed off.

"We believe you are rejecting the kidney." The doctor's voice was soft and kind.

Marc's eyes widened and his face went slack as he tried to mask his emotions. "So what now?"

"I'm increasing your immunosuppressive medication. The drug will block a specific region of your immune system T-cells, preventing the cells from multiplying and attacking your kidney." He put a hand on Marc's shoulder. "Most people go through several bouts of rejections before their body settles into a routine, so try not to worry."

"I went through a few before and that kidney lasted a long time," Marc said, more to Rebekka than to the doctor. The words should have comforted her, but they didn't. His eyes were darker and conveyed a hopelessness that she had never seen before, and his hand gripped hers tightly as though he used every effort not to weep.

After the doctor left, Marc turned to her. "It'll be fine. Don't worry."

"I'm not worried." But she was. The song she had written for Marc once more sounded a haunting melody in her mind. Would she ever play it for him? Would it ever have a name?

"I guess I won't be going to Claire's funeral tomorrow," he said.

"Would you like me to tell André?"

"No. I'll call him." He sighed. "His problem certainly puts ours into perspective, doesn't it?"

Rebekka nodded solemnly.

* * * * *

By Wednesday, the day of Claire's funeral, the cutting agony André had first felt at his wife's death had begun to fade into a determination to live worthy of being reunited with her. At times the aching and emptiness were too much to bear, and he would collapse onto his knees next to the single bed he had slept in as a youth and pray until the desperation eased, or until he fell asleep. He spent much of the first few days after his wife's death kneeling.

He and the girls had been staying with his parents, as he didn't feel emotionally capable of returning to his own apartment. He knew he would have to face it soon, and was glad his mother and sisters had promised to help him go through Claire's possessions. There would be items he should put away for the girls—objects with only material value, like her jewelry and her collection of pewter. Other items he would save were priceless, like her diary, the letters she had written to the girls on each birthday, or the knickknack of the kissing couple he had bought for her on their honeymoon. Someday Ana and Marée would want to know the stories behind the items, and he would want to reminisce.

Someday.

It was hard now, when his soul still cried out for her. When his ears longed to hear her voice, and his body craved her touch.

The girls had cried when he had tearfully but steadily informed them of their mother's passing. He had held and rocked them until they fell asleep, and continued to stay with them the entire night, in case they woke up and needed him. Sunday they had spent together quietly at his parents, and on Monday he had taken them to see Claire at the funeral home. She looked peaceful in death, and though the girls cried again as they touched and kissed their mother, he felt he had been wise in letting them say good-bye in this manner. The funeral home director and the counselors at the hospital had urged him to be open with the girls about the death, but he had feared their grief as much as his own.

Now as he helped them into the matching dresses Claire had made for them last Easter, he pondered his wife's life. Her ill health early in their marriage had encouraged her to search for more sedentary occupations, and not only had she become an excellent seamstress and cook, but she was also an avid reader of anything from novels to nonfiction of all types. When he'd experienced troubles at work, she had drawn from her learning to counsel him. Her mind had become a veritable library of which he had made frequent use. It was only now as he fingered the material she had cut and sewn with such preciseness that he realized he had taken many of her talents for granted. "I'm sorry, dear," he murmured.

"That's okay, Daddy. It didn't hurt. I didn't feel anything."

André's hand paused as he zipped Ana's dress, realizing she thought he'd been addressing her. "I'm glad it didn't," he said. "Now for the shoes."

"I don't know where mine are," Marée wailed from the floor where she was sitting with a small doll her grandmother had given her the day before.

"They're right here in this suitcase," André said. "Grandma went and got them at our place yesterday. See? She even remembered your tights." He scrunched up the white tights and slid them onto her tiny feet. Ana began pulling on her own. Claire had stitched a small X on the bottom of each foot so the little girls could tell which way to wear them. André knew it had been for him as well, since he had as much trouble as they did with the awkward things.

André tried to lift Marée to finish pulling up the tights, but she was staring at her shoes and not cooperating. He stifled his irritation and the urge to jerk her to her feet.

"Marée, I need you to stand up," he said, voice carefully controlled.

Her small face swivelled toward him, and by her expression he realized she hadn't heard anything he had said. "Marée," he called.

Her eyes focused on him, blue-green orbs that so reminded him of Claire. "Did I make Mommy die for not getting my shoes on?" she asked. Her voice was heavy and sad, and tears began falling from her eyes.

André was shocked. How long had this worry been weighing upon her young mind? He gathered her stiffened body into his arms and cuddled her close. Ana paused with her shoes in hand, every bit as curious for the answer as Marée.

"Of course you didn't cause Mommy to die," he said. "Never, never think that. She just got sick. It had nothing to do with you."

"But she always got better before," Marée protested with a trembling frown. "Except this time when I couldn't find my shoes."

"That's because it was time for her to go home to Heavenly Father. I know it's hard to understand. She loved you so much and didn't want to leave, but she had to. And now we just have to keep on and someday we'll see her again."

Marée buried her face in his chest, her stiff body finally relaxing. "I miss her." The words came out as a plaintive cry. Ana began crying with them, and André reached out to pull her into their embrace. "It's going to be okay," he whispered. "I promise."

* * * * *

Rebekka and her family had been invited into the Relief Society room to take part in a Perrault family prayer before the funeral. She was surprised and happy to hear occasional gentle laughter as people conversed quietly, waiting to share a final moment with Claire. An air of reverence and love hung over the room. Many members of the extended family had traveled to be there to support André and to pay their last respects.

Perhaps that was why Rebekka was startled to see Raoul walk in the Relief Society room alone, just in time for André's father to offer a prayer.

"Where's Desirée?" Rebekka whispered after it was over.

Raoul frowned. "She didn't come."

"Why?"

"She didn't know Claire well, and she hates funerals."

"She should be here to support your partner," Rebekka insisted. She looked across the room at André, who stood by the recently closed coffin, talking quietly with his parents. His eyes were rimmed with red, but he had managed to maintain his composure throughout the viewing and the condolences. The girls were at his side holding his hands tightly, and Rebekka was gratified to see him smile at something one of them said. "André needs all the support we can give him. As your wife, she owes it to him to come."

Her comments fell on deaf ears. Obviously, Raoul could hear no evil when it came to his new wife. "I know she's not really connecting with the family," he said, "but she really is a nice person. You should see her with her friends."

"*Her* friends?"

"Our friends. She's warm, fun to be with, and—well, sexy." When Rebekka punched him on the shoulder he said, "Hey, I can say that about my own wife!"

"Not at a funeral you can't. And I still say she should be here."

Raoul sobered. "Honestly, Rebekka, it's okay. She has this thing about funerals. She'll get depressed for days remembering her grandmother's funeral. They were pretty close. At least she sent flowers."

Rebekka couldn't help the pity that formed in her heart. If only Desirée would listen to the gospel. Maybe then she would be able to accept them.

"Come on," she said to Raoul. "There's still time for you to say a word to André before we go in."

* * * * *

The funeral services comforted André more than he had expected. His parents each spoke, recalling Claire's special talents and how much she cared for her family. Then Josette recounted stories of her faith, how close Claire had been to the Lord, and the example she had been to them all. As they talked, André found himself thinking of the day he had met Claire, how there had been an air of purity around her. He had known instantly that she was to be his companion. How fortunate he felt to have loved and shared his life with such a wonderful woman!

The Spirit of the Lord descended and filled André's heart with comfort and sweet hope. He would see Claire again, of that he was sure. He would touch her soft face and love her for eternity. Even at that moment he felt her close, almost as if her arm rested on his.

When the funeral was over and Claire had been interred at the cemetery, André felt a strong need to be in his own home. He thanked everyone who gathered at his parents' to express their condolences and then carried the tired girls to his car, suddenly anxious to be back where he and Claire had lived and loved.

In their apartment, he brushed the girls' teeth, though he had never been the stickler for it that Claire had been (seeing as all their baby teeth would soon be replaced by new ones anyway) and snuggled them into separate beds in their shared room.

Afterwards he was restless, and he paced from one end of the apartment to the other. His mother had been at work here, and the place was clean. Every room—even the bedroom where Claire had been so sick that last day—smelled fresh. *Thank you, Mom,* André thought.

As he walked through the apartment, memories of how they had purchased and arranged their belongings crowded into his head. Their furnishings were simple yet elegant, with deep hues of mauves, greens, and off-white instead of pastels. Claire had never gone for frills, but for solid value and timelessness. The furniture and accessories fit him perfectly. As had Claire.

He slumped onto the sofa in the TV room, staring at the blank screen while his hands fingered the crocheted lap blanket Claire had made. He held it to his chest, closing his eyes, breathing in her smell that was comforting and yet filled his heart with longing. Tears squeezed out of his swollen eyes, even when he thought there were none left. "I miss you, honey." His voice was but a whisper in the silent stillness of the room.

The buzzer sounded in the hallway, signaling that someone was outside the apartment building wanting to come up. He walked wearily into the hall and pushed the black button without asking who was there. Then he waited, peeking through the tiny spy window. Depending on who appeared from the steps or elevator, maybe he would answer the door. And maybe he wouldn't.

Rebekka came into view from the staircase, her fine features pensive. Even to a member of his family, he might not have opened the door. But to her he must. She had been with him when he needed her most.

"I'm sorry," she said apologetically, as he emerged before she could ring his doorbell. "Your mother said you'd left these and since I was going home anyway, I thought I'd stop by and deliver them." In her hand she held the dolls Ariana had purchased for Marée and Ana. "She said that Marée was particularly attached and that she might need it tomorrow."

"Thank you." He took the dolls and waited for her to say good-bye. Instead she continued to stand in the hall, hesitating. "Are you all right?" he asked.

She sighed, and her eyes that were already red and swollen turned desolate. "Marc didn't want me to tell you . . . said you had enough to worry about, but I think you should know. Yesterday he started rejecting my kidney."

André felt as though he'd been hit. Marc had been on the phone the past few days taking over the part of his work that Raoul didn't have time to handle. All this time André thought his brother was recovering steadily, but instead he had become more ill. "So what does this mean?"

"Well—" she stared at the ground "—so far nothing. They're controlling it by medication. But it still . . . Oh, André, I'm so worried." Her gray eyes were like storm clouds again, huge and threatening rain. "After all these years of waiting for him to notice me, I'm afraid I'm going to lose him."

André put an arm around her and led her into his apartment.
"Come on in. Let's talk about it."

"I knew giving him my kidney was right," she said, hitting her
right fist into her left palm. "But now I just don't know what to do. I
keep asking myself why we're having to go through this, what lesson I
should learn. But I just don't see the necessity of his rejecting the
kidney for some stupid lesson!"

He helped her settle on the sofa, the cream color of her knit pants
blending in with the color of the leather, while he sat in the glider-
rocker nearby. She fingered Claire's white lap blanket. "I've thought
about marrying him now while he's in the hospital, just in case. That
way if anything happens, I could still seal us later in the temple." Her
eyes met his reluctantly. "How's that for faith?"

André shook his head. "I think your faith is fine, Rebekka. You
were always great at planning things and going for what you want."

"But I'm afraid to tell Marc," she answered, relief in her voice.
"It's important that he keep up his spirits. If he thinks he's . . ." She
couldn't finish the words.

"What does the doctor say?"

"Only that we have to wait and see. If the medication works, he'll
eventually be released and we'll go on. If it doesn't, they'll have to
remove my kidney from his body and put him on dialysis until he can
get another operation."

"Then it sounds like you have some time."

A frown marred the smooth face. "Maybe." She leaned toward
him, rubbing her fingers together. "I feel like it's so close, our being
sealed, and yet life is so fragile. Everything can change overnight."

Yes, I know. His thoughts must have shown in his face because
Rebekka placed her hand on his arm. "Look at me, carrying on this
way, when you've already been through so much. And today of all
days. I'm so sorry, André." A single tear escaped the confines of her
luminous eyes and slid down her left cheek. "I guess that shows the
true me—how selfish I am. But I've no one else I can tell this to. Well,
Raoul, maybe. If he weren't so caught up with his own problems."

André's momentary agony subsided. "It's all right, Rebekka.
That's what family's for." He realized that he had always considered
Rebekka family. Once, before meeting Claire, he had actually imag-

ined himself in love with her. Rebekka had only been sixteen or so at the time, though she possessed a maturity beyond her years. But even then he had seen her passion for Marc and, never being the type for unrequited love, he hadn't let himself fall too deeply. Then he had met Claire, just eighteen, and had never looked back.

André still cared for Rebekka, though more in a removed sense since she belonged to Marc, and also because his love for Claire hadn't let thoughts of other women enter his mind. Claire had filled his every emptiness. Now suddenly, his life stretched out before him, long and lonely without her. He sighed.

Rebekka glided to her feet with the gracefulness that was always hers. "Thank you for listening. And if you need help with the girls, please let me know. I want to help."

"They'll be going to school next week," he explained as they walked out the apartment door and into the hall. "And I'll be going back to work. Since Marée only goes part-time, she'll stay at day care until Ana finishes, and then at least for the first week or so, I'll knock off early to pick them up. Maybe after a while I'll need help for the few hours between the time they get out and I get off work. My mother has volunteered of course, and Marie-Thérèse and Josette, but I'm sure there'll be enough to go around." He smiled sympathetically. "Maybe by then you'll know where you're headed with Marc."

"Thank you, André. I appreciate it. You've always been such a good friend." She hugged him briefly and was gone.

André stared after her long after the automatic lights in the stairwell shut off. He prayed fervently that Marc would be all right and that Rebekka would be happy. Then he went into the apartment where the girls lay sleeping. Ana was no longer in her bed, but had curled up with her sister. They looked like miniature Claire-angels. He had meant only to check on them and go to his own room, but all at once he couldn't face the queen-size bed without Claire. Not yet. Instead, he let himself fall onto Ana's bed. Tomorrow he would sleep in his own room, but tonight he needed to be with his girls.

CHAPTER 15

Rebekka called her brother early the next morning from the transplant hospital. "Marc's making me call you," she said without preamble. "The doctor has forbidden him to do any more work from bed, so here is a list of people for you to call."

"Hi Rebekka," said Raoul. "And I love you, too. It's good to hear your voice."

She ignored him. "As you know, André won't be in today, and that's going to leave you—"

"Actually, André did come in this morning."

"What!"

"Yeah, he got worried about a deal we're working on. He's been our main representative on it since I've been busy with another client, and he thought he should meet with them on-site."

"But the girls—"

"They're with him. André took along one of our secretaries to keep an eye on the girls in the car while he walks around the site. He came—"

"But—"

"—stocked with lots of snacks, books, and the like. You know, stuff kids need. And there's a restaurant nearby if they need food."

"He's just lost his wife!" Rebekka felt angry at her brother for not being sensitive to André's emotional state. Were work and the resulting profit so important that André couldn't have time to grieve?

"It's good for him," Raoul said firmly. "He needs something to focus on right now, and I thought this would be the easiest thing for him—not a lot of time, but something to help him feel useful. That's why I called him."

"You *called* him?" Rebekka was aghast. "I can't believe you'd do that. You're an insensitive . . ." She struggled to find the right words.

"Easy, Rebekka. You know I'm your favorite brother."

"I'm not fooled—you're my *only* brother. And I think you should have given him time."

"He's a man. It's what he needs," Raoul insisted.

"I'll remember that the next time you're suffering."

"Thank you."

Oooh! she thought. *Talking to Raoul is like talking to a wall. He should have stayed on his honeymoon with that prissy wife of his.*

"Well, at least Marc's not part of your manly scheme," she said. "I'm not going to lose him now because of some client. The doctor says no work and that's exactly what Marc's going to do. Nothing. Period. The only thing he's going to do is play chess or read those stupid science fiction books everyone keeps bringing him."

"I wouldn't dream of asking him," Raoul assured her. "Besides, with the work he's already done, and with what André's taking care of, I can handle the rest. You and Marc can even take a nice long honeymoon."

Don't do me any favors, Rebekka wanted to retort, but she didn't because she wasn't really mad at her brother. Life was simply so uncertain at the moment. She desperately wished she could wind back the clock and marry Marc in Utah, and that André could have gotten Claire to the hospital on time.

She closed her eyes and rubbed her temples, feeling a headache coming on. Her side was hurting too, since she was standing at a payphone in the hospital, not willing to call from Marc's room where he would insist on talking to Raoul himself. She was already breaking the doctor's rules by passing on the information, but Marc had been so agitated that she had agreed.

"Rebekka," Raoul's voice was soft. "You take care of Marc and I'll take care of André, okay? They'll both be fine."

"Okay," she managed, gulping back the threatening tears. "And I love you."

"I know. I love you too. Later." He hung up the phone, and for some undefined reason, Rebekka felt better.

CHAPTER 16

Two weeks dragged slowly by. Then a third. Physically Rebekka grew stronger each day, but she was emotionally drained. Marc's condition continued to worsen, despite various medications.

She had finally let Danielle postpone their wedding, seeing as Marc was too ill to go anywhere, much less travel to a temple. Rebekka was terrified that she would lose him forever. Just when the walls of despair were close to burying her, the idea she'd had of marrying Marc in the hospital returned to her mind, lifting her spirits.

She went to the transplant hospital on a Wednesday morning in a better mood. Marc was slumped in bed staring at the wall, the remains of his early breakfast still sitting on the counter.

"Hi, honey," she said brightly.

He focused on her and smiled, but the happiness was forced. "Hi. I'm glad to see you." He frowned. "It was a long night."

She kissed him and with her hand smoothed the creases in his forehead. "You're bored." She knew him so well.

"I feel useless, that's what. I just wish this would be over one way or the other."

She must have made a sound or her torment must have been apparent in her face because Marc was immediately repentant. He squeezed her hand. "I didn't mean anything by it. I'm just sick of being here."

Rebekka made her voice calm. "I understand. But you will get better. I know it. Come on," she tugged on his hand, "the nurse said I could take you for a little stroll. It's fairly warm out, but you'll need a sweater." She helped him into a sitting position before retrieving the navy argyle sweater from her bag.

"You've been to my apartment."

She grinned. "You mean *our* apartment—or soon to be. Yes, I stayed there last night." She wasn't about to admit how she had slept on his bed, wetting his pillow with her tears; the knowledge would only distress him. "And before you ask, yes, you still have a plant on the kitchen windowsill."

"You remembered to water it? Wow, now I'm impressed."

She hesitated before replying, "I watered it today . . . Okay, so it *was* the first time and it *was* dead, but I planned to buy you a new one before you found out." Her words made him laugh, which had been her intent. "You knew I wasn't good with plants," she added.

"Yeah." His voice was warm, like the old Marc. He pulled her down to sit with him on the bed, hugging her. "I love you, Rebekka," he murmured in her ear.

"Whew, and I was beginning to think that you wouldn't marry me after all."

He pulled back slightly, eyebrows raised in question.

She had been going to tell him her plan outside in the fresh air, but her idea couldn't wait. "Marc, I want us to get married next week. If it has to be here in the hospital, so be it. That way we'll be together no matter what."

"You think I'm going to die." His voice was even.

This was the reaction she had feared, and the reason she had not brought the suggestion up sooner. "No, of course I don't think you're going to die. I just want to be your wife. Please, hear me out, Marc. I know we've always had the temple as our goal, and I'm not losing sight of that, not at all. But there's no temple here in France—you know that as well as I do—and we'll have to get married civilly first anyway before we can fly to Switzerland or Germany to be sealed. We've lived with that knowledge our whole lives. So why not get married in the hospital now and when you're better in a few months we'll take the first available plane to the temple? Waiting's not a big deal, right? We both know people who've waited to be sealed because they couldn't afford to travel to the temple—"

"But you and I *can* afford it."

Rebekka was beginning to feel desperate. "I know, but you're sick! You're worthy, but can't physically make it to the temple—yet. It's the same thing!"

He gripped her hands and stared earnestly into her eyes. "Oh, Rebekka, I want to marry you more than I can say! I lie awake at night thinking about it. But I want to be able to walk to my wedding, not have it here in the hospital. And then I want to fly to the temple immediately afterwards, papers in hand, to make our marriage official in the temple. I promised the Lord long ago that when I married, I would do just that. I really don't feel that waiting to be sealed once we're married is an option. Please try to understand. I love you more than life, but I can't do what you're asking."

Rebekka looked defeated. "Well, then I guess we'll have to wait until this bout of rejection eases."

"And if it doesn't?"

"We'll face that when we come to it!" Rebekka answered passionately. "Oh, Marc, at least we'd be married!" She didn't add that if he died she could still seal them in the temple, but what she was saying was clear to both of them.

"I—I—" Marc suddenly turned a pasty white. "Rebekka, I don't feel so well."

Fear sliced through Rebekka's heart. She pushed him gently into a reclining position on the bed before signaling the nurse with the call button.

The nurse immediately checked Marc's vitals signs. Clicking her tongue in worry, she gave him a shot and insisted Rebekka leave. "He really needs to rest now."

Rebekka felt miserable, not only because of her fiancé's failing health but because of his reaction to her grand idea. Logically, she could understand his objection to marrying in the hospital, but her terror at possibly losing him for eternity went beyond all reason. She wanted to spend happily ever after with him, to forever see him looking at her with that attractive grin and the gleaming brown eyes that so fascinated her.

Numbly, she returned to Marc's apartment, wanting desperately to be with him, but also hurt at his reaction to her proposal. She ate a rye-bread sandwich for an early lunch before falling asleep on Marc's bed, wearing one of his old T-shirts. With her entire heart, she wished he could be with her.

Later a phone call pierced her awareness. Rebekka yawned, stretching carefully because of her still-tender abdomen, and picked it up. The clock on the nightstand read ten minutes after three in the afternoon.

Ariana's voice sounded loud in the silence. "Marc's been rushed into surgery. He's had a violent case of rejection and they have to remove the kidney. And they're also putting in a permanent catheter in his neck so they can give him emergency dialysis."

Rebekka's heart pounded loudly and her hand shook so that she could barely hold the phone to her ear. "Is he going to be all right?"

"I don't know." For a moment, Ariana's voice sounded forlorn. "But of course, he has to be all right," she added firmly.

"Have you called the Ukraine?"

"Jean-Marc's doing that now. Don't worry, we'll take care of it."

"I guess we should have called Louis-Géralde home from the first," Rebekka said bitterly. She began to sob. "I'm so sorry. I thought I was doing something good and now it's all been for nothing."

"It's not your fault, Rebekka. You did a very wonderful thing. No one can help that he's rejecting your kidney, or that he has trouble with dialysis. Many others endure dialysis for half their lives or more."

Rebekka was still crying, but she held her hand over the phone so Ariana wouldn't hear. Why, when Marc had finally recognized his love for her, did everything seem to be conspiring against them?

She was changing to go to the hospital when the doorbell rang. With surprise, she opened the door to André. He took in her red eyes and tear-streaked face and without hesitation, gathered her into his arms. The tears came again, but with André holding her shaking body, the pain was at least bearable.

"What if I lose him?" She met his eyes briefly before raising her face to the ceiling. "Please, dear God, don't let me lose him now."

"You're not going to lose him," André said. "But come, the girls are waiting in the car. I just picked them up from school."

"Alone?" she was appalled. Marc's apartment was in a commercialized section of town.

"No. Valerie, one of the secretaries from work, is with them."

"How did you know where to find me?"

"Mom called. She said you needed help. Valerie, the girls, and I were just headed off to do an on-site inspection, but it can wait. I'll give you a lift to the hospital."

"But you shouldn't have to be there." The ache in Rebekka's heart renewed for both herself and André, who had recently lost so much.

"Of course I should. He's my brother."

"But the girls."

"I was going to have Valerie take them home, but they want to stay with me. They'll be all right. The whole family's going to be there."

Gratefully, Rebekka let him lead her out of the apartment, down the elevator, and out to his car. Once there, he introduced her to Valerie, a girl barely out of her teens with straight, shiny black hair, a wide smile, and hazel eyes. She was average height and size, and her features were also average, even plain, except for the charming smile, and for her eyes which were alive with such friendliness that Rebekka could hardly look away.

"It's so nice to meet you," Valerie said as André introduced them. She grinned and her smile filled her face with warmth. "I mean, I've seen you around, but we were never introduced."

Rebekka thought that meant Valerie was relatively new or her position far removed from Marc's, who was not only a partner, but CEO of the company.

"Pleased to meet you."

Valerie bobbed slightly and then took a few steps back. "I'll take the subway from here," she told André. "It's not far."

"Thank you so much," André said.

"You're welcome. And any time you need me to help you with the girls, just ask. I really like them." Valerie cast him another brilliant smile and was gone. For a moment, Rebekka felt a sense of jealously as her protectiveness rose to the surface. Was this girl out to snare André, who was so vulnerable at this point in his life—whose wife had been dead scarcely a month?

Oh, stop it, she told herself. *So what if she is? She's obviously a nice girl and she likes André's children.* Despite the family's loyalty to Claire, the best thing for André and his little girls would be for him to remarry.

If Marc died, I would never remarry, she thought as she entered André's car. *Never.*

But what if he died before they married? Would she live her entire life alone? The thought was too terrible to bear.

"Are we almost there?" asked Ana, bringing Rebekka's thoughts back to the car.

"Just a few moments more," André replied.

"Is Uncle Marc going to heaven with Mommy?" Marée's tiny voice trembled with the words.

Rebekka looked compassionately at the child. She wanted to tell her that Marc would not die—words Rebekka desperately wanted to hear herself—but she didn't dare say something that might end up being a lie. These little girls had been through enough with their mother's death, and preparing them for any possibility was the only way Rebekka felt she could help them. But what to say?

To her relief, André answered, "We don't think so, but we don't know yet. Whatever happens, the Lord will be with us. I promise you that. And everything will be okay."

The girls looked trustingly at their father, faces sober but not tearful.

Once at the hospital, they had to wait another two hours before finally hearing that Marc had made it through surgery and was receiving emergency dialysis. "He should be feeling better afterwards," Dr. Juppe told them. "With his history, I doubt we'll be able to use dialysis as a long-term solution, but we can pray that it works until we can come up with an alternative."

An alternative. Meaning another transplant.

"We've left a message to be delivered to our youngest son," Ariana said. "He should be home soon."

"Well, I couldn't imagine doing anything before a week or two anyway," Dr. Juppe replied. "If that soon. He needs some time to recover. Of course, if we run into problems with the dialysis we may have to move forward anyway."

The relief Rebekka had temporarily felt was overrun by terror. She began shaking so badly that she almost collapsed onto the sky-blue carpet.

Making a sympathetic noise in his throat, André half-carried, half-led her to a couch. "He's all right, Rebekka," he reminded her.

"For now." It wasn't good enough.

Her shaking gradually subsided, but the tight, convulsive fear remained in her heart. André's presence was like an anchor in the midst of her sea. Seeing that the others were still talking intently with the doctor, Rebekka whispered to him, "Remember what I said to you the night of Claire's funeral? About marrying Marc? Well, I want to do that—as soon as possible."

He blinked. "You will."

"No, I mean in the hospital."

"But what about the temple? And the guests and. . ."

"I don't give a dang about the guests!" she snapped. "And if he can't get to a temple then—" Tears began to drip from the pool in her eyes. "Well, then at least I can seal us later." She lifted her chin slightly. "Don't you see? I thought you understood. You seemed to the last time."

He put an arm around her and leaned forward, talking quietly but firmly in her ear. "Marc *is* going to get better. He is. And you two will be able to get married as you planned."

"I know that," she whispered, hating the uncertainly in her voice. "But isn't it better to be prepared, just in case?" Her hand tightened on his arm. "Oh, André, I couldn't bear it if he died and we didn't even have the hope of eternity together."

"He's not going to die," André said fiercely.

"Claire did!" She saw anguish flare in his eyes and wished she could take it back. He pulled from her and leaned back on the sofa, defeated.

Rebekka grabbed his limp hand. "Oh, I'm sorry, André. I'm just not myself. I can't think straight because of the fear of losing him. But the truth is that Claire was one of the most special people I know, and she still died. Why not Marc? What's so special about us that he wouldn't die when someone as kind and as good as Claire did?"

"Okay, then marry him. I'll support you."

"Marc won't."

His brow furrowed. "What do you mean?"

"Well, I brought it up to him this morning." Rebekka's whisper was low and urgent. "But he says he won't marry me unless it's in the temple. I just don't understand why he wouldn't want to marry me now, just in case. Why? Can you even imagine? He has to see reason! Will you talk to him? Will you make him see how important this is? He'll listen to you."

André let out a long sigh. "All right. I will." He squeezed her hand. "But I still say he's going to be fine."

Rebekka knew her relief showed clearly in her eyes. "Thank you, André. And I'm sorry for putting this on you, but you're the only one I knew would understand. Claire may be gone, but you'll have her again. But unless Marc marries me, I have no such guarantee. I've been waiting so long for this . . ." She trailed off, not wanting to admit more, though he was already aware of her lifelong love for his brother.

He squeezed her hand. "I know, Rebekka, and I'm here for you."

A warmth filled her heart, pushing out much of the dreadful fear. "You always have been. And I can't tell you what that means to me."

"You've been here for me, too."

She smiled at him. "I hope so, André. I wish Claire . . ." *Dang!*—she was crying again. André said nothing, but put a comforting arm around her shoulder.

* * * * *

Shortly after the surgery and Marc's emergency dialysis, Dr. Juppe announced that Marc was out of immediate danger. Most of his family went to their homes, including André and his daughters, but Rebekka kept vigil with Marc's parents, Ariana and Jean-Marc. Watching their closeness and the way they supported one another in this crisis made Rebekka ache more acutely for Marc.

She wasn't allowed to see him until the next morning, when at last they allowed her to visit for a brief time. He lay on the bed looking up at her with a grin. "Sorry about this," he said apologetically. "After you left yesterday, I tried to get up to use the bathroom and the next minute I'm mopping the floor with my face. Then things got worse."

An intense joy filled her heart, a sort of fierce gladness, as she rejoiced momentarily in the fact of his life. "Oh, Marc, you scared me!" She kissed his cheek instead of his mouth, aware of the nurse's presence in the room. "You look much better, though, than you did yesterday. How do you feel?"

"Pretty good, all things considered—except here where they reopened the wound. They gave me dialysis so my blood's clean, and that means I should have more energy. It wasn't as bad as I remembered. I was nauseous during the whole thing, felt like I was going to puke all over the bed, but it's subsiding now."

"They put in a catheter?" She eyed the white bandage poking out of his pajama top.

He nodded with a grimace. "In my neck here. Can't get it wet. I'm going to have to take only baths for a while. Very careful baths."

"Marc, about the wedding. We—"

"Louis-Géralde will be here soon."

Rebekka rubbed impatiently at the tears on her cheeks. "Don't you want to marry me?" She lowered her voice, hoping the nurse who was intently studying Marc's chart near the door wouldn't hear.

"Of course I do." His voice was equally quiet, but intense. "You know I want to marry you, but I want to do it right. Look at me, Rebekka. Look!" His hand slapped on the bed.

"I've seen you and I don't care how horrible you look. It doesn't matter! I love you!"

"I know." His voice was weaker now. "And I thank God every day for my good fortune."

Rebekka clung to his hand and cried. She tried to be brave but she couldn't be—didn't want to be. She was losing him; she felt it.

Marc caressed her hand until her tears subsided. "I'm sorry," he offered wearily.

"I know. So am I. It *is* going to be okay, isn't it?"

But Marc was already drifting back to sleep. Rebekka felt guilty for letting out her anger and frustration on him. He needed rest and here she was pouting like a teenager.

I can't lose him. Dear Father, I can't. Please.

The nurse made her leave. Rebekka returned to the waiting room, where she had plans to stay until she could see Marc again. She found her mother there.

Danielle embraced her, smelling fresh and clean. "How is he?"

"Better now." Rebekka again fought tears. "I think. They gave him dialysis. But he was sick during it, just like the last time. Oh, Mother, what am I going to do?"

"Come home and rest. Come on, now. They'll call you if Marc needs you." Danielle put her arms around Rebekka and led her from the hospital.

* * * * *

Philippe was waiting in the car when Danielle brought Rebekka from the transplant hospital. Her normally pale complexion was even paler, reminding him of the porcelain dolls Danielle collected. The gray pinstriped pants and white shirt she wore were rumpled from her night at the hospital, and her long auburn hair, pulled into a ponytail at the nape of her neck, was in disarray.

"I shouldn't leave," she said.

Philippe made his voice firm. "Nonsense. You need to rest now. I know you think you're all better from your surgery, but it's not doing you a bit of good to wear yourself out."

"Oh, Father, that was ages ago." Her face crumpled, and she began to cry. "I'm so afraid."

Although she didn't call him Daddy, Philippe was reminded of the day of her surgery, and his subsequent miracle in the alleyway. Why had his life been spared that day? Was it because of his prayer? He had tried to brush off the memory of the whole occurrence, but it kept bothering him. And he felt somehow changed.

They had planned to take Rebekka out to breakfast, but she was obviously not in any condition to go. In silent communication, he met Danielle's gray eyes. She nodded once, and he pulled out into traffic in the direction of home.

Philippe walked Rebekka to her room while Danielle went to the kitchen to see about breakfast. "What about your work?" Rebekka asked him as she sat at the edge of her bed. The eyes that had been so unfocused now met his with complete clarity. Philippe was a top executive of a large banking chain, and he had long drilled into his family the importance of his job.

"It can wait." Philippe had planned to go in but changed his mind when he saw Rebekka.

Her gaze became unfocused again as she stared at the floor. "Well, you won't have to worry about me getting married without you," she said dully. "Marc can't get married now."

The words hurt him more than he would admit. Perhaps he *had* been upset for not being able to give his only daughter away, but never would he wish for this circumstance.

"Marc will get better," he insisted.

She met his gaze. "He has to, doesn't he? Oh, I wish you—" She broke off and sighed wearily.

What had she been going to say? The anger in him began to rise as he wondered. Had she stopped short of disrespect? Disdain? What?

Rebekka must have glimpsed the fire in his eyes because she cringed slightly. Taking a deep, cleansing breath to douse the flames, he tried to reason with himself. Perhaps she had only been going to ask him to bless her. Obviously she didn't know how much hearing the plea had cost him the last time.

And yet . . .

He carefully helped her lay back in the bed, under the covers. Then slowly, methodically, he knelt by the bed, holding his daughter's hand. Slow realization came to her face and her mouth opened in awe. He bowed his head. Rebekka didn't move at all, and he wondered if she was still staring at him. Risking a glance through his lashes, he saw her clutching his hand, eyes closed and face pointed to heaven. Tears leaked from her eyes. The expression on her face was one he had never seen before, as if he had given her something she had longed for her entire life. A warmth filled his heart and spread to his extremities.

"Dear God," he prayed, his voice rough with emotion. "Please bless my Rebekka . . . and Marc. Please." His voice faltered and failed, but she didn't seem to mind. She wrapped her arms around him.

"Oh, Daddy."

He held her for long minutes, feeling a bond he had never known possible to share with another person. It was nothing short of miraculous.

Another thought entered his mind: what if he had prayed like this with his beloved Danielle? She had asked him to many times during the first few years of her membership in the Church, but he had always refused. Now he couldn't remember the last time she had asked.

What surprised him even more were that the hurt, anger, and uncertainty he had felt moments before were completely gone. For the moment at least, his heart was free from the terrible fury that almost continuously plagued him like an insidious illness. By contrast, he felt light and free. Could a simple prayer hold so much power? Or had it been the embrace of his precious daughter?

Danielle came into the room with a tray of juice and rolls. With a surprised glance she registered his kneeling position by the bed and Rebekka's arms around him. "Is everything okay?" Her soft voice urged Philippe to tell her his newfound feelings, but he rose to his feet, gently disengaging himself from Rebekka.

"Yes," he replied confidently, knowing that she would accept his words even if she suspected otherwise. Leaning over, he kissed her, suddenly anxious to be alone to examine what had occurred. "I'm going to work. I'll call later."

With another kiss on Rebekka's cheek, he strode from the room.

CHAPTER 17

Thursday morning, the day after Marc's emergency surgery, André dressed the girls and drove them to school. He had to reassure them three times that their Uncle Marc would be all right. "You were there when I called this morning," he reminded them. "He's doing great. And I'm going to take you to see him after school, aren't I?"

He hated the vulnerability in their eyes, and questioned his motives for sending them to school that day at all. But the counselor they had been seeing in the almost four weeks since Claire's death had recommended that their life follow as smooth a routine as possible. That meant a full day of school for Ana, and morning school and a few hours of day care at the school site for Marée. Then, work allowing, he would pick them up and take them home for some family time. On the days when he had to work late, he either took the girls with him, or Ariana watched them. He had also begun bringing projects home from the office to work on after the girls were asleep.

I keep busy so I won't miss Claire.

And it worked . . . sometimes. When it didn't, he fell quietly apart, and then picked up the pieces in the morning before waking the girls.

Before heading to the office he stopped at his parents' apartment, knowing they were home waiting for word from Louis-Géralde. Ariana opened the door, her face tight with worry. Fine lines that André had never noticed before stood out around her mouth and eyes. "What's wrong?" he asked. "Is Marc okay?"

"He's doing well, but we haven't had any luck reaching Louis-Géralde. Apparently, he's off in some remote area and they use a pay phone to stay in touch. They're due to check in on Sunday night, so the mission president will talk to them then."

"He knows it's an emergency, doesn't he?"

Ariana sighed, her brown eyes filling with water. "Yes." The tears didn't spill, and André was glad. He was too close to crying himself.

His father came into the entryway. "We were going to have some breakfast, want to join us?"

"No. I'll grab something at work."

"You're losing weight and that's not good," Ariana said. "You need to keep healthy."

"I *am* eating. At least enough to feel satisfied. But I'll eat more, I promise." Anything not to worry her further. How could he admit that without Claire, food had lost its flavor. What he wouldn't give for one of her stews—as long as it meant she was there across the table from him.

Not voicing any of these feelings, he left his parents. Following a sudden urge, he diverted from his usual path and headed to the transplant hospital. The nurse on duty was one he didn't recognize and she wouldn't let him in to see Marc. "We're keeping visitors to a minimum," she explained. "He's still in serious condition."

"But I'm his brother. That's immediate family, isn't it?"

"The doctor said just the parents and the fiancée. You could talk to her, but she left about an hour ago." Then her eyes brightened. "Wait, are you André?"

"Yeah, André Perrault. His brother."

"Well, he's been asking for you. Won't let it go. Let me ring the doctor. I bet he'll let you go in."

Within a few minutes André was ushered into Marc's room. The nurse didn't stay in the room, but she made him leave the door open.

"Oh good, I've been waiting for you to show your ugly face." Marc tried to lift himself on his arms, but grimaced and fell back. "They made me walk around again after Rebekka and our parents left. Ooo, it hurt. Whatever you do, don't make me laugh."

"Poor baby. Then I guess I shouldn't remind you that my ugly mug looks a lot like yours. Except I have more muscles. Or used to."

Marc peered at him, brow furrowed. "Hey, you've lost weight. You do look more like me."

"Well, we can't all be good-looking." André settled into the stiff armchair next to the bed, wondering where Rebekka's easy chair had gone.

"They feed me too much here," Marc grumbled. "But it's all a certain kind of food. Yuck. I'm sick of it all."

"Well, how about some wedding cake?"

Marc's smile froze. "Rebekka told you."

"Well, who else was she going to tell? You certainly weren't listening."

"I've been a little preoccupied."

"*You've* been a little preoccupied!"

"Sorry, man. I know you've had it bad—worse than I have."

"No, Rebekka's had it the worst."

"What do you mean?"

André sighed. "What I mean is that Claire is dead. But as horrible as that was and as much as I miss her, at least it's over. I don't have to torture myself with the hope that a miracle's going to happen. Rebekka, however, feels like she's watching you die a little at a time, which is even worse. Why don't you just marry her and give her some peace?"

Marc looked away from him. "I can't." His jaw tightened. "I won't."

"Why? Are you nuts? I thought it was your kidney they took out, not your brain."

Marc's face whipped toward him. "Because I love her!"

André stood, abruptly tired of the conversation. The pain of losing Claire was once again fresh in his mind—what did anything else matter? But he had made Rebekka a promise, and Rebekka had always been important to him.

He sat down again with a little more force than necessary. His chair bumped the small table next to the bed, knocking several of Marc's science fiction books to the floor. "Are you going to explain what you mean? Or should I just go to work and make up for this little *vacation* you're having here."

"Vacation!" Warmth seeped into Marc's face. His jaw clenched and his nostrils flared in anger. "Okay, look, I'll tell you why I can't marry her while I'm in the hospital. I had this feeling back in Utah. A feeling like I wasn't going to have a lot of time with Rebekka. I accepted it. I vowed that I would take the time we would have and enjoy it to the fullest."

"You think you're going to die." André couldn't believe what he was hearing.

"I do *not* think that . . . Well, I'm trying not to."

"That's all the more reason to marry her now."

The muscles in Marc's jaw worked furiously, and André had the distinct impression that had he been able, Marc would have begun pacing. "But I can't do that to her, André!" he continued tensely. "If I marry her and then . . . die, she'll mourn me the rest of her life. You know she's like that. Look at how long she's waited for me already. Rebekka's faithful to a fault." Marc's hand brushed impatiently at his dark hair, which had fallen forward into his face.

He's serious, André thought.

Marc took a deep breath and plunged on, "If I can't be here to help her through this life, I still want her to live. I want her to find another man, and I want her to get married and have his children and be happy."

"She could still do that."

"No!" Marc's answer was explosive. "I've thought a lot about this—I've done nothing but think about this. I love Rebekka more than I love life, and I'm not going to tie her down unless I'm going to be around to be her husband."

"But marrying you would make her happy!"

Marc's face was ashen, as his energy had evidently been funneled into their conversation. "In the short term maybe, but Rebekka could live another seventy years. Alone as my widow, or with a man who will always resent that she is sealed to me. Don't you see, André, I can't let her bear that pain or make that choice. I'm the idiot who waited so long to let her into my heart, but I won't be the one to make her suffer anymore."

André had no answer. His brother had a valid point. Rebekka was young and could eventually go on with her life. But a temple sealing to a husband who passed away could complicate that immensely. Admiration crept into his heart; if he were in Marc's place, he didn't think he'd have it in him to give her up, even if it might be for her own welfare.

"You understand." Marc's utterance was a statement, not a question. "I believe that rules are set in place for a reason, André, and I'm trusting in God. I hope and pray that I'll be the one to take Rebekka to the temple, but if I can't . . . Promise me that you'll take care of her. Please? See that she goes on with her life and is happy. Will you do that for me?"

André felt his brother's eyes gouging into him, demanding, pleading for an answer. He took a deep breath. "Of course I will."

"And you'll see that she finds someone and gets married?"

Anger coursed through André, an anger unlike any he had felt since his little sister Pauline had died and her boyfriend had, upon first request, refused to come to the funeral. When he spoke, his voice was savage. "I will *if* you do your part! Because that's when this martyr attitude of yours ceases to make sense. I want you to live! You got that? You have to fight every inch of the way. You don't give up and go toward any stupid bright lights or Pauline calling you. I don't want to hear any of those excuses. You must live! Not just for Rebekka, but for me. Got it?"

Marc studied him silently. "Yeah. I do. I will. And thank you."

André gave his brother a hug, awkwardly because of Marc's recumbent position. "I love you, buddy."

Then he walked out the door without looking back, not wanting his brother to see the tears in his eyes.

CHAPTER 18

On Saturday, Marie-Thérèse was in the sitting room with Brandon, looking over the family financial files, when Larissa finally dragged in from spending an afternoon with Jolie. She snorted when she saw what her mother was doing. "Don't tell me—now you're going off to the Ukraine to get yourself some kids while Uncle Marc's dying in the hospital."

Marie-Thérèse gaped at her daughter in amazement. "Larissa!"

The girl didn't look penitent. She tossed her dark head. "Well, isn't that what you got those papers out for?"

Marie-Thérèse's hands shook, and she shoved the papers back into their folder. "For your information, little girl, these have nothing to do with the adoption. You father and I've postponed our trip to the Ukraine because of Marc. We did it weeks ago. Haven't you heard anything we've said?"

"I've been a little busy, you know," Larissa replied tartly. "After all, members of my family keep up and dying like flies."

"Uncle Marc's not dead," Brandon said, glancing up from the book he was reading.

An emotion resembling hatred filled Larissa's face. "Too bad it's not you, pig face."

"Hey, I'm not afraid of death," Brandon shot back. "*I've* got nothing to be ashamed of."

"Stop it!" Marie-Thérèse wondered when things had tumbled out of control. One minute her life had held so much promise and the next Claire was dead and Marc was in the hospital. And Larissa, her dear sweet daughter, was acting like a stranger. A hateful stranger.

Marie-Thérèse clutched the financial folder to her chest and ran from the room, not bothering to fight the tears.

"Way to go," she heard Brandon mutter. "You're going to get it when Dad comes home."

"Oh, shut up!"

"You know how much Mom wanted to adopt a kid."

Marie-Thérèse shut the door to her bedroom so she didn't hear her daughter's response. She tossed the financial folder onto the dresser and lay on the mattress under which she had hidden the adoption application papers—safe and out of sight.

Yet when she closed her eyes, she could imagine the little baby that was supposed to be hers. Was he crying in some orphanage? Or was it a little girl, longing for a mother to hold her? Was it so wrong to want another baby?

How terribly ironic that she would want a baby so very badly when once she had cried upon discovering she was pregnant. Yes, the timing hadn't been right when Brandon came along—she'd just had Larissa, and she and Mathieu had been newly married and still adjusting to each other and to parenthood. There were a thousand excuses for her feelings, but sometimes she wondered if her longing now wasn't a fitting punishment for her rejection then.

But no, the Lord would never hold that against me. He isn't like that. This is simply my lot to bear.

Before she knew it, Marie-Thérèse was on her knees by the bed, her hands under the mattress touching the folder. She wiped her face on the bed. "Dear Father," she began. She poured out her soul to God, and slowly her sorrow faded. Heaving a deep breath, she climbed to her feet, steeling herself to face her daughter.

Larissa and Brandon were still in the sitting room, Brandon with his face in his book, and Larissa staring at the television set. They both glanced up as she walked in the door, taking in the red-rimmed eyes. A brief look of remorse passed over Larissa's face.

Marie-Thérèse grabbed the remote from the coffee table and flipped off the TV. "Come on," she said to her children. "Let's go for a walk."

"I don't want to go for a walk," mumbled Larissa.

Marie-Thérèse held out her hand, wondering if all twelve-and-a-half-year-old girls were so belligerent. "Come on anyway. Afterwards we'll go see Dad at the church, and if he's done helping install the new lights, we'll go catch dinner and a movie."

"Could we go by the mall so I could show you those new pants I told you about?" Larissa asked. "Jolie got some today."

Marie-Thérèse knew her daughter was trying to make the most of the family outing—as she always did—but it didn't matter. At least they would be together. "Why not?"

Larissa smiled and bounced to her feet, heading toward the door. "All right. I'm just going to change."

Brandon stood more slowly. "Did you see her new earring?" he whispered.

"What?"

He pointed to his belly button. Marie-Thérèse was stunned into exclaiming, "She better darn well *not* have a belly ring!"

Brandon winked at her. "Gotcha!"

Marie-Thérèse nearly wept with relief. She hugged her son. "That's enough of those kinds of jokes." *It's too close to reality,* she added silently.

"You sure you don't want to send her away to boarding school?"

"Of course not. Who would you fight with?"

"The new baby?" he asked hopefully.

Gladness spread through Marie-Thérèse. At least one of her children looked forward to the new addition. She sighed. "Well, Brandon, at this rate I don't know if there ever *is* going to be another baby."

"Don't give up hope yet, Mom," Brandon said with a wisdom far beyond his years. "Miracles still happen."

"Good." Marie-Thérèse figured a miracle was just what she needed for Larissa

CHAPTER 19

Philippe attended church on Sunday with his family. He could feel curious eyes on him, but tried not to feel self-conscious. After all, he had attended before and his presence meant nothing. At least that's what he told himself. But inside he knew that this time *was* different. He was there not because Danielle had asked or because one of the children was in a program, but because he wanted to learn about the changes that had begun in his heart. All at once, everything seemed to make sense to him as it never had before. God did exist, so it naturally followed that if He cared about His children, He would have surely organized a church for them, and set out a plan by which they could return and live in His presence. Why hadn't he understood this before? For so long he had blamed the Church for stealing his children from him, but all this time had he himself prevented a deep relationship?

This last thought sat uncomfortably on Philippe's mind as he watched people file into the chapel for sacrament meeting. One young boy's eyes caught his. The teen stiffened and blanched as he stared at Philippe. *Must be looking at someone else,* Philippe thought, but he knew the boy was staring at him. There was a clear fear in his eyes, and Philippe had the distinct impression that if two missionaries had not been directly behind the teen, he would have bolted from the chapel.

That's strange. I know I've never seen him before. Why would he be afraid of me?

Of course there was the possibility the boy had seen Philippe before at church and had been told something negative about him.

Since Philippe had always been careful to maintain an emotional gap between himself and the members, he had likely wounded some tender feelings over the years. Perhaps even this boy's.

The teen walked stiffly to the back of the chapel to sit with the missionaries. Philippe let his eyes slide over the rest of the congregation. Many he recognized, many others he didn't. *I've never set eyes on that boy before either. I'd swear to it.*

He glanced once more at the two missionaries in their neat suits and ties. The boy was staring at him again. When he noticed Philippe's attention, he gazed carefully down at his brown corduroy pants, plucking at something Philippe couldn't see. He wore a tie against his blue shirt, but not comfortably. *Borrowed,* Philippe thought.

He nudged Rebekka, sitting on the padded bench next to him. "Who's that kid, the one with the missionaries?"

"That's Thierry," whispered Rebekka, following his stare. "He's been taking the missionary discussions for the past few months. He's come a long way. Used to wear jeans to church and had hair as long as mine."

"Have I seen him before?"

Her eyebrows rose in surprise. "I don't know. You probably met him at the Perraults. Just about everybody came over that Sunday after the farewell, and he knew Louis-Géralde fairly well. Still, you didn't stay long enough to do anything but give Louis-Géralde a check, so you probably didn't talk to him or anything. Why?"

"I'm not sure. There's something about him. He's not familiar, but I would swear that he knows me."

Rebekka peeked over her shoulder at Thierry. "Hmm," she said. "He does seem to be checking you out."

"Or maybe it's you," Philippe said, more comfortable with that idea. Rebekka was a striking woman and it was very possible the teenager was staring at her, not him.

Rebekka's reply was doubtful. "Hmm, maybe."

The bishop began conducting, and Philippe tried to concentrate, but felt eyes burning into the back of his head. Why that single stare stood out among the host of other curious stares he always garnered, he couldn't say, yet he felt it meant something. What?

On either side of him, Danielle and Rebekka were intent on the speaker. Philippe closed his eyes. *God, hello, it's me again. So what's up with that boy? Is it anything I should worry about? And how are You coming along with the Marc thing? Rebekka really needs some help. Thanks for thinking of her.*

Feeling utterly foolish and sure that he had done it all wrong, Philippe quit praying and listened to the speaker. Heat filled his chest and at that moment, he couldn't think of a single place he would rather be.

CHAPTER 20

Rebekka spent Sunday afternoon with Marc at the hospital before going to his parents' apartment for dinner. The entire Perrault clan had gathered in hopes of hearing from Louis-Géralde. They actually wouldn't be talking to him, but to President Bradley, the mission president, who would let them know when Louis-Géralde would be coming home and how he had taken the news of Marc's illness. They were grateful President Bradley's mother was French and that he had learned French as a child, though his father had been American. It would make communication easier.

Everyone seemed more somber than usual. Marie-Thérèse's daughter, Larissa, sat sullenly on the couch and didn't speak to anyone. The other children seemed to pick up on her feelings and the adults' nervousness, becoming whiny and irritable as a result. After dinner Josette and Zack took them into the TV room to play a few board games. Rebekka was glad to see them go, secretly amazed at Josette's patience and ability with the children. Even Larissa came out of her ill humor while talking with her aunt.

As they waited for the phone call, Rebekka surveyed each of the remaining faces. Ariana and Jean-Marc were pensive and always close to one another, sharing support. Ariana's parents, Géralde and Josephine Merson, appearing older than usual, were seated on the sofa. André sat in an easy chair, elbows on his knees, hands clasped together. This situation was perhaps the toughest for him, having so recently lost his beloved wife. But Marie-Thérèse and her husband Mathieu Portier looked worse than anyone, as though neither had slept in weeks. Since Rebekka knew they hadn't been at the hospital with Marc, she wondered if Larissa was the real root of their weariness. Or was it because they hadn't followed through with the adoption? Rebekka wished desperately that they hadn't postponed their plans for the baby. New life was what they all needed right now. Hope.

The phone rang. The family members looked up, tense. Jean-Marc answered, signaling with a nod of his head that it was Louis-Géralde's mission president.

After identifying himself, Jean-Marc listened soberly for a long time. Then, "Please let us know the minute you find out. Thank you."

"Well?" The word came from almost everyone at once.

Jean-Marc held up a hand. "Louis-Géralde didn't call in tonight as he was supposed to. But that isn't necessarily a bad thing. The pay phone he normally uses could be out of order, a bus he was using could have broken down. Since he's way out in the country, a lot could have happened. President Bradley is sending the zone leaders to look for them. They should have word for us by tomorrow afternoon."

Tears stung Rebekka's eyes. Jean-Marc was talking more, recounting a few instances the president had told him of when missionaries had been out of contact. Each case had ended happily.

But they didn't have a dying brother at home, Rebekka thought. She wanted to scream and yell and cry, but how could she? This was Marc's family and they loved him as much as she did. And now they had the additional worry of wondering about Louis-Géralde.

Rebekka's eyes were so full she couldn't see. A hand reached for hers. *André.* She clung to him.

"You said you were going to visit Marc again tonight. Need a ride? The girls and I can wait in the car."

"No, I can drive." Her voice trembled, and she was grateful for the warm, comforting hand on hers.

"Please, Rebekka. It's early yet. The girls won't mind."

Rebekka gave in. "Thank you, André."

They said good-bye to the rest of the family and made their way to the door, each holding the hand of one of André's daughters. "Did you ever get to talk to Marc about the wedding thing?" she asked in the elevator.

He nodded, but inclined his head toward Marée and Ana. "I'll call you tomorrow to talk about it, okay? Maybe we can go out for lunch."

She had the sense that he was stalling for time, but she couldn't insist that he tell her—not in front of the girls. The only other thing she could do was agree to the lunch. "Ah, a nice restaurant without the smell of antiseptic and medicines. I think I'd like that."

"Can you meet me at the office?"

"I'll be there at one."

* * * * *

The next day in his office, André sat back in his leather chair with a sigh of relief. Things at the company were finally under control. It hadn't been easy with Marc gone, but he and Raoul had worked out the problems so well that now, with suddenly nothing to do, he felt at a loss.

A large picture of his family stared at him from the wall opposite his desk. It had been the last they had taken together, three months before Claire's death. At the time he had been annoyed at having to take time off work for the picture, though he'd tried not to show it. Now he was grateful to have it. More than grateful.

"Well, I guess tonight I'll take the girls somewhere nice for family night," he said to Claire. "I might not get them in bed on time, though. They've been wanting to go to the zoo. It's not too cold, do you think? First of November already. Is the zoo even open in November? I really don't know. You always took care of that." He grimaced. Until she was gone he hadn't known just how much she had taken care of. "Sorry about that," he said with a sigh. Then he purposely forced a smile as though Claire were really there. "Well, I'll do better." He pressed a fingertip to his lip, kissed it gently, then waved it in the direction of the picture.

The gold watch on his wrist slid down his arm with the motion. When did the band become so loose? He'd have to tighten it soon, or regain his lost weight.

He noticed it was almost time for Rebekka to arrive for lunch. An undefined emotion arose in him. Excitement? Pleasure? Well, he always enjoyed Rebekka's presence. She was both kind and intelligent . . . and also a good friend.

Thinking of Rebekka reminded him of what he would be forced to tell her that day: Marc wouldn't marry her unless he was certain he was going to live. André's heart ached with his love for both of them. If only things could be different. If only they could start over and change the future.

A thought came to him seemingly out of the blue, though he realized as soon as he examined it that its seed had been germinating in the deep recesses of his mind since his conversation with Marc. *What if Marc had never opened his eyes to Rebekka's love? Neither of them would be going through this conflict now about the marriage, and she might even have found someone else to care for.*

It was an absurd, unworthy thought and André felt immediately ashamed. No one could change the present or remove the pain someone else suffered, especially not by wishing. Nor should they. For instance, there was no way he could wish he and Claire had never met just to spare himself the pain of losing her. He snorted. *I might as well wish that I had chased after Rebekka when I first had that crush on her and spared us both the pain of losing . . .* His thoughts trailed off, and he swallowed hard.

Claire was gone and Marc had asked him to take care of Rebekka if he died.

Don't think about it. Marc has to live.

André took a deep breath and headed for the door. He had taken only two steps when it burst open. Desirée Massoni strode flamboyantly into the room, chin held high, dark eyes daring him to protest. He felt no surprise at the intrusion; he had learned in the past month that Desirée never did anything quietly.

"Do you know where Raoul is?" she asked, smoothing her tight leather skirt. She also wore a matching black leather jacket and tall leather boots with the highest heels André had ever seen.

"Out at one of the sites," he said.

Desirée's well-outlined lips puckered into what she obviously thought was an appealing pout. "Oh, dear. And I was coming to go out to lunch with him. Now the surprise is ruined." She removed her leather jacket to reveal a tight white top with a low neckline.

André was briefly embarrassed for Raoul. Desirée was a beautiful, alluring woman, and as a man he could see why Raoul was attracted to her, but her choice of clothes today was inappropriate. And not because they were made of leather—he'd seen many women wear leather tastefully and attractively. This outfit was simply too tight. She also wore too much makeup for his taste.

And yet there was a certain part of him that did react to her presence—the lonely part of him that longed for a woman's touch. But it was Claire's wholesome, caring touch that he longed for, not this wanton creature's.

André felt suddenly uncomfortable, as though he had jumped from an ice-cold stream into a warm hot tub. He immediately stepped away from her, but she closed the space again with two steps of her own. Her full, dark hair fell over her shoulders in shiny waves, and her brown eyes, accentuated by long, painted lashes, studied him. He noticed that she had a smattering of freckles across her nose, almost hidden by makeup.

Strange. Rebekka should have the freckles, he thought. *She's the redhead.* Yet Rebekka's hair wasn't really red, but more a dark auburn, and her skin was almost unnaturally smooth and clear of any marks that he could remember. *Still, she should have freckles,* he thought irrationally. *At least one. Maybe I never noticed.*

For the life of him he couldn't understand why he was comparing the two women. One was Raoul's wife, the other nearly Marc's. They had nothing to do with him. He loved one as a longtime friend and tolerated the other because of Raoul. That was all.

Desirée took another step toward him, a teasing smile playing on her lips. "Do I make you nervous?" she asked.

"Of course not," he lied. At that moment he wanted to be anywhere but in that room alone with her. "I do have an appointment right now. I was just leaving."

Her hand reached out to adjust his tie. "That's too bad. I thought maybe you could take me to lunch since Raoul's not here." Her long, plum-painted fingernails raked softly down the pattern on his tie. She looked up at him under those long lashes, meeting his gaze firmly, and he saw an invitation there that utterly terrified him.

Violently repelled, he took a step back. His mind refused to work. An invitation for what? Was he going crazy? But, no, he had worked in the world long enough to have run into this before—he knew without a doubt what he was seeing. Desirée had tried to flirt with him often—as she flirted with everyone. André had decided it was simply her nature and had not taken her seriously. He even went out of his way to be nice to her when his real urge was to avoid her.

Desirée continued to gaze at him as if reading his thoughts. She stared up at him with her painted lips slightly parted, offering . . .

Worst of all, had he not been so horrified—she was his partner's wife, and he had just said good-bye to the most wonderful woman in the world—he might have considered her invitation, maybe even believed her feelings were genuine.

His stomach churned in disgust. Claire had been gone almost a month—the longest, most difficult, and painful month of his entire life, and he still longed for her almost constantly. Her touch, her laugh, the sound of her breathing at night, the feeling of connection. It was all gone, and yet he knew logically—while his heart rebelled— that someday he might find a companion again. Perhaps even find love. He yearned for it, for the normalcy it represented, and at the same time was utterly appalled at the suggestion. No one could ever replace Claire in his heart and in his life, and he felt guilty even enter- taining the thought for a mere second. Certainly, he would never look twice at a woman like Desirée. No, he would go on with his life. He would make his daughters happy. He would wait to see Claire again. Beyond that . . .

Dear Lord, he prayed for strength. A distinct memory of Joseph from the Bible fleeing Potipher's wife came to his mind. Yes, that was what he needed to do: flee. Or get her to flee, since this was his office.

He purposely retreated. "I can call him for you if you wish," he offered, reaching for a phone on the desk.

"No!" her voice was sharp with barely hidden anger.

Something inside him broke. "Look at you!" he said, not both- ering to hide his repulsion. "Look at what you're wearing and what you're thinking! Raoul is my friend and I would die before I would do anything to offend him. Or the memory of my dear wife."

"It's not Raoul you're afraid of. It's your God!" she hurled back at him.

"Either one," he declared firmly. "I believe in God and do my utmost to obey His commandments. And I believe in friendship, and in the sanctity of the marriage covenant. What do you believe in, Desirée? Isn't it time you find out?"

Her face had become sneering, her voice vindictive. "I believe that you're lonely. And I believe that you are going to die a lonely, shriveled-up old man who will forever wish this day had turned out differently." She shook a finger at him. "And don't you dare try telling Raoul. I'll just deny it. I wouldn't have you now if you gave me the moon."

"I see right through you," he murmured softly, dangerously. "I only hope you change before Raoul sees what I already do. I don't want to see my friend hurt."

With a sound of disgust, she turned on the heel of her boot and flounced from the room, leaving André trembling with barely concealed fury. How dare she play upon his emotions, so volatile and erratic since Claire's death! Yes, he was lonely—how dare she take advantage of that! Worse, how could she treat Raoul so carelessly? And should he tell his friend and partner? Or would it put a wedge between them that could never be removed? Raoul would have to believe Desirée's account of the event, whatever that might be, or leave her, and André didn't think Raoul was ready to do that, not yet. He was too blinded by his love.

André gave a long sigh. Maybe he should keep quiet and leave well enough alone.

* * * * *

Rebekka stood up as André entered the large reception area outside his office. As usual, he was dressed like a successful businessman, complete with a dark double-breasted suit and tie. She considered the tie more closely. Not all successful businessmen wore ties these days, a habit she was sure André would never give up. Marc might, but not André. "Hi," she said more brightly than she felt.

"Have you been waiting long?"

"No, just a little while."

He smiled. "Sorry. I had a last-minute visitor."

"I saw Desirée."

His eyebrows rose. "She say anything?"

"No. She didn't even see me. But whatever you said to her must have made my sweet little sister-in-law furious. What's wrong? Wasn't Raoul there to do her bidding right when she wanted him?"

"Uh . . ." André looked decidedly uncomfortable.

Rebekka felt her face flush. "Oh darn, I'm sorry. I shouldn't say anything like that about her. I don't know why, but try as I might to like her, she just rubs me the wrong way. Please don't think too badly of me for judging her. Although I wouldn't blame you if you did. I should at least like her for Raoul's sake, shouldn't I? I used to think she was a nice girl before I actually talked to her. Oh no, there I go again." She glanced toward the exit. "Can we go now before I say anything worse?"

André chuckled and felt inside his jacket for the dark sunglasses he had taken to wearing outside during the day. "For what it's worth, I agree with your assessment of Desirée. I just hope she doesn't cause your brother too much pain."

She checked to see if his expression was as hard as his voice. It was, and the atypical behavior made her stare. "What really happened in there, André? Anything I should know?"

He put on the sunglasses and shook his head. "No. You already have too much to worry about."

They were silent as they walked across the cobblestone sidewalk to the curb. Rebekka had been about to cross the street when a taxicab pulled from the side of the road.

"Watch out, there's a car." Andre tugged her back.

She waited until it passed before asking, "Well?"

"I mean it, Rebekka," he said as they crossed. "I definitely don't want to spoil this day further by talking about Desirée."

She knew she would get nothing more from him. "All right, then, let's talk about something more pleasant." Of course, what she wanted was to hear what Marc had said to André about her idea of getting married in the hospital. She had mentioned it many times over the past few days, but Marc had been almost downright belligerent in avoiding the conversation. She felt ready to hit him over the head with a rubber hammer, and would if he wasn't so weak.

But because they had a whole lunch to get through, Rebekka decided to wait until near the end to bring up the issue. Her stomach was growling fiercely—she had forgotten breakfast—and she didn't want to start crying before she filled the emptiness with something. Besides, there was much to be said for not knowing. That way she could still hope that André had made her stubborn fiancé see the light.

The restaurant André had chosen was nearly full with the lunch crowd, but they were immediately ushered to a table in the back room. In this area, the tables were partially sectioned off with portable linen screens. She chose the chair across from André and allowed the waiter to seat her. "Did you call ahead?" she asked when they were alone.

He smiled. "No, but since it's so close to the office, I come here a lot—usually with clients. Business lunches. They like me. I think they save a few tables back here for preferred customers."

She surveyed the tasteful wallpaper and paintings with interest. "Marc and I've eaten here before, but it's usually out on the sidewalk. I've never even been inside."

His smile became wistful. "Marc likes the fresh air. I do too, but sometimes the privacy is preferable when you're discussing business." He gave a short laugh, and his eyes, freed now from the dark sunglasses, held a private memory. "Or for private assignations. You know, sometimes Claire and I would come here. She'd have one of the waiters call over to the office saying that Madame so-and-so was at the restaurant waiting for me to buy her lunch and to discuss business. She'd use a different name every time and speak with an accent. She also would wear these ridiculous cat-eye glasses we bought on our honeymoon and smile mysteriously. She never fooled anyone, of course; they all knew she was my wife, but it was a lot of fun. I think they enjoyed it as much as I did."

The melancholy in his voice was almost palpable, and Rebekka had to swallow twice before she could speak. "Oh, André, maybe we shouldn't have come here." She put her hand on his briefly. "We could leave right now. They won't mind."

"No. I need to stay. Claire has gone to a better place, but I'm not going there anytime soon. I have to adjust." His eyes asked her to understand. And maybe she could, just a little.

The maître d' arrived with their regular waiter, and before Rebekka and André could order he placed a gentle hand on André's shoulder. "First let me say that I am so sorry for your loss," he said with sincerity. "We will all miss your wife."

"Thank you," André responded. "That means a great deal to me."

The maître d' bowed slightly and turned to Rebekka. "And you, Mademoiselle, perhaps will be the one to bring the smile back to his face, no?"

Rebekka smiled, deliberately misunderstanding. "Of course. All of his family and friends will do their best."

"Very well." He bowed again. "This young man here will take good care of you. I must get back to my post."

The situation could have been awkward, but they didn't let it become so. André quickly ordered and Rebekka did the same, though once the waiter left she couldn't remember what she had requested.

They shared an enjoyable meal—Rebekka was relieved that she had asked for a salad of mustard greens and barbecued chicken chunks, with dressing on the side—and she hardly noticed when the restaurant cleared out as the business world returned to work.

"So, I guess you're going to make me bring it up, aren't you?" she said finally.

André sighed. "It's just not good news. I'm sorry, Rebekka, but Marc wants to make sure he's going to recover before he lets you commit your life."

Her voice rose slightly. "But I'm already committed."

"I know that and he knows that," André replied calmly, "but if he takes a turn for the worse, he doesn't want you to be tied to him. He wants you to find someone else and be happy."

Helpless anger boiled up in her heart. "And you agreed with him! Admit it. I can tell! Why?"

André rubbed his hand through his hair, much as she had so often seen Marc do. The watch on his arm slid with the motion as though it were loose. "I admire him for it," he admitted reluctantly, staring deeply into her eyes. "And quite honestly, I don't think I could refuse you if I were in his place."

She was so angry, the words she wanted to say came out in a splutter. "Why . . . you . . . I think . . . so mad . . . kill you if . . ." She groaned in frustration and gave up.

André regarded her with compassion. "Rebekka, think about it logically. I know you love Marc, but you're only twenty-five. You have your whole life before you! If something were to happen to Marc, you'd eventually find someone else and be happy."

"Nothing's going to happen to Marc!" she snarled.

His eyes shot sparks. "Then why are we having this conversation!"

"Because I—" Rebekka's eyes filled with tears.

"He just wants you to be happy," André said gently. "That's all. And you can hardly fault him for that. He loves you, Rebekka, but he won't marry you unless he knows he's going to be around to see that you're happy. He knows how you feel about him now, but what if he died and you did find someone else? Over the years you would grow and change with that person and you might just love him more than you loved Marc. I know you can't see that now, but couples do grow together and love does deepen. And if that were to happen, he feels as if he'd be an obstacle to your happiness."

Rebekka's chin lifted in defiance. "Is that what Claire is to you now that she's dead? An obstacle?" Even as she spoke Rebekka couldn't believe she was voicing such a malicious thought.

"Fair enough." The compassion still reflected in his eyes, but his voice was tight and controlled. "As a question, I mean. But my relationship with Claire is not the same as yours with Marc. We've been married for seven years, and we have two daughters. I know you've loved Marc for a long time now, but that's not the same as being married."

Rebekka knew it wasn't the same—and she was desperately trying to remedy that. But no one else seemed to understand. "And I envy you," she said through gritted teeth. "Oh, how I envy you!"

André inclined his head in acceptance. *Perhaps he does understand,* she thought.

From across the table, he reached over and took her hand. "He's still alive, Rebekka, remember that! Marc still has an excellent chance. Louis-Géralde will soon be home and you'll see."

His words turned her thoughts in another direction. "Have you heard from them? Did they find out why Louis-Géralde didn't call in?"

He released her and drew away, though the comforting warmth of his touch remained. "No, but we could call now. He felt for the cell phone she knew he carried in his jacket pocket. In a few seconds he was talking to Ariana.

"Well, have you heard? Good. What did—" He broke off and listened for a long time, a disbelieving expression stealing over his features. Rebekka could faintly hear the rise and fall of Ariana's voice, but could make out nothing of the meaning. She stifled the urge to rip the phone from André's grasp.

When at last he ended the connection, he was visibly shaken. Rebekka's voice abruptly failed her, and she couldn't form the words to her questions.

"It's Louis-Géralde," André said heavily. "The zone leaders apparently arrived and found him. Don't worry, he's okay." He added this hurriedly, obviously reading the fear in her eyes, "But he won't be coming home as soon as we hoped. He and his companion are in jail."

"Jail?" It was all too preposterous to believe.

"Yes. Don't know what the charges are. Seems no one does. Maybe they haven't even been charged yet."

"But that's—"

"Apparently they've offended some high official in the small village where they're teaching. So things are stalled."

"When can they get him out?"

André shrugged. "That's just it. The president doesn't know. He's getting the French Embassy involved, but it still may take awhile. Possibly weeks."

"Weeks!" Rebekka was horrified. "But that'll be too late. Marc's getting weaker every day. You see it, don't you? Oh, André!" She started to cry, grateful now for the privacy screens and the few customers.

He slid into the chair to her right and put his arm around her. "It's going to be okay. Please, please don't cry. We'll find a way to help Marc. My father already told the president that we were going to do everything possible from this side. We're an influential family, the lot of us. We'll call in favors if we have to." He gingerly wiped the tears from her face with a crumpled napkin. She leaned into him, grateful for his presence.

"What would I do without you?" she murmured.

He had one arm around her, pulling her close so that their cheeks were touching, and his other hand held hers firmly. *Such a kind and wonderful man!* Rebekka thought. Throughout their lives they had been friends and his comfort during this rough time in her life was just about all that was keeping her sane.

"Marc asked me to watch out for you," André said. "And I will. You can always count on me, Rebekka."

She was touched. "Marc asked you to take care of me? That's so sweet."

But then almost immediately, she wondered what Marc had meant by the words. Was he talking about after his death? Did he mean for her to find someone else—perhaps someone like André?

No! What a ridiculous thought! Rebekka told herself.

Rebekka met André's gaze, noticing how handsome he was, how like his brother. She could also see the apparent loneliness in him, and for the first time in her life, a feeling other than friendship for him rippled through her heart.

Rebekka's surprise was so great that her tears ceased and she stared at him in open-eyed wonder. All at once, there seemed to be a powerful electric link between them, and Rebekka's thoughts raced crazily, unable to comprehend the new feelings in her heart.

After a few brief, powerful seconds, their eyes broke away. "What were you saying?" he asked, shaking his head as if to clear it. There was an apology in his eyes, but she didn't understand why. Had he seen and understood her fleeting feelings? She hoped not—she certainly hadn't.

It's nothing, she wanted to tell him. But if she spoke, she would actually give credence to the experience. Guilt arose in her heart. How could she even begin to notice her brother-in-law in that way? *Stress,* she told herself. *It's the stress. I love Marc and I'm worried that he's going to die. And André is here, strong and healthy—everything I want for Marc. That's all.*

There was so much tension between them, she almost couldn't breathe. She forced herself to answer his question. "I said, uh, that it was sweet for Marc to want you to take care of me."

He smiled, but it didn't reach his eyes. "Yes, that was it. Well, it's not as if it's a burden. You and I have always gotten along. Been friends." He chuckled. "In fact, a long time ago, after my mission and before Claire, I had a huge crush on you, Rebekka. But——"

"But I was too young," she said bitterly. "The story of my life."

"No, not that. I mean you *were* very young, but you were always mature. The reason I didn't pursue it was because I knew you were in love with Marc and I realized that would never change. Then I met Claire, and I knew we could be happy together. We *were* happy. I love her so much."

Rebekka understood what he was saying. When she had given up on Marc and fled to America to work for Damon Wolfe, she had come to care for Damon a great deal—before she had become involved with Samuel. While she had never really loved Damon, knowing him and experiencing his kindness had taught her that somewhere in the world there would be another man that she could love. Someone who didn't have to be Marc. She had believed it enough then to give Samuel a chance, but now that Marc had come around, she didn't want to entertain such notions. Marc was everything to her. And yet—tears came to her eyes at this next realization—he wouldn't marry her until he was sure he would be around to take care of her. Did that mean he thought she would find someone else the minute he died?

"But why not tell me since—I mean, now that you don't feel that way anymore?" Rebekka asked.

He shrugged. "A guy thing, I guess."

She felt there was still much he wasn't telling her, but she wasn't about to push. She was already confused enough by the odd thoughts about André. What would Marc say if he knew?

The tension between them had faded significantly, but everything was by no means as it had been before. Now when Rebekka looked at him, there was an awareness in her heart that hadn't been there previously. What did it mean?

She pushed the thoughts guiltily aside. "I have to go see Marc," she said, half-apologetically. "I have to make sure he's all right. This news about Louis-Géralde isn't going to be encouraging."

"Good idea," André answered easily. "Tell him I'll stop by this afternoon after I pick up the girls. They aren't going to Mom's today."

"I will." Rebekka's heart thudded in her chest. They were pretending that nothing had happened—as best they could. Nothing had. They were friends and soon would be in-laws. She loved Marc with her entire heart, and André was still mourning Claire. That was it.

They emerged from the restaurant, side by side, careful not to touch one another. With regret, Rebekka realized that the days when they had so innocently comforted each other with siblinglike physical affection were over—and she missed him already.

He smiled at her, squinting slightly in the sunlight. With a fluid gesture, he placed his sunglasses on his face, covering his warm brown eyes. Was it her imagination or did he seem even more lost than before?

"You know, Rebekka," André said, voice teasing. "By rights you should have more freckles than you do."

She shrugged, wondering where this comment came from. "I did once. As a kid. They've faded away, that's all."

"You still have thirteen," he said. "Here and here." His finger pointed out the marks without actually touching her skin.

"Oh, great." She rolled her eyes. "That's some number."

Then his eyes widened. "No. There's another right above your lip. Fourteen. I don't know how I missed it. It's darker than the others."

She laughed. "That's a relief." She wondered if she really did have that fourteenth freckle or if he was just trying to make her feel better. "I've never had anyone count my freckles before."

"Well, now you have."

The tension of earlier was back and Rebekka nearly began weeping. What was wrong with her? Why did she suddenly not want to go to the transplant hospital at all? It didn't make sense; she loved Marc.

And André was only an old friend.

It was all too much to think about. "Good-bye, André," she said firmly.

"'Bye, Rebekka, and try not to worry. The Lord knows what He's doing."

On the way to the hospital, Rebekka pondered André's parting words. "I'm glad someone knows what he's doing, then," she whispered in the quiet of the car, "because I certainly don't."

CHAPTER 21

In the days after the surgery to remove Rebekka's kidney from his body, Marc had been incapacitated by severe anemia. Dr. Juppe tried to compensate with drugs, but even then Marc had only enough energy for a brief walk in the halls. Though he longed to leave the confines of the hospital, there was no possibility of his returning home.

He was dying, he could feel it. And every day he felt worse, not better, as the nurses kept telling him he would. Rebekka came to visit faithfully, and talked about their wedding—especially about getting married in the hospital. He could see the hurt in her eyes when he refused to be drawn into the conversation. He loved her so much that he wondered what hurt more, his body or his heart. If only he could make her see that his all-encompassing love for her prevented him from tying her down to a ghost. He had spent many years as a blind idiot, but now he would do right by Rebekka, even if she couldn't see it. Someday, if worse came to worst, she would thank him.

By worse you mean leaving Rebekka to someone else, a voice in his head clarified. The idea was terrifying and horrible to consider. His whole being ached with the possibility of not having her sealed to him.

Please, Father, he prayed fervently. *I knew I wouldn't have much time, but not like this. Can we have a little more?*

He was still repeating this prayer when Rebekka came in Monday afternoon. She'd been with him a few hours in the morning, but left to run a few errands and to have lunch with André. Marc hoped his brother had explained to Rebekka why he couldn't marry her in the hospital. Maybe André had been able to make her understand.

"Hi, sweetheart," she said, bending to kiss him. She smelled like fresh flowers instead of the impending death odor Marc knew hung around his own body.

He returned her kiss. "I missed you. Did you have a good lunch?"

"Yes. Very nice."

"What about that book I asked for?"

"First stop I made." She held it up. "Want me to read a few chapters?"

"Sure." He was relieved she didn't bring up the subject of marriage. Maybe André had been able to help them after all.

"Okay, then." She started reading and he relaxed, holding her hand and listening to her soft voice as it flowed over and around him.

"Don't go to sleep on me, Marc,"

He started. Had he been drifting off? That happened a lot now. He was always so tired.

There was a noise at the door, and from far away he seemed to hear a nurse talking, but couldn't understand the words. It wasn't important enough. Not even the book in Rebekka's hand could tempt him now. His eyes shut. He felt Rebekka leave to talk to the nurse, but knew she would be back.

When she did return, she was silent and pale. With effort he asked, "What happened? No one else died, did they?" The joke fell decidedly flat.

"Nothing's wrong. Maybe you should rest. Do you want me to read some more of your book? If we're going to get married—" she stopped and swallowed hard "—then I'd better get used to reading them. And you'd better start reading my mysteries."

She wasn't fooling him. Even in his drugged state he could see that something was wrong—something besides everything else. "Rebekka," he said softly but with determination, "please tell me."

Tears sprang to her eyes. "I just talked to the doctor. He's bumped you up as far as he can on the transplant list. Thank heaven money isn't a problem." Her voice was unsteady as she added, "Your condition is . . ."

"Worse, huh? But why the list? Louis-Géralde should be home soon. Uh-oh, what happened? Rebekka, I can see it in your eyes. What's wrong with my brother?"

"Nothing." Her gaze didn't quite meet his.

"Rebekka. I can take it."

"He's okay. Really. It's just that he can't come home right now. There's been some sort of a mix-up and he's been put in jail. They're working on getting him out now. I didn't want you to worry."

"Jail!" Marc's desire to sleep fled. "I've heard about Ukrainian jails. He might be there for weeks!"

"I've already called my friends at the embassy to see if they can do something. If I still worked there it might be faster, but they'll come up with a plan. He'll be okay. It's you we're worried about."

He tried to sit. "I can go get him."

"You aren't going anywhere." She pushed him down. "Louis-Géralde is fine. Or will be soon."

Marc bitterly acknowledged that he wasn't well enough to even sit up, much less get on a plane bound for the Ukraine. Tears threatened to fall, but he fought the familiar sensation. Rebekka held his hand and they stared at each other. His eyes roamed her face, every inch known and beloved to him. The fear in her eyes was so prominent and deeply etched that he wondered if it would ever go away.

Once again, he began to pray.

* * * * *

Back at his desk, André couldn't concentrate. *Fourteen freckles,* he thought. What had possessed him to count them? He didn't understand the urge, would never have believed possible the odd thoughts that were coming into his brain. During their life together he had loved Claire completely and totally. Any feelings he might have once harbored for Rebekka had been eradicated from his heart the moment he had seen Claire. She had been his *life.* Yet now she was gone, and he knew that whether he wanted to or not, he had to find some semblance of happiness, if not for himself, then for his daughters. But his plans for happiness did not include another woman.

So what happened at that restaurant with Rebekka?

Marc put it into my head, that's all, he told himself. *It never crossed my mind until he asked me to take care of her.*

Then why did you tell her that you once had a crush on her? He still had difficulty believing he had confessed this, seeing as how she was engaged to his brother. The whole confession had been a mistake. But he had been so terribly lonely and she bursting with a visible need for comfort.

At least he hadn't admitted everything.

He hadn't told her how he had wondered—however briefly—what might have happened had Marc not come around, or if he hadn't met Claire. Would such a relationship ever have worked?

Guilt assaulted André from every side. How could something like this even cross his mind? Was he so desperate to fill the emptiness inside that he would betray his brother and so soon forget his wife?

No! his soul cried. He had loved Claire—with his entire heart. And he would never hurt his brother.

Then why all these feelings? Yesterday, he had sworn it would be years before he might be able to think about another woman romantically.

Yet Rebekka wasn't another woman—she was his friend. She had always been his friend.

Did these feelings stem from the fact that Rebekka had known and loved Claire? Or perhaps because she could teach Claire's daughters what a wonderful person their mother had been?

André put his head in his hands and moaned. The pain he'd felt at Claire's death seemed to double. He longed to have her with him, to have their family whole. That must be why he had been drawn to Rebekka at the restaurant. She represented all that he had lost.

Marc asked me to take care of her, he thought.

His hands tore at his hair, and the pain helped him focus. What it all boiled down to was this: Marc thought he was going to die, and Rebekka thought he was going to die. Even the other members of the family seemed to be preparing themselves for tragedy. *I'm the only one who believes he's going to live,* he thought. *The only one. And yet if he doesn't live he wants me to take care of . . .*

The thought was not one to be finished. Suddenly André had to do something about his brother's condition. He absolutely wouldn't stand by and watch Marc die. He loved him too much—him and Rebekka both.

He grabbed an envelope of money reserved for emergencies from the back of his desk, picked up his briefcase, and strode to the door, locking it behind him. "I need the next flight available to the Ukraine," he told his secretary. "If there's a choice, I need only enough time to stop by the hospital to see my brother. Call me on the cell as soon as it's set. Leave a message if I don't answer. Then find Mr. Massoni and tell him I'm going out of town for a few days and he'll have to go solo in the meeting tomorrow. Tell him I'll call to explain later. Oh, and call my mother and get the number of the mission president in the Ukraine. Leave the number on my cell messages as well."

If she thought his commands a little strange she didn't let on. With a hurried thanks André ran out of his building and hailed a taxi. If everything went as planned, he wouldn't have time to worry about his car.

At the transplant hospital, André sauntered purposefully past the nurses' station and into Marc's room without permission. He was at once met with the antiseptic scent of death that hovered over the room. Rebekka was there, and both she and Marc looked with surprise in his direction. Marc's eyes were too dark in his pale face, and André knew Rebekka had told him about Louis-Géralde.

"André!" Rebekka flushed slightly as she said his name. She was so beautiful and uncertain that he wished to wrap his arms around her and tell her not to worry. But that was Marc's job.

"I'm going to the Ukraine," he announced. "I just stopped by to let you know."

They stared at him, but he shrugged. "Hey, I had planned to go there for a week anyway with Marie-Thérèse to pick up the baby they were going to adopt, just in case they ended up having to stay three weeks instead of two. Mathieu couldn't take more time off work. Since I'm all clear to go, I'm the logical one to bring back Louis-Géralde. I'm going to call the mission president on the way and see if there's anything I can do to speed his release."

"Thanks," Marc's voice was gruff and the gratitude in his eyes all too apparent. André felt uncomfortable, unworthy. His gaze strayed to Rebekka.

"My friends at the American Embassy might have some connections in the French Embassy in the Ukraine," Rebekka said, rising from the bed. "It's worth a try anyway. Let me see your documents.

I'll fax copies to my friends, so they can help you if you run into any problems. You never know."

With a click André opened his briefcase where he had kept his passport and other documents since he had received them over a month ago. He handed them to her.

When she had gone, André turned to Marc. "Why are you staring like that?"

"Because it's what I wanted to do—go get Louis-Géralde. I'm the oldest and I feel responsible. Thank you for going in my place."

"He's my brother too, and you're not the oldest, Josette is. Remember?"

Marc snorted. "By five minutes."

"And there's Marie-Thérèse—she's four months older than both of you—even if she was adopted later."

"I know, but a man's responsible for his younger brothers."

André cleared his throat. "Maybe. But I'm not going for Louis-Géralde. He'd be okay. The mission president would take care of him."

"You're going for me." Marc's voice was flat, hopeless, and André's anger flared to life.

"Yes, I'm going for you, and for Rebekka, and for our whole family." He leaned closer. "But you aren't doing your part like you promised. You're giving up." He swept his arm in a wide arc, indicating the room. "Is this the last place you want to live in before you die? Marc, you have to try!"

Marc nodded, tears filling his eyes. "Will you give me a blessing? Please, little brother, I need it."

André inclined his head, feeling oddly inadequate for what his brother needed. He took two steps closer to the bed and put his hands on his brother's head. What if he didn't have faith enough for this task? What if his new feelings for Rebekka got in the way?

"Father in Heaven, by the power and authority of the Melchizedek priesthood which I hold . . . ." he began. Words that hadn't been in his mind a moment before sprang to his lips as though from a prepared speech. Power coursed through his body and hands to Marc's head. He felt how he imagined Captain Moroni in the Book of Mormon had when he blessed his generals before traveling to Zarahemla to free his people from the king-men: "and I will leave the strength and the blessings of God upon them, that none other power can operate against them."

"You will live to see my face," André promised, hands trembling on his brother's head. "No power on earth can take you until I return."

Shaking, he finished the blessing. Marc's wondering eyes met André's. "Thank you. I needed that."

"I know it's been tough." André forced his voice to become hard—a difficult thing with the love and power of the Spirit that had permeated his heart, mind, and soul. "But you know that this blessing is predicated upon your own faith and your desire to live. You will live to see my face again—if you fight!" He sat on the edge of the bed and added softly, "And if you're ever tempted to give up, just think of Rebekka." His voice grew in volume. "Think of how desperately she wants to spend her life with you! She needs you, Marc, and you have to fight for her!"

"I will." Marc's eyes flicked to the door.

André followed his gaze and saw Rebekka watching them. How much had she heard? Then he decided that it didn't matter. She needed to hear it as much as Marc.

He strode to the door. "Good-bye, Rebekka." He accepted the travel documents from her outstretched hand. "Take care of him."

"What about the girls? Don't they get out of school soon?"

"I was going to call Mom or Josette on the way to the airport."

"I'll pick up the girls. I know where."

Her gray eyes pleaded for something to do, so he nodded. "I'll let the school know you're coming. Thank you." He smiled and moved into the hall. Once he would have hugged her or kissed her cheek good-bye, but now he couldn't trust himself to be near her. Only his determination succeeded in carrying him outside to his waiting taxi, where he sank thankfully to the seat. "The airport," he said.

He checked his messages and saw that his secretary had called while he was in the transplant hospital with Marc. She had scheduled his flight for four o'clock that afternoon, but instead of a direct three-hour flight to Kiev, he would have to first fly to Vienna, Austria, where he would have a two-hour layover before he picked up his next flight. That meant he would arrive in Kiev at about 10:40 P.M., local time. Because of the hour time difference he would spend six hours in transit, four of which would be inside a plane. While this wasn't the direct flight he had preferred, it was all the choice he had until the next day. And that might be too late.

Sitting back, he sighed deeply and began to make the promised call to the girls' school and then another to Raoul to explain his absence.

"Don't worry," Raoul assured him. "I'll take care of everything."

Lastly, André called the number his secretary had left for President Bradley in the Ukraine, already practicing the arguments he would use if the president refused his help. President Bradley wasn't at the mission office, but the missionary who picked up the phone gave him another number to call.

When President Bradley picked up, André quickly explained who he was and how grave Marc's situation had become. "I know you're doing your best, President, but I can't sit and watch my brother die. I need to see if I can hurry along Louis-Géralde's release. So I'm on my way now."

The mission president was silent for a moment, and then spoke in a deep voice. His French accent was good, but his vocabulary limited. "You know, you just might be the answer to my prayers. There's, uh, something you don't know about. A . . . complication. But I will explain when you get here. It's the reason the zone leaders haven't . . . uh, been able to free him yet. I was on my way, but unfortunately another . . . crisis has shown up here, and I must take careful it—take care of it. But I have the idea that with your presence and a little . . . invention, we'll be able to get your brother free much sooner than the usual two weeks."

"I'll call you when I arrive then."

"Call me at this number," the president replied. "It's my mobile phone—I am not sure where I'll be."

André disconnected and leaned back in his seat. So much had happened since that morning. *I miss you, Claire,* he thought. Staring out the window, he blinked the tears from his eyes.

CHAPTER 22

Rebekka loaded the dishwasher as André's daughters brought the dinner dishes from the table. She had enjoyed preparing the meal for them in their apartment, and was looking forward to reading to them before bedtime.

"Are we going to see Uncle Marc?" asked Ana, taking Rebekka's hand.

"No. It's getting late and you two have school tomorrow. Besides, your grandma and grandpa are hanging out with him tonight."

While at first she been reluctant to leave Marc, Rebekka was grateful for the distraction the girls provided. Of course, Ana and Marée could have gone to their grandparents' or to one of their aunts', but everyone had agreed it would be best to keep the girls in their own home. Rebekka had found herself volunteering to stay with them there and to see that they went to school on time the next morning. Unlike the members of André's family, she had no children or elderly parents to depend on her, and it wasn't a problem to pack a small suitcase of her things for the night. She was like a nomad—no real home of her own except the apartment she and Marc were planning to share, and she could stay with the girls for as many days as it took André to complete his task in the Ukraine.

The terrible ache inside her had dulled to a sore throb. She had heard what André said after he gave Marc the blessing and believed that Marc would live—at least until André returned with Louis-Géralde. But what about after that? Would Marc survive another transplant?

And, as if her fears weren't enough to already drive her insane, ever haunting her were the feelings she had experienced toward André at the restaurant—the confusing emotions that didn't fit within the established boundaries of their relationship. Rebekka bit the inside of her bottom lip. Oh, why did an already difficult situation have to become more complicated?

"All done," Marée said brightly, handing Rebekka the last of the dinner dishes. Her turquoise eyes gleamed, reminding Rebekka so much of Claire that she sat down on a chair and drew the girl to her.

How distressed Claire must have felt to leave them. Though André was a good father and would certainly do his best, Rebekka felt strongly that little children needed a mother, too. Would he ever find a woman who could love them as Claire had?

I could try to help André with them. She smiled in satisfaction. Yes, she would help André with the girls. And she would continue to befriend him. She would marry Marc, and set André up with that pretty secretary, Valerie or whatever her name was. It was decided. There was no reason to think about it further. Leading the girls from the kitchen, she pushed any lingering thoughts of André from her mind.

* * * * *

Upon arriving in the Ukraine nearly a half hour later than he had expected, André spent a terrible night at the airport while officials checked out his paperwork. There seemed to be some sort of complication no one could explain to him. Their French-speaking translator kept talking in circles, saying nothing intelligible—at least nothing André could decipher. Finally they contacted the French Embassy, and to his great relief, Rebekka's contacts in the American Embassy in France had forwarded requests and documentation.

It was all very disconcerting to have the airport officials stand in the way of his goal of reaching his brother. André suspected that what at least a few of them wanted was a bribe from an obviously successful businessman in a hurry. He wondered if he should comply, but worried that he would land himself into even more trouble. Finally, an important-looking man came into the little room where André had been placed. His short black hair was smooth except for a small part in the front that looked as though he had been pulling on it in exasperation.

"I'm sorry to have kept you," he said in heavily accented French. The lines on his face were deep and he looked as exhausted as André felt. "Your documents are now in order. There was some problem with the date only. Please forgive my men for holding you up." He clicked his tongue, indicating that André should not have been detained at all. "Thanks to the French Embassy, all is under control and you are free to go."

"Thank you." André tried to keep his anger from showing in his voice, knowing his delay was not directly this man's fault. Instead he focused on his gratefulness to Rebekka for her prudence in sending his documents through bureaucratic channels. At least this terrible night was behind him.

Once released, he searched for a pay phone, since his cell no longer worked now that he was out of France. Before he could use the phone he had to exchange the ample amount of euros he had brought for Ukrainian hryvnias.

At last he placed the call to the mission president. "I've been worried," President Bradley said. "I was just going to send someone to the airport to see if we could find you."

"I think they wanted a bribe," André said.

"Likely. Look, I'm about an hour's drive away from where you are now. If you'll, uh . . . jot down the address and grab a taxi to come to my . . . location. Ask the driver if he minds taking us on to the jail. That will be the fastest way. Are you ready to write the addresses of both . . . locations?"

"Yes. Go ahead." André wrote the information on the back of his used airline ticket.

The Tuesday morning rush hour was already underway when he emerged from the darker confines of the Kiev airport, blinking in the bright sunlight. André was relieved to see a row of waiting taxicabs. There were also several children who approached him, asking for money. André eyed their mismatched, ragged clothes, and gave them each a bill, pleased to see their happy grins as they dipped their dark heads in thanks.

André searched the row of waiting cabs to find a driver who spoke French. The first two drivers glared at him blankly, but the third, a small, swarthy man with a long moustache, smiled. "I do speak but a bit of French. Where you need to go?" Unlike the mission president, both his accent and grammar were atrocious, but it was better than the one word André knew in Ukrainian.

André showed him the unpronounceable names and addresses President Bradley had given him. The man smoothed his moustache. "Sure, I know where these are. I take you there. But both are far away. This one—" he tapped the address of the jail "—is half hour outside Chernihiv. We drive two and a half hours, maybe three. Cost a lot. Even if you don't come back, you pay both the ways."

"That's okay. But I want to come back. I'll pay you a tip, too, if you get me there fast. The only stop is to pick up a friend."

"Get in, then. We go."

As André did, three more children showed up to ask for money, obviously alerted by the first children. The taxi driver shooed them away, yelling in what André assumed to be Ukrainian. The children answered back in high, angry voices, but they retreated.

On the long drive André fought the urge to doze in the back seat. His teeth felt dirty, his clothes were rumpled, and he was decidedly irritable. To keep himself awake he explained his situation to the taxi driver. He wasn't sure how much the driver understood, but the man kept smiling and nodding. He spoke French only brokenly, but André knew from his own experience with English that it was easier to understand than speak a foreign language.

They arrived at the first address and found President Bradley waiting outside. He was shorter than André had expected from his deep voice, but had a large chest and a full head of wavy black hair that added to his presence. His blue eyes twinkled as they shook hands.

"We will talk on the way," he said as he entered the taxi.

André reentered the car. "You speak French rather well," he said.

President Bradley grinned. "My mother was French, and a school-teacher. I learned from her."

"And your father?"

"An American. He was in the military and we spent a lot of time overseas. My mother had school at home when we were younger. We joined the Church in Germany and shortly after returned to the States. I went to college there." He grinned. "Funny thing is, I always thought I would go to France on my mission, but I ended up serving in New York. I spent most of my time there in two different areas—each of which had a large group of Ukrainian-Americans. When I received this call, I finally understood why I needed that experience."

"So you could learn Ukrainian."

"So I could learn to love the Ukrainian people," he corrected, "and bring them the gospel."

André let a moment pass before saying, "You said you had something to tell me. About why you couldn't get my brother out of jail."

"Yes." President Bradley glanced at their driver and lowered his voice. "Life is much different here than in France or in America. Bribery isn't, uh, discouraged as in our countries. In fact, it really is a way of life. The average person does not make a lot of money and they depend on bribes to make it through the month."

"How does this relate to Louis-Géralde?"

"We've decided to create a 'no bribe policy' for the mission. The Church has a rather high profile with all these clean-cut missionaries walking around, and in the past they've been a real target for such things. But I have found that while legal measures are much slower here—without bribery, of course—they do work. So we go through legal methods, and it is starting to pay off."

"You mean they realize you won't pay, so they speed you through to get rid of you."

President Bradley nodded gravely. "Precisely. Except we have tried this with your brother's situation to no avail. I mean, it will work eventually—I've made a few calls and set things in motion—but it will take time."

"Time that we don't have."

"That is where you come in."

"Oh?" André was puzzled, but willing to hear the president out.

"When the zone leaders were unsuccessful in . . . uh—what's the words—extracting your brother, I was ready to go in and pay whatever it took. But I knew word would get out and this would set us back some, especially in that city. And I didn't want that. So I was praying for a way to free him and to maintain our 'no bribe policy.' Then a situation with another missionary came up—one of my elders received a Dear John letter and disappeared. Don't worry, we found him, and I think that after a bit of soul-searching he may just finally become the missionary his Father in Heaven knows he can be. Of course, you understand that while he was missing, I had to start a search for him. And all this brought enough of a delay that you decided to come. See? The answer to prayer."

André still didn't know where the president was going. "What can I do exactly?"

"Well, I've already placed a call to a good friend of mine who works for the government here. He promised to call the authorities who are holding your brother and mention that the Church never pays for the release of their missionaries, and holding him will end up being a burden for them in the long run. Then I will show up in person, demand their release, and restate that claim. Then I will leave. And you will come in, not connected to the Church, but to one of the missionaries."

A smile began to work its way across André's face. "Ah-ha. I see. Then it won't matter if I pay to get him out. Because it's not you."

"Theoretically." President Bradley folded his arms across his chest.

"And if it doesn't work?"

"It will. Did you bring enough money?"

André pulled out his wallet and spread out the bills.

"Looks like plenty."

For the rest of the drive, they chatted amicably. André noticed that President Bradley's French was improving by the minute; apparently, he had simply needed a bit of practice. When at last they arrived at the small jail where Louis-Géralde was being kept, President Bradley said, "Now give me a half hour. It'll only take me a few minutes, but give them some time to stew. I'll meet you at the elders' apartment afterward. Here's the address." Smiling with determination, the president left the car and strode down the walk.

"Let's drive for a bit," André directed his driver.

"A half hour, yes? Isn't that what the man say?"

"Yes, please."

As the minutes passed, André tried to take in the sights, but he was too preoccupied to notice much. What was he going to do—walk into the jail waving around his money? What if no one understood that he needed Louis-Géralde to be freed *today*. They had already lost so much time. He prayed for guidance and in the midst of his prayer, realized that the answer had been in front of him all along.

"Hey, you wouldn't want to earn an extra bit of money, would you?" he asked the driver casually, as the taxi finally headed back toward the jailhouse. He picked five of the largest bills—one hundred hryvnias each—out of his wallet and waved them in the air. "If you come with me and try to explain that I need to see my brother, I'll give you this."

The hryvnias disappeared into the driver's front pocket before André realized he'd taken them. "Sure. This I will do. I will help you . . . how do you say it? . . . rescue this brother you tell me about."

"Oh, and one more thing. Don't mention the man who was with us. They can't know that we're together." He was pretty certain the driver hadn't heard much of their conversation, and it was unlikely he would know who the mission president was anyway, but André wanted to be sure.

Once inside the small jailhouse, André was glad he had enlisted the help of the taxi driver, because as poorly as the man spoke French, he had no problems with his native Ukrainian. He talked to the men behind the desk rapidly, and soon André was being ushered past the main desk and down a narrow, white-painted hallway. One of the doors in the hall led to a larger room with two cells for prisoners, complete with the classic iron bars. André saw Louis-Géralde immediately, lying on an uncomfortable-looking cot and reading the dog-bitten scriptures Rebekka had given him before he left France. He was comparing them intently with another set of scriptures that André assumed were in Ukrainian or Russian. On another cot in the same cell, another young boy—an American by the look of his blonde hair and facial structure—slept soundly under a thin blanket. The other cell was empty.

Louis-Géralde looked up as the guard stopped at his cell, barking out something in Ukrainian. "André," Louis-Géralde said, leaping from his cot in surprise. The other missionary stirred but did not wake.

"Hey, little brother."

"What are you doing here?" Louis-Géralde grabbed hold of the bars and brought his face up close. "President Bradley knows, doesn't he? We're not supposed to get visits from family, and I don't want to get in trouble."

"He knows. We're trying to get you out." André placed his hands over his brother's in greeting before sitting obediently on the chair the guard indicated. He watched as the man locked the door behind him as he left, presumably returning to the front office where André hoped the taxi driver still waited for him. The locked door made André uneasy. *Well, at least I'm not inside the iron bars,* he consoled himself.

"Good." Louis-Géralde's anxious expression relaxed. He pulled his cot closer to the bars and sat on it.

"So what are *you* doing here?" André asked, mildly amused that his brother was worried about breaking the rules when he was obviously not doing any missionary work.

Louis-Géralde looked sheepish. "Well, I thought I was doing everything right, but apparently things aren't done here exactly the way I think they should be."

"I'll say," a voice said in English.

André glanced at the other missionary, who was sitting up and rubbing the sleep from his very blue eyes. A myriad of freckles seemed to dance across the missionary's face.

"He learned a word or two of French in high school," Louis-Géralde explained in rapid French, his voice low. "I think that's why the president put us together. In fact, he speaks it better than Ukrainian or Russian, despite being here already six months, which isn't saying much because his French is really terrible. Mostly we speak in English when we're alone."

"Darn know-it-all greeny wouldn't listen to what I told him," the elder continued in English. "If he'd just slipped them a hundred hryvnias like I told him, we wouldn't be here. While you're explaining things, be sure to explain *that*, Elder Perrault. Eighteen bucks, that's all it was. Not worth being here for three days."

Louis-Géralde's face reddened. "You understand what he's saying, don't you?" he asked.

André nodded. "Sort of." Like most people in France, he had studied English over the years, though he wasn't close to speaking it as well as Louis-Géralde.

"Well, he's right," Louis-Géralde continued with a frown. "It *was* my fault. But I just didn't feel like giving the guy my hard-earned cash when I wasn't doing anything wrong."

"Well, what did you do?"

"I told you—nothing."

André sighed. "What did they charge you with?"

"I'm not sure. But what happened was that our investigator's husband started hitting her one night. We arrived in the middle of it, and I told him if he touched her again, I'd throw him out the window." Louis-Géralde smiled apologetically. "I couldn't just let him do that to her. I'm not as tall as you are, but I'm just as big, and the guy got scared and called the police. The next thing I know, the policeman is asking for some money to smooth over the threat, but I said I'd rather hang than give him or that wife-beater any money. Imagine, paying the guy to beat his wife—it's unthinkable! Elder Barney warned me just to pay it, despite the president's 'no bribe policy,' but I had to uphold mission standards . . ." Louis-Géralde made a face. "And now you've had to come all the way from France to save me. How embarrassing. No offense, André, but couldn't the president send the zone leaders?"

"He did. But I guess they weren't allowed to see you. And the president himself was here a few minutes ago, but he says going through the regular channels will take weeks—and we don't have the luxury of waiting."

For the first time, Louis-Géralde gazed at him with fear showing in his eyes. "What do you mean?"

"You know that Marc got a transplant, don't you?"

"Yes. Mom said Rebekka was the donor. I was a little relieved because I was just getting the hang of this missionary stuff. I didn't want to leave so soon. I mean, the language was fairly easy for me to pick up—probably because of all the years I've taken it in school—but the rest isn't as simple as I thought."

"It never is."

"But if Marc got the transplant, why are you here?" He suddenly blanched. "He's not dead, is he?"

André arose and again covered his brother's hands where they were clutching the iron bars. "No. But he *is* dying. He rejected

Rebekka's kidney, and he's going downhill fast. Without another transplant, he'll die for certain. They've put him near the top of the transplant list because he's so critical, but with his blood being so rare, you're the best match—at least until Marc and Rebekka get started on kids of their own."

Louis-Géralde sagged with relief. "Then it's not too late. We have to get home. Can you get me out of here?"

"I don't know. I can't understand a thing the guards say. The only reason they even let me in to visit was because of something my taxi driver told them. I don't know what. He could have promised them anything, for all I know. It worries me since your zone leaders weren't even allowed in."

"Let me talk with my companion," Louis-Géralde said. "And see what he says. He's been here longer. Maybe he'll have an idea."

"Okay, but hurry. I don't know how long they're letting me stay."

Louis-Géralde explained the situation in English to his companion. They spoke so quickly that André didn't follow much of what they said. When they finished, Elder Barney stood and walked over to André. "So you're Elder Perrault's brother," he said in slow English, sticking his hand through the bars, "and I thought you were from the embassy or something. Nice to meet you."

"Nice to meet you, too," André replied, shaking the elder's hand.

"And thanks for coming."

"I'm going to explain your idea now," Louis-Géralde told him in English. Then he turned to André and began to speak in French. "My companion thinks that if you explain about Marc it might get some results. But could you say that Marc's family is offering a reward in order to get me back in time for the transplant, a reward you are willing to share with whoever can get me out? That way, they will have a little more . . . uh, incentive."

"I think the taxi driver already told them that I'm your brother. They looked at my identification."

Louis-Géralde scratched his cheek, and then raked his hand through his dark hair in a manner that reminded André of Marc. "I don't think it'll matter much," Louis-Géralde said. "They might go along anyway, especially since they know they have nothing on us, and since they know by now that they aren't getting anything out of the Church. Plus, if our case gets to the attention of the French Embassy, they might have big problems on their hands."

"Okay, I'll do it." André started for the door, but Louis-Géralde stopped him.

"Just so you know, they aren't *all* corrupt here. It's a way of life— to some more than others. The economy is so tight and the people aren't paid very much. They do what they have to in order to survive. I've met some of the most wonderful people—people who would give you the shirt off their back if that was all they had. There's even a guard here I've been giving the discussions. He's okay. You understand that, don't you?"

Memories of his own mission in France came flooding back to André, vivid and precious. "Your president and I already had a talk about this very thing. And I think I do understand. But what I'm sure of is that you love this people already, and I'm glad to see it. When we get you back here after the operation, you are going to be a wonderful missionary—if you'll just learn to stop threatening to throw people out of windows. Bullies included."

Louis-Géralde smiled wistfully. "Do you think they'll let me come back to the mission? I don't know that they will . . . because of the surgery, you know."

"Of course they will. You'll be just as healthy as before. You don't need two kidneys to live a normal life. If there's any problem, I'll talk to President Bradley myself. I promise. He's a great guy."

"Thank you. Because as much as I want to help Marc, I feel I belong here for my mission. I need to bring the gospel to these people."

André nodded and turned to the door, pretending not to see the tears in his brother's green-brown eyes.

He tried the locked door, of course to no avail, then he banged on it. After four times, he finally heard someone in the hall. The guard let him out and led him to the front office, where the taxi driver was having coffee with the jailers. André smiled at the others and motioned to the driver for a private consultation.

"Look, my brother says they really haven't got anything on them. He was only defending the woman from her husband."

"Yes. I hear that from these guys," the driver thumbed over his shoulders. "They take the boys here only because that man has a brother who is big guy in town. They say they also want to protect boys, but this I do not believe."

"Okay, then tell them the French boy's family is offering money for his return. A reward, not a bribe. Because of the kidney transplant, got it?"

The driver's eyes gleamed. "You think they will better buy that kidney story if you give them money."

André fought his growing irritation. "The story is true. My brother needs a transplant, and if you don't believe it, contact the French Embassy. They know about it. If we don't get back soon, my brother is going to die!"

"Good idea!" The small taxi driver nearly danced with excitement. "The mention of embassy. Very good! And the time thing—makes them fast. I do it!" He looked admiringly at André. "You are very good with this. Never have I hear a better story." Before André could reply the driver turned and launched into his explanation to the guards.

"No better story than the truth," André muttered.

He watched as the driver conversed animatedly with the others. Once he pointed at André and then put his hands to his heart. The guards looked unimpressed and continued to listen dispassionately.

Then, after what seemed like an hour, the little driver was at his elbow. "Where is the money?"

André pulled out his wallet, noticing one of the guards leaving the room. "How much?"

"Four times what you give me before. Two thousand hryvnias. You have it, no? I tried to talk them down but . . . And you will still have enough to pay the cab fare, yes?"

André examined his wallet. "Yes."

"Then . . ." The taxi driver held out his hand.

André didn't debate, but gave him the money. In turn, the driver passed it to the man at the desk, who exchanged the bills for a piece of paper. "You have to sign it," the taxi driver informed him.

"What does it say?"

"That charges are dropped. But you responsible for their actions. If more happens, you pay."

André signed, hoping he was doing the right thing. To his relief, Louis-Géralde and Elder Barney were coming into the room, accompanied by the other guard. They were each given a manila envelope containing their previously confiscated belongings.

"Hey, they took my money anyway!" Louis-Géralde exclaimed.

"Stow it!" André said shortly. He smiled his thanks at the guards and led the missionaries from the room.

"How much did you have?" Elder Barney asked in English.

"Almost two hundred hryvnias."

"Let's see," the American elder said, concentrating. "That's about thirty-six dollars and I had about twenty. And ask your brother how much he paid." André told him about the two thousand hryvnias, and Elder Barney was incredulous. "That's what . . . three hundred and sixty dollars and with what they took from us . . . wow! They got away with over four hundred American dollars! That's a *lot* of dough here." He slapped Louis-Géralde on the back. "And all for standing up for an investigator. Personally, I think your brother could have gotten us out for a lot less. I bet the taxi driver took a cut."

Louis-Géralde didn't translate the words, nor did André let on that he had understood as much as he did. The American dollar figures meant nothing to him, but he knew exactly how many euros he'd exchanged—not a small amount—and he would barely have enough to pay the expensive cab fare back to the airport. He decided not to tell the boys that he had also paid the taxi driver another five hundred hryvnias to act as a translator.

André had the taxi driver go to the apartment where the missionaries rented a room from an elderly couple. President Bradley was there, and he embraced the missionaries warmly. "Pack up," he said without delay. "Elder Perrault has to leave for France and Elder Barney is going to be transferred. I think it's time we saw a pair of native sisters in this area, don't you? That ought to keep things quiet for a while."

"Just so long as they take care of our investigators." Louis-Géralde pulled out his suitcase. He grimaced. "We have a lady whose husband isn't always nice."

President Bradley chuckled. "Don't worry, Elder, I know just the sister missionary. Your investigators will all be fine. I'll make sure of that."

André waited impatiently as the missionaries packed their few belongings. The nearly two-hour drive back to where the president had left his car went by even more slowly than the journey to the jail. At last they bid President Bradley and Elder Barney good-bye.

"Louis-Géralde will probably need several months to recover before he can return," André warned.

"Let him take as long as he needs," said President Bradley. "I'll talk it over with Salt Lake to see if they'll extend his service so that he can make up those months."

Louis-Géralde extended his hand. "I'd be grateful for that, President. Thank you."

"Well, thank you too, Elder. And we'll miss you. You are a good missionary."

"And will be again," André put in.

"Yes. And meanwhile, I'll keep you in my prayers." President Bradley's voice showed compassion and Louis-Géralde hugged him.

When they arrived again at the airport, André gave the driver the rest of his hryvnias. At the ticket counter, they booked the next available flight home at three. The direct flight was only three hours, and with the hour they gained from the time difference, they would be back in Paris at five o'clock.

"Let's get some lunch while we wait," André suggested, realizing he hadn't eaten a thing since his lunch with Rebekka the day before.

Rebekka, he thought. *Better not go there.*

"I'll have to change a few more euros, but it doesn't take long," he added.

Louis-Géralde brightened noticeably from the somber mood he had fallen into. André knew exactly how the boy felt. What if they were too late? The blessing he had given Marc was dependent upon Marc's will and faithfulness. Had he given up?

Another thought came, just as tormenting. What was Rebekka thinking and feeling and doing right this minute? He hoped his spilled-over emotions hadn't ruined their friendship.

They arrived at a small restaurant in the food court of the airport, where Louis-Géralde broke the silence, his smile returning. "Good, they have borscht."

"Borscht?"

"A soup made from potatoes, cabbage, and beets." He pointed to a customer at a nearby table, eating from a bowl filled with a dark red mixture. "That's it right there. There's beef in it too, and they top it with fresh dill, parsley, and a dab of sour cream. They give you black rye bread to go with it. You have to try some. You'll love it."

André hid a grimace. "I bet I will."

Louis-Géralde eyed the soup appreciatively. "Too bad we can't take some home. It's really good after it ages in the refrigerator a few days."

Looking at the red soup, André was glad they wouldn't be taking it home.

CHAPTER 23

At six-thirty on Tuesday evening, Rebekka was putting a roast into the oven when she heard a key in the lock. Instinctively she looked to where the girls were coloring at the kitchen table. No, neither had escaped when her back was turned. Who could it be? She knew that André's parents had spare keys, as did Marc, but when she and the girls had left the hospital barely a half hour before, Ariana and Jean-Marc had been visiting their son.

André? Maybe he was back from the Ukraine! Tucking a piece of hair behind her ear, she headed toward the entryway.

André looked up at her as she came from the kitchen, startled. He kicked the door shut behind him. "Rebekka, I . . . Mom said you had the girls, but I didn't know you'd come here. I was going to clean up quickly and then call you."

Rebekka noticed that he was still wearing the same clothes he had worn yesterday at lunch. The suit was rumpled, the tie askew. Her heart pounded furiously, and she reasoned that was because he had news of Louis-Géralde. "We all felt it best not to interrupt their schedule more than necessary. You know, like the grief counselor suggested." She spoke softly so the girls wouldn't hear, not only for their consideration, but for herself; somehow she didn't want to share his attention with them just yet. "I brought them here yesterday after school. Today I took them to the hospital to see Marc and then back here. Your mom is coming later to sit with them after they're in bed while I go back to Marc."

Go back to Marc. The words hung between them, cloying, impenetrable.

"We arrived in Paris at five," he said, his voice suddenly growing weary, matching his rumpled attire. "I took Louis-Géralde to the transplant hospital on the way here. Since he's already had all the preliminary blood-typing tests, they think they'll be ready to do the surgery tomorrow."

"Tomorrow?" Rebekka gulped.

"The doctor would like to wait until Marc is stronger, but that's just not going to happen."

She knew. Marc was dying and she had understood by the doctor's manner the past few days that this transplant would be Marc's last chance; he was too weak for more.

André regarded her for a moment without speaking, then he made a move toward her, as though to take her in his arms. Rebekka would have welcomed the comfort, but knew she had given up that luxury when she had let those guilt-filled thoughts enter her mind the day before. Their friendship was now forever clouded by that memory.

"Oh, André," she said, her voice filled with pain and longing. Longing for what? She couldn't say, not even to herself. If only Marc had been well!

"He'll be fine," he said. "We must believe." He touched her arm gingerly. "I'm going to say hello to the girls and then take a shower and change. Will you stay until I'm done?"

"Yes. I have dinner in the oven. Are you hungry?"

A half smile turned up the corners of his mouth. "Yeah. I didn't eat much in Kiev."

She watched him go into the kitchen to greet the girls, who squealed and gave him exuberant kisses. Both children began talking rapidly, recounting every minuscule thing that had happened to them since his departure.

Rebekka didn't follow, but walked slowly into the living room and sat on the sofa. She picked up the white crocheted lap blanket and smoothed it with her fingers.

What was wrong with her? Why did she feel so frightened, confused, lonely? Was it only because of Marc's illness?

Closing her eyes, she began to pray for strength and endurance . . . and also something else she could not name.

* * * * *

André let the delicious hot water beat into his tired muscles until the steam in the bathroom was so thick he could hardly breathe.

Not taking Rebekka in his arms was the hardest thing he had ever done. But it was the *right* thing. Whatever was between them—was it only his imagination?—had to come secondary to her feelings and her prior commitment to his brother.

When he emerged from the shower, Rebekka informed him stiffly when to take out the roast, hugged the girls, and left. To Marc.

André was satisfied that he had done all that he could do for his brother. The rest was in the Lord's hands. He only wished the knowledge hadn't come with a vision of the future he would never have.

* * * * *

"Thank you, brother," Marc said to Louis-Géralde. The words were difficult to utter because the emotions inside him churned and bubbled so violently that it was all he could do to hold back tears.

"Hey, no prob." Louis-Géralde smiled.

"We'll help him get checked in and settled in his room and then check back on you," Ariana said.

Marc nodded, not trusting himself to speak aloud. When his parents and Louis-Géralde left the room, he took a deep breath and murmured, "Thank you, Father."

The tears came then and he started to cry deep, racking sobs that came from the depths of his soul. But unlike the other tears he had shed in private since rejecting Rebekka's kidney, these originated in hope.

Hope!

Maybe he would live after all! Maybe the impression he had in Utah didn't mean what he thought it had. He could have misinterpreted it. Or perhaps the time for their separation was yet in the future.

Oh, Rebekka, I might just be able to have you for eternity. It's the only thing I want now. Nothing else matters.

The uncertainty of his situation had caused him more agony these past weeks than he would admit to anyone. Not to the Lord in his prayers, not even to himself. The truth was, Marc had looked many years for a partner, and not one woman had remotely aroused stronger feelings than the ones he held for Rebekka. He knew there was no one else he would ever love the way he loved her. Even his supposedly once-strong feelings for Danielle were revealed to be nothing more than a boyish crush.

Yet it was this same burning love for Rebekka that made it possible for him to refuse her offer of marrying him in the hospital. Marry her and die. He couldn't do that to her—he wouldn't! Oh, he desperately wanted to give in to her wishes because without her he would spend eternity alone. There was no one else for him—of that he was certain.

Now there was hope. He had exercised his faith and the Lord had seen fit to bless him, despite the obstacles in his way. At last he and Rebekka would be happy and together!

"Thank you, thank you, thank you!" The words formed a continuous litany. Marc felt so grateful to his God and his brothers that he was almost too full of emotion.

The wrenching sobs were at last subsiding, and Marc dried his face on the soft white sheet. He took long, cleansing breaths and began to think about the future.

Rebekka entered the room a scarce fifteen minutes later, her face flushed with her hurry. She practically flew to his bedside.

"What's wrong?" she asked anxiously, searching his face. "You've been crying." Her soft hands touched both sides of his jaw, cradling his face. He could smell her sweet perfume. His arms went around her and he pulled her closer.

"Louis-Géralde. He's here."

"I know." Her cheek felt deliciously cool against his own.

"I'm going to make it, Rebekka! At least I'm going to try. Will you pray for me?"

"Now?"

He nodded.

They held hands as Rebekka offered a prayer of thanks, followed by a loving petition for Marc's well-being.

A warm feeling entered Marc's heart, engulfing his entire soul with light. "Can you feel that, Rebekka?"

She nodded, tears escaping from her eyes. "I can."

* * * * *

"It'll just be a little while now," Rebekka told Marc the next morning as they waited for his surgery.

He smiled weakly at her from the bed. "You know, I can't help thinking that I'm the most fortunate man alive. Look at all the sacrifices people are making for me—André flying to the Ukraine, Louis-Géralde coming back to give me his kidney, and you, Rebekka. You are the best. Have I ever told you how much I love you?"

He had, but every time he said it, she felt the thrill of it again. She looked at his familiar, beloved face, now so much happier and hopeful than she had seen it in a long time. "Yes. And I love you." She bent her head and kissed him tenderly. He shut his eyes and sighed with her touch.

"Now be a good boy and come back better, okay?"

"I'll do just that." He gave her the youthful grin she adored, the one that had so frustrated her when he hadn't returned her affections while growing up. "And three weeks from today we'll get married, okay?" He kissed his finger and held it up to her lips as the orderly pushed his bed from the room. Rebekka held onto his hand for as long as she could, but let him go at the door. She watched until he was out of sight

Then she began to pray.

Hours passed as they waited for Marc to come out of surgery. Rebekka stayed in the waiting room with Marc's family for most of the time, talking quietly or reading a magazine. Her parents checked in occasionally, but knowing that her father had already missed too much work, she insisted they leave. "I'll call you with any news," she promised.

Before lunch she was permitted in briefly to see Louis-Géralde, who was doing well after his surgery earlier in the day. "Hi, Rebekka," he groaned when she came into the room. "They made me get up and walk, the brutes! Can you believe it?"

She shook her head sympathetically. "I remember it all too well." Her hand went to her side where she would forever bear the scar of her attempted gift to Marc. They made small talk for a minute and then Rebekka paused, "This is a great thing you're doing," she told him. "I can't tell you how much this means to me."

Louis-Géralde's face grew sober. "They say he still might not make it. That even if the kidney works fine, he may be too weak to recover."

Rebekka reached out and touched his shoulder comfortingly. "It's in the Lord's hands now." And almost miraculously she felt the Lord's love surrounding her like a warm embrace.

Back in the waiting room, her eyes met André's, and almost instinctively she found herself walking in his direction. She had always been so grateful for his support; perhaps she could offer him some of the comfort she had felt in Louis-Géralde's room.

He smiled tentatively as she approached. "Where are the girls?" she asked.

"With Josette. She's feeling sick right now, with the baby due next month and all."

Rebekka felt a mild surprise that the months had passed so quickly. "Worrying about Marc hasn't been helping her. Josette and Marc are close."

"She always tried to protect him as kids. This time there's nothing she can do. It's tough for her."

Rebekka nodded, knowing exactly how Josette felt.

They sat together on the couch without speaking, far enough away from one another that not even their clothes touched. The silence was comfortable, but the memory of the incident at the restaurant returned. She quickly shoved it to the back of her mind, and forced her thoughts elsewhere.

At long last Dr. Juppe came into the waiting room, and the Perrault family and Rebekka gathered around him. "The transfer went really well," he announced. "The kidney's working, but he's still very weak. The next twenty-four hours will tell. Since the match is so good, I worry a lot less about his rejecting the kidney than I do his surviving the surgery. He's a strong man, though, and he's got a lot to live for." The doctor winked at Rebekka. "I would go so far as to say that if he makes it until morning, he'll be just fine."

Joy sang through Rebekka's heart and tears of gratitude sprang to her eyes. Marc was going to live. He was!

"Thank you, Dr. Juppe," Ariana said for all of them. "We appreciate everything you've done." Jean-Marc shook his hand and asked if he could take the doctor and his wife out to dinner later that day. Dr. Juppe agreed.

Rebekka's eyes met André's and for some reason her stomach churned. He frowned and drew her aside from the group. "Are you all right?"

"I'm fine," she replied a bit tersely. More gently she added, "I should call my parents with the news, though. They're waiting to hear." But what she really wanted to do at that moment was find out why she felt so uncomfortable whenever she spoke to him.

It's nothing, said an inner voice, but her guilt returned in force.

André said nothing, but his eyes didn't leave her face. Suddenly, Rebekka was acutely aware of her rumpled jeans and her pink T-shirt. Pink? Why had she worn pink? She knew it contrasted with her auburn locks, despite their being so dark. She must look a sight!

For a moment she felt utterly miserable.

"You, André!" came a tight, angry voice from across the room. Rebekka was relieved to feel André's searching eyes leave her face. Raoul strode quickly across the carpet toward them, looking furious.

"What?" André asked.

Rebekka had never seen her brother so angry except for the night their father had informed Raoul that Desirée was nothing more than an overly made-up, money-digging tramp. Rebekka hadn't agreed with her father's assessment then, but now? Could it be that he had seen something she had missed? Like Raoul, Rebekka had been so willing to overlook any initial warning signs. After all, Desirée had been taking the missionary discussions at the time.

"I've just had an interesting discussion with my wife," Raoul said, nearly spitting out the words.

"Raoul, calm down!" Rebekka cast a glance at the rest of the Perrault family, who quickly averted their interested gazes. "I'm sure we can work this out."

"Not this we can't!" Raoul cast a threatening glare at André.

"Just spill it, Raoul." André said crisply. "Your timing couldn't be better. Marc just finished his surgery and we're waiting to see if he's going to live or not."

A look of regret passed over Raoul's face, but was almost immediately lost again to the seething anger. "My wife says *you* made a pass at her last Monday when she came looking for me. Says it happened in your office. What do you have to say for yourself?" Raoul's expression was venomous.

Rebekka grabbed Raoul's arm. "Stop it, Raoul! If you can't discuss this civilly, then leave."

Raoul strained against her grasp. "I'm not going anywhere until I hear what he has to say for himself. And if I'm not convinced, then you'll be glad we're in a hospital because he'll need one!"

"He didn't do it!" Rebekka looked at André, confident that he would explain what had really occurred.

"She did come looking for you on Monday," André answered steadily, "but nothing happened between us. I was leaving right then to eat lunch with Rebekka."

"That's right," Rebekka volunteered, continuing to grip her brother's arm. "I arrived just as Desirée came out of his office. She looked fine to me." Then because he had not asked about Marc's well-being, she added spitefully, "Except she was wearing too much lipstick, and that skimpy white shirt she had on was way too tight for my tastes. She should have worn her leather jacket instead of carrying it."

Her words had an odd effect on Raoul. He was still tense under her grasp, but not fighting to get free. "Leather jacket? You mean a black one?"

"Yes. She was carrying it."

"She took it off while we were talking," André added. His color deepened and for the first time Rebekka wondered what *had* occurred between him and Desirée. Had something actually happened? No, she couldn't believe that of him. More likely, Desirée had been the one . . .

Oh, no . . . Rebekka stared at her brother in dismay.

"I—I wanted her to wear the jacket today," Raoul explained in a lost-sounding voice. "But she said she'd left it in André's office. That he was holding it when she escaped from—"

Rebekka understood then that Desirée had been protecting herself. She must have honestly thought she had left the jacket in

André's office, and then had believed André would use it to convince Raoul of what had really occurred between them.

"She must have left it somewhere else," André said softly, obviously coming to the same conclusion. "Would you tell her that I don't have it, and that I'm sorry if she mistook anything I might have said on Monday?"

"Maybe it was all a misunderstanding." Rebekka gently released her hold on her brother's arm. "Ask her to think about it and see if maybe there was some misinterpretation." *Misinterpretation, my eye,* she thought. *Desirée is nothing but a menace.* Her heart completely went out to her brother.

Without another word to either of them, Raoul turned and walked stiffly to the elevator.

Rebekka looked at André. "It was her, wasn't it?"

He sighed and glanced mournfully in Raoul's direction. "She's young. She doesn't understand . . . she wasn't raised the way we were."

Rebekka shook her head. "Excuses. When you're married, you're faithful. There is no other choice."

"What if there were a choice? What if she were only dating or engaged to him?" André stopped talking, face paling, and Rebekka knew he was no longer talking about Desirée. "Uh, Rebekka," he continued hastily. "I have to leave. Now."

She watched pensively as André fled the waiting room.

* * * * *

When Rebekka was finally allowed to see Marc late in the day, he was in good spirits. "They didn't make me get up this time. I guess I was too weak. But they did help me move my legs and hips a lot. Sort of like walking in bed. Tomorrow they said they'll help me give standing a try."

Rebekka sent up a prayer, thanking her Father in Heaven for the success of the surgery.

So far.

She stayed all night with Marc, fearing that despite how well he looked, he would die if she went away. Occasionally she dozed in her chair, and once she dreamed of André. She awoke shivering slightly, annoyed that the thoughts intruded on even her sleeping hours.

Dr. Juppe arrived the next morning and ordered a battery of tests. Rebekka read aloud to Marc as they waited for the initial results, but her heart thumped so thunderously she wondered if Marc could hear her words. Finally the doctor came in smiling. "I think you two better call the preacher," he announced. "This has every indication of a keeper."

"Yes!" Marc threw his fist triumphantly into the air, and then winced. "You'd think I'd remember by now."

Rebekka laughed and kissed his cheek, blinking away tears of relief.

"Louis-Géralde wants to see you," Dr. Juppe added. "Is it okay if I bring him in here? Says he wants to play chess."

"Sure. I feel great."

Dr. Juppe threw him an amused smile. "Well, you won't later when the nurses get done with you."

"Walking?"

"Yep. Walking."

Marc sighed loudly, but his face was content.

As the doctor left, Rebekka stood. "Look, I'm going home to shower and change." She glanced down at the pink T-shirt that looked even worse than it had the previous evening. "Goodness, this is an awful color. I think I'll just throw it away."

"But it's my favorite shirt! You can't throw it away. You look so adorable in it."

For a moment Rebekka was speechless. How could she have forgotten that he loved this shirt so much? Of course he did. He told her that every time she wore it, which must have been the reason she put it on.

"Okay. I'll keep it."

He gave her a smile that melted the odd feeling growing in her heart. "Thank you. And hurry back after you change. I want to find out what's going to happen next in that book."

"Well, try reading it yourself. You're obviously feeling much better." She winked at him, grateful the words were true.

"And miss hearing your voice? Not a chance. Besides, you'll wonder what happened and I'd have to explain it anyway."

"But I—" She had been going to say that she hated science fiction, but the truth was, she did want to know what happened in that particular book. "See you later then." She gave him a quick kiss on the lips and escaped before he could comment on the brevity.

What was wrong with her? Didn't she love Marc? She felt as if she had asked herself that question a million times. The answer was the same: of course she did—passionately. Then why did she feel so confused?

In the waiting room she found Dr. Juppe talking to Marc's parents, who had just arrived. Instinctively she glanced around for André, but he was nowhere to be seen.

Ariana hugged her. "Isn't this wonderful? Dr. Juppe tells us that Marc is definitely going to survive the surgery and that already his creatinine levels are lower than even a week after the other surgery. Our prayers have been answered!"

Rebekka started to say how grateful she was that everything was going so smoothly, but instead yawned.

"Go home and get some rest, Rebekka," Jean-Marc suggested. "You've been here all night. We'll keep our sons company."

"Yes, go on," Ariana agreed. "Don't worry about them."

"I think I'll do just that."

She left the hospital, but instead of going to her car she walked aimlessly, thinking about her life and trying to make sense of it all. For so long her normal life had been put on hold—her job, her marriage, her family. But it wasn't as if she didn't know where life was taking her. Her future was decided.

Or was it? Why the sudden thoughts that plagued her conscience?

"Rebekka!"

She stopped and searched for the source of the voice, and saw Ariana emerging from the hospital doors. Rebekka waited for her to catch up.

"I thought you were going home," Ariana said, slightly out of breath.

"I guess I needed a walk. I've been cooped up a lot."

"I know what you mean. I'm just on my way to get some fresh pastries from that café down the street. For the boys. And I promised to call André. He wanted to know how Marc was doing."

Rebekka thought she knew why André hadn't come himself. He was avoiding her. She sighed. "He should come to see Marc," she said, choosing her words carefully. "I probably won't be back until after lunch and you and your husband might not want to stay with him that long."

"I'll tell him."

As they walked, Rebekka felt Ariana's gaze acutely, but didn't lift her eyes from the cobblestone sidewalk. She kicked at a loose stone and sent it flying with more force than intended.

"Do you want to talk?" Ariana asked softly.

Rebekka stopped walking and looked up at her with a jerk. "What?"

"You seem rather distracted lately. I've noticed." Ariana put a hand on her arm. "It's about André, isn't it?"

She closed her eyes, willing her emotions to steady themselves. Tears seeped out anyway, as if mocking her control. She took a breath, held it, then slowly let it out and opened her eyes. Ariana was watching her, blurred by Rebekka's tears.

"But how?" Rebekka asked. "I don't understand. I love Marc so much. I think I loved him so long I wouldn't know how to begin not to love him. But . . ."

"You feel something for André."

"We're friends," Rebekka insisted.

"But . . ." Ariana prompted again.

"But every now and then I wonder what would have happened if he hadn't met Claire, and if Marc hadn't come to love me."

At this confession, a tight ball of pain grew around Rebekka's heart. There was Marc, the man of her childhood dreams and the knight of her adulthood—strong, loving, and finally ready to be all hers. She had dreamed about him for nineteen years, had wanted nothing more than to be his bride. Yet suddenly there was André, who was always there for her, his quiet kindness belying the suffering he had endured. The vulnerability in him evoked a tenderness in her heart that she had never expected—and wasn't sure she wanted.

"It can't be," she whispered. "I can't feel this way."

"Why not?" Ariana said, seeming to follow her private thoughts. "You grew up with both of them. They were your friends. It's natural that you would develop feelings for them."

"But it's Marc I've always loved."

"And Marc loved you, although he never understood that until recently. But André was attracted to you too, before he met Claire."

"He never told me at the time."

"Well, perhaps he was a little hung up on how much younger you were. Just like Marc. What was it, seven years between you?"

"Yes, and there's almost ten between Marc and me."

Ariana put an arm around Rebekka. "What I'm saying is that there's a lot of history between the three of you. You just have to sort out what is real." She smiled. "But I know you'll do what is best—for you and for everyone else involved."

Rebekka wanted to deny everything Ariana said, but how could she when it explained the feelings in her heart? And the awful guilt. "What am I going to do?" she asked.

Ariana gave a low laugh. "Marc's getting better now, so I say take your time and be sure about what you want to do."

"I feel so sad for André," Rebekka said. "He's so alone."

"Yes, but he's strong. He's already faced one of the worst things a man can endure. He'll be all right." Ariana prompted Rebekka with a light touch on her back and they resumed walking. "Emotions are such interesting things," she continued. "Especially love. Sometimes it happens when you least expect it. You know, I fell in love with Jean-Marc while he was serving a mission. Oh, we had to keep rules, but I went to a different mission and we were able to write. At the time it seemed like a miracle for me to have such strong feelings for him.

"You see, before I joined the Church, I used to believe there could be only one person you could really love, but now I know that's just not true. I loved my first husband, Jacques, very much. He could have been the man of my dreams, if he had wanted to progress in the same direction. But he didn't. Not then. Perhaps he never would have with me. But I know that he loved me and that under other circumstances, we could have made our relationship work. Like Jean-Marc and I have done. On the other hand, Jean-Marc was ready for an eternal relationship from the first. We had the same goals. We grew together. And I have never once regretted loving him."

Rebekka wiped the tears from her face with both hands. "Are you saying that I should—should—" she stumbled over the words. "—pursue a relationship with André?"

"No, not at all. I'm just saying that the idea of a soul mate simply isn't true—at least for most people. As long as two people love each other and put the Lord first, they can make it work. That's all I'm saying."

Rebekka gazed down the street to avoid the stare of an interested passerby. This was a discussion she would have preferred to have inside somewhere, out of the view of others, but she couldn't help that now. "I'm so confused. I used to be so sure of myself. Of my decisions. But I've learned that I'm not always right—look at my kidney for example. My insistence almost cost Marc his life—may still do so."

Ariana stopped and hugged Rebekka's trembling body. "Oh, Rebekka. Never think that! You did nothing wrong! You sacrificed a great deal for Marc, and we are so thankful."

Rebekka let herself sink into the other woman's arms, grateful for her comfort. "But now I don't know if I can ever trust my feelings again, Ariana. Even the ones I feel for Marc. And how can I even begin to think about André romantically? That would kill Marc, and I might just die too—of guilt. Oh, I just don't know what to do."

"Pray. A lot. It'll come to you." Ariana paused and when she spoke again, Rebekka could hear the smile in her voice, though she didn't meet the older woman's eyes. "Be true to who you know you are, and trust in the knowledge that your Father in Heaven has given you."

Rebekka's gaze flew to the older woman's. "Thank you."

Ariana reached out for her hand. "Rebekka," she said gently, "I don't know why any of this has happened, but I do know the Lord has a reason, one we can't see right now. Just have faith in Him."

"I will . . ." *Try,* she amended silently.

They began to walk again. When they reached the pastry shop with all its delectable smells, Rebekka's stomach grumbled loudly. "I think I'll have one of everything," she mumbled. Ariana laughed. A short time later they emerged, each carrying a flaky pastry. Tucked under her arm, Ariana also had a small box filled with a variety of pastries for Marc and Louis-Géralde.

Ariana walked Rebekka to her car. "Go home and sleep on it, Rebekka. I believe you have the answer inside your heart. Pray for guidance and it will come. Don't worry about getting back for Marc. We'll stay with him and call you if he needs you."

"Thank you." Rebekka popped the last of her warm pastry in her mouth and slid inside her car. As she drove off, she looked in the rearview mirror and saw Ariana looking after her thoughtfully.

CHAPTER 24

"Thierry Lorrain, you say?" Philippe asked, adjusting his grip on his cell phone. He had parked his car and was making his way into the corporate offices of the banks he managed when the phone had beeped.

"That's right. He's supposedly staying with his father, a Basil Lorrain, but the neighbors haven't seen too much of the guy. Apparently, he comes and goes. Sometimes for months at a time. Landlord said—and I quote—'ain't none of my business, so long's the rent's paid.'"

"Hmm, interesting. And how old do you think the kid is?"

"Fifteen tops, I'd say, given the school classes he's taking. Looks older though."

Philippe was only listening with half his mind. The other half hummed, *Lorrain, Lorrain. Where have I heard that name before?*

"Anything else you want me to find out?"

Philippe could tell the private eye was curious about Philippe's connection to the boy, but Philippe had no more information to give the man. Thierry Lorrain was simply a teenager who had stared at him in church.

"No, that'll do. Wait. I know. Find out what the last date was anyone saw the father. And how long until the rent is due again."

"That last I already know. Seems the kid paid it a week ago, so nothing's due for another three weeks."

"I see."

"I'll let you know on the other."

The private eye hung up, and Philippe clicked his own phone shut. Lorrain—where had he heard that name before? He tried to think back if Rebekka had mentioned the boy's last name. No, he distinctly remembered that she hadn't. Thierry was all she had said.

Philippe was sure he had heard the name in connection with someone he knew, but the memory eluded him. He sighed. What was the point? Thierry Lorrain was another neglected child who would resent interference from anyone trying to help. Not that Philippe planned to interfere; he just wanted to know why the boy had stared at him so intently. He felt compelled to discover the reason.

Philippe greeted his secretary as he approached his office. "Two young men are waiting to see you," she informed him. "They said they had an appointment, although I couldn't see it in your book. I put them in the conference room. Is that all right, or should I send them packing? They look like they're selling something."

He smiled. "Actually, they're giving it away. And I do have an appointment with them. Could you please send them into my office?"

When the two young American missionaries were ushered into his spacious office, Philippe met them with a warm handshake. One was tall and somewhat portly, his brown hair atrociously uneven, while the shorter one had a wiry build and sandy hair. "Thank you for coming, Elders." He stifled the urge to laugh at the name. He had always thought it amusing that the male missionaries from the Church used the title of *Elder* instead of their first names. There was certainly nothing elderly about them.

"Thank you for asking," replied the shorter elder in decent French. Philippe peered at his tag; *Elder Ferguson*, it read. The other man's tag said *Elder Pike*.

"We, uh, are rather curious as to the nature of the business you want to conduct," said Elder Pike, his large face clearly showing his trepidation. His face, framed by the uneven brown hair, turned crimson. "I mean . . ." Whatever Elder Pike meant he really wasn't prepared to say. Philippe doubted he would understand anyway, as the elder's nervousness made his American accent a hairbreadth short of atrocious.

"What my companion means," Elder Ferguson said quickly, "is that we've known your wife and children for some time now and they've told us that you weren't interested in our message." He shifted uncomfortably. "So we are naturally curious."

"Of course." Philippe motioned to the plush, black leather sofa and easy chairs that were tastefully arranged in a corner of his office. He went to the bar behind the sofa. "May I offer you a soda?"

"Sure," the elders said simultaneously.

Philippe searched the contents of the bar, glad that his secretary had kept a small variety of nonalcoholic drinks for his wife and the occasional customer who did not drink. He had heard that Jean-Marc Perrault, also the manager of a large banking firm, didn't keep alcoholic beverages in his office, and wondered how he explained the lack to important clients. Did it make a difference in his career? Philippe realized abruptly that he didn't care. The desire to know God had been growing since his first clumsy prayer in that alleyway. Philippe wanted to know once and for all why the anger in him had diminished, and what his family had found with the Mormons. As with this Thierry business, he felt compelled.

He turned to the missionaries, who had seated themselves on the sofa. "I brought you here for the same reason anyone invites you into their homes. I want to hear your missionary lessons. But I don't want you to tell my family or anyone else yet. This has to be between us."

Elder Ferguson dipped his head, and a short, sandy lock of hair fell to the front. "Between us and the Lord," he corrected gently.

"Ah, yes. Him, too." Philippe felt a burst of emotion in his chest at the thought. Did the Lord really care what he was doing?

Of course, a gentle voice whispered in his mind, but Philippe couldn't put a source to it.

"My wife's been a member of your church a long time," he said quickly, settling himself into one of the leather easy chairs, "and I don't want her to get her hopes up. I'm still very skeptical."

"What made you want to hear our discussions?" Once again it was Elder Ferguson who spoke, and his intense hazel eyes seemed to burn a path to Philippe's heart.

"Because my daughter asked me to pray for her." Philippe wanted to explain more, about how it hurt to see his daughter plan for a marriage he couldn't attend; how he and his son had barely exchanged ten words since his elopement; how his beloved wife looked up to him with such faith even though he was an unbeliever who at times barely managed to conceal the rage inside him. But he couldn't tell these personal things to anyone—he hadn't even voiced them to himself. He was relieved when the elders seemed to accept his explanation without question.

"I can see that you love your family very much, Monsieur Massoni," said Elder Ferguson. "That is why the gospel is so important."

Philippe nodded absently, for an idea had suddenly occurred to him. "You're teaching that young boy, Thierry, aren't you?"

Both missionaries looked surprised. "Yes, we are," said Elder Ferguson.

"He's going to be baptized soon," added the tall Elder Pike hesitantly.

"He is?" Philippe made a mental note to suggest a visit to his own barber for Elder Pike. Although it probably wouldn't put a cramp in his ability to carry out missionary work, having the world's worst haircut couldn't be the highlight of this young man's mission.

"Yes. He has prayed about the Church and knows it's true." Elder Ferguson said. Philippe waited for him to elaborate, confident that with a little urging these young boys would tell him what he wanted to know. The other missionaries he had spoken to over the years were always too anxious to tell about the lives of future converts, perhaps believing these soon-to-be members would somehow change Philippe's longtime decision to *not* listen to their discussions.

"Tell me about this boy," Philippe pressed. "How can a child so young know whether a church's teachings are true? For that matter, how do you boys know?"

Elder Ferguson answered both questions with fervency. "Because the Lord told us," he said. There was strength in his voice, a strength Philippe envied. "Age is not what's important," the elder continued, "but the intent, the seriousness of the request is. The Lord will answer prayers."

"Ah." Philippe tried not to be impressed with the elder. But he was. "So you're going to baptize Thierry soon." He was fishing again, hoping the elders would bite.

"That's right." Shy Elder Pike's tongue loosened and he was suddenly anxious to speak. "Except he's only fifteen and he needs his father's permission to be baptized. But he's gone away on business, we think."

Ah, the missing father. "Any idea where he went?"

This time Elder Ferguson answered. "No. We're waiting to hear from him." He fell into silence, seeming to sense that Philippe's interest was unusual.

Philippe wouldn't let it go. "Fifteen is too young to be alone."

He had touched just the right chord, as Elder Ferguson's face plainly betrayed his worry. "Yeah, we're worried."

"What are you doing about it? Maybe I can help."

Elder Ferguson smiled. "I think many people have been wrong about you. You do care about the ward members."

For some reason the words stung, but Philippe ignored them. "I care about my wife and children," he corrected. "I would do anything for them. And since they are members of your church, I know they would be concerned about this boy." He wasn't really stretching the truth. If Danielle knew that Thierry was alone, she and half the women in the ward would be at his apartment right now, smothering him with food and places to live. But it wasn't time for that, not yet. He had to get to the bottom of the mystery first.

"I suspect he's surviving on the one meal he gets at the school and what the neighbors share," Elder Ferguson went on. He took a drink from the glass in his hand. "We try to take him along to our dinner appointment with the members most nights. They don't seem to mind."

"What did you say his last name was?" Philippe was beginning to feel a little guilty at his probing. The missionaries were too young, too gullible, too easy to give their trust. Then he realized that what he thought was gullibility was actually a Christlike innocence. *They are like Danielle.*

"Bernard," Elder Pike answered in his awkward French. "Well, sort of."

"Officially it's Lorrain," said Elder Ferguson. "He thinks of himself as Thierry Bernard because he was raised by a stepfather for most of his life after his mother's death. When the stepdad died, the social workers found his birth father, and he's been living with him for the past year. Poor guy. He hasn't had an easy life."

"Well, he has you now." Philippe hadn't meant for the words to come out sounding as sincere as they did.

Elder Ferguson laughed. "He has the ward family now. That's what he needs—a steady family who's not going to desert him."

Philippe wondered briefly if that steady family was what had attracted his own spouse to the Church. Or could the message it taught actually be true? For the first time in his life he hoped that it was. "Tell you what, Elders, I'll send a few feelers out to see if I can find Thierry's father. Don't tell him—no sense in getting his hopes up. And meanwhile you keep a careful eye on him. If the father doesn't turn up soon, we'll come up with another idea. And before you leave, I'll give you some money to buy him a few groceries and things he might need. No need to tell him it's from me. In fact, I'd rather you didn't."

"You have our word." Elder Ferguson smiled.

Philippe smiled back, finding himself liking this elder more and more. "Thanks. Okay, I'm ready to begin our discussion."

CHAPTER 25

Thursday morning after she had seen Larissa and Brandon off to the middle school they both attended, Marie-Thérèse opened her apartment door to her sister Josette and Josette's three-year-old son, Stephen. "Did you hear?" Josette said excitedly. "Marc is doing great this morning! That means he's going to be just fine as long as he doesn't reject this kidney. And I know he won't do that—I just know it!"

Marie-Thérèse didn't have her sister's confidence, but the successful surgery certainly merited celebration. "Mom called me from the hospital just now. She sounded happy."

"I'm going over to see him in a little while. But I came here first because I wanted you to go with me." Josette shifted her son's weight to her other hip.

"Sure. I'll need to grab some breakfast."

"I can wait."

"Then come on in." Marie-Thérèse took Stephen from her sister's arms. "Boy, you're a heavy kid," she teased. "It's a wonder your mom can carry you with that big belly she's got."

Stephen laughed. "It's a baby and I'm gonna play with him. I'm gonna teach him to kick the ball, put on his shoes, and go pee in the toilet." He grinned proudly.

"Yes, I'm sure you'll be the perfect big brother."

"Yep, 'cause he's little and doesn't know anything yet. Anton says we even gotta teach 'im how to talk."

Josette laughed. "The list of things to teach the baby keeps getting longer. I think it'll be a shock when he sees that it's going to be a long time before the baby will do any of those things."

"Baby?" asked Marie-Thérèse. "Does that mean you still haven't come up with a name?"

Josette followed her into the kitchen where she slumped gratefully to a padded chair. "Well, before I had kids I had a hundred names ready for a girl," she admitted. "But after having four, I'm running kind of low on the boy side."

"Maybe next time."

Josette groaned and laid her face on the table—or tried too. She couldn't reach it over her huge stomach and had to be content with resting her face in her hands. "I don't think there's going to be a next time. I've done my share of multiplying and replenishing the world, don't you think? Five kids, and you'd think I had twenty from the way people count them when we go anywhere."

Marie-Thérèse smiled. "Reminds me of that missionary who baptized Mom. Do you remember when he and his wife visited with all those kids? Eight, wasn't it? They were quite a sight."

"I think the hospital emergency room admitted a lot of people with cranked necks around that time." Josette replied with a giggle. "And remember how we both liked the oldest boy, whatever-his-name-was?"

"I think he has around seven kids now."

"Wow, and me with five." Josette kneaded her stomach. "I'm so tired of being pregnant. It seems like I've spent my whole life being pregnant."

"An awful thought."

A silence fell between, not an uncomfortable one, but one of deep thought. Marie-Thérèse was thinking of the baby that could be hers at that moment if she hadn't postponed her trip to the Ukraine. She also thought of pregnancy—how she wouldn't mind being pregnant like Josette!

"You could go now," Josette said. "Marc's out of danger."

As always, Marie-Thérèse was amazed at how attuned her sister was to her thoughts. She sent up a silent prayer of gratitude. Death had separated her from her biological sister, but she had been blessed with an adoptive sister who was every bit as close as any blood sister could be. She and Josette were the best of friends. Adoption was a wonderful alternative to those in her situation, and she wanted so badly to be able to raise more children. If only the fertility doctors could have found something wrong with her or Mathieu, something they could fix! *No, I won't go down that road again.*

"Well, there's still the wedding," Marie-Thérèse said, becoming aware that her sister expected a reply. "I can't miss that."

"Yes, but it will take weeks for Marc and Rebekka to get things ready again."

"As will rescheduling the adoption. They go by certain dates, not just when people can make it. I have to let them know months in advance."

"Oh, of course." Josette's face drooped. Then she brightened. "Well, then you could at least sign up again."

"Yeah, I guess." The longing inside Marie-Thérèse's heart became biting.

"What about Larissa? Has she come around?"

Marie-Thérèse let out a long sigh and walked over to the refrigerator. "Not in the slightest. Sometimes I wonder where I went wrong with that girl." She pulled out the milk and set it on the counter before continuing. "It's like she and Brandon came out complete opposites. He's so understanding, patient, and considerate, while she's selfish, impatient, and obnoxious. I wish I could put them into a bag and shake them real hard so that they even out a bit."

"Well, I like Brandon just the way he is. Larissa, too. She's just going through an identity crisis kind of thing."

"I hope that's all it is," Marie-Thérèse said. "You know, sometimes it's hard for me to believe that I actually had feelings of bitterness when I found out I was pregnant with Brandon. I mean, he's not perfect—as you can tell by the mess in his room—but he has really turned out to be my salvation these past months."

Josette smiled. "Are you really *that* surprised? Pauline told you he would be okay. And he is."

Marie-Thérèse smiled at the memory. At the time of Pauline's death she had been pregnant with Larissa, and since everyone knew she was expecting a girl, Marie-Thérèse had thought Pauline was confused when she spoke of a little boy being okay. It wasn't until much later that she realized Pauline had been talking about Brandon, not Larissa. Near the end of her short life the veil had been very thin for Pauline.

Marie-Thérèse fished two mugs out of the cupboard, poured milk into them, and set them to heating in the microwave. In three minutes the milk was hot. "You did want milk, didn't you? I forgot to ask."

"Are you kidding? I just about live on milk now." She made a face. "It's the best thing for my stomach. But I swear that after I have this baby, I'll never drink another drop again!"

They laughed together comfortably. Marie-Thérèse sipped her hot milk plain while Josette stirred in chocolate powder. They both ate one of the flaky croissants Marie-Thérèse had purchased early that morning from the corner shop.

They began to talk again, staying away from sensitive subjects like adoption and children's rebellion. Marie-Thérèse cupped her hands around her mug, wishing the warmth of the milk could reach to her heart. Why couldn't she avoid the painful subjects in thought as she could in speech?

After they were finished with breakfast, Marie-Thérèse helped Josette collect Stephen and they walked to the door. Josette touched her shoulder as they waited for the elevator. "I know it's hard now, but Larissa will come around. We'll keep praying."

"Would you talk to Larissa? I mean, I think of everyone in our family, she listens to you the most. She really likes you. And if you could share some of your past experiences with her when you have a chance, and she could see how your choices affected your future . . . Oh, I don't know. I just think it might help."

"I would be happy to talk to her," Josette said. "Heaven knows I had my rebellious days, however much I hate to admit it. And maybe something I say will be useful. But you know, I'm not as worried about her as I am about that poor little girl she hangs out with. Larissa has a pretty wonderful mother to get her through—and a really great father. Not to mention the rest of the family. Together I bet we can help her realize where she's headed before something really goes wrong." Josette reached out a hand to stop the elevator from closing. "Come on, we'd better hurry or Marc will wonder if he still has any sisters. Don't worry, Marie-Thérèse. Everything's going to be fine. You'll get your baby, and Larissa will come around. The Lord has a way of working out problems, and all in His own time. We just need to be patient."

Marie-Thérèse's heart felt considerably lighter as she rode down the elevator with her sister. Josette was right. The Lord had a plan, and now she had to have faith. That was easy, right? She had been living by faith her entire life. While it was true that nothing worthwhile came easily, the Lord had always promised His help. Surely that would make the difference. And when she finally held her new baby in her arms, all the waiting would fade into nothing.

Lifting her head in resolution, Marie-Thérèse pushed her negative thoughts aside and followed Josette into the November sunlight.

CHAPTER 26

After dropping his daughters off at school, André stopped by the transplant hospital to see Marc. At least that's what he told himself he was doing. As he entered the corridor, he saw his mother coming down the hall from the direction of his brother's room.

"Where's Rebekka?" André asked, scanning the area. Ariana smiled at him gently, as though reading his inner thoughts. *But no, she can't know my feelings,* he told himself. *No one must ever know. I am ashamed of them myself.*

"She was tired," Ariana said, pausing as she approached him. "She'd been here all night. We sent her home to sleep. What is it, son?"

André felt like sobbing in his mother's arms and letting her soothe away his pain. But he was a man now, and should be able to handle this alone. "I'm fine, Mom. I'm just worried that something I said earlier might have upset her."

"She was upset. But I think that's because of all the emotions she's been dealing with lately."

He folded his arms over his chest. "What do you mean?"

Ariana placed her hand over his folded arms. "I've been watching you—and Rebekka this past week. And I'm worried about you both."

"There's nothing to be worried about."

"Are you telling me you aren't attracted to her?"

André tried to wave the comment off. "Rebekka's a pretty woman. Who wouldn't think that?" He unfolded his arms and rubbed a hand over his face. "Oh, Mom. I didn't try to—"

"I know."

"I've done nothing to compromise her—I promise."

"Son, walk with me for a while."

André let his mother take his hand and lead him to the exit. They walked down the cement sidewalk of the hospital that soon met up with the older cobblestone walkway running in front of the property.

"André," Ariana began. "I know your life has been difficult, what with losing Claire and all the recent changes in your life. There are some things we're just never ready for." Her dark eyes grew sad. "I think every loss is met with a lot of struggle and emotional highs and lows. And I think you are experiencing that right now."

He snorted. "You can say that again. But, Mom, I—these feelings. Suddenly I'm seeing Rebekka in a new light. And I find that I care for her a great deal. Today I woke up so envious of Marc that I wished I was in his place—even if it meant I'd need a new kidney. Can you believe that?"

They took a few more steps before Ariana spoke again. "Perhaps you need to step back a little before you say or do something you'll regret."

"I don't want to hurt either of them," he said hoarsely.

"Well, then I think this needs to be Rebekka's call. Give her some space. Keep in mind that she's struggling with difficulties just as you are." Ariana paused. "André, don't take this the wrong way: I know it's only natural to want to replace the relationship you had with Claire—"

"Rebekka is not Claire," he snapped.

"That's right. I just want to be sure you know it. You knew and cared for Rebekka long before you met Claire, but that doesn't mean you can pick up those feelings where they left off. Healing takes time."

André let out a sigh. "I need to talk to her."

"Perhaps," Ariana said slowly. "But maybe you should see your brother first."

André didn't think he could do that. He didn't know if he could ever look into Marc's eyes again. What would he say? "Hello, brother. I think I'm falling in love your fiancée?"

"I'm sure he'd like to see you now," Ariana pressed. They were headed back up the walk to the hospital now.

André shook his head, backing away from his mother. "No. I have to see her first."

"André, no! I can't pretend to know how this will end up, but no matter what happens, you're going to lose her or Marc—at least for a time."

André didn't listen. His heart ached for the comfort only a woman he truly loved could give. And she was gone.

* * * * *

Rebekka awoke from a restless sleep. She had come to Marc's apartment rather than to her parents because she had wanted to be alone to think and to pray. She felt guilty coming here, though, since after today she might no longer be Marc's fiancée. She wanted more than anything to marry Marc, but how could she unless she resolved these feelings for André?

Rivers of uncertainty carved through her heart. *Why, oh, why did this happen? Why am I even contemplating a relationship with André?*

She tried to tell herself that André certainly didn't feel anything for her, but she had seen the truth in his eyes. Moreover, he had understood that the choice was hers even before she had.

She put the pillow over her head. The cloth smelled fresh since she had changed the case yesterday and hadn't slept on it last night, and she longed for Marc's familiar smell.

A noise barely penetrated through the down filling in the pillow. She couldn't even tell what it was or from where it had come. The door?

She sprang to her feet and ran down the hallway, her heart racing unevenly. Everyone who knew Marc also knew he was in the transplant hospital. So the only people who would ring the bell were salesmen, missionaries from another church, or someone looking for Rebekka.

Possibly André.

She hoped it was him . . . and feared that it was.

Hands pressed against the door for support, she peered through the peep hole. Though distorted by the thick, reducing glass, she saw it *was* André. Quickly, she ducked out of sight, overwhelmed by the flood of mixed emotions.

"Rebekka, are you there?" he called, voice muffled by the barrier between them.

She put her hand on the door, but something—what?—cautioned her against opening it. Why shouldn't she talk to him? It might clear things up—wasn't that what she needed more than anything?

Tempted by the thought, her hand stretched to the doorknob, but she pulled it back before it reached the metal. *Oh, Marc, I don't know what to do!*

"Rebekka, I've just come from talking to my mom. I tried to call your house, but they said you were here. Come on, let's talk."

Had he seen her? Or a movement? Her heart thudded violently in her chest. She pressed her hands against the door in an attempt to push away an invisible danger.

Then abruptly, he was gone. She hadn't heard him leave, but she knew that he was no longer behind the door. A gasp escaped her lips and she realized she'd been holding her breath. As she drank in air, relief of another kind also flooded her body. There was no reason she shouldn't have opened the door to talk with André, and yet for some reason *not* letting him in had been the right thing to do.

But why?

She ran to the window and peered down in the street, hoping to catch a glimpse of him. The street below was empty.

* * * * *

André left Marc's apartment building more than a little disgruntled. Was Rebekka there? He thought he had sensed her presence behind the door, but why hadn't she opened it? Was it because she wanted him to stay away from her? Or was it because she was afraid to look him in the eye, afraid that maybe she would see the same feelings that were in her heart?

Logically, he knew he was vulnerable because of Claire's recent death, and the same logic dictated that he shouldn't even think of Rebekka in this way. But how could he tell these things to his heart? These past few hours of hope contrasted so completely with the devastation of losing Claire. He needed Rebekka. And so did his girls.

So did Marc.

Why hadn't Rebekka opened the door? Possible answers swarmed in his mind until he thought he would go insane.

He drove aimlessly about Paris, knowing that he was no good for work. Things would run smoothly enough with Raoul at the helm. If not, his secretary would call or page him on his cell phone.

Marc would have a key, he thought. Maybe he should force Rebekka to talk to him. He wouldn't try to persuade her or make any foolish declarations, as Ariana had warned him. All he wanted to do was clear up the confusion of feelings. He had no intention of betraying his brother.

But aren't you betraying him even now?

The pain inside his heart was almost unbearable. *Dear God,* he prayed. *Please help me know what to do. I love my brother so much. And I am so lonely.*

Without realizing it he had arrived at the transplant hospital, presumably to get a key from Marc. *Why did my mother want me to see Marc before Rebekka?* The thought was unexpected but not really surprising. But he certainly couldn't tell Marc how he was feeling—he would never do that. If anything was done, it would be up to Rebekka.

He walked in the door, rode up the elevator, and was outside his brother's door before another traitorous thought entered his heart. *If Marc died, Rebekka would be free.* Immediately, he felt repulsed. What kind of a man was he to wish for the death of his own brother?

I don't want him to die. I don't! I love him.

He needed all his strength to open Marc's door. Inside, his brother lay on the bed as though he were waiting for something, looking more fragile and unprotected than André had ever seen him. André faltered, the words he had formulated in his mind dying on his lips.

"How're you doing?" he asked instead.

Marc gave a low chuckle that held a refreshing mirth. "I'm going to live, André." Tears gathered in his eyes. "You were right, I'd given up. I was sure I was going to die and leave Rebekka. I know you're not going to believe this, but you're the only reason I fought. Your faith. Well, that and Rebekka's love."

"I'm glad." André's throat had gone so dry he could barely utter the words. "I knew it was up to you."

"I have the two best brothers a man could ask for," Marc continued, "and soon I will marry the only woman I will ever love."

André couldn't reply, and was thankful Marc didn't seem to notice his silence.

"So, since I'll be out of here in a week or so," Marc's said with determination, "I was wondering if you would have my office at home fixed up for me. You know, files I need to look at and such. The doc won't let me go back to work for at least four weeks after the surgery, but he did say that I could peruse a few files at home. No on-site stuff, and I have to promise not to work longer than an hour the first week out, two the next, and so on." He smiled and fished in the drawer of the nightstand next to the bed, straining with the effort. "Here's a key." He tossed it to Marc. "Rebekka has one, of course, but she might not be there."

André stared at the key. *If he only knew what he has just given me.* With deliberation, he put it in his pocket. He felt like a thief.

"So you'll do it?"

"Sure."

"I'd appreciate it if you wouldn't make too big a deal about it to Rebekka or Mom. You know how they are."

Numbly, André nodded. *Why did you ask me to take care of her?* He wanted to ask. *Don't you know what you started?*

After a few more words of detached encouragement, he left Marc and turned back the way he had come, tears burning under his eyelids.

He reflected on everything that had transpired in the past months, and on Rebekka and Marc, the two people on earth that he loved more than any others save his small daughters. Why had he been trapped in such a position when he was so in need of comfort?

One thing was sure: he needed guidance. Not the earthly kind, but the kind he could receive only from his Heavenly Father. And a little perspective wouldn't hurt either. He knew he should go home and kneel to ask properly. He also knew he should forget he had the key altogether. Maybe toss it out onto the street where some little child could find it and keep it for his collection of odd and ends. But throwing this opportunity away seemed like discarding all chances with Rebekka, and he couldn't do that. Never.

Never?

Still, he prayed as he drove, and when he arrived at Marc's apartment, he bowed his head and prayed harder. *I just want to look into her eyes,* he promised the Lord. *That's all. I have to know how she feels about me.*

* * * * *

Rebekka heard the bell again as she was combing her hair in preparation to visit Marc. Her body jerked when she heard someone enter the apartment. Pulse thumping with fear, she crept from the bathroom to the hall and down to the entryway, wielding her brush as a weapon.

"André!" she exclaimed, the fear changing to something quite different, something to which she was reluctant to give voice. "You scared me!"

"Sorry." He smiled, but it was a tense smile that didn't reach his eyes. He stared at the key in his hand for a long moment before pocketing it. Without looking behind him, he gently kicked the apartment door shut.

He nodded toward the kitchen, indicating for her to follow. "We need to talk," he said.

"Okay." Her voice was unsteady and he glanced at her quickly. He sat at the small table and indicated the seat across from him.

Rebekka took the chair, relieved at the physical distance.

"You were here when I came earlier, weren't you?" His voice held a rough edge she had never heard before.

She traced a pattern in the marble tabletop, not looking at him. "Yes," she admitted softly.

"Why didn't you let me in?"

She was silent a long time and then, "Because I was afraid."

"I would never hurt you."

Rebekka ignored the slightly wounded tone. "I wasn't afraid of you."

"Then who?"

Still she didn't look at him. She could feel his gaze—hurt and inquisitive—and struggled to gather her thoughts.

"Tell me . . . please."

I was afraid that you would take me in your arms and ask me to leave Marc, she thought. But aloud, she said, "It was nothing." Tears pooled in her eyes.

André glanced at the ring on her left hand. "You were right to not open the door, Rebekka," he said quietly, firmly. "I hadn't thought things out before I came to see you. Or prayed. I've done both now."

The tears continued to gather in her eyes, as did the confusion in her heart.

André proceeded in a low voice. "Rebekka, I know you love Marc. I love him too. And I don't know what's going to come of all this. All I know is that I'm confused, I'm lonely, and I miss Claire so much. I don't want to hurt you or Marc—ever."

His sincerity made her want to weep. "I know."

"I may be a little presumptuous in thinking that if things had worked out differently in the past, then maybe you and I . . ." He stopped, as though he had stepped too close to an invisible line.

"You are not presumptuous," she answered in a small voice. The pool in her eyes spilled over.

He made a sound in his throat. "I wish I could take away your tears. I never wanted to hurt you. I'm sorry." He stood abruptly. "Go see Marc, Rebekka. I'll be around."

She followed him to the door, trembling inside. His message was clear. He would not do anything to come between her and Marc. Any decision was up to her. Once her path had been so clear, but now she couldn't help wondering what might happen if she didn't marry Marc, if several months down the road she began to date André. Could they be happy together?

But what about Marc? She loved him—how could she even consider not marrying him after all the years of waiting?

But I can't marry him if I'm not sure, she thought. *I can't do that to him, either.*

She had her doubts about André as well. He was an honest man, but what if he was only trying to find Claire again, or the family life he had shared with her? It was too soon after Claire's death to know if anything he felt now was real. Or was it? One thing she was sure of: a relationship with André would mean more waiting. And there was always Marc.

Only after opening the apartment door did André turn to look at her. "This is a fine mess we've gotten ourselves into." He leaned over without warning and gave her a brief, affectionate hug that reminded her of simpler times. Rebekka blinked to see through her tears.

André turned away. He didn't wait for the elevator, but took the stairs two at a time. She watched after him until she could no longer hear his footsteps. Then she went back inside and shut the door.

CHAPTER 27

Larissa lounged against a wall at the far end of the main school hall, watching her best friend Jolie flirt with Neven and Serge, two boys from their grade. Since their location was partially hidden by the stairs leading to the second floor, it was a good place to ditch math class. Jolie leaned back so that her belly-button ring was in full view. The boys laughed and tugged at their own earrings, clearly visible with their ultrashort hair, bleached to a white-blonde.

"You got one?" Neven asked Larissa. Of the two, he was the most talkative and the most handsome.

"Just in my ears." Larissa wanted to tell them that she thought making holes in belly buttons was stupid, but how could she when Jolie was so proud of hers? And she certainly couldn't admit that if she came home with a belly ring her parents would flip. She wrinkled her nose in thought. Jolie's green hair was another matter. Maybe her parents would allow something like that. Only she would prefer blue for herself.

"Larissa's a Mormon," said Jolie, her brown eyes glinting in the weak sunlight coming from the large window opposite them. "They don't do things like that."

"Really?" asked Neven, raising an eyebrow. His dark eyes and olive skin contrasted sharply with his white hair.

Way cute, thought Larissa. *Even though I'm taller than he is.*

"Don't worry, she's not a weird Mormon, or anything," Jolie assured them. She pushed off the wall and slung an arm around Larissa. "She's not really one of them. She's cool."

The boys laughed, and so did Larissa, though she didn't think it was very funny. Jolie was her best friend, but she could say some hurtful things.

Why do I care? thought Larissa. *She's only telling the truth. I don't belong. Not in my family or anywhere.*

The bell rang and Jolie let her arm drop from Larissa's shoulder. "Finally the lunch bell. I'm starved."

"Hey, Larissa!"

She looked up the stairs to see who was calling her name. "Oh, it's my little brother," she grumbled, stressing the *little*. "He's a pest, but I'd better talk to him. Wait a minute, would you?"

"Sure." Jolie leaned back again, one foot bracing her body against the wall

Larissa met Brandon as he reached the foot of the stairs. "Did you ditch math?" he asked. "You're not usually out before me."

"Shush." She pulled him across the hall by the windows, wishing he was back at the grade school. But no, he had skipped an entire year and now seemed to have nothing in the world to do but check up on her. "You'd better not tell."

"They'll find out anyway," he said, his light brown eyes serious. "I don't know why you bother ditching. I thought you were good at math, like Mom."

"I'm not like Mom," she snapped, "and I don't like math."

"So you're like *them*?" He glanced at Jolie and the boys, now separated from them by a thick stream of students coming down the stairs from their classes.

"Why not? They're my friends."

"Friends?" he snorted. "They're brainless is what. Brainless clones. All dressed up with earrings and funny hair. You can't tell one from another. Look at them."

In spite of herself, Larissa glanced over and sure enough, the two boys were almost indistinguishable at this distance. Even Jolie, chatting in the hallway with several other girls who had gathered, could have been almost any member of their crowd.

"So?" she demanded. "What's wrong with that? They're nice to me and I like them. You're just like Mom and Dad. You act like they're not good enough for you. Is that what they teach us in church? Funny, I must have missed that lesson. I thought the Savior told us to love everyone."

Brandon's eyes grew troubled. "Oh, Larissa, that's not what I meant. Honestly. And it's not just that you're friends with them, it's that they're your *only* friends. You don't hang out with anyone else, anyone who knows what's right anyway. That's what makes our parents crazy."

She didn't want to listen. "Look, pest, my friends accept me for who I am. Got it? No one else does. Not at church or anywhere."

"I just think you're being stupid about this."

"So? I think you're stupid all the time."

He looked hurt. Staring at the ground and biting his lip, he muttered, "I just wanted to help. Excuse me for caring."

Larissa knew he would tell her parents about her skipping math class because he believed it was the right thing to do. And she knew she would get in trouble. She would be reprimanded, and snotty little Brandon would be praised. The pressure inside her built until she couldn't stand it anymore. "Go ahead and tell. I don't care," she said in a vicious whisper. "And they don't care, either. Not about me or about you."

He looked at her with wide eyes that said, "What are you talking about?"

"They didn't want you, you know." The words tumbled out of her mouth without her bidding. "When Mom found out she was pregnant with you, she cried. You think you're so special, but they didn't even want you! And now the only reason they're nice to you is because they feel guilty."

"It's not true!" He shook his head, tears forming in his eyes. "Mom and Dad love us both! But you, you don't love anyone. Why do you have to be so mean?" With that he lurched away into the crowd. Larissa stared after him, feeling suddenly lost. How could she be so mad at him one moment and then sad for him the next?

Jolie and the others came to where she stood, sweeping her along with them as they walked. "Hey, is it true Mormons have a lot of kids?" asked Neven. "I heard they always have a dozen or so."

"There's just my brother and me in my family."

Jolie nudged her. "For now anyway. You poor thing."

Larissa was relieved when the others didn't respond. Talking about the impending adoption was not something she could bear today. She let herself be carried by the crowd toward the lunchroom. "Hey, isn't that your name, Larissa?" asked Neven. "I think they're calling you over the intercom." Larissa listened hard, barely catching the request to go to the office.

She stopped walking, trying not to show her trepidation. Surely her parents couldn't have found out about her missing class so soon. "I'll catch up with you later," she called. Jolie waved and turned the corner to the lunchroom.

As Larissa walked into the school office, Aunt Josette rose from a chair and came to meet her. "Oh good. You heard the page. I was afraid you wouldn't over the noise. I meant to come earlier, but I was late dropping Stephen off at Grandma's."

Larissa looked at her blankly. "Why are you here? I mean, it's good to see you and all, but I was just on my way to lunch." Seeing her aunt reminded her of what she had said to Brandon. If her parents found out, she'd likely be grounded until she was married.

Josette smoothed the material of her dark blue suit over her large stomach. Larissa noticed how beautiful her aunt looked, despite the mound she carried around her middle. Her hair was long and thick and shiny, and her facial features perfectly formed and unblemished. Larissa wished she could look like that, but compared to her poised, beautiful aunt she was a thin, gangly nothing.

"Actually, I've come to take you out to lunch," Aunt Josette said. "I've been meaning to for a while. Things have been pretty crazy around here lately, and I've missed talking with you. But now that Marc's feeling better—he should be out of the hospital in a few days— I thought I'd come in and surprise you. You don't mind, do you?"

Larissa shook her head, but she wondered if her aunt had been sent by her mother, and a resentment began smoldering in her heart. Whatever they had planned wouldn't work. She wouldn't be happy about a new baby, and she wouldn't stop seeing Jolie. That was that.

She followed her aunt as they left the office. Before going to the car, they stopped at Larissa's locker for her coat. She felt a little self-conscious walking through the halls with a pregnant lady, but no one seemed to give them more than a passing glance. Aunt Josette smiled and nodded to the students, acting as though she knew them personally. Larissa wished she could feel so relaxed among her classmates.

Instead of a regular restaurant, Aunt Josette drove to a pastry shop. Larissa grinned. "Yeah!" she exclaimed.

Aunt Josette laughed. "I know. I'm terrible. I would never come here for lunch if I had my kids with me. I'd have to be responsible. But you are my niece and I can spoil you as much as I like. So order anything you want."

They giggled together and Larissa felt the past months peel away. She was like a small child again—one who had worshiped her aunt and had lived for the time they spent alone.

They each ordered several pastries and then settled around a small table. As they ate, nothing about her parents or the baby came up, and Larissa began to relax.

"Aunt Josette," she asked, thinking back to her conversation with Brandon. "What kind of friends did you have when you were young?"

Aunt Josette's smiled wavered. "Oh, honey, I knew you'd ask me that some day, but I'm not sure I want to answer."

"Why?"

"I made some huge mistakes." She smiled grimly. "But then again, if you really want to know, maybe I should tell you."

Larissa stuffed the last bite of her second pastry into her mouth. "I do."

"Well, I wasn't anything like I am now. I was young and pretty—"

"You still are!"

Aunt Josette reached over and squeezed her hand. "Thank you. But I was much prettier then. I had even longer hair, and best of all, I had a really good figure." She patted her stomach and they both laughed. "But all I really cared about was having fun, you know? My mother would talk about the choices I was making, and I'd just tune her out. What did I care about eternity? That was so far off."

Larissa felt that way a lot. Sometimes she thought her parents were so busy living for tomorrow that they forgot all about the present. They certainly couldn't remember what it was like to be young.

"My mother also taught me that I had the right to demand respect from boys. But I didn't understand that either. I liked to live fast and dangerously. I stayed out late, dated people I shouldn't, and wore clothes that were way too immodest. I thought I was invulnerable to everything. All my mother's warnings meant nothing."

Larissa put her hands under the table and pulled down the hem of her skirt a bit. Her mother had told her it was too short, but she had sneaked it out of the house today under her long coat. "What happened?"

"I went to college in America. BYU, actually. My parents practically forced me to go. There I continued to have my fun. It was the only important thing in the world. Then I met a guy who was fast and dangerous and good-looking. He had a lot of money, and treated me well—until one night when we were alone." She sighed and her forehead wrinkled. "And then he tried to rape me. Said I owed him. He beat me up pretty badly, but luckily your mom and dad had been looking for me that night. They found me just in time and called the police."

Larissa felt an ugly pit form in her stomach. How could someone have done such a thing to her beautiful aunt? "But he was just one guy."

"Yeah, but he was the type I went out with. Not all of them would have done what he did, but none could have taken me to the temple like Zack. None of them treated me like a princess."

Larissa shrugged. "I'm not really into guys anyway." She thought of Neven and blushed.

"Well, I guess I wanted to tell you this so that you'd understand that I barely escaped. And the worst part was that it all happened because I made a lot of bad choices. I had my priorities all wrong, and everyone could see it but me."

Now Larissa knew where this was going. "You think the same thing about me, don't you? That I'm making bad choices."

Her aunt shook her head. "Honey, I don't know. I just see that you're miserable and your mother is worried."

"It's because she wants a baby."

"And you don't."

Larissa looked away from the compassion in her aunt's eyes. "No. I don't. She just wants another perfect little Brandon." *I'm not good enough.* Tears began in her eyes and she hoped her aunt couldn't see.

"Your mother loves you."

Staring at her hands in her lap, Larissa said, "What if I didn't believe? What if I think the Church and its rules are stupid."

"Then I'd say it was time for you to do some soul-searching. It's not going to be easy, but it must be done." Aunt Josette paused for a moment and then added, "Larissa, I just want you to do one thing for me. I want you to remember that I know the Church is true, and that you can lean on my testimony until you develop your own."

Larissa shrugged and stood, still avoiding her aunt's stare. "I'd better get back to school now. Thanks for lunch."

As they walked to the car, Aunt Josette put her arm around Larissa. "I love you," she said. "Remember that, too."

Then you're the only one, thought Larissa.

Aunt Josette let her off in front of the school. For a long time Larissa stared after her, thinking about everything she had said. She felt on the verge of understanding something very important, but it flitted away when she heard a loud whistle behind her.

"Hey, where ya been?" Jolie called. "We've been looking for you all over."

Larissa glanced once more in the direction of her aunt's car, and then went to join her friends.

CHAPTER 28

On a Friday, ten days after his transplant, Marc left the hospital. Though his parents had wanted him to stay at their place, he had insisted upon returning to his own apartment. Rebekka picked him up, looking more beautiful than ever. He marveled at his good fortune. Health and Rebekka—what more could he possibly want?

"I can't stay long," Rebekka said as she carried his small suitcase into his apartment. He reached to help her, but she playfully slapped his hand away. "No lifting for you for at least another five weeks," she reminded him. "Besides, it's not heavy."

"Why can't you stay?" Marc followed her to the bedroom where she opened the suitcase and began removing the contents. He studied the room, drinking in the furnishings—bed, dresser with mirror, armoire, bedside table, pictures and wall hangings, and a small new television set and stand next to the French doors leading to his bedroom balcony. Everything besides the TV looked familiar but strangely new. He had expected some of Rebekka's things to be mixed in with his in preparation for their marriage, but saw nothing that hinted of her presence. He glanced at her and found her staring out the window.

"Rebekka?"

She started, her gaze coming back into focus. "I'm sorry, did you say something?"

"Why aren't you staying?"

"I have to do the translation for Damon and Jesse. I'm supposed to have it done by Monday." For the past week, Rebekka had been working again for Hospital's Choice, Inc., the company she had been employed with in Utah. Marc had understood her decision to continue working, though he had missed her presence in the hospital. *She's not avoiding me,* he had told himself repeatedly in his boredom. He had tried to focus on his books, but there were only so many novels a person could read without a break.

Rebekka returned to the kitchen. He followed her, feeling the ache where his clothes chafed at the light bandage covering his incision. The kidney itself worked wonderfully, but the aching and itching of the healing wound sometimes drove him to distraction.

"I bought you a new plant," she said, pointing to the windowsill. "See? So you won't be lonely."

"Did André bring some stuff over from my office?" He regretted the words once he'd said them.

Rebekka paled. "He better not have! I bought you a ton of books and movies. You're supposed to take it easy." She clenched her fists and glared at him.

Marc laughed, gathering her rigid body into his arms. "Don't be mad. I will read and watch every one, I promise." He scattered little kisses over her left cheek and ear until her smile reappeared and her body relaxed.

"Now," he said, releasing her. "What about our wedding?"

Rebekka backed away, her face even more pale than before.

"What's wrong?" he asked with a sense of dread. All at once, he realized that he and Rebekka hadn't talked about marriage for over a week. Why was that?

"Nothing's wrong. I—you're too weak."

He took a step toward her. "I'm fine, and I can prove it." He took her hands in his, pulling her close for a tender kiss. Rebekka responded with equal emotion, but after a while jerked away, her eyes half-closed, masking her inner feelings.

"Rebekka, tell me what's wrong. I know you're upset about something."

Her eyes looked panicked as she glanced around the room. "Marc, I really have to go."

"But it's Saturday. No one works on Saturday."

"You always did," she said with a wry grimace. "Don't worry, we'll talk about this later."

He released her. "Okay."

She gave him an unsatisfactory kiss on the cheek and flitted out the door.

Marc slumped into a kitchen chair and shook his head in frustration. He knew Rebekka well enough to know that something wasn't right. When had it started? A week ago?

Yes, he had first noticed her strange behavior a week ago, when she had gone back to work for the American company, Hospital's Choice, Inc. Marc frowned. He knew that Samuel What's-His-Name from Cincinnati was still connected to the overseas marketing of the company. He had been in love with Rebekka when she had been in America, and she had been attracted to him as well. Had Samuel come back into the picture? Did Rebekka still have feelings for him?

The thought disturbed him more than he was willing to admit. He and Rebekka had finally come together—he couldn't bear to lose her now. The nagging pain in his side from his wound diminished with the possibility of losing Rebekka.

How could he find out?

And what if she actually loved the other guy?

I would have to let her go.

The thought was ridiculous. He was allowing his imagination to run away with him. He and Rebekka were in love and would be married. Her lack of enthusiasm stemmed from worry over her job. She was simply anxious to finish, much like he himself itched to get back into things at his company.

Work. The word came like an invitation to his mind, and he arose and walked purposefully down the hall. In his home office, he immediately saw that André was as good as his word. Piles of papers and reports had been laid out on the desk in order of importance.

Marc spent the next hour familiarizing himself with the happenings of the firm since his collapse near the river. He was happy to see that André and Raoul had kept everything under control, though there would be plenty to keep them all busy in the upcoming months—including several new construction projects they had bid on and won.

After only an hour he was thoroughly exhausted. Remembering his promise to both Rebekka and the doctor, he left his office, went to his bedroom, and popped in a video. Before the credits were over, he was asleep.

* * * * *

Rebekka knew she should tell Marc that she was having doubts about their relationship, but every time her mouth opened to do so, her love for him sealed her utterance. How could she hurt him when she wanted to marry him?

The problem was that André inspired similar feelings in her heart, and despite the long prayers she sent up to the Lord, she couldn't find direction. She felt that her Heavenly Father considered both men worthy companions and that she would have to decide what to do on her own.

Well, duh . . .

Rebekka felt like an idiot. How did she come to be in this situation? She felt so guilty and dishonest that she found it difficult to look Marc in the eye.

Paralyzed by indecision and a dreadful fear of making the wrong choice—not to mention hurting those she loved—Rebekka threw herself into her freelance work for Hospital's Choice, Inc., to avoid thinking about the problem. She didn't lie about having deadlines, but no one knew they were self-imposed, since Damon and Jesse weren't aware of the time and effort involved in translating English to French. They trusted her to be fair with both her time frame and her billing.

Well, she was honest in the billing, but the time frame was drastically underestimated, which was why she wasn't going to make it on time. *It's all the medical terms I'm having to research,* she thought. She was working on translating the manuals for the hospital software the company had written, and had told them the first fourth of the largest manual would be finished by Monday. *Not a chance.*

The software was successful in over three dozen American hospitals, with more becoming interested in it every day. With their affiliate company, Corban International, Hospital's Choice planned to market the same program in Europe the following year. That was where she came in. Many terms would be left in the universal English, but much more needed translating. It was hard, grueling work, even with the helpful translation software, and every minute Rebekka (who had always considered herself fluent in both languages) found more words she didn't know—in French as well as English. Already she had placed ten phone calls to a member of the ward who was training to be a doctor. After the fifth time she offered him a consulting wage, dependent upon approval from America.

Now at her parents' apartment, she worked for as long as she could in Raoul's old room—recently converted into her office—until she was almost in tears. Then she gave a quick call to Damon Wolfe. "I just can't do it by Monday," she told him bluntly in English.

"Take a few more days."

"I'll need at least two weeks to do a perfect job, maybe three. And then two or three months for the rest of the manual."

"That's fine, Bekka." He was silent for a minute. "Look, quite frankly, I figured you didn't give yourself enough time, so I'm not surprised at the delay. Translating is even more work than actually writing a manual from what I hear. But I do know you're the best one for the job, and I'd much rather you take a little more time to ensure it's done well. And I want to know all the hours you work. Every single one."

"I will. But don't be surprised at the bill," she said, mentally calculating that she had already worked eighty hours in one week.

He gave a low laugh. "Bekka, I've got more money than I know what to do with. I might as well give it to someone who actually works as hard as I do."

"I don't know about that."

"I do. I've seen you. Who else would give herself five weeks to translate an entire manual that took us a year to write?" There was another long pause, and then he said quietly, "Bekka, are you all right? Your fiancé hasn't had a relapse, has he?"

"No," she replied, her voice quavering. "Everything's fine."

"I don't believe you. Look, take some time off, starting right now. Go see Marc, or do whatever and don't even think about translating another word until Monday. Got it? This is Saturday, for crying out loud. Take a break."

The relief Rebekka felt was so great she almost couldn't speak. "Okay. I will."

She had no sooner hung up the phone than it rang again. Warily, Rebekka picked it up. Was it André? Marc? The tension flooded back into her body.

"Hello, Rebekka?" a female voice said. "This is Josette. Look, we thought we'd arrange a quick get-together tonight to celebrate Marc's recovery. Think he can make it?"

"I'm not sure. He's not here."

"That's odd. I called his apartment and there's no answer. I figured you two would be together."

Rebekka's heart started beating erratically, and her breath caught in her throat. "I had to work," she said. "But he's probably asleep. Or maybe he went somewhere. Why don't I just run over there and check?"

"Okay. I'll keep calling the others." Josette's voice plainly showed her worry. "Everything's probably just fine, but I'm so emotional when I'm pregnant. If anything happens to Marc after all this, I'll kill him!" Sniffing loudly, she bid good-bye.

Rebekka ran out of her office and nearly collided with her mother in the hall. "Sorry, Mom," she said.

"Have you seen your father?"

"Not since this morning."

Danielle looked puzzled. "He said he had to meet with someone this afternoon, but he hasn't gotten back. We were supposed to go shopping and then out to eat."

"He's just been delayed again." Rebekka smiled apologetically. "Look, Mom, I have to run. I'm worried about Marc."

Her mother didn't answer, but had already gone through the kitchen to the balcony. Rebekka grabbed her coat and ran out the door. Down in the underground parking lot, she quickly started her car. She often walked the three blocks to Marc's, but now she was in a hurry.

Half a block from her house, she saw a strange sight. Her father was parked on the side of the street, and two missionaries were emerging from his car. Rebekka quickly parked in the open place behind him and bounced out of her car. "Dad," she said, tapping on his window.

He looked over at her, surprised, and then at the missionaries' backs. He rolled down the window. "Hi, honey. What are you doing?"

"I might ask you the same thing. You're late and Mom's worried."

His face became contrite. "I should have called."

Rebekka took a step toward her vehicle, but curiosity overcame her. "What on earth were you doing with the missionaries?" She remembered vividly the day he had prayed with her. Had he finally seen the light? He had attended church twice in a row, and her mother had high hopes that he would be going tomorrow as well. Rebekka had wanted to talk with him about the Church, but she had been too wrapped up in her own problems.

"They needed a ride," he said blithely. "They had a meeting planned with someone in that building over there."

"Oh." Her hopes were dashed. Still, the odd coincidence merited more investigation. "Well, how did you run into them?"

"What is this, the Inquisition? I called them. I wanted to talk to them about that young boy in your ward. There's something about him."

Rebekka was disappointed, but she tried not to show it. "Well, Mom's waiting for you, and I need to go."

She kissed her father's cheeks before returning to her car. Once inside, she pulled into the street and hit the gas, the passing buildings becoming a haze in her hurry to get to Marc.

I shouldn't have stopped to talk to Father, she berated herself. And what had she been thinking to leave Marc alone on his first day out of the hospital? What if he had started bleeding internally or had some delayed side effect from the surgery? She would never forgive herself.

CHAPTER 29

"Marc! Marc!" Rebekka called as she let herself in the apartment. When there was no answer, her voice became panicked. "Marc!" His car had still been in the underground lot when she had parked in his extra space, and now she spied his keys on the wall table near the coat rack, which still held his coat. *So where is he?*

She sprinted down the hall, stopping briefly at the open door to his office, where papers lay scattered over the desk. A burst of anger at André flooded her body. *How dare he give him work when he needs rest!*

Almost frantically, she ran to Marc's bedroom. He was there lying on the bed in unnatural stillness. "Marc." Her voice was now agonized. What had happened to him? *It's all my fault!*

Then there was a movement on the bed and his eyes fluttered open. "Rebekka?" he said. "Thank heavens! I thought I had an intruder. I was lying here wondering how I was going to fight them off." He struggled to a sitting position and reached for her. Rebekka came into his arms, trembling.

"What's wrong? You look like you've had a scare."

She buried her face in his neck. "I thought I'd lost you." In a rush she told of Josette's phone call and her fear of finding him dead. He held her until she quit shaking, then kissed her tenderly.

"I'm so sorry," he whispered in her ear, sending a delicious shiver down her spine. "But will you forgive me if I say that I'm glad you came? I missed you."

"I missed you too."

"Can I get you something to eat?" he asked. "I'm starved, and you look like you could use something. You've lost weight these past months."

"I'm not hungry. And besides, I'm sure there'll be plenty to eat at your parents' tonight. Oh, that reminds me, I'd better call Josette. She was worried."

"She does that a lot when she's pregnant," he said with a laugh. "Remember how the last time she called me to go find Zack when she couldn't get him on his cell phone? She was sure he'd been hurt while showing real estate or whatever he was doing that day."

Rebekka smiled in remembrance. "I think she was about due—just like this time."

They laughed as she dialed Josette's number. After Rebekka assured Josette they would be at the celebration, she and Marc put in a video and settled down to watch it.

"What about your work?" Marc asked during the opening credits. He twirled the engagement ring he had given her around her finger, watching the five diamonds catch the light.

She shrugged. "It can wait."

For an hour and a half, all was right with the world. She and Marc were together and her contrasting feelings relegated to a remote corner of her mind. This was how their love was meant to be.

All too soon, it was time to go to Marc's parents' apartment for the celebration. "Why don't you pack a few things and stay with them tonight?" Rebekka asked.

He snorted. "What for? I feel great."

"Please." Rebekka remembered her earlier fear, and knew she wouldn't sleep at all if he was here alone. "I'm worried about you."

Seeing her determination, he yielded without further argument. "But only until Monday," he warned.

They took her car to his parents, and it was only as they rode up the five flights in the elevator that she realized the inevitability of seeing André. Of course he would be invited, and given the insistence and curiosity of his expectant sister, it was doubtful he would refuse.

Marc's mind was apparently also on his brother. "Have you seen André lately?"

Rebekka's stomach flip-flopped. "No. But he'll probably be here tonight."

"Well, if you get a chance, check how he's doing. He's been looking rather miserable the past few times I've seen him. I think he's having a hard time, but when I ask he brushes me off—I guess he thinks I have enough to deal with and doesn't want to burden me. It's probably about Claire. I know he misses her. But he might open up to you. Will you try? Maybe there'll be something we can do to help him."

"Sure," she agreed, swallowing with difficulty. He couldn't know what his request might mean to their relationship.

He hugged her. "Thanks. I knew I could count on you."

André himself opened the door when they knocked, flanked by Ana and Marée. "Rebekka!" the girls cried, throwing themselves into her arms.

"What, none for me?" Marc teased.

"Daddy said not to pester you," Ana announced.

Marée's lips formed a pout. "He said you can't lift us."

"No, but I can still give hugs." Marc knelt and gingerly hugged each girl.

Rebekka's eyes met André's. *Why have you been avoiding me?* he seemed to ask.

That's a stupid question, she told him silently. But how could she know what he was thinking? Was she putting words into his mouth?

"You've been working too hard," André said to her. "You've lost weight."

Rebekka's confusion returned in force upon seeing him. She wished she could turn around and go home.

"That's what I think," Marc said, climbing awkwardly to his feet.

André looked concerned. "Are you remembering to eat, Rebekka?"

"Yes," she snapped, then felt immediately guilty at the expression in his eyes. Still, she couldn't help adding, though a little more gently, "Honestly, you two treat me like I'm five years old. Besides, if anyone's lost weight, André, it's you."

She pushed past them and went to the kitchen where most of the Perrault clan was already gathered. Some of Josette's children were playing cards with Brandon, but Larissa sat on a chair with a pouting expression. "What's with Larissa?" she asked Marie-Thérèse in a low voice.

"She wanted to go somewhere with her friend," Marie-Thérèse whispered back. "Actually, she's as much the reason for this party as

Marc is. I didn't want to let her hang out with that girl, so Josette and I came up with this. When she's with this certain friend, I can't trust Larissa to be where she says she'll be. Last week, her friend had a party when the parents weren't home. I only found out because I called the mother to make sure." She sighed. "No way I want her involved in that. I wish something could change her attitude."

Rebekka made a silent vow to pray for Larissa's well-being and to go out of her way to include the girl in the conversation. Perhaps all Larissa needed was more love and acceptance.

Soon another table and more chairs were set up in the kitchen, including a padded easy chair for the guest of honor, and another one for Louis-Géralde, the hero of the hour. He had been released days before Marc, but would not be returning to the mission field for at least another month—and only if he held to an increasingly rigorous exercise schedule.

Rebekka basked in the Perrault family's friendship and acceptance. She remembered too well how this apartment had been a haven for both her and Raoul while growing up. They had especially admired Jean-Marc for being what their father wasn't. Or at least that was how she had seen her father then. Now she wasn't so sure.

She searched the room. "Where's Raoul?"

"I left a message with his wife," Josette said, frowning. "But I honestly can't tell you if it got through. I'm sorry to say this about her when I've only met her a few times, but she confuses me."

"She confuses everybody," André assured her.

Rebekka nodded in agreement. She and Raoul had not talked about Desirée since that day in the hospital. Whether he had been purposely remote or their paths just hadn't crossed, she couldn't be sure. Yet he wouldn't have stayed away tonight, not if he'd known about the special gathering to celebrate Marc's release. Not only was Marc his partner, he was soon to be Raoul's brother-in-law. *Or supposed to be*. Rebekka sighed inwardly. Her eyes burned and she blinked for relief.

"Rebekka, don't you have anything to say about it?" Josette's voice pierced her thoughts. She paused in passing out the playing pieces for the next game.

"Yeah, after all, it is your wedding," added Larissa.

Rebekka glanced at all the expectant faces. "What?"

"We were asking Marc when you were getting married," Zack explained, popping a potato chip into his mouth. He put an arm around Josette's shoulders. "Our baby is going to be born in another three weeks and while we don't want to be too demanding, Josette would like to make it to her twin's sealing."

"So that means right away, or at least two weeks after the birth." Josette looked at her expectantly. "My visiting teacher said she'd travel to Switzerland with us so she could watch the baby while we're in the temple with you."

A rush of noise filled Rebekka's ears. She could feel Marc's hand on hers tighten encouragingly. On the outside, the decision appeared simple, one she once would have made easily and confidently. But from across the table, André watched her silently.

"No," Rebekka said.

"What do you mean, 'no'?" Josette asked, puzzled. She shifted her body uneasily.

Marc's eyes met hers. She focused on him for a long moment, loving him so much that she knew she had to tell him the truth—or at least some of her confusion. But not here, in front of all these people. She gazed around the room at the beloved family members anxiously awaiting her next words. Only André's face was unreadable. Next to him sat Ariana, her stately features frozen into an expression of sympathy.

"I mean we haven't talked about it. There hasn't been time." She smiled. "But as soon as we do, you will all be the first to know."

The subtle tension that had entered the room dissipated as quickly as it had come. The conversation rolled on. Rebekka stood, feeling Marc's hand slip from hers. "I'm going to get some water," she said. "I'll be back."

She walked to the cupboard for a clean cup and then to the refrigerator for ice water, though her insides were already cold. Eyes seemed to follow her, but she didn't look around. Whose would they be? And how was she going to get through this evening?

She couldn't. *I have to tell him now. It'll be better here for him with everyone nearby. I couldn't bear to think of him being alone after I . . .* After what? After she broke his heart?

Marc made it almost too easy. He came to stand beside her and put an arm around her waist. "I think I need a little air. How about a little walk to the balcony?"

"Okay." She swallowed hard, letting him take her hand and lead her from the kitchen. No one seemed to notice their departure, but she knew differently. André would notice. And so would Ariana.

There was only one balcony in the fifth floor apartment, and to get to it they had to go through the TV room. Once outside, Rebekka stood at the railing, gazing down at the few cars that ventured in front of the apartment building.

"Rebekka, what is it?" Marc asked, touching her elbow. "You've been acting odd for the past week or so. What's wrong?"

Rebekka turned to face him, her heart feeling as if it would break. "I can't marry you, Marc. At least not now."

He blinked in disbelief. "Why? . . . But you love me!"

"I do love you," she said miserably. "It's not you, Marc. Please. There have been so many changes in our lives, and I just need some time."

"Time for what? Rebekka, I thought we agreed that we had already wasted too much time."

She struggled to stop the tears. "You're right. I know you're right. But, Marc, there's something I need to be sure about. If I marry you, I want to do it without any doubts. With my whole heart."

They stood in silence for a long while, and then, "Is there someone else, Rebekka?" he asked.

"This is between us," she said. "It's about needing to be sure. I gave you years to find out how you felt about me. And now it's me who needs time! Please."

Marc looked stunned. Without waiting for him to reply, Rebekka fled. André was in the hall and he smiled quizzically at her, but she ran past him. From the kitchen she could hear laughter, and she was grateful she wouldn't have to pass Marc's family before she reached the door. What would they say about what she had just done to Marc? She didn't wait for the elevator, but stumbled down the five flights of stairs, her tears blinding her path.

* * * * *

André was shocked at the change in Rebekka since he had last seen her in Marc's apartment. She was only a shadow of herself, and the misery in her huge gray eyes was almost too much for him to bear. Worse, he had to watch from a distance as she sat by Marc, who occasionally held her hand and stared at her lovingly. André had to summon all his will to stay at the table and take part in the games and conversation.

When Marc and Rebekka left the room, André was restless. He paced the kitchen, wondering for the millionth time what would have happened if he had been more honest with Rebekka in the past. But what about Claire and his daughters? He could never give them up. The confusion that had been André's constant companion for the past few weeks seemed to eat into his very soul.

He left the kitchen in search of a quiet place that he could pray. To his surprise, Rebekka came running past him, not meeting his gaze.

André stared after her, his heart thundering. What had she done? A noise behind him made him turn around. It was Marc, so pale and weak-looking that André feared for his life. "What happened?" he asked.

"Rebekka—she said she wasn't going to marry me. I have to go after her."

Guilt filled André. *This is all my fault,* he accused. He wanted to run after Rebekka and force her to stay with Marc. But then, if Rebekka wasn't sure about marrying him, maybe he had spared them both a lot of pain. "You just got out of the hospital," he said quietly. "You'll hurt yourself! I'll find her."

"She's *my* fiancée!" Marc pushed off his hands and strode to the apartment door. André stumbled after his brother.

Suddenly, Ariana blocked their path. "Neither of you is going after her!" she declared, her chin lifted in challenge. Though both sons were a head taller than their mother, they stopped in midstride.

"She said she's not sure about us, Mom." Marc's face was pleading. "I have to talk to her!"

"No. Not now. What you have to do is give her time. She cares very deeply for you, son, and I know it hurts, but you have to let her go. If it's meant to be, she'll come back. I promise."

Marc drew himself up to his full height, masking his emotions. "Of course. You're right. I can't force her. It's just . . . I don't know what I'll do without her."

Ariana put her arms around Marc. Her eyes met André's over his shoulder. "You'll be all right," she murmured. André wondered if she was talking to him just as much as Marc.

Ariana pulled away. "Now, I'm going back into the kitchen or the others will wonder why I'm gone. I want you both to go into the living room and calm down a little. André, stay with him." She stepped away from the door, but paused to shake a finger at them. "And don't you dare set one foot outside that door!"

Without looking back, Ariana marched across the entryway and into the kitchen.

Marc stared hungrily toward the door leading out of the apartment. His look of devastation cut deeply into André's heart; he knew only too well what Marc was feeling. How could he have let his thoughts and his loneliness ruin his brother's life? He put a hand on Marc's shoulder. "She'll be gone already, anyway. Give her some time. I'll help you find her later."

Sighing in defeat, Marc retreated into the living room. He stood by the unshuttered window, looking out into the night as though to search for Rebekka, while André reclined wearily on the long blue couch.

"I think it's another man," Marc said.

Guilt made André's mouth dry. "What makes you say that?"

"I don't know. She's acting different. I mean, for a while, everything is fine and then suddenly, she'll close up and I can't get through. At first I thought it was because she was mad at me for not marrying her in the hospital, but now . . ." He spread his hands helplessly. "She said she wasn't sure what she wanted. André, what am I going to do?"

André would have given almost anything to take the pain from his brother's face.

Anything?

He swallowed hard. The two people he loved most were hurting because of his actions. *But I didn't do anything,* he thought. *I backed off. Whatever happens is Rebekka's choice.*

Suddenly he *needed* to ask Marc about Rebekka. He had to know how his brother really felt about her. Did he love her as deeply and as soul-searchingly as André had loved Claire? Would he work to make her happy? Or had he simply turned to Rebekka because over the years he hadn't found anyone else?

"What if it *is* another man?" he asked.

Looking away from the window, Marc met André's stare, his voice coming as a growl, "I'd kill him."

André held his voice steady. "What if she cared for him and just wanted to see where things might lead?"

Marc's face crumpled, and his eyes were bleak. "I don't know."

"Are you sure *you* love Rebekka?" André hated himself for asking, but he had to be sure. Rebekka deserved a wholehearted love, the kind that held nothing back. "I mean, with the once-in-a-lifetime kind of love?"

To his surprise, Marc grinned, and color seeped back into his pallid face. He eased himself into the comfortable chair by the window, favoring his wounded side. "I know this will come as a big surprise to you, but I used to have a terrible crush on Danielle."

"Rebekka's mom?" Indeed, that was a surprise.

"Yeah." Marc's voice came from far away. "It was rather a childish thing, but I clung to it over the years. I used to hate Philippe for not being the man she deserved, and thought I could do so much better. But she just kept on loving him, and I noticed that he began to treat her like a queen. He was living up to her expectations." He paused for a long moment. "I think I was wrong about him. I was certainly wrong to believe in my little crush."

"And Rebekka?"

"I've always loved her," Marc said. "I just didn't know it. Stupid, huh?" He laughed lightly and looked down at his casual, dark blue slacks. "Once I thought I spent so much time with her because that way I could be with Danielle, but after Rebekka went to America, I learned that it was the other way around. I enjoyed being with Danielle because that meant I would be near Rebekka. It was her all along." He lifted his gaze, eyes showing his earnestness. "I'm thirty-four years old, André. I've dated a long time and I've never found anyone like Rebekka. I love her so much it hurts when I think about not being with her. And when we're together . . . I can't explain it. I see eternity in her eyes, and I feel it in her arms. I would do anything to make her happy."

So would I, André thought.

"That's why I couldn't marry her and die," added Marc, shaking his head. "But I regret it now. I mean, I can hardly believe that after all this time I may not end up with her." He propped his elbow on the armrest and let his chin rest on his fist. "I have only myself to blame. I should have married her long ago." He clenched and unclenched the fist, making his head move up and down. Then he dropped his hand to his lap, and his voice became determined. "But so help me, I can't just let her slip away without trying. I'm going to fight for her every inch of the way. I love her so much, and I want to spend the rest of my life making her happy, for however long the Lord allows. I know she still loves me, and as long as there's a chance, I'll fight for her."

"But what if she still doesn't marry you?"

Marc's expression was one of pure torture, matching the feeling in André's chest. "Then I guess I would have to let her go. Her happiness is what is most important." He paused and said in afterthought. "And I would never marry. There is no one else for me. I know there is for most people, but I think I've waited so long that all my chances are used up. I feel it."

André believed that his brother was telling the truth as he saw it. Yet there was something else he had to know, one more thing that would reveal Marc's worthiness of Rebekka. One more thing before André could be sure. He let the silence grow between them before saying almost casually, "Rebekka's certainly a beautiful woman, but did you ever notice her freckles?"

A slow smile spread across his brother's face. "Are you kidding? I love those freckles. She has exactly fourteen, you know—some so faded you can hardly tell they're there. My favorite is the one just above her lip on the right side." He laughed in self-deprecation. "You probably haven't even noticed it, but I even have dreams about that little spot. I guess you can tell that a man's really gone on a woman when he starts counting her freckles."

"I guess so." To his relief, André didn't feel pain at the statement, only a calm numbness. "I wish you the best, brother," he said sincerely. "And I will do anything to help you win Rebekka."

Marc's eyes grew wet and he arose from his chair, holding out his hand. His handshake was surprisingly strong. "Thank you, André. I appreciate all your support. I owe my life to you and to Louis-Géralde. I *owe* you."

André shook his head. "We're brothers. I know you'd do the same for me."

"I would. Anything you ask, I would give you. Even my life."

"Anything?" André tried to make his voice light. "Better be glad I'm not asking for Rebekka, then."

Marc cocked his head and said thoughtfully, "As much as I would like to believe otherwise right now, Rebekka's not mine to give. She's her own person. But I would trade my happiness for yours, André. If I could give you back Claire—"

André stood abruptly. "Are we going to find Rebekka or not?"

"It's not going to be easy. She was pretty determined." Marc's eyes reflected agonized uncertainty.

"Why don't we make a few phone calls?"

"Okay. You go ahead." Marc gave him a strained smile. "But do it from the kitchen, okay? I'm just going to say a prayer and then I'll be in."

André kept the smile on his face until he was out of his brother's sight. Now he knew why his mother had asked him to talk with Marc in the hospital that day when he had been so intent upon finding Rebekka, and why she had forced him to stay with Marc in the living room tonight. She had wanted André to understand the depth of his brother's love for Rebekka. And now he did: Marc loved her without reservation.

Not like him. André's feelings were mixed up with what-ifs and a longing for Claire and the family life they had shared. He had feelings for Rebekka that came from a long relationship, but could he promise her that they were anything deeper than friendship? That they didn't originate from his loneliness or the desire to replace what he'd lost? He couldn't allow her to gamble on that—or to destroy Marc.

But it's her decision. True, but he could make things easier for her.

When André entered the kitchen, all eyes turned to him, and he knew that his mother had told them the news about Rebekka's uncertainty. "How's Marc?" Josette asked.

"He'll be all right," André answered. His mother's eyes bored into him, but there was nothing he could say in front rest of the family to reassure her further.

"Do you think Rebekka really isn't going to marry him?" asked Ana.

André was about to reply, but it was Marc who spoke from the doorway. "Yes, she's going to marry me," he said confidently. "After all, she didn't give me back the ring. Besides, Rebekka and I were always meant to be together. I just need to remind her of that."

Once again André felt his mother's eyes digging into him, but he had nothing to add. He already knew what he had to do.

CHAPTER 30

As she drove from the Perraults' apartment, Rebekka wished she had ignored her parents' objections and had leased her own apartment upon her return from America. Then she would have somewhere to be alone without worrying about either Marc or André.

At home she would have to endure her parents' questions at best, and Marc or André following her at worst. Marc's apartment was out of the question, as were the homes of all of his siblings. They were too close to the situation and she couldn't involve them. She had friends, of course, but none with whom she wanted to share her predicament.

Raoul!

Yes, she could trust her brother to let her stay with him and to insulate her from the others. She could even face her brother's silly wife, if only she could have time alone to think.

Now that she was alone, her desperation had subsided once again into quiet confusion. She recalled with longing the peaceful hours she had spent with Marc earlier in the day, but had little hope of regaining that feeling. Why was she so confused? Over and over in her mind, she replayed her refusal to marry Marc. What must he think of her?

With a sigh of relief she found a parking space near her brother's apartment building and rang the outside buzzer to his apartment. There was no answer over the intercom, nor was there a click signaling a release of the doors. Where was he?

A couple came out of the building, and before the door could shut, Rebekka ducked inside and rode the elevator up the six floors to his apartment. She rang the bell, but there was still no answer. She knocked.

"Raoul," she called, knowing it was hopeless, "it's me, Rebekka."

Now I'll have to go to a hotel.

Why are you running? a voice inside her head questioned.

I can't hurt Marc. I won't! At least not more than I have already. I need some time.

She was about to signal the elevator when she heard something in Raoul's apartment. She rang again and as she did, the door opened. Her brother stood there, eyes bloodshot and auburn hair disheveled.

They stared at each other for a full thirty seconds without speaking before he opened the door wider and ushered her in. She fell into his arms. "Oh, Raoul. I'm so glad you're here! I was debating whether to stay in your stairwell or go to a hotel."

"What is it?" he asked quickly. His face was pasty and he looked as though he hadn't slept in days.

"Oh, it's just awful. I don't know what to do!" She glanced around the small entryway. "Can we talk alone a minute? I don't want to disturb Desirée." *Or have her listen in.*

"We're alone," Raoul said dully.

The sadness in her brother's face demanded that she ask, "Where's Desirée? And why didn't you come to the Perraults tonight? Josette said she talked to Desirée. Did she even tell you about the party?"

He was silent a full minute, and then said, "She left me. Just an hour ago." His eyes rose slowly to meet hers, his face crumpling as he gave into tears. "Two and a half months we were married, and now it's over."

Horrified, Rebekka hugged him tightly. "What happened?"

The dejection in his voice nearly broke her heart. "Earlier today, I found the jacket she claimed she'd lost in André's office—at a place she liked to go before we met. A bartender had it. He didn't know I was her husband, and he told me stories of what she has been up to while I was at work or doing my Church calling. Or when I thought she was with friends. Drinking, dancing, flirting—and she's been unfaithful." He shuddered and closed his eyes briefly to regain control. "I confronted her after I got home. The stories were all true. She wouldn't admit to them, but I could see it in her eyes. She knew I didn't believe her. So she gave me an ultimatum: her or the Church." Tears leaked from the corners of eyes that begged for understanding.

"I turned my back on my beliefs once before when I married her, I realize that, but I won't—I can't—deny my faith again."

"I'm so sorry." Rebekka led him to the kitchen and helped him sit in a chair. He looked about the room with unseeing eyes as she stood next to him, a comforting hand on his shoulder.

"You were right all along, Rebekka. I shouldn't have let what I wanted right then get in the way of my eternity. I let what I thought she was blind me to reality. I loved her so much that I just couldn't stand another day without having her with me, without being a husband to her. But now I can't help thinking that if I had waited, and insisted on marrying her in the temple, things might have been different." He turned into her and let his face burrow into her stomach. "I don't really blame her. I was foolish, and now I don't know if she'll ever gain a testimony. Or come back to me. And I don't know if I can be happy without her." He struggled to breathe as sobs wracked his body.

Rebekka rubbed his back awkwardly. *Some of the guilt is mine,* she thought. Though she hadn't been in France when he had eloped, she distinctly remembered the e-mails where she had *not* warned Raoul against marrying Desirée. She had felt that she couldn't tell him to wait when he had been so completely in love. After all, their parents had made their marriage work despite their religious differences, and while it was not the best scenario, she had believed it was possible that Raoul and Desirée would do the same. But her heart had *known* it was wrong; she should have warned him. But would he have listened?

"I'm so sorry," she repeated with a sense of failure. "Is there anything I can do?"

He shook his head and continued to weep.

For long moments Rebekka comforted her brother until at last there were no tears left. He pulled away from her, his face red and blotchy. Rebekka slumped into the opposite chair.

"So why did you come tonight?" he asked after a long silence.

Rebekka blinked in surprise. Wrapped up in her brother's pain, she had put aside her own dilemma. How trivial her problem now seemed in light of Desirée's desertion.

"It's nothing."

"Tell me. You can't hide it from me. I know something's wrong." He sounded more like the old Raoul, the one who hadn't yet learned of betrayal.

She knew he would have it out of her one way or the other; they had always been close. "I love Marc, but recently I've had feelings for someone else. Well, not feelings so much, but I wonder if I'm making the right choice."

His eyes widened in surprise. "Is it that guy in America? Samuel or whatever?"

"Oh, no. I haven't even talked to him. I've been using my boss as a go-between."

He lifted a hand in a silent request for her to continue.

"André," she said in a low whisper.

The implications were almost too much for Raoul. His hand fell to the table with a loud smack, and he stared at her in disbelief. "Does he know?"

"He has an inkling, but he's certainly not pursuing me or anything." She looked at him beseechingly. "He was sad and needed a friend when Claire died, and I needed to talk about Marc. I kept wondering what I would do if he died, and there André was saying that he would take care of me—that Marc had asked him to take care of me! And I just started thinking about what a wonderful man he was, and that led to me thinking what might have happened if he had asked me out before my mission, before he met Claire. Don't you see? It was all so gradual that I didn't know something was happening before it hit me. We've been friends for so long. Good friends—close friends. And now I'm wondering what to do. What if I'm not supposed to marry Marc after all? You know how long I've loved him, and I can't believe I'm even considering not marrying him. But how can I if I'm not absolutely sure? I don't know what to do—I don't want to hurt either of them."

His head shook in sympathy. "Oh, Rebekka, I'm so sorry. I wish I knew what to tell you. I wish I knew the answer." He grimaced before continuing more softly, "Although I'm not too sure you'd want to follow any advice I gave you. As you can see, I didn't do so well myself."

Rebekka sniffed twice and wiped the tears from her face. "Maybe I really should go back to America."

Her brother looked at her quizzically. "Running away isn't going to solve anything. Marc has proven that he'll come after you, and André won't because he loves Marc. So you'll have found out nothing. No, you need to stay here and sort this out. You owe that to yourself and to them."

"I pray and pray but I just feel confusion."

"Then when *don't* you feel confusion? Think about that. It's what I've been asking myself this past month. I found that in church I don't feel confused, with you I don't feel confused, and at work there's also no confusion. It's only when I'm with her. So that's why I let her leave tonight."

His words held a great deal of wisdom. "I'll think on it," she said as the phone rang, making her jump. Her breath caught in her throat. "I'll bet it's them."

Raoul picked up his portable phone from the table. "Hello?" he asked, grinding his toe into the green ceramic tile. "Oh . . . hi, André." Not until she saw the disappointment on Raoul's face did Rebekka realize that he had hoped the call was from Desirée. Her heart ached with pity. But if his description of Desirée's behavior was true, how could he begin to want her back?

"Don't tell them I'm here!"

Raoul motioned for her to stay and walked out of the kitchen. Annoyed that she couldn't hear at least his side of the conversation, she waited tensely for his return. In a few moments Raoul reappeared and tossed the phone onto the table. It slid across the smooth surface toward her, as though begging her to talk to the person on the line. Rebekka clenched her fists. The engagement ring Marc had given her was suddenly heavy on her finger.

"He already hung up," Raoul said. "He was calling for Marc. I told him I'd heard from you and that you were all right, but that you didn't want them to look for you. I said you'd call him and Marc tomorrow."

She sighed with relief and unclenched her fists. "Thank you. Though I don't know what good another day is going to do."

Raoul scratched his head in what she recognized as his stalling gesture. There was obviously more he had not told her. "Well, here's the bad news," he said. "André and I got to talking about Desirée. I told him she left, and he said he'd be over in a minute."

Rebekka felt the strength drain from her limbs. Her temporary sanctuary had ended. "I'd better get going then. I can't talk to him, not tonight. Not until I know what I'm going to do."

"Wait!" Raoul searched her face, not missing the desperation in her eyes. "It's just André. He's not going to force you to talk if you don't want to do. Besides, you could just stay in the bedroom. I'll go down and move your car so he won't see it."

Rebekka nodded, relieved. "You have an old T-shirt I could wear to bed?"

"Use whatever you want. Desirée left some stuff—you could use that."

"No thanks. One of your shirts will be fine." She stood and walked to the door leading to the hallway.

"Rebekka?"

She stopped. A shadow had crept over his face, and the sadness in his eyes made her want to cry. "Could you take our room?" he asked. "I think I'd rather sleep in the den."

"Sure, would you like me to make the couch up for you?"

"No. Actually, it's already out. I slept there yesterday."

She wondered how long he and Desirée had slept apart, but didn't ask. Her brother deserved some privacy. "I'd like to meet Desirée in a dark alley," she muttered on her way to the room, though it wasn't really true. For Desirée there would be no rules of fairness or pity. How had she fooled them all with her act? But still, there had been some good in her, something Raoul had loved. Rebekka wondered if she would ever really understand what that was.

Rebekka sighed as she rummaged through her brother's tall dresser for a T-shirt that would be long enough to use as a nightgown. None were, so she used an old pair of his sweats for bottoms, pulling the drawstring tight. The entire outfit was rather large on her, but she would be warm. The digital radio clock on the nightstand read only nine o'clock, and she wasn't tired. Her nerves felt taut, like a guitar strung too tight.

"I need a book." She spied a thick romance novel near the clock and began to read, but by the third chapter threw it on the floor where she could pick it up the next morning and toss it in the trash. "Junk. How can she read such garbage? It's porn, not romance."

In the top drawer of the other nightstand she found a *Book of Mormon* and began to read. The noise of the doorbell caused her to abruptly set the book down, realizing she hadn't understood a thing she had read. *No wonder I'm so confused,* she told herself. *I don't pay attention.*

She jumped from the bed and began to pace in front of it, for the first time noticing how small the room was with all the new furniture Desirée and Raoul had purchased after their marriage. *Maybe he should have agreed to move,* she thought. *Or maybe they should have bought less furniture.*

She heard voices in the kitchen and recognized not only André's voice, but also Marc's. *Of course he would come too. They are both Raoul's friends . . . and business partners.* For the first time the full impact of what the brothers meant to each other hit her. They loved one another deeply, and she was coming between them. No matter what decision she made, life would never be the same for anyone ever again. For an intense moment, she longed for their childhood, where love meant tweaking ponytails and skating in the street.

Rebekka listened in utter stillness as the murmur of the men's voices rose and fell. Her chest swelled with the familiarity of them until her heart nearly burst with longing. Within minutes, she heard them leave, and she tiptoed into the kitchen, expecting to find Raoul there alone. Instead he'd left a note, scribbled hastily.

> *Gone to the office to get some stuff done. Don't worry. See you tomorrow.*

The note was generic enough that the others would think it was for Desirée if they had seen it, but Rebekka knew Raoul meant it for her.

Gone to the office indeed, she thought with disgust. She remembered too well how Raoul had sent André to work the day after Claire's funeral. Now it seemed André and Marc were returning the favor. *What is it about guys and work?* She didn't admit, at least not in words, that she would love to go into her own office at her parents' apartment and work—anything to take her mind off the confusion in her heart.

"It's your own fault," she chided herself, retreating back to the bedroom. She picked up her scriptures and read until finally falling asleep.

CHAPTER 31

On Monday, Marie-Thérèse accepted Josette's invitation to eat lunch out. At twelve-thirty they left three-year-old Stephen happily playing with Ariana and drove to a nearby restaurant. "I just can't stand staying at home," Josette confessed when they were seated. "I feel so restless."

"That's because you're sick of being pregnant and you want the baby to come."

Josette sighed. "Yeah, I guess. You know, I never really knew what 'endure to the end' meant until now. I mean, I love my kids and wouldn't trade any of them for anything in the world, but some days all the work is so overwhelming and endless that I want to run away and hide. I sometimes think about all the things I could do if I didn't have so many kids."

"Like me?" the words escaped before Marie-Thérèse could stop them.

Josette regarded her silently. "Maybe." Her eyes became imploring. "Don't hate me. I know these are my hormones talking, but I sometimes wonder why you even want to adopt any more kids."

Marie-Thérèse couldn't be offended at her sister's apparent earnestness. "I'll tell you how you would feel if you didn't have all the boys. You'd wander around the house wishing you did."

"Not me. I'd clean the floor or go shopping."

"That's because you have the kids and know what it's like not to be able to do those things. When they grow up, I've no doubt that you'll clean and go shopping, but you'll appreciate the time only because of where you've been."

"Actually, I think I'd rather do more interior decorating." In conjunction with her husband's real estate job, Josette often helped new owners decorate their homes. Marie-Thérèse knew she enjoyed it thoroughly—and missed it when she couldn't take the time.

"Yeah, but the point is, I know you. You and Zack decided you wanted a lot of kids and you had them. Now you know what it's like. If you didn't have them, you'd always wonder."

Josette stared at her solemnly. "Like you."

"Like me." Marie-Thérèse leaned back in her chair, not wanting any more of the gourmet sandwich she had ordered. "Although, I always knew I couldn't handle a lot of kids. I do want just one more. A little girl, I think."

Josette leaned forward. "Could that be because of Larissa?"

"Yes. It probably is." Marie-Thérèse sighed. "She grew up too fast. Do you know that yesterday she told me she wanted to bleach the brown from her hair and dye it blue?"

"I bet Mathieu loved that."

Marie-Thérèse snorted. "He told her that she most certainly could do it—after she turned eighteen and moved out. Larissa, of course, yelled that she couldn't wait until she turned eighteen and that the minute she did, she would be out of here. And she'd get her blue hair."

"Well, we weren't much older than that when we left home."

"Two or three years makes a lot of difference. Besides, we left to go to BYU."

"Yeah, and I had you." Josette's eyes were far away. "If I hadn't, I think Mom and Dad would have preferred to chain me to the bed."

"Not a bad solution," Marie-Thérèse said lightly. "I just hope that Larissa's path won't be too hard. I pray every night for something to wake her up—something that won't be permanently damaging." She grimaced. "I guess I want it both ways."

Josette placed a comforting hand on her shoulder. "You're a mother—of course you want that for your daughter."

Her comments brought a question to Marie-Thérèse's mind. "And how do you feel not having a daughter?"

Josette shrugged. "It used to bother me a great deal, but now it's okay. I don't want to go through another pregnancy, and I see all the problems you've had with Larissa. I guess I'm pretty content." She gave a low laugh. "I've always been good with boys anyway."

"You got that right." Marie-Thérèse threw her napkin onto the table. "You about ready?"

Josette nodded, coming awkwardly to her feet. "Maybe I should take Larissa out to lunch again. Although I don't know if anything I said the last time helped."

"You tried. That's all I could ask."

"And we'll keep trying."

"Mom said she had plans for Stephen all afternoon," Josette said when they reached the car. "And that means I've got nothing to do."

"I thought you had floors to clean."

Josette laughed and punched her playfully on the shoulder. "I do, but I'm too big to do any cleaning right now. Some women get the nesting instinct when they're close to delivery, but I get the fleeing one. I want to be anywhere but cooped up at home. Besides, I have a lady coming in today to help out. So if you don't mind, I'll tag along home with you so that I can stay out of her way while she cleans."

"Oh, I don't mind." *It'll save me from my own thoughts,* Marie-Thérèse added silently. She unlocked her car door for Josette.

"Do you really think that Rebekka and Marc won't get married?" Josette asked. "Mom said she didn't see her or Raoul at church yesterday. And Marc said he hadn't talked to Rebekka yet, but that Raoul had promised she'd call."

"She probably just has the prewedding jitters," Marie-Thérèse answered. "I bet she'll come around." She hoped it was true.

When they arrived at her apartment, Marie-Thérèse checked her answering machine as she always did. The light was blinking, signaling a new message. She poked at the play-back button.

"Hello. This is the secretary at your son's school. He's had an allergic response to something. A bee, I think. He's with the nurse now. Can you come down as soon as possible? We'll call your husband's number too, to see what you want us to do. Thanks, and good-bye."

Abruptly, Marie-Thérèse felt a heavy substance form in her stomach, as though the sandwich she had eaten had petrified inside. She wanted to run away. Instead, she snatched up the phone and dialed the geological department at the firm where Mathieu worked. His message service answered, and she hung up in frustration.

She explained the situation quickly to Josette. "Let's just go down there," her sister said. "I can call Mom and everyone else on the way to see if they've heard anything. Thank heaven Zack made me charge this stupid cell phone since he's so worried I'll go into labor at any minute."

"Okay." Marie-Thérèse seized her purse, trying to subdue her fears. The message the nurse left hadn't sounded too threatening, and Brandon was forever coming down with something. Surely the school would take care of it. She forced a nervous laugh. "You'd think with all the times I've had to take him to the doctor for one reason or another that I'd have grown used to it."

"It's like labor," Josette agreed. "You forget how hard the pains are until they begin. Although I have to admit, my births have been relatively easy compared to most."

And I had to have double epidurals, Marie-Thérèse thought. As they left the apartment, for some reason she thought of Claire.

* * * * *

Marie-Thérèse was in a nightmare from which she couldn't awake. They had arrived at Brandon's school only to find that the nurse had called for an ambulance, which had taken him to the hospital.

"He'd gone into anaphylactic shock," she explained. "He began to swell and could barely breathe. I gave him a shot of epinephrine to delay the reaction but . . ." She let the sentence dangle.

Marie-Thérèse gripped her sister's arm. "We have to get to the hospital. I have to be there for him."

"Mom!" Marie-Thérèse turned to see Larissa running in the school corridor toward her. "They told me what happened! Where is he?" Her eyes searched the area frantically for Brandon.

Marie-Thérèse felt numb and couldn't make herself move to comfort her daughter. She blinked relief for her dry eyes, wondering why her body wouldn't respond to the brain signals she was sending.

Josette put her arms around Larissa. "He's at the hospital. We're going there now."

Without asking permission from either her teachers or her mother, Larissa followed them to the car. *She has a right to be here,* Marie-Thérèse thought.

Once at the hospital, Josette continued to call family from a pay phone, while Marie-Thérèse and Larissa waited to talk to the doctor. Time ticked slowly, interminably by, and all the while Marie-Thérèse's fear grew. At last the doctor came to see them. "The nurse at your son's school saved his life," he began.

"Then he's okay?" Josette said quickly.

"Well, yes and no."

"What do you mean?" Marie-Thérèse felt dizzy from holding her breath.

The doctor frowned apologetically. "Your son had a severe allergic reaction to some food he ingested—strawberries and kiwi to be exact. Apparently, he had fruit salad for a snack. Strawberries and kiwis come from the same family, and apparently he got too much. Now that the swelling has gone down he can breathe fine, but he hasn't regained consciousness. We are still unsure if that's because the lack of oxygen damaged his brain, or if the damage occurred when he fell and hit his head on the cement when he collapsed on the school grounds. We don't really know."

"He's in a coma?" whispered Marie-Thérèse.

"Yes, he is. Most likely he will awake, but there's always the chance that he won't. I've called in a specialist who's with him right now, but when he's done, you can go in to see . . ."

Marie-Thérèse stopped listening. The numbness she had felt at the school had vanished, replaced by a piercing agony. After all these years, the thing she had so dreaded was happening.

"The men will be here soon to give him a blessing," Josette told her when the doctor had gone. "Mathieu arrived at the school shortly after we did and they directed him here. Come on, let's sit down. Brandon'll be fine."

Rage enveloped Marie-Thérèse. She wanted to lash out, to hurt someone as badly as she was hurting inside. "Don't you see?" she nearly screamed, knowing that she was on the edge of hysterics. It didn't matter—nothing mattered but Brandon. "Pauline said before she died that something was going to happen to him ! Don't you remember? She said that she was going to watch over him until he could be with me. Don't you remember that? This is what she was talking about—Brandon's going to die!"

"No!" Josette put a firm hand on either shoulder. "That's not what she meant! I remember it well. I wrote it down in my journal. She said 'Your little boy is going to be just fine. I'll help look after him until he gets to you.' That's what she said. 'Until he gets to you.' And we agreed long ago that it's because she knew that when you were carrying him, you and Mathieu would have problems with money, and that you wouldn't want to be pregnant—that you would resent it terribly because you didn't know how you could manage to feed another mouth. And that later you'd worry how your rejection would affect him. That's what Pauline was talking about. And she told you not to worry about it! She meant to take care of him until he was born—that's all!"

"But what if that's not what she meant?" Marie-Thérèse demanded, squashing the hope that hurt more terribly than the pain. "What if she meant now? And that she'd watch over Brandon until I died and could be with him!"

"We felt the Spirit when we first talked about this," Josette insisted. "We both did—all those years ago. You knew he'd be okay and not be affected by your rejection when you were pregnant. And he wasn't, not one bit. Brandon's a wonderful boy."

Marie-Thérèse shook off her sister's hands. "But what if she meant then *and* now! So many spiritual things are directed at more than one circumstance—look at the scriptures!"

"Well?" there was a flare of anger in Josette's eyes. "Then he'll be okay now, too."

Marie-Thérèse faced her with equal anger. "But people are okay when they're dead! Aren't they? Aren't my mom and dad and *my* sister Pauline okay? Of course they are. Well, I don't want to lose my son to that kind of 'okayness.' I've lost too many already!" Marie-Thérèse began to sob bitterly.

Josette's mouth rounded to an O, and she tried once again to comfort Marie-Thérèse. But Marie-Thérèse backed away. "No, don't touch me!"

And she ran. Away from the loving sister who had been blessed with so much; away from the rebellious daughter who didn't love her;

away from her faithful Brandon, who would now get his wish to see what it was like to be dead.

Inside the bathroom, Marie-Thérèse paced in a stall, tears running freely down her cheeks. *No! No!* her heart moaned over and over. Time passed, but for Marie-Thérèse there was nothing but the bathroom stall and her silent pleas. She closed her eyes and let the agony consume her.

"Mom?" Larissa's voice came, tremulous and frightened. "Mom, are you here?" After several loud sniffs, she added. "I see your shoes. I know you're there."

Marie-Thérèse had stopped pacing at the sound of the voice and now she opened her eyes. With distaste, she noticed that the previous occupant of the stall had not only been messy, but had neglected to flush the toilet. She burst from the stall, feeling ill.

"He's going to be okay," Larissa said tentatively, but there was a question in her voice.

Marie-Thérèse didn't reply, but put her arms around her daughter and held her, enjoying the life that pulsed in her gangly body. Larissa clung to her, tears wetting her young face. "Dad's here," she said softly.

They emerged from the bathroom and found Mathieu waiting for them. Marie-Thérèse released Larissa and fell into his arms. "Our little boy," she whispered. "He's dying."

"That's not what the doctor said. We must have hope." There was no reproach in Mathieu's voice, but Marie-Thérèse became even more despondent.

"What will we do if he dies?"

"We go on."

"I don't know how," she replied wearily, pulling away from her husband and the comfort he offered. "I've done it so many times. I can't do it again. I *can't* lose him."

Larissa made a rude noise in her throat, and her face suddenly flamed with hurt. "Maybe if he died, you'd finally pay some attention to me! Isn't that a stupid thought? Like it would ever happen. You've always loved him more than me. Just because you didn't want him when you were pregnant with him and you were afraid he'd grow up to be a mass murderer or something. It's like you try to make it up to him, but you can't so instead you love him more."

"Where did you hear that?" Marie-Thérèse demanded, horrified. She had been so careful with the secret.

"I heard you talking about it with Aunt Josette today, and about a million times over the years." Larissa's chin lifted. "Well, what about me, Mother? When does anyone start caring about me? With my luck Brandon really will die and you'll cry about it the rest of your life. And I'll pay for it. This really stinks!"

Mathieu's face turned thunderous. Marie-Thérèse had seen him angry before, but never so completely. "That's quite enough, Miss Smarty Pants!" he said tightly, almost viciously. "You had better get some respect and get it fast. I'm through putting up with your antics. Through! You are our daughter and you're going to start showing us the respect we deserve. Think about others for a change, instead of yourself!"

"You always take her side!" Larissa shouted. "Always!"

"I'm not always on her side," Mathieu said, his color deepening. "Was I on her side when I let you go to that concert with your friends? Was I on her side when I agreed that you should be allowed to cut your hair? What about when I said I didn't think you should have to share a room with the new baby? A dozen instances come to mind when we've both been more than fair with you, but it's over. As of today, I'm laying down the law. You will obey and pay respect or else!"

Larissa stared at her father in surprise which quickly gave way to anger. "I hate you!" she said venomously. "I hate you both! You can have your precious Brandon—I'm leaving!"

"No you aren't!" Mathieu grabbed her arm and marched her into the emergency room waiting area where Josette and an elderly couple were the only occupants. "Now if you so much as rise from that chair until I give you permission," he said with barely concealed anger, "your bottom will be redder that it ever has been! And believe me, I don't care how old you are. I mean what I say! If you keep acting like you're three instead of almost thirteen, you're going to be treated like it!"

Larissa's face twisted in an ugly grimace, but she stayed in the chair. Marie-Thérèse felt her daughter's hateful stare ripping into her like the claws of a cat.

Yet at least for that moment, Marie-Thérèse was distracted from her terrible fear for Brandon's life. Larissa was her daughter and she loved her deeply. "Please, Larissa," she pleaded. "I might lose Brandon; I can't bear to lose you, too."

Larissa said nothing, but her glowering seemed to abate slightly.

The doctor emerged then, to Marie-Thérèse's relief, and escorted her and Mathieu to Brandon's side. "We'll be moving him to a permanent room in a while," he informed them. "But take your time with him."

Brandon lay on the pillow, face red and blotchy against the stark white. Other than the slight rise and fall of his chest, he was motionless. An IV dripped steadily into his veins.

Marie-Thérèse began to sob again, stroking her son's hair, while Mathieu gripped his hand. "We're right here, son. Come back to us. We need you."

Marie-Thérèse continued to cry.

After a long time, they moved Brandon to another room, where Marie-Thérèse took up immediate occupancy in the chair to the right side of the bed. She rubbed at her son's lifeless arm. The rest of the family arrived and she listened as her father, assisted by Mathieu and André, gave him a blessing. She noticed that Jean-Marc also blessed the family to accept the Lord's will.

No! I won't. I can't. I won't! I can't let him die!

She prayed as she had never before prayed in her life. She begged, pleaded, and bargained with the Lord, promising every good thing if He would allow her son to live.

But her prayers lacked faith—she knew it. And Brandon was going to die.

CHAPTER 32

Rebekka returned to her parents' home on Monday morning, more exhausted than the night before. She should have contacted Marc as she had promised, but since she still didn't know what to say, she didn't, though her heart ached for comfort—his comfort. To be fair she had left a message on his cell phone, though she called when she knew he was in sacrament meeting and would have it turned off. She had promised to call again the next day.

Today.

She sighed. She had spent the entire Sunday feeling very ill because she had slept so poorly on Saturday night. Raoul had finally returned home at nearly three in the morning—alone—and she had heard him in the kitchen. They talked for hours and then finally fell asleep on the living room floor together, waking up stiff and sore, but just in time for church meetings. Raoul looked as terrible as Rebekka felt, and getting themselves ready took longer than they expected. They ended up going to a different ward an hour away, and Rebekka was glad that she wouldn't have to face anyone she knew—especially Marc and André. She almost hadn't gone to church at all, but Raoul reminded her that after the first time it was easier to miss, and one day she might not go back at all. He was right, she decided, and had forced herself to dress, though finding something in Desirée's closet modest enough to wear to church had been a challenge.

At church, she had felt a peaceful calm enter her heart, and she was intensely grateful she had attended. *Only Marc should be at my side,* she had thought.

Or should it be André?

Now the harsh confusion was back. Rebekka rubbed her temples, where a headache was steadily growing.

At least there was no one home who would demand an explanation. She had called her parents on Saturday night so they wouldn't worry, but Danielle would most certainly want to know why she hadn't been in their sacrament meeting the previous day, and all about Raoul's separation. She would likely have also heard from Ariana about Rebekka's break-up with Marc, and want to know the reason.

At least for the time being, Rebekka was spared the questions.

Going into her office, she plunged into her work. She paused several times to stare for long moments at the phone. What would Marc be doing now? She hoped he wasn't overworking. Surely his family would check up on him.

He's a full-grown man. She told herself. *He doesn't need a babysitter.*

In the afternoon, her stomach reminded her that she hadn't eaten anything. She turned off her computer and made her way to the kitchen. Danielle, who was standing by the counter, glanced over at her in surprise.

"I didn't know you were home, honey."

"I didn't know you were, either." Rebekka poured herself a glass of orange juice from the refrigerator. "I've been working in Raoul's room—I mean, my office."

"I was doing the grocery shopping," Danielle said, motioning to the counter where there were three large, reusable shopping bags, all made of sturdy material with wide, padded handles. "Here, these are still warm." She rummaged in one of the bags and offered Rebekka a cloth sack filled with fresh rolls.

Rebekka took a roll gratefully, biting into the flaky crust. "Mmm," she said with a sigh. The bread in France was the thing she had missed the most while living in America.

Well, that and Marc.

Had she even missed André?

Of course, he and Claire had been together then, so why would she have missed him in *that* way? In fact, if Claire hadn't died, Rebekka and Marc would nearly be married, and she wouldn't be in this predicament.

Rebekka felt she was on the verge of discovering a truth that might be terribly important, but her mother interrupted her thoughts.

"So, how's Raoul?" Danielle asked.

The truth Rebekka had almost realized instantly vanished. "He's at work." She took another bite of the bread and chewed slowly. "Apparently, Marc and André came up with a new project and they put Raoul in charge of it. He has to leave town tomorrow."

Danielle paused with a carton of juice in her hands. "That's good."

Rebekka set her cup forcefully on the table, dropping the half-eaten roll next to it. "What do you mean, good? I think he should find Desirée and either talk some sense into her or get a divorce, not bury himself in work. What good is that going to do?"

"I don't know. Why don't you tell me?" There was amusement in Danielle's face. "I mean, you seem to be doing pretty much the same thing."

"I am not . . . I'm—my situation is different."

"Of course it is." Danielle resumed shelving her purchases, the amusement gone. Rebekka knew then that someone must have filled her mother in on the details of what had happened on Saturday night, or at least some of them. But surely she didn't know about her feelings for André. Neither Ariana, Raoul, nor André would break her confidence.

"Dear," Danielle continued, "men generally tend to bury their problems in work, while women turn to their friends and their children. Now maybe that's because men have traditionally been the breadwinners—I don't really know—but that's the way it is."

"Did you do that?" Rebekka's curiosity overrode her anger.

Once again Danielle paused in her work. "Rebekka, believe it or not, there was a time when I almost left your father. And I did turn to you and Raoul and to my friends. But we made it through. He loves me and I love him." Danielle's face glowed. "And he even went to church again yesterday. I didn't have to ask him."

Rebekka knew what that meant to her after a lifetime of hoping and praying . . . and waiting. "Do you think he's really interested? Or is it that boy—Thierry?"

"He's interested," Danielle said with assurance.

Rebekka wasn't so sure, but she didn't want to hurt her mother's feelings.

Danielle put her hand on Rebekka's shoulder. "Someday you'll look back on this trouble you're having with Marc and see the reasoning. I promise you. It won't be tomorrow, or even next month, but someday. And Raoul will do the same. The Lord loves both of you, and He's aware of your needs."

Ariana had said much the same thing. Rebekka sighed.

"Why don't you get cleaned up and we'll take a break—go for a walk or something. If you want, we can talk about what is bothering you. And we still need to get some shoes to go with your wedding dress."

Rebekka looked down at her rumpled linen pantsuit—the same outfit she wore Saturday night. "I don't even know if I'll be wearing the wedding dress," she mumbled.

Danielle didn't appear to hear her. Resigned, Rebekka trudged to her room, dragging her feet. Once there, her eyes rose to the closet where she kept her wedding dress in a specially designed blue bag. Carefully, she unzipped the bag and fingered the delicate folds of shiny satin. Marc had never seen her in this dress, but she knew it made her beautiful, and she ached to try it on again. Instead, she headed for the shower.

In the bathroom, she slipped off the engagement ring Marc had given her. She examined it carefully, remembering the expression on his face when he had offered it to her near the river. His gaze had held so much love and hope, and now she didn't feel worthy to wear it, not when she had betrayed their love.

I didn't!

With a heavy sigh, Rebekka returned the ring to her finger. She wasn't going to take it off until . . .

Until what?

Huffing in frustration, she cut off her thoughts and hopped in the shower.

When she emerged from the bathroom, wrapped in her white terry-cloth robe, her mother was waiting in the hall, her face etched with worry. In her hand she gripped their portable phone.

Marc! Rebekka's first thought flitted across her mind.

"Josette called," Danielle said. "Brandon ate something at school and had an allergic reaction. He's in a coma and they don't know if he'll come out."

Rebekka felt the color ebb from her face. "Oh no!"

* * * * *

Rebekka and Danielle went immediately to the hospital where Brandon was being treated. Rebekka was stunned. How could such a terrible thing happen to such a nice kid? And how could something as benign as a strawberry cause such a disaster? Rebekka felt disillusioned. Brandon was such a wonderful boy. How could this happen to him?

All the Perraults had gathered at the hospital except Marc and Louis-Géralde. Ariana gave them a small smile as she embraced Danielle.

"How is he?" Danielle asked. The distress in her voice reminded Rebekka that not only was Danielle a good friend of the Perraults, she was also Mathieu's cousin. Brandon was family in more ways than one.

"He's in a coma," Ariana told her, "but the doctor seems to think he still has a good chance of waking up. Marie-Thérèse has taken it very hard, though. Mathieu says he doesn't know how to comfort her."

Rebekka's own problems suddenly became trivial; at least Marc was going to live. "Poor Marie-Thérèse," she said. "Is there anything I can do?"

"They're giving him a blessing now. Other than that, they won't let anyone in to see him besides immediate family. So I guess we're just here for moral support."

"We'll do anything we can to help," Danielle inserted. "Organize meals, read to him. Whatever we can do. Please let us know."

Rebekka was about to add to her mother's comments when she saw André saunter through the heavy wood door that set off the waiting room from the rest of the hospital wing. The confused emotions of the previous day returned and Rebekka bit the inside of her bottom lip nervously.

"Is something wrong?" her mother asked, touching her elbow in concern.

"No," Rebekka lied. "Nothing."

André's eyes locked onto hers and for nothing could she tear them away. She was vaguely aware of his father and grandfather behind him, branching off to talk with their wives. André came straight toward Rebekka.

"We have to stop meeting like this," he said.

Danielle gave a wry smile at his poor attempt to joke, but Rebekka couldn't even manage that much. Her heart hammered in her ears.

"I'm so sorry about Brandon," Danielle said. "I know that you two are close."

Rebekka saw the naked mourning on André's face. But almost immediately he masked the emotion. He took Rebekka's arm firmly and led her away down a hall, away from the others.

"Where is Marc?" she asked. "I mean . . . how's he doing?"

"He's all right—physically. I was with him earlier today at his place. But he doesn't know about Brandon yet because no one answered at his place when I called. And he must not have his cell on. I was going to see him now."

"He wouldn't have gone to the office, would he?" Rebekka said anxiously. "He promised me he wouldn't but—" She didn't know if all promises were void after the incident Saturday night. She bit her lip.

He stopped walking and turned to face her. "No, he's not at the office. But I doubt he's sleeping. He's probably looking for you."

A wave of guilt hit her. "I should have called him. But . . . but . . ." Tears filled her eyes and she could barely see André through the haze.

"Look, Rebekka." He broke off and stared at the ring Marc had given her for a moment before continuing. "There—there's something I need to tell you."

She blinked hard, but his face was still blurry. "What?"

"I've done a lot of thinking this weekend and I want to tell you that I think you should marry Marc."

"I should marry—What?" She was so stunned that she wondered if she had heard correctly. Had she imagined that he was attracted to her?

André cleared his throat and continued. "I know that in your heart you love Marc, and that he loves you more than life itself. I can see you two belong together." Her eyes had dried and she saw his face now, earnest, convincing.

"Then you don't—?" She couldn't finish.

"I'll always be your friend Rebekka. And hopefully, I can learn to be your big brother." He tried to laugh but it sounded flat to her ears. "It might take a little time, but I'll be okay," he continued, eyes full of compassion. "I care a great deal for you, I really do. You are a special, incredibly talented woman, and under other circumstances, I think . . . well, it doesn't really matter. The fact is, I'm still in mourning. I believe I've been too ready to try to fill the void Claire left in my life, and that was wrong of me. I need time to heal. I really miss her." His voice had grown hoarse.

Rebekka thought there was more truth to his last statement than anything else he had said.

"You and Marc are ready to go on with your lives." André hugged her with a finality that ripped at her heart. "I want you both to be happy."

"What should we tell Marc?" she asked.

André shrugged. "What is there to tell? We comforted each other, and somewhere along the way the lines were blurred. But they were always there, and we always knew that."

A weight seem to lift from her shoulders. He was right. André was still in love with Claire, not her, and she loved Marc. She did! All at once, her confusion was completely and utterly gone.

"I'm going to get back to the family," he said, thumbing casually over his shoulder. "And I think maybe you ought to be the one to go see Marc. You two can check in here later. It doesn't look like Brandon's in any immediate danger—he's unconscious, but stable."

She glanced down the hall, nodding. "I'll do that. Please tell Mathieu and Marie-Thérèse that I'm praying for them . . . and for Brandon."

"I will."

They stood looking at each other, and Rebekka was acutely aware of how differently this moment might have ended in other circumstances.

Or would it? An incredible calm filled her soul, similar to the peace she had experienced in church yesterday.

Like the times she spent alone with Marc.

The answer was there all along, Rebekka marveled, *just like Ariana said it was.*

Finally she saw what had been hidden from her these past weeks. When everything was said and done, she could imagine being happy with Andre, but she could *never* imagine living without Marc. He was her hero, the man of her dreams.

She had to find Marc! Her anticipation to be with him outweighed any other emotion. She couldn't wait be in his arms, and feel his lips on hers.

"Good-bye, André," she said somewhat breathlessly.

He nodded and she was relieved to see not pain, but understanding in his eyes. She smiled thankfully and walked away.

CHAPTER 33

André watched until Rebekka walked away, knowing he had helped her see the truth that had always been in her heart. Her reaction to his words proved that if forced to choose between them, she would have eventually turned to Marc. André could have tried to persuade her to wait, to get to know him better, but in the end, he believed that she would still have married Marc. By encouraging her to do so, André had given them a chance at the happiness they deserved. He would still be a part of their lives, and that was a deal he could live with. A deal he *had* to live with.

Heaving a sigh, he walked in the direction of the room where his family had gathered. *One foot in front of the other,* he told himself. *That's the way I'll survive.* He knew it wouldn't be easy, seeing Marc and Rebekka together and wondering what might have been, but he had done the right thing. Over the years, his ache for what she represented would fade.

"André!"

With surprise he turned to face the newcomer. "Hello, Monsieur Massoni." He used the formal title for Philippe, as he had done since childhood, despite the closeness of their two families.

"My wife called me. She seemed really upset. How's Brandon?"

André shook his head, the worry about his nephew coming to the forefront of his thoughts. "They don't know yet. They have a few more tests to run, but basically, he's stable. We just have to wait to see if he'll wake up, and if he does, how much damage there is."

"He's a strong boy," Philippe replied, "and he has a lot of support. That should help."

They walked together in silence. As they approached the waiting room Philippe spoke, "Look, if it's going to be a long wait, do you think you could make a visit with me?"

André didn't hide his surprise. "A visit?"

"Yes, to a young boy in your ward." Philippe hesitated. "I really don't want to explain right now, but I could use your company. And I think you'll find it worth your while."

"Okay." André was curious about Philippe's request. Though they had shared an amicable relationship since the day Philippe had helped Raoul raise the money to become a partner in the engineering firm, neither had made any social overtures toward the other. The nearly two and a half decades between them, not to mention their differences in faith, had made a deep friendship improbable. "But I have to pick up the girls at school soon," André added. "Will that be a problem?"

"No. Besides, the young man in question should be just finishing school himself. That is if the missionaries are keeping up their vigil."

André wondered what the missionaries had to do with Philippe, but he had learned in business that sometimes his best recourse was to wait. Philippe would explain when he was ready.

Philippe greeted everyone and then drew his wife aside for a private conversation. André noticed that his parents appeared more gray than usual, but when he approached they smiled. Ariana looked deeply in his eyes. "Where's Rebekka?"

Her name hit into him with a painful slap. "She went to find Marc," he said with only a little hesitation. "They belong together, and I told her so."

Her hand rested on his arm, comfortingly. "You did a good thing. You can be proud of that." But André knew that true sacrifice held no pride, only a sense of right that couldn't be faked.

His father clapped him on the shoulder. "I know it wasn't easy, and I'm sorry."

"Thanks, Dad."

"You ready, André?" Philippe asked from across the room.

André nodded. "I'm going to get the girls," he told his parents. "Call if you need me."

They took André's car because it had the seatbelts adjusted to accommodate the girls. "I know it may not seem like it," he told

Philippe, "but these metal clasps are a lot more difficult than they look."

Philippe smiled. "Believe it or not, I do remember. As a child, Rebekka was forever complaining about the shoulder belt."

This time the mention of Rebekka didn't slap as it once had, but instead penetrated his body and evaporated. It was gone. Gone. Not like the pain of losing Claire that had seemed to burrow permanently into his soul.

Oh, Claire! I miss you!

"Do you mind if we stop first at the boy's place?" Philippe asked. "If we have time, it might be better to go there without the girls. It's not an exceptionally rough area, but I can't vouch for what this boy might say or do."

André glanced at his watch. "As long as it's not too far."

"He lives near the high school. Just go there and I'll direct you."

"Let me ring the day care first, just to make sure. They watch Marée for part of the day, and if I'm late, they'll keep both girls for a while."

Philippe waited while he made the call. André returned the phone to his suit coat pocket, then asked, "I take it you've been to this boy's house before?"

"I drove by it on the way over."

André glanced at him and then back at the road. "Do you want to tell me what this is all about?"

Philippe gave a laugh. "I guess I owe you that. Does the name *Basil Lorrain* ring any bells?"

André nodded slowly. "Yes. Claire had a brother by that name."

"She did?" Philippe's surprise told André he hadn't expected that answer. "Do you know anything about him?"

"As far as we know, he left France when Claire was just a little girl. Presumably to find work. She has a few pictures of him, but—" He broke off, realizing that he was speaking of his wife in the present tense. "She wanted me to find him. It was one of the things she asked me that last day."

An odd look came across Philippe's face. "This just gets stranger and stranger," he said. "Maybe there really is a God who cares."

"Of course there is." André spoke quietly but with conviction.

"You can say that after all the tragedy your family has suffered?" Philippe's voice wasn't mocking or vicious, only curious.

"God tests those whom He loves."

Philippe laughed. "Must not love me very much, then."

"No?" André raised his eyebrows, thinking of the stories Rebekka had told him about her father's upbringing. "You haven't endured difficulty?"

Philippe looked thoughtful. "Maybe you're right."

"So, what about Basil?" André asked. "He's not in trouble at your bank, is he?" Though if he was, at least Philippe had saved André the effort of looking for Claire's long-lost brother.

"No, nothing like that. And truthfully, I'm not sure exactly where he fits in with this child we're going to see, but I feel almost driven to find out. The boy is living in an apartment with a Basil Lorrain. I had no idea before today that he might have any connection to Claire, but when my wife came by my office before lunch this morning with some old wedding announcements—apparently she's planning to have new ones made up for Rebekka and Marc if they ever settle on a date—and one of the announcements was yours. I saw your wife's maiden name and finally it clicked where I'd seen the name Lorrain. So then I started wondering if somehow you were related to the boy, or to the man he lived with." Philippe pursed his lips. "I never thought he would be so closely related, if this all turns out to be true. It was a long shot from the beginning, but as Danielle always tells me, the Lord works in mysterious ways."

But what André thought was mysterious was Philippe's sudden preoccupation with how the Lord worked. From what he had seen, Philippe had never depended one iota on anyone for anything other than himself. Not even his wife.

"That's all very interesting, but you still haven't told me what your connection is with the boy." André stopped at a light and studied the other man.

Philippe's brow furrowed before relaxing suddenly. "Just an inspiration," he said. "That's something you should understand, being a member of your church. Isn't it?"

André sighed and pushed on the gas as the light changed, wondering if Philippe would ever admit the reason for his involvement.

He followed Philippe's directions, and soon they arrived at their destination, where a double row of tall apartment buildings flanked both sides of the street. The buildings were old, though most were in passable repair; the sidewalks were worse, having lost large patches of cobblestone.

Approaching the outer door of the apartment building, Philippe checked the time on his gold wristwatch. "Might be home already. Hope not. He might not open the door."

As he spoke, André spied one of the sets of full-time missionaries that covered the ward boundaries. Both American, one was tall and stocky with brown hair, the other of average height with lighter hair and a wiry frame. Between them was a boy with dark brown hair, standing about the same height as the shorter missionary. André recognized him immediately from the ward house, and even remembered talking briefly to the teen. What was his name? Thierry, wasn't it? Ordinarily, he would never have noticed the boy, since he usually spent Sundays speaking in other wards in connection with his high council calling, but since Claire's death he had been given time off his usual speaking schedule and had greater opportunity to see those attending his own ward. He distinctly remembered seeing this boy sitting with the missionaries for several Sundays, perhaps more. He recalled that his attention had kept returning to the boy for some unknown reason, but each time he had dismissed the incident.

The three youths were laughing openly and lightheartedly. For a moment, André recalled his own childhood laughter. How many times had he, Marc, and their sisters, and even Rebekka walked the streets together, talking and laughing? Those were days he would never forget. And while he wouldn't trade his experience for those days, he felt a bittersweet melancholy and a longing for simpler times. Innocence was its own kind of bliss.

In that moment of longing, the teen looked up and saw Philippe. He stiffened and abruptly halted. The elders looked at him, confused, and then toward the door to the apartment building where the two men waited. Thierry continued to stare at Philippe, seemingly glued to the spot. With voices too far away to hear, the missionaries talked at length to Thierry, who looked about to flee.

Why is he so afraid of Philippe? André couldn't put the pieces together, but a glance at Philippe told him the boy's reaction wasn't a total surprise—at least not to Philippe. In less than a breath, André grew angry. He didn't know what game this new Philippe was playing, but he wouldn't allow him to harm this boy. He strode forward and Thierry's glance shifted to him, relaxing slightly. Under the missionaries' urging, he took a few cautious steps.

"Hello, Elders, Thierry." André held out his hand, all the time studying Thierry's face. The boy had dark hair and brown eyes, nice-looking, but nothing out of the ordinary. The teen smiled and suddenly André recognized what it was that had drawn his attention to the boy at church—he had Claire's smile. He was so stunned that for a moment he could hardly breathe, but then it was gone, so quickly that it might not have happened at all. If Philippe hadn't discovered the boy's real last name, André would never have given the occurrence another thought; in all the billions of people in the world, it was logical that a few might resemble Claire. But with the coincidence of him living with a father whose name was the same as Claire's own brother, it could only mean one thing.

Thierry must have seen something in his eyes because he immediately tensed again. "Hi," he muttered, sounding sullen next to the hearty welcome of the elders.

André glanced at Philippe, but the older man shrugged and inclined his head, inviting André to continue.

But this is your party, André wanted to say. Yet he knew that if this child really was related to Claire, it was his responsibility to find out.

"I just dropped by to talk to you and your father," André told Thierry.

"He's not here."

"Is he at work?"

Thierry shrugged.

"Look, Thierry, if you know anything, you should tell these men," Elder Ferguson said. "They'll help. We all want what's best for you."

Elder Pike rested a large hand on Thierry's shoulder. "You know we're your friends," he encouraged. "We'll stand by you."

"I don't know where he's at!" Thierry insisted, his foot toying with a loose cobblestone. "But he'll be back." He shot a nervous glance at Philippe, who remained quiet. "At least I think he will." Abruptly, the boy looked deflated.

"Could we go inside and talk?" André asked, noticing the interested stares of several neighbors as they leaned halfway out of their
second- and third-story windows on their elbows.

Thierry grunted something André took to be assent, and followed
him into the apartment building and up the worn marble staircase to
the sixth floor. The missionaries and Philippe brought up the rear.

André surveyed the studio apartment with compassion. The carpet
wasn't bad and the empty white walls had probably been painted within
the past two years, but the ceramic tile in the kitchen had dirt-caked
spider web cracks throughout and the overpainted cupboards drooped.
The laminate on the short counter was relatively clean, but peeling, and
the single curtainless window looked as though it had been painted shut
too many years ago to count. A large, battered television sat on a crate
against the wall. Another crate sat next to it, filled with dusty books and
what André thought might be picture albums. The only other furniture
in the room was a rickety old dresser, a double bed hiding under a
mound of blankets and clothes, and a sagging blueberry-colored sofa.

Thierry pointed at the sofa, inviting them to sit. André and
Philippe settled on the too-soft cushions, while the missionaries
sprawled on the floor with an ease that suggested they had done so
many times before.

"How long have you lived here with your father?" André asked
gently as Thierry threw his backpack onto the bed.

"A year." Thierry didn't look at him, but concentrated on settling
himself on the crate of books next to the television.

"And before that?"

"I used to live in Toulouse with my stepdad, but he died a couple
years back and I lived in some foster homes until they found my dad.
Then we came here."

"Is he gone a lot?"

Thierry met André's steady gaze. "Yeah." Then he shrugged. "But
I take care of myself. I'm not some baby."

"Of course you're not," Philippe said, speaking for the first time.
"But your father's been gone about a month, hasn't he? Or just over
five weeks, to be exact."

Fear leapt into Thierry's eyes and the boy's chin jutted out defen-
sively. "So, are you from the cops?"

"No. Look—" André cast Philippe a hard stare. "We're not here in any official capacity." He glanced at the missionaries, to include them in his words. "We're here because we are concerned, but—"

"What do you care?" interrupted the boy. "Don't tell me—you're just worried my dad'll get in the way of my baptism. I tell you, he won't. He and I do what we want. I only stay with him because he pays the rent."

"Well, the rent's due again, isn't it?" Philippe said. "Or very soon. You have to admit, you're a little worried that he won't be coming back to pay it."

"He will too!" Thierry jumped to his feet, hands clenched.

Philippe's blue eyes glinted. "What I really want to know is why you stare at me in church. These last weeks, every time I look up, you're there. You've seen me before somewhere and I frighten you. Why?"

"I'm *not* afraid of you!" Thierry exclaimed.

But André knew better. The boy was terrified of Philippe, but trying hard not to show it.

Thierry strode to the door and opened it. "Look, I want you to leave. All of you."

Everyone remained motionless, stunned by the request. André stood and walked over to Thierry. "I apologize for Monsieur Massoni's outburst," he said softly. "To tell you the truth, I'm here because he asked me to come. But before you kick us out, I want to tell you about my wife."

Watching him warily, Thierry shut the door, folding his arms across his chest. "Okay, I'm listening."

"She died a little over six weeks ago." André spoke to him, but knew the others were listening. He was glad his back was to them; only Thierry would be able to see the tears glistening in his eyes.

"I know," Thierry said, less angry now. "I liked her. She was nice. We talked a few times."

The knowledge made André happy. "Well, what you probably don't know is that she was raised in a very poor family. Her father died when she was young, then her little sister and her mother. She had a brother, who went away when she was small. She never saw him again."

The boy shifted, obviously wondering impatiently what the story had to do with him. André smiled gently. "His name was Basil. Basil Lorrain."

Thierry stared, jaw gaping. He blinked and shook his head once. "You're saying my dad's her brother?"

André shrugged. "Could be. I hope he is." He said the words with all the sincerity he felt in his heart.

"But I talked to her. I never guessed."

"There's no reason you would have recognized each other. You were using the name Bernard and she was using her married name. The name Lorrain wouldn't have come up in casual conversation. You both have dark hair, but your eyes are brown and hers were turquoise. There is really no resemblance between you." *Except the smile.* But he didn't say it aloud. "Claire was very young when her brother went away and her memories of him were faded. Even if you looked like him, she wouldn't have placed you as his son."

"I look like my mom," Thierry said. "I'd hate it if I looked like *him*."

"Well, I would be very happy if you turned out to be my nephew. Very happy." André let that sink in before asking, "How would you feel about it?"

"I—I . . . don't know." Thierry was struggling with something, and André thought it best to allow him do it on his own—for now. "It's just so weird. My . . . uh, dad, well, he told me about his family. Said they lived in Strasbourg, but that they died while he was working in Germany. He went back and asked the neighbors about them."

"That's true. They did live in Strasbourg, and they all died. Except my wife. I'm not surprised the neighbors didn't know what happened to Claire. She and her mother were pretty much ostracized in the neighborhood after they joined the Church. Her mother died suddenly, soon after I met her, and she moved here to live with my parents until we were married. She never went back."

"He said he only had one sister, not two."

"The other sister was probably born after he left. He was quite a bit older than Claire."

"I don't know." Thierry moved away from the door, his expression glazed.

"If you have any pictures, it might help," Elder Ferguson suggested.

In response, Thierry walked to the crate full of books and rifled through them. "Here," he said after a long moment.

André took the frayed album eagerly and sat on the sagging sofa, the others gathered closely around him. He saw immediately that the photos were not in order, but placed haphazardly. With ease, he picked out Thierry's father because the resemblance to the boy was strong. Except Basil's eyes were turquoise.

Like Claire's.

Of course, a million people in the world had turquoise eyes.

"That's my mom," Thierry said, pointing to a thin, unhappy-looking woman with brown hair. "And that's me. There's more of me and my mom, but the rest of the people I don't know. Must have been people he met." The sadness in his voice was the longing of a son to know his father.

At last, buried in the middle of the thin album, André found what he was looking for: a picture of Claire as a small girl, holding onto her mother's hand. Unlike the other photos in the album, it was not inside the protective plastic, but looked as though it had been simply shoved into the book to take care of later. He flipped it over and read the careful manuscript writing: *I miss you, Basil. Claire asks about you all the time. Please come home.*

André's heart ached at the pain Claire's mother had endured. How had Basil felt about the words his mother had written? Was this why he had eventually returned to Strasbourg—only to find his family gone?

"It's Claire," he said through the sudden lump in his throat. He looked at the young boy, who stared at him with a strange yearning in his eyes. "I know it's going to take some getting used to, Thierry, but it appears I'm your uncle. I can't wait to talk to your dad."

Thierry's tentative smile faded instantly. "He's not coming back."

André studied him. "I thought you said . . . Why's that?" He tried to make his voice light, but the weight of the world was in Thierry's eyes, and he had to know the reason Basil would desert his son.

"I can't tell you! But he's not coming back! And I don't care!" Thierry grabbed the photo album from André and threw it across the room. It hit the wall and broke apart, spilling several photographs onto the floor. "I don't need him or anybody!"

"But *we* need you!" André answered. "Listen, Thierry, we're family. I don't know what that means to you, but it means everything to me. If Claire were alive, she'd thank God she found you. I'll do the same. If you're in some trouble, I want to help. Please. There isn't anything I wouldn't do for you. Anything. And the same goes for any member of my family."

Thierry gaped in amazement, apparently not knowing quite what to make of him. He looked at the missionaries and they nodded encouragingly. Lastly, his gaze drifted to Philippe.

"He means what he says," Philippe said. "My wife is only a member of the Perrault clan by way of her cousin's marriage to André's sister Marie-Thérèse, but they've always been there for her." He smiled warmly.

Thierry searched their eyes another time before André added. "If Basil's in trouble, we need to know. You can trust us. I promise you that."

Elder Ferguson nodded. "You can trust Brother Perrault," he said. "Can't you feel that? Isn't that the same feeling you had when you prayed about the truthfulness of the Book of Mormon?"

Thierry relaxed, as all the fight went out of him. He stared at the ground. "We were in the alley that night," he whispered.

For a moment André didn't understand. He glanced at Philippe, who spoke. "Your father was the one who hit me, is that right? That's why he left town. He was afraid of the police."

Thierry nodded once, quickly, but didn't look up. "Yeah. We needed money. He was going to hit you again, but I recognized you from Louis-Géralde's farewell. I knew you were married to Sister Massoni, and I couldn't let him do it. I thought he would kill you. He's done it before. Not when I saw; he told me about it. And when I didn't let him hit you again, he pushed me down and ran. I haven't seen him since. I think he was afraid I'd tell, though I wouldn't have. I just didn't want him to kill anyone. I took your money, though. I knew I would have to pay the rent." Thierry let his gaze slowly rise. He looked not at Philippe, but at André. "I'm sorry. Are you going to call the cops?"

André brought his hand to Thierry's shoulder. "No, I'm not, though Philippe might want to talk to them about your father. And I don't think you have anything to feel guilty about—except for taking Monsieur Massoni's money, and that we can make up later. One thing I do know is that our meeting is no coincidence, Thierry. Claire prayed every day for her brother and any family he might have. I bet those prayers are what led the missionaries to you, and you to us." While still addressing Thierry, he turned his gaze to Philippe. "What happened in the alley is that you possibly saved Monsieur Massoni's life. I'm proud of you."

Thierry's eyes glistened and he smiled the smile that was so like Claire's. In that instant, André saw not the brash, independent teen, but a small boy who desperately needed someone to love him, the son André never had.

André glanced at his watch. "I really have to pick up my girls," he announced. He pretended not to see the disappointment on Thierry's face. "You want to come with me, Thierry? We have a lot to discuss. And I'm sure the girls will be so excited to know they have a new cousin. What do you say? We could grab a bite to eat afterwards."

"Well, I guess so," Thierry said with false reluctance. "I do have some homework, though."

"Bring it along. And why don't you bring a change of clothes too, just in case? We might not have the time to come back tonight. If you don't mind, you could crash out at my house. My office there has a sofa bed." André was determined that Thierry would never sleep in this apartment alone again.

"Okay. I guess. I don't have plans." Thierry moved toward the bed and the clothes lying on top.

Philippe drew André aside. "Are you sure you want to do this?" he asked quietly. "You don't have to, you know."

"He's family," André replied in a quiet voice. "I don't pretend it's going to be easy, but he belongs with us." He laughed at Philippe's doubtful face. "Look, I won't be leaving my daughters alone with him any time soon, or leaving my credit cards lying around, but there's nothing in my apartment that can't be replaced. He's what's important now. Claire would want it this way. Besides, he's a good kid, can't you see that? He saved your hide, didn't he?" He slapped Philippe on the back. "I owe you one."

Thierry had finished his hasty preparations and was talking quietly with the missionaries when André approached. "You ready?" André asked. Thierry nodded and followed him to the door.

"Yeah."

André waited while Thierry locked the door and then followed him down the stairs. Outside, André put his hand on the boy's back and gestured toward his car. "See you around, Philippe, Elders."

"But isn't he going with you?" Elder Pike asked, glancing at Philippe.

"No." André flashed a smile at Philippe. "He came with me, but he can find his own way home. This conversation is between Thierry and myself." He almost laughed at Thierry's relieved expression.

"Well, then I guess I'll just phone a taxi," Philippe said, pulling out his cell. "Elders, would you accompany me? There's a guy I want you to meet—if you have time, that is. He cuts hair."

As he drove off, André wondered why Philippe was setting people up with the missionaries. *He really has changed,* he thought.

He chatted easily with Thierry on the way to the girls' school, keeping the conversation light. Together they walked in to collect Ana and Marée.

"So what do you think of engineering or architecture?" André asked as they waited for the girls to gather their things.

"Don't know much about it," the boy answered. "But I'm a fast learner. I'm best at languages, though."

André smiled at Thierry, who was now being inundated with questions from his daughters. How grateful he was for their cheerful faces! So much of his precious Claire was in them.

And how grateful he was for Thierry! One way or the other, André would make them all happy.

And I'll be happy, too, he promised himself. *With the Lord's help.*

"Okay now," he said brightly. "Ana, Marée, I know you're dying of curiosity, but before you kill our new friend here with talk, Thierry and I are hungry. Where do you want to go eat? I'll explain everything on the way."

He didn't tell the girls about Brandon. Not yet. Before doing so, he would check in at the hospital. He prayed that by then Brandon's condition would have changed for the better.

And if it hadn't?

Then we'll go wait with the others. And I'll tell them about Thierry. They'll be glad for some good news. The anticipation of that moment left him feeling happy. He had a son . . . of sorts.

Thank you, Father, he prayed. Whether Thierry realized it or not, he was the answer to many prayers, and André was determined to make his life a good one. Not only for Thierry or for the girls, but also for the memory of Claire.

CHAPTER 34

When Rebekka arrived at Marc's apartment, there was no answer. She used her key to let herself in, the gnawing fear of losing him growing every minute. She wished she could turn back the clock to Saturday and change her reaction that evening. If only she could have understood her true feelings then!

She quickly glanced through the rooms. The scattered papers in his office showed signs of its recent use, but the bed was made and there were no dirty dishes. Where had he gone?

She tried to think like Marc, but was uncertain if her reasoning was accurate. Last month she would have felt in her heart where to find him, but now she wondered if she had lost that intuition.

Ridiculous, she told herself. *I still know him. And I love him.*

The thought steadied her. "When I didn't call him, he would have gone to my house," she said aloud. "But I wasn't home. He can't go to the office, and all his family is at the hospital, so where else would he go?"

She snapped her fingers suddenly and headed for the underground garage. But after a moment's hesitation she left the elevator on the main floor and went outside, nearly jogging the block to the metro station. Where she was going it would be a lot easier to not worry about her car.

She had to pay a train ticket because her pass had expired when she had been in America, and she hadn't needed to renew it since most of her traveling had been to and from the transplant hospital, for which she had used her car. Impatiently, she counted the stops.

Please be there, Marc, she said in her head. *Please be there.*

When she arrived at her station, she was the first one out the doors and raced down the marble steps two at a time. She blinked briefly in the weak winter sunlight and buttoned her long leather jacket against the chill in the air. With a flood of other people, she crossed the street at the crosswalk but hurried on alone to the Seine River. A single artist painted on the parapet overlooking the river, his hands encased in gloves that left his fingertips bare. His nose and cheeks were reddened with wind, as though he'd been there for hours. Next to him in a midsize wooden crate was a stack of unframed paintings lying on their sides, separated carefully from one another by white tissue paper. He looked hopefully at Rebekka as she passed, but she was in too much of a hurry to stop. Smile fading, he turned back to his work.

Rebekka hurried down a flight of cobblestone steps to get closer to the river. This was the same place she and Marc had come that day so long ago when he had collapsed. He *had* to be here. Her eyes anxiously scanned the area, her thumb toying with the engagement ring on her finger. How often they had come here over the years. Surely he would remember!

The music she had composed for Marc, to be played for him on their wedding day, began in her mind, slowly building to a loud crescendo. Vivid, turbulent, warm, tender, and passionate—like her feelings for him. The warnings that had once haunted her were gone.

But he wasn't in sight.

A couple of teenagers lounged on one of the stone benches, and an old man with a cane walked farther down the cobbled path next to the river.

How could he not be here? Rebekka's heart ached with longing. Would he listen to her explanation? Would he believe that she loved him, not with a portion of her heart as she did André, but with her entire soul?

There was a movement behind a tree growing from one of the few squares of dirt placed periodically in the cobblestones. Rebekka's heart lurched. Marc! She would recognize him anywhere.

He turned and saw her at that moment. He took a step, revealing the rest of his body that had been hidden by the trunk of the tree. Rebekka also took a step in his direction, marveling at the emotions in her breast. How much she loved him! Having almost lost him gave her new insight to the extent of that love.

Their eyes met. "Rebekka." His mouth formed the word, but she was too far away to hear. He was wearing jeans and a polo under his long, black leather jacket, and had two sets of roller blades slung over one shoulder.

Roller blades?

They closed the distance between them until they were only inches apart. Rebekka wanted to throw herself into his arms, and searched his face for a similar desire. Had she destroyed all her dreams?

His eyes were unreadable and the fear of losing him grew to a stabbing pain in her breast. "Marc," she whispered.

He fingered one of the metal blades. "I went to your house," he said softly. "I thought that . . . I wanted to remind you." His hands shot out and grabbed hers. "Oh, Rebekka. I know there's someone else, but you are my life and I'm going to fight for you! We're meant to be together!"

The silliness of him going to her apartment with roller blades when he couldn't possibly use them during his recovery brought a lump of tenderness to her throat. His expression turned to one of torture as she struggled to speak. "I know," she managed finally, simply.

With a finger, he unhooked the pairs of roller blades from his shoulder and sent them crashing to the stones at their feet. He reached for her, and she stepped into his arms.

"Hey, you've been crying." His thumb smoothed a tear on her cheek.

"I was so afraid of losing you."

He held her tightly and she could feel his body tremble. "When I was here just now, I kept thinking the same thing. I was sure that I had lost you."

Rebekka smoothed his brow and kissed his cheek. "Don't be silly," she murmured, vowing never to hurt him again. "I've waited almost twenty years to become your wife, and I'm not giving up now. I love you. And I'm sorry for Saturday night."

"But I was wrong." He stared earnestly into her eyes. "I should have married you right there in the hospital. If I had to do it over again, I would. Oh, Rebekka, I know it's selfish, but I can't stand the thought of eternity without you!"

No, you were right, she wanted to say. *If you had died I might have married André. I might have grown to love him.*

Love him more than Marc?

It really didn't matter anymore, though she was honest enough with herself to admit that if Marc had married her and then died, she might have eventually come to resent him later. But from this moment, she vowed to never look back. Instead, her mind raced with plans for the future.

"Kiss me," she murmured, lifting her lips to his. "Just kiss me." He did and in his arms, nothing else mattered.

After a long time, they wandered from the river. Rebekka spotted the artist, still painting in the cold, and pulled Marc to a stop to peruse his work. "He's really quite good," Marc said.

Rebekka smiled at the young artist. "Will you do one of us?"

A flush covered the already cold-reddened face. Without speaking the artist turned his easel toward them, and Rebekka saw that he had already begun a rough rendition of a couple embracing by the river.

"That's us!" Rebekka exclaimed with wonder, marveling at how the artist had captured their joy.

"It'll take me a few days to finish," the man said, smiling at her contentment. "I'll need half the money now and half when I deliver the painting. And it would work best if I could take a few pictures of you up close—to work from in my studio. So that the faces are right." He held up a camera. Rebekka suspected that he had already taken their picture while they had been embracing below, but she was glad. Now she would always have something to remind her of this moment.

"Shoot away," Marc said, encircling Rebekka with his strong arms. He kissed her again.

CHAPTER 35

Night fell and Marie-Thérèse was alone in the room with Brandon. The extended family had departed and Mathieu was with Larissa somewhere. She rose slowly to use the bathroom, careful not to turn on the overhead lights. Once there, she fell to her knees near the tub and began to pray again. But though she prayed long and fervently, it was without hope, because she knew Brandon's fate was already decided. Inside, she felt her testimony dying. *I pray and pray,* she thought, *and they still die. Mother, Father, Pauline. And now Brandon.*

As she came from the bathroom she felt someone in Brandon's room, and heard the person talking in a low voice. Marie-Thérèse's steps faltered as she recognized Larissa.

"I wish it was me," she was saying, her voice a brutal kind of sad. "You should see Mom. She's a basket case. I thought she was going to have a heart attack on the spot when they told her. If it was me, she wouldn't be so bad. So don't die. You gotta come back . . . for her. And I'm so sorry I told you last week that they didn't want you. I know it's not true. It's me they wish they'd never had." Larissa shuddered deeply and continued through intermittent sobs. "I love you so much, Brandon. And I know why Mom loves you the way she does. You deserve it. I wish I did." She bent over Brandon's body, weeping heartbrokenly.

Marie-Thérèse came forward slowly, her own agony dimming in the realization of her daughter's pain. She reached the bed and drew Larissa into her arms. "Oh, honey," she murmured, turning her daughter to face her. "I've never loved Brandon more than you.

Never. Please believe that, even if you believe nothing else I say. If it were you—" Marie-Thérèse gulped "—on that bed right now, I would be in every bit as much pain. The only difference is that Brandon would help me face it, and I would be stronger for the help." She paused. "Can you help me, Larissa? I need you so much."

Larissa clung to her and for the first time in more than a year, Marie-Thérèse felt loved by her daughter. The feeling was delicious, and she knew suddenly that her love for Larissa and Mathieu was what would keep her living after the Lord took Brandon.

"I wish it was me," Larissa said in the dark.

"And I've been here wishing that it were me," Marie-Thérèse replied. Then out of habit she added, "I guess this is how Jesus felt in the Garden of Gethsemane, why He was willing to die for us." Why did she say it? Did she really believe? She was no longer sure.

"Yeah." Larissa gave a little sigh and snuggled closer. "I'm sorry, Mom. For what I said earlier. I didn't mean it. I was scared. I know Brandon and I fight a lot, but I—I love him."

"Shhh, I know. We all say things we don't mean when we're angry."

Larissa hiccuped gently. "Not you."

"Even me." Marie-Thérèse was glad that her daughter couldn't see the feverish upheaval in her heart.

"Is Brandon really going to die?"

Yes, Marie-Thérèse wanted to say, but instead she answered softly, "I don't know."

They stood together silently for a long time, until Marie-Thérèse's knees ached. She slid to the chair, bringing her daughter to her lap. Larissa was nearly asleep when Mathieu came in quietly, peering at her in the dim glow of the headboard nightlight.

"I've looked everywhere," he said. "I can't find Larissa. Do you think I was too hard on her?"

"She's here with me."

Mathieu breathed a sigh of relief. "Thank heaven!" When his eyes adjusted to the dark, he moved forward. "Maybe you should take her home. I'll wait with Brandon."

"I can't leave him."

"Well, I'm not leaving you." Mathieu's voice had a stubborn tone Marie-Thérèse recognized all too well.

"Okay, stay. But at least take Larissa to sleep out on a couch in the waiting room. This room is so small there's not enough space for all of us. I'll let you know if anything happens."

Mathieu knelt by her chair, taking the hand that was not supporting Larissa. "I love you, Marie-Thérèse, and we'll get through this. Try to have faith. Please. You have always been such an example to me. I need your strength."

Marie-Thérèse felt she had none left to give, but she nodded because he had asked and because if it came right down to it, she loved him even more than she loved Brandon. He kissed her mouth gently and then offered a prayer.

A last family prayer, Marie-Thérèse thought sadly. Her stomach twisted, but as she hadn't eaten since her lunch with Josette, she was in little danger of losing any contents.

Mathieu carried the sleeping Larissa out of the room, leaving Marie-Thérèse alone with Brandon. She took his hand. In and out he breathed, seeming only asleep. How deceiving!

New tears slipped down her face.

* * * * *

Larissa was only pretending to sleep as her father carried her from the room. She felt so warm and secure in his arms, and during his prayer, she had heard the love in his voice and it was as if she *knew* for the first time that her parents loved her. The warm, tender emotions that filled her heart were so wonderful she was afraid if she moved they would disappear.

Her father laid her gently on the couch and smoothed her hair. She heard a noise and peeked through her lashes to see him wiping tears from his cheeks. His lips were moving as if in prayer.

Would prayer really help? Her dad obviously thought it would, and so did her mom. But Larissa hadn't prayed. She wasn't sure God would want to hear anything from her. Yet Brandon might die if she didn't and then she would remember forever that she had told him he wasn't wanted. He might die actually believing her.

She squeezed her eyes shut. *Dear Father in Heaven,* she began. *I don't know that You exist, but Mom and Dad say You do. And Aunt*

Josette, too. I want to believe. Please. . . make Brandon be better. Or let it be me instead. Not Brandon. He's too good. I'm the one who deserves to be punished. Take me instead!

Her pleas increased in fervor. *Please, Father in Heaven. Help us! I'm sorry for everything, and I promise to try to be better to my family. Please bless Brandon!* Tears squeezed out of her eyes and made a path down her cheek to the couch cushion.

"Larissa?"

She opened her eyes as her father gathered her into his arms. "It's going to be all right," he said. "You have to understand that."

"But Brandon could die," she said in a small voice.

"He could, but that doesn't mean things won't be all right. And we still need to have faith. All of us. Can you do that for me?"

"Yes." She felt she could do anything for Brandon. And anything to ease her parents' suffering.

Her father's arms tightened around her. "Then trust me when I say it's going to be okay."

Larissa shut her eyes again and pressed her face against his shirt. Once again she felt warm and secure. Was it the Spirit? Or was it the warmth of her father's arms?

Maybe right then they were the same thing.

* * * * *

Eyes tightly closed, Marie-Thérèse prayed. She pleaded, begged, and sorrowed until there was no strength left in her body.

At long last a voice whispered inside her soul, *Trust in Me.*

I did trust You, she answered silently. *And You took my mother, and my father, and my little sister. And the other babies I might have had. You can't have Brandon too!* She never thought she would be angry at God, but she was now.

What if I told you it was his time to come home? Marie-Thérèse wasn't sure where the words came from, but suspected they originated in her own thoughts.

She had no answer for the question. She wouldn't let Brandon go. Opening her eyes, she placed her arm over Brandon's inert form, as though she could keep his spirit from leaving.

Trust in Me. The thought came again.

You can't have Brandon, she countered. *Please! I'll have nothing left!*

But that wasn't quite true. What of Mathieu and Larissa? What of the rest of her family and all the blessings the Lord had given her over the years? The strains of a familiar hymn came to her mind: *Count your many blessing, see what God hath done.* But she wasn't in the mood to count them. Not when so much was at stake.

She could barely make out Brandon's face in the dim light, but the steady displays of the monitors comforted her. He was alive. But what if it was his time to go? Was she holding him back? Was he longing to fall into the arms of his loving Father in Heaven?

Yes.

Marie-Thérèse's heart ached at the unwanted truth. But what about her?

Count your blessings.

As directed, she began to count her blessings and see how much the Lord *had* given her. Loving family and friends, a roof over her head, years of happiness, forgiveness for sins, and hope of eternal life. The list could go on, but these were the most important.

"Oh, Brandon," she said with a sigh.

Rising to her feet, she felt his face that was neither hot nor cold to the touch. Could she give him up if that was what the Lord required of her? Where did the bounds of her faith end? If she couldn't give him wholly to the Lord, what kind of faith did she have? And how could he be healed if his own mother didn't have enough faith? It was a paradox that puzzled her.

So what *did* she believe? She thought about it a long time as she stroked her son's unmoving cheeks. Her life's trials ran through her mind, and in all honesty she had to admit that her Father had been near, guiding and protecting her. Could she give Him any less than all He required?

"But I'm so afraid," she whispered to the dark. "Maybe I need more faith, yet if I pray for it, I'll only receive another trial. And I don't want another one of those—especially not the trial of losing my son."

Was that what it came down to? Another trial?

Suddenly the irony of her words struck her with full force. She didn't feel she had enough faith, and yet if she prayed for faith, she would be given a trial designed to increase her faith. So obviously, she had faith that the Lord would answer her prayers—at least about some things.

She wiped the tears from her cheeks. Maybe she wasn't lacking faith so much as she lacked the strength and the will to exercise the faith she did have.

Okay, she said, looking at the dark ceiling and trying to picture His face. *I'll trust in You, Father. I'll trust You with Brandon's life. And I will exercise the faith that You will take care of him and us . . . one way or another.*

"Brandon," she said aloud, taking his hand in hers. "I want you to fight as you have never fought before. I want you to live. Live!"

Her voice became softer, but still urgent. "But if you must go, I understand. Or at least most of me does." She faltered and then continued unsteadily, "I'll miss you so, so much, but we *will* be together again. Obey the calling within you. The Lord will show you the way. Follow Him."

Looking once again heavenward, she added, "Father, Thy will be done."

The invisible load that had dragged on her shoulders lifted. She smiled wistfully at the quiet assurance that entered her heart, infusing her with a spiritual warmth that she knew was love coming fom her Heavenly Father. She kissed her son and left the room to find Mathieu.

He wasn't asleep, but staring at the ceiling in the waiting room, partially holding a sleeping Larissa in his arms. Tears were drying on his face. He looked at her, a question in his eyes, but she shook her head. "Nothing new." She kissed his cheek gently. "I just wanted to tell you that I know our son is in the Lord's hands now. I wanted you to know that I do have faith, and that I know God loves us."

Mathieu met her gaze and smiled. Without his saying a word, she understood how happy he was that she had found her faith again. Brandon's death would still be a difficult trial, but the Lord would sustain them.

She returned to Brandon's room to resume her mother's vigil. Sitting forward in her chair, she laid her head on his bed, holding his hand until she fell asleep.

When she awoke, the room was lighter, as rays of sun streamed through the gaps in the curtains. Without lifting her head, she felt for her son's hand again, searching for a pulse. Surely the end was near.

"Mom?"

Stunned, Marie-Thérèse raised her head to see Brandon's eyes fluttering. Her tongue had turned to stone.

"Mom, are you there?" His voice was weak and wavering.

Finally, she could speak. "Yes, Brandon. I'm here. Of course I'm here. I would never leave you."

"I saw it," he said. "I wanted to stay, but they made me come back." He paused. "I'm glad I came back, though. I missed you."

Marie-Thérèse's heart lifted in a silent prayer of gratitude. "I missed you, too."

* * * * *

Later, Marie-Thérèse, Mathieu, and Larissa met with relatives in the waiting room to pass on the doctor's assurance of Brandon's full recovery.

"I told you it was going to work out," Josette whispered, hugging her. "And I think this experience with Brandon has changed Larissa. I doubt the changes will be overnight, but she's going in the right direction. You'll see."

Marie-Thérèse nodded, too choked up to speak. There would be battles ahead, she was sure, but with faith in the Lord, anything was possible. She returned her sister's hug, struggling for composure. "One thing I think you should know," she said quietly. "Mathieu and I have decided to withdraw our adoption papers completely. We talked about it this morning after Brandon awoke. We want to concentrate on Larissa and Brandon now. It's the right thing to do. Especially for Larissa."

"But you wanted another baby so much!" Josette's face showed her curiosity.

Marie-Thérèse shook her head solemnly. "What I want—need— is a close relationship with my daughter. And that's going to take my full attention." She spoke with confidence and met her sister's gaze steadily, willing her to understand.

"You're right. Of course you're right. Maybe someday—"

"Well, you never know how things may change, but for now I have a new dream. And I'm going to be happy. The Lord has blessed me with so very much; I won't take it for granted again."

Larissa appeared at her side, and Marie-Thérèse put her arm around her daughter. Yes, everything was going to be just fine.

CHAPTER 36

One week later, Rebekka's heart sang as she arose and dressed in her Swiss hotel room. After days of handling airline flights, hotel reservations, and arranging a brief civil ceremony in France, she and Marc would finally become husband and wife for all eternity.

Carefully, she applied her makeup and arranged her hair, paying special attention to detail on this important day. As required by French law, she and Marc had legally married in France the day before, but they agreed to treat that civil ceremony as one more "reservation" to make before the real wedding. This morning, she would take a taxi to the Swiss Temple, where in the afternoon she and Marc would be sealed, not only for the span of life but for forever. A lifetime of dreams come true!

Marc's doctor hadn't been too enthusiastic about their plans for the wedding in Switzerland, but Josette, due to give birth in two weeks, insisted they have it before her baby was born so that she would be able to make the trip to Switzerland.

"When she's like this, you just have to give in," Zack had said, winking adoringly at his wife. The offended stare she cast in his direction melted immediately at the love so clearly etched in his eyes.

"He'll only be getting married in the temple once," Josette had replied with a shrug. "And there's no way they'll want to wait a month for me to have the baby and recover. Look at them all goo-goo-eyed, like a couple of calves. Besides, I'll be fine. None of our babies except Preston have come early, and my labors are so easy, you could probably deliver the baby yourself if you had too." Then they had all laughed at Zack's suddenly pale face. With the couples' past births the nurses spent as much time making sure he didn't faint as they did comforting Josette.

So it was decided, and almost three weeks after Marc's second transplant, Rebekka and Marc would have their temple wedding, and Josette would be there to see her twin sealed. Since Josette wasn't allowed on a plane for fear of an early delivery, she and Zack had gone ahead by car and picked up the rest of the family at the airport the night before.

Rebekka still worried constantly about Marc's health, but he had assured her repeatedly that although he wouldn't be skiing any time soon, he felt fit enough to at least walk to his own wedding.

"I promise to take it easy on you," Rebekka had teased with a glint in her eyes. With relish she had taken care of nearly all the wedding arrangements, assisted by her mother and Ariana. Marc's sole contribution had been scheduling their stay at an oceanside resort in Nice, where they could depend on fairly good honeymoon weather despite their December wedding.

As she walked into the sitting room to place her makeup bag with her other luggage, Rebekka heard her parents' voices coming from the largest bedroom of their shared suite. *Good, they're up,* she thought, ready for some company. She had taken a few steps toward their door when her father's words caused her to pause, unsure if she should interrupt them.

"Why did you put up with me all these years?" Philippe was asking.

"Because you're a good man and you've been good to me," Danielle answered. "And because I love you."

"But I've been so blind."

Danielle gave a low, silky laugh. They fell quiet and Rebekka assumed they were kissing.

"I can't wait to see the look on Raoul's face when I ask him to baptize me," Philippe said after a long while.

Rebekka ran to knock on the door. At her parents' invitation, she pounced into the room. "What?" she demanded of her parents, who smiled at her eagerness. "Did I hear you say baptized?"

"We thought you were still asleep, dear," Danielle said. "After all, we don't have to be at the temple for another two hours." She winked at Philippe.

Philippe grinned. "It was your wedding gift, Rebekka. I planned to tell you after the ceremony. I may not be able to see you sealed today, but I will be able to help bless your first child."

Rebekka ran to the bed and flung her arms around her father as she hadn't done since she was a small girl. "Oh, Daddy, that's the best present ever!"

"Then why are you crying?" He chucked her gently under the chin. "Come on, this is my little girl's wedding day. We can't have your eyes all red now. What will Marc think?"

"I'm just so happy," she blubbered. She searched her father's blue eyes and found no trace of the smoldering anger that had for so long lurked behind them. There was a new peace in its place, one she had never seen before.

As though reading her thoughts he said, "I should have listened sooner. I've wasted a lot of years."

Danielle patted his arm lovingly. "But you're ready now." There was a tremor in her voice and a new happiness in her face that told Rebekka how much Philippe's decision meant to her.

She's waited even longer than I have, Rebekka thought. Aloud she asked, "But when did all this happen? I thought you said were talking to the missionaries because of Thierry."

"That's what I wanted you to believe." Philippe's face sobered. "I didn't want to raise any false hopes."

"But all these weeks you've been listening to their discussions?"

"That's right. Of course, I was working on finding Thierry's family, too."

"It's a good thing you did," Danielle put in. "Thierry's thriving under André's care. I'm glad he plans to adopt the boy. I just hope his birth father doesn't return and make trouble."

"He won't," Philippe said confidently. "He doesn't want to go to jail. Besides, he never really cared about Thierry. André does."

Danielle laid her hand on Philippe's arm. "I'm proud of you for getting them together."

"Me too." Rebekka had noticed a new peace about André, and was glad for it. She hugged her father again.

"Enough already. Your mother has just about smothered me a million times since I told her last night!" But he held onto Rebekka as he spoke.

She laughed. "I can't wait to tell Marc! He'll be so excited about your baptism."

"Stunned, more like," Philippe quipped.

Rebekka laughed again. Could life get any better?

"Come on," she urged her parents out of bed. "I can't miss my appointment at the temple."

Philippe laughed. "Yeah, like there's any chance of that happening."

"I don't know," Rebekka said. "Raoul's not here yet, and I can't get sealed without him. But I wouldn't put it past André to arrange another business trip for him at the last moment."

"Now, Rebekka." Danielle clicked her tongue disapprovingly. "Work has been good for him. You know that."

Rebekka became serious. "Of course I do. He does seem to be happier. Maybe he's finally getting over Desirée."

"I think it might take longer than a week," Philippe put in with a sigh. "And I'm not too sure we've seen the last of her, either. We don't know all the details of what happened, but we do know Raoul really cares for her. I just hope he's learned something from their relationship, if only that he's more careful if he decides to take her back."

Rebekka didn't know what to make of that statement. Raoul had loved Desirée, and still did. Perhaps only time would tell if there could be any future between Raoul and Desirée. She hoped not, but couldn't discount the principle of repentance—or her brother's feelings.

Her parents were dressing when Raoul finally arrived, directly from the airport. "Thank heaven," Rebekka said. "I was beginning to worry."

He hugged her. "I wouldn't let you down."

"Oh, Raoul, this is the best day. Just wait until I tell you about Dad!"

"No fair," Philippe said, coming from the bathroom. "It's my news."

Danielle didn't smile or join in the laughter. She walked up to her son and put a hand on either side of his face and stared into his eyes. "How are you doing?"

"I'm fine, Mother," he answered, though his face was lined with stress. "And I've learned a lot—especially about how blind I was not to see where Desirée and I were headed. There were signs even before we were married, but I chose to ignore them."

"I'm sorry." Danielle hugged him and Rebekka saw her mother blink tears from her eyes.

"I'll be okay," Raoul said. "I'm finished beating myself up about it. I'm looking toward the future now, and keeping busy. Oh, that reminds me, I'm going on another business trip. I'll be flying out after the ceremony."

"So that's why your suitcase is so big," Rebekka said, stifling a protest. "You look like you brought as much as I did. And Marc and I'll be gone two weeks."

Raoul drew away from Danielle, a genuine smile breaking through his grave expression. "I can't believe you two are finally getting married."

All at once Rebekka's entire being felt alive with light. "I know. Neither can I."

* * * * *

Later in the afternoon, Rebekka and those she loved gathered in the sealing room of the Swiss Temple. Her eyes wandered over the beloved faces of family and friends who had come to share this special day. Here they had gathered as one, despite the separate trials many had endured the past months.

Her gaze stopped on Mathieu and Marie-Thérèse, who sat holding hands, a new serenity on their faces. Marie-Thérèse had asked the entire extended family for help and advice on dealing with Larissa, and Rebekka had to admit that in the past few weeks Larissa's attitude had shifted drastically for the better. Everyone hoped it was a permanent change.

Rebekka's eyes wandered past Josette and Zack, who seemed to be carrying on a private conversation with their unborn baby. The scene was so touching that Rebekka could hardly wait until she was expecting her own baby. Marc's baby.

Her mother was there, of course, as were Marc's parents and grandparents. Even Marc's Aunt Lu-Lu and her husband Jourdain had come from Marseille to see them sealed. Next to Jourdain sat Louis-

Géralde, scheduled in a month to return to the mission field in the Ukraine.

And then there was André.

He smiled encouragingly as he saw her gaze, though the expression in his eyes was partially hooded. She knew he had found contentment in the relationship with his girls and newly found nephew, and she thanked the Lord for it. There would always be a special place in her heart for André.

As she surveyed the rest of the guests, she also imagined unseen family members on the other side of the veil. Surely they were here and rejoicing with her and Marc!

At last Marc took her hand and led her to the altar. "I love you," he whispered in her ear.

She returned his tremulous grin. "I love you, too."

* * * * *

After the simple, deeply profound temple ceremony, Rebekka and Marc headed to the airport in a taxi. The flight was uneventful, except for the teasing garnered when the other passengers discovered their newlywed status. Even the taxi driver who picked them up at the airport had something to say. Almost immediately he launched into a series of disastrous honeymoon stories, seeming particularly fond of one where a groom had been so badly sunburned on his first day at the beach that he had to spend the rest of his honeymoon at the hospital

"Good thing it's winter," answered Marc good-naturedly. The driver laughed and Rebekka joined in.

"Ah, alone at last," Rebekka said with a heartfelt sigh when they finally reached the hotel.

But there was a message at the front desk from Ariana, and when Marc returned her call, he blinked with amazement. "It's Josette," he told Rebekka. "She went into labor on the drive home. Zack barely made it to a hospital before she gave birth. Both mother and baby are doing fine, though, and he should be able to drive them back to Paris tomorrow or the next day—once he recovers from the slight concussion he gained when he fainted in the emergency room."

"Well, that's one nephew's birthday we won't forget!"

They laughed together and made their way to the elevator. When they arrived at their spacious three-room hotel suite, Marc glanced around and whistled. "I don't remember ordering a piano."

"I did that." Rebekka took his hand and led him to the sofa. "I found out where you had our reservations and changed the room to one with a piano."

He pulled her onto the sofa and held her close, staring deeply into her eyes as their lips met. How happy she was! Adding to the joy of being wrapped in his arms was the assurance that they were now husband and wife, joined for eternity.

After a time she pulled away, remembering there was something she needed to share with him. "I have a surprise for you. Just sit here and wait." She arose, sat at the piano, and paused before beginning the song she had written for him. Her parents had planned a huge wedding dinner after their return, and she would play this song again in front of their guests, but today's performance would be solely for Marc.

She began to play, at first caressing the keys softly, gently, slowly, and then coaxing more from the instrument, increasing in both tempo and volume, hoping that all the love and longing she had put into the music's creation over the years came through in the notes. The chords pounded through her heart and into the still room. Never had she played so well or with so much emotion.

Upon finishing, she turned to see him sitting at the edge of the sofa, staring at her, tears wetting his cheeks. "I've never heard you play that before. It's beautiful—what is it?"

She had debated on several titles for days, yet none seemed perfect for the piece. But as he asked, an idea came to her mind. "It's called 'Ties that Bind,'" she answered with sureness. "I wrote it for you."

"Absolutely perfect." He came to her, grabbing her hands, pulling her tightly to him. "Because that's exactly how I feel. We are bound with love—a tie that will last forever."

"Forever," Rebekka echoed. She lifted her lips to seal their promise with a kiss.

About the Author

Rachel Ann Nunes (pronounced *noon-esh)* knew she was going to be a writer when she was thirteen years old. She now writes five days a week in a home office with constant interruptions from her five young children. One of her favorite things to do is to take a break from the computer and build a block tower with her two youngest. Several of her children have begun their own novels, and they have fun writing and plotting together.

Rachel enjoys traveling, camping, spending time with her family, and reading. She served an LDS mission to Portugal. She and her husband, TJ, and their children live in Utah Valley, where she is a popular speaker for religious and writing groups. *Ties That Bind* is her thirteenth novel to be published by Covenant. Her *Ariana* series is a best-seller in the LDS market.

Rachel enjoys hearing from her readers. You can write to her at P.O. Box 353, American Fork, UT 84003-0353, send e-mail to rachel@rachelannnunes.com, or visit her website at http://www.rachelannnunes.com.